Teia screwed her eyes shut, though it made no difference. Blood and death and darkness come again, the Wild Hunt sweeping across the plains. A sob thickened her throat, then another. Fire-eyed Hounds that bayed in tones to curdle her soul, waved on by a dark hunter. Nothing but ruin behind them and the harsh clatter of the gallows-birds.

More sobs shook her, though the tears would not come, nothing but a hot prickle behind her eyes. She pressed the heels of her hands into them as if to blot the visions out, but they marched on. Nightmare after nightmare, one after another. Teia sobbed and sobbed and sobbed.

Finally, exhausted, she lay staring at the oil-lamp in its niche in the wall. Its tiny flame danced on the merest breath of air, bright and brave against the thronging shadows. The Wild Hunt. Now her visions made sense. The Hounds in her dreams, the dark hunter—oh, Macha preserve her, she recognized him now. Or rather, Her. Maegern, the Raven, Keeper of the Dead. And Ytha had summoned Her.

If Teia had been standing, she would have fallen to her knees. Her bones could not have supported the weight of the realization crashing down on her. Ytha and the other Speakers had summoned the Raven to aid them, but Teia had seen Her Hounds scouring the plains like a firestorm. Already the goddess's bloody hand was reaching out from Her exile. Her powers would only grow now, and She would not be satisfied with just the plains. Devastation would follow the prints of Her Hounds all across the world.

Teia's fingers spasmed closed over her wounded palm. Dread clawed at her stomach. *Oh, Speaker, what have you done?*

TOR BOOKS BY ELSPETH COOPER

Songs of the Earth
Trinity Rising

TRINITY RISING

THE WILD HUNT
BOOK TWO

ELSPETH COOPER

A TOM DOHERTY ASSOCIATES BOOK | NEW YORK

This is a work of fiction. All of the characters, organizations, and events portrayed in this novel are either products of the author's imagination or are used fictitiously.

TRINITY RISING

Copyright © 2012 by Elspeth Cooper

First published in Great Britain by Gollancz, an imprint of the Orion Publishing Group

A Tor Book
Published by Tom Doherty Associates, LLC
175 Fifth Avenue
New York, NY 10010

www.tor-forge.com

Tor® is a registered trademark of Tom Doherty Associates, LLC.

ISBN 978-0-7653-6851-5

Tor books may be purchased for educational, business, or promotional use. For information on bulk purchases, please contact Macmillan Corporate and Premium Sales Department at 1-800-221-7945, extension 5442, or write specialmarkets@macmillan.com.

First Edition: February 2013
First Mass Market Edition: February 2014

Printed in the United States of America

0 9 8 7 6 5 4 3 2 1

For Rob. He knows why.

TRINITY
RISING

1

THE KINGDOM WAITS

❧

Spangles of light dusted the air, like a cloud of pallid butterflies. Silver goblet in hand, Savin stepped through them and with a gesture of his other hand drew the Veil closed behind him, as if drawing a curtain across a window overlooking a sunlit terrace garden. A tingling as his fingertips touched the edges together, a shiver over his skin, and the weave was restored as if it had never been disturbed.

A useful trick, that one. It allowed him to move freely in places where it was unwise to attract too much attention and it impressed the gullible. As the fairground shills and bunco-men knew, sometimes a little showmanship was worth more than gold.

One by one, the spangles faded into the gloom around him and he frowned. The tower room in Renngald's castle should not have been dark, nor chill enough to make his breath steam, even after the late-summer heat of Mesarild. He rarely felt the cold, though he'd had to learn the trick of ignoring it rather than being born to it like his hosts, but the damp that came with it in these far-northern climes was ruinous for a library so he'd left a fire burning. Now the fire was dead, and there was no sign of the servant girl he'd left to tend it.

Where was the useless creature? He sent a thought questing through the castle's bedchambers and sculleries

and found her at last in the foetid warmth of the sty,
bent over a hurdle with her eyes shut and her skirts
around her waist as a lank-haired lad ploughed her for
all he was worth.

He clicked his tongue irritably. Gold certainly hadn't
been enough there. She'd have to be replaced. Acquir-
ing his books had cost him too much time and trouble
to let them be ruined by mildew because some dull-
witted slattern was less interested in minding her duties
to him than in being stuffed by the pig-boy until she
squealed.

A snap of his fingers called flames to the logs in the
wide hearth. Another thought lit the wall-lamps, pushing the shadows back into the corners. Despite the lus-
trously polished Tylan cabinetry and thick Arkadian
carpets, there was no disguising that this was a room in
a fortress. Granite corbels peeked between the fine wall-
hangings, and no amount of swagged and draped velvet
could pretend that the windows were anything more
than arrow-loops. Not quite the exotic wood screens
and perfumed silks of his rooms in Aqqad, but it was a
comfortable enough place to work – if only he didn't
have to travel quite so far in search of a decent bottle of
wine.

He lifted the goblet and swirled its contents around,
inhaling the bouquet. Tylan lowland red, dark and rich
as blood. Not an outstanding year, but quite good –
certainly far better than anything his hosts could offer:
mead, or that thin, bitter beer they made here, good
only for sour stomachs and dull heads. His lips twisted
in distaste. This far north, good wine was one of the ci-
vilised comforts he missed the most.

A change in the texture of the quiet alerted him that
he was no longer alone. The clicks and rustles from the
fireplace were muted by a sudden, expectant stillness,
yawning like a grave waiting to be filled.

Goblet halfway to his lips, he turned. The sight-glass

stood in the middle of the table, covered by a velvet cloth. It was impossible for a mere object to stare, but somehow it did, pulling at his attention, reeling away and yet looming closer as if he was looking down at it from the top of a monstrously high cliff.

He took a mouthful of wine, then flipped away the cloth. The glass was no larger than one a lady might have on her dressing table, if she did not mind the disturbingly figured silver frame that appeared to shift under one's gaze, writhing around and through rather more dimensions than the usual three. Within the frame was darkness, void and absolute. It had no surface to reflect light or colour, and yet it seethed.

We have been waiting, breathed a voice as cold and prickly as hoar frost. *You have found it?*

'Not yet.'

Another delay. The darkness shifted again, like ripples in ink. *Our master grows impatient.*

For a creature outside time, their master appeared to feel the passing of it most keenly. 'The Guardian has a new apprentice.'

Irrelevant.

'Perhaps.' He sipped his wine. 'And perhaps not.'

You told us the Guardians are a spent candle, of no consequence.

'I may have been . . .' he hated the taste of the admission '. . . too hasty.'

Silence. Then: *This apprentice concerns you.*

'He wouldn't let me read him,' Savin said, 'and I like to know what I'm dealing with. I don't much care for surprises.' Swirling the last of the Tylan red around the goblet once more, he frowned into its ruby depths. Alderan on the move again. The old meddler was planning something, without a doubt, but what? That was the puzzle, and puzzles had to be solved.

The apprentice was forewarned.

That was unlikely. It was not the old man's way to

give answers to questions before they were asked, and sometimes not even then. Besides, he couldn't have known that his latest pet would come under scrutiny quite so quickly. What was he up to?

'There was no reason for him to be prepared for our meeting. It was pure chance – I happened to be in Mesarild and sensed the Guardian weaving something. I wanted to know what it was.'

The old man was usually more careful with his colours, so Savin had cut short his visit to the wine merchant and followed them to an unremarkable house by the tailors' guildhall, then to an inn in the old city, and what he'd found there had been . . . intriguing.

Chance so often governed the lives of men. The turn of a card, the face of a coin, and empires fell. A smile tugged at the corners of his mouth. Now that was an appropriate image.

Something amuses you.

'I'm curious about this one. He was wary. All he would say of himself was that he had escaped some entanglement with the Church, and his left hand was bandaged. Unless I'm much mistaken, he knows what he is.' Dressed like a ragged little nobody, but with the manner and bearing of a man who lowered his eyes to no one. Whoever he was, he was someone to watch.

A threat, then.

'More likely just another piece of the puzzle. The Guardian wouldn't come this far from the Isles simply to wet-nurse a minor talent – he was in Mesarild for a reason.' A germ of an idea began to form. Perhaps the talent *was* the reason . . . Even more intriguing.

The idea grew, took shape. Anything special was precious, and anything precious was a point of vulnerability. A weakness. Weaknesses could be exploited. Like shucking an oyster, it was all about knowing where to insert the knife.

You should have brought him to us. Let him answer our questions.

'Your questions tend to be the sort from which there is no coming back, except as food for the pigs,' he said sharply, irked by the interruption. 'I may yet have a use for him.' A way to get behind those bloody wards, for a start.

Prevarication. In the sight-glass, the darkness seethed. *We made a bargain with you. We taught you what you wished to learn. We expected progress.*

'I *have* made progress. I am close to finding what you seek.'

The twisting of the silver frame grew more frenzied, the ever-changing shapes still more unsettling. Amongst them, fangs glinted and jaws snapped.

Make more. Be closer. Our master's patience is not without its limits.

Savin tossed the last of the wine into his throat and swallowed it down. 'I have not forgotten the terms of our agreement.'

Good. If you had, the consequences would have been ... unpleasant. The blackness in the glass trembled, no longer void now but choked, crammed with shadows that coiled in endless, restless motion, sullen as a stormy sky. *Be swift, human. The Kingdom waits.*

2

SPEAKER OF
THE CRAINNH

❦

Drwyn set a torch to his father's tent at dusk, in accordance with tradition. The flames licked at the painted leather tentatively, as if savouring a strange new food, then found their appetite and leapt up to devour it. In minutes the pyre was well alight, fire swaying and snapping in the perpetual east wind. He cast the stump of the torch into the blaze and stepped back from the searing heat. By morning, it would all be over.

A sigh rippled through the assembled clansmen. Out of the corner of his eye he saw the shadowy figures fall back, melting into the gloom amongst the huddle of tents as others came forward. Twenty warriors would stand vigil with him, one for each year of his father's rule. They formed up in a rough circle around the pyre, faces stripped of identity in the sooty orange light, honed by sharp shadows. Spears upright before them, they would stand with him until the fire died or the sun rose.

The tent collapsed in a gout of flame, the old man's body and the grave goods heaped around it now an unrecognisable huddle in the heart of the fire. When morning came, nothing would be left but ashes and a few bits of charred metal, shattered pottery. Little to show for a man who had led his people for two decades and seen them grow and prosper under him.

The last few years had been good to the Crainnh.

The elk had flourished, bearing more calves than anyone could remember, and the rivers had run silver with fish. Even the winters had felt less cold, coming later and lingering less, though the plains were still snowbound for half the year.

Prosperity had made the waiting especially difficult for Drwyn. His father had remained in stubbornly good health, appearing to grow more vigorous not less as each winter passed. But Ytha had counselled him to patience, to bide his time and wait. Though it had taken another three years of Drwyn bowing his head and biting his tongue, he'd got his wish: the old buzzard had finally breathed his last between the thighs of a fifteen-year-old girl. Maegern had carried away his soul to the Hall of Heroes to sit at Her right hand and drink *uisca* from a silver cup, and now, at last, Drwyn would be chief.

In time, youngling, said a voice in the back of his head. *All in good time.*

Ytha watched him through the fire. Her gaze swept over his face like an icy wind, dissipating the heat-haze between them until her face was as clear as if she had transported herself to stand before him.

Drwyn blinked, startled, then ground his teeth at being caught out by one of her tricks. Sun-browned skin creased as one brow lifted and her lips quirked mockingly – as if she knew his secrets and the knowing amused her. He ground his teeth all the harder. He would not look away.

Ytha's lips quirked again. She was laughing at him, blast her! By the Eldest, he would not stand for it!

Green eyes dulled to grey in the darkness fixed his, no longer showing any trace of amusement. They were hard as agates, sharp as frost. *Remember who is the kingmaker here, Drwyn. The torc of the Crainnh is not yours yet.*

He swallowed. Sweat prickled on his palms but he

couldn't move his hands to wipe them on his trews. Ytha's presence in his mind was a weight pressing on his brain; he could no more disobey her than fly.

Better, she said. *You must be patient, my youngling. All things come in their season. Tomorrow you will be chief, and in time Chief of Chiefs. But not yet. You must wait for the fruit to ripen before you bite, else the taste is bitter and the fruit is lost.*

Wavy hair, more white than ruddy, blew across her face. She lifted a hand to push it back and the starseed stone in her ring flared in the firelight, bright as a winter star. Then it winked out and her presence in his thoughts along with it.

Drwyn exhaled slowly. There he was, man and warrior, due to be named chieftain of the Wolf Clan in a few short hours. He shouldn't be afraid of a woman. But everyone in the clan, his late father included, walked light and spoke soft around the Speaker. He could do no different. The powers she commanded froze the marrow in his bones.

And he needed those powers, as well as her counsel. No mistaking that; without her he would never be Chief of Chiefs. With her, anything was possible, and in the morning, it would begin.

⚙

The Crainnh celebrated Drwyn's succession with a feast. Twenty elk were butchered and dressed for roasting and baskets of fish and fowl were caught by the hunters. Every woman in the clan baked or brewed or gathered her own contribution to the festivities. A huge fire was built on the ashes of the pyre, around which the new chief, his war band and the clan elders raised their cups to Drw's departed spirit before toasting the coming glories of his son.

Ytha, however, was frowning. Choice cuts of meat lay untouched in her bowl as she sat cross-legged on a cushion and watched the clanswomen serving bread and beer to their menfolk. She was watching one young woman in particular. Occasionally she sipped from her cup, but mostly she just watched.

With Drw and his dearth of ambition gone to ashes at last she should have been in a mood to celebrate, but she was not. This was only one obstacle removed; it did not guarantee that there would be no others, no further pits or deadfalls that could trip the most well-prepared plan and break its legs. Always, always she had to be wary of what might be hiding in the long grass.

Drwyn tossed a bone into the fire and scrubbed his greasy fingers on his trews. 'What troubles you, Ytha?'

'That girl, there.' She nodded towards the indistinct figure passing around the far side of the fire, a basket balanced on her hip. 'Do you see her?'

There was little to see, apart from a mane of brown hair and a light-coloured dress. 'I see her,' Drwyn grunted, reaching for his cup. 'She was in my father's bed the night he died.'

'It was the bedding of her that killed him.'

'So? My father took a dozen wenches like her after my mother passed. One of them had to be the last.'

There'd been plenty of women before his mother passed, too: casual tumbles, warm beds on cold nights, but none like this, offered for and won, and none he'd kept for so long.

'She may be a threat to us, in the future,' Ytha said. 'She has an aura I cannot read.'

'And that is dangerous?' He laughed. 'You're starting at shadows.'

'Maybe.' Ytha tapped her cup against her chin and asked the question that had pricked at her all day like a thorn in her shoe. 'What if your father had another son?'

'Drw's dead. All his sons are dead, save me.'

'And he was dipping his *daigh* in her for two full

seasons! What if she conceived?' Ytha gestured towards the girl, who was handing out hunks of bread. 'What if the girl is carrying?'

'My father was too old for getting bastards,' Drwyn scoffed. 'Besides, what threat is a brat? I'd throttle it with one hand.'

'I don't doubt you could, assuming she let you anywhere near it. She's only young, Drwyn, not stupid.' Oh, the man was a trial, always acting, never thinking. He scowled at her rebuke and Ytha moderated her tone.

'Age only weakens the stalk, not the spark in the seed,' she said. 'Ever since that girl became your father's bedmate, she's shied away from me. If she bears a child, and enough of the captains think it's Drw's get, it could split the clan.'

The war captains had to be united in their acclamation of a new chief, just as the clan chiefs had to be united behind the Chief of Chiefs. Without that, all Ytha's planning would be for naught.

'Clan law, yes, I remember,' he said with an impatient gesture, clearly irked at being reminded. 'Can you tell if she's going to crop?'

It was possible, but she'd need to delve the girl to be sure – and that one would not allow anyone to lay a finger on her if she thought she might be carrying the dead chief's son. If only her aura could be read!

'Yes, I can tell, but I have a better idea. If she is a threat, I would rather have her where I can watch her. I shall send her to you tonight. If you bed her a few times, we can pass off any child she might bear as yours instead of your father's. You look enough like him to make it believable.'

Drwyn showed his teeth. 'As I recall, she's pretty.'

Not that a girl needed to be much more than passable to stiffen his *daigh*. In that, at least, he was his father's son. 'Oh, she is very pretty, Drwyn. Eyes the colour of bell-flowers and lips like ripe berries, just waiting to be plucked. You'll enjoy her, I think.' Ytha took a deep draught of beer. 'It is time for you to speak to them. Remember what I told you.'

'I remember well enough,' he grunted and stood up. Sourness twisted his mouth as he gulped down the last of his beer.

She frowned. Drwyn did not like to be led; she had learned that much. But he even seemed unable to bear it well when it was for his own good. 'Be careful, my chief.' She spoke softly, deliberately.

He stared at her, sullen as any youth. His eyes were black in the firelight but hot, like embers. Tossing his cup onto the crushed turf, he made her a mocking little bow. 'Yes, Speaker.'

Ytha lashed out, snatching hold of him with her mind. Bands of solid air tightened around his chest. He opened his mouth to speak and she squeezed the breath out of him.

'Do not mock me, Drwyn. You know I can make you into whatever you want, but never forget that I can unmake you just as easily. Do you hear me?'

His dark eyes remained belligerent. Ytha tightened her grip. He struggled for air, his hands pinned to his sides by the grinding pressure of her weaving. His face had turned the mottled red of spoiled liver when finally panic overtook stubbornness and he dipped his head.

She released him and had the satisfaction of seeing him stagger a little. 'Do you hear me?'

'I hear you, Speaker,' he gasped, sucking in great heaving breaths. Ytha selected a slice of meat from her plate and bit into it, leaning back on her arm whilst Drwyn's colour returned to normal.

'I am glad we understand each other now,' she said. His expression was hard and flat, not in the least repentant. His eyes burned. She took another bite of meat. 'I would hate to see anything go awry because of a misunderstanding.'

'Nothing will go awry, Speaker. You can trust me.'

'Can I?'

Drwyn bristled like a startled prickleback. 'You can,' he said harshly.

'There will be no further misunderstandings between us?'

'None.'

'Good.'

She finished the meat, watching him all the while. Despite the restless flexing of his hands his gaze was steady, holding hers without flinching. Not many in the Crainnh could do that – fewer still who would choose to, especially after tasting her displeasure.

Drwyn had all the fire of his father at that age. Quick-blooded, eager to prove himself, too impatient to be taught, but where the passing of time had sharpened her ambition, it had made Drw fat and old and content to leave things be, as long as they suited him. Now all her plans rested on the son to achieve what the father would not – if he ever learned to control his temper.

Ytha wiped her mouth and put her plate aside. Irritation flickered across Drwyn's face when she picked up her cup and took her time drinking, her eyes never leaving his. One of the first steps to wisdom was patience, and by the Eldest she would teach him that, if nothing else.

When the cup was empty, she set it carefully on her plate and stood up, arranging her robes around her.

'The war band is waiting, Speaker,' he said at last, with gruff diffidence. 'May I go?'

Ytha nodded. 'You may. You know what to say to them.'

She extended her hand, her ring glittering in the firelight. Drwyn hesitated for no more than half a heartbeat before he dropped to one knee to press it to his forehead. She suppressed a smile. So the boy was capable of some restraint after all; such a shame he hadn't demonstrated more of it over the last three years.

Ytha watched him walk back into the circle of fire-light. His warriors were on their feet the instant they saw him, although some were less than steady and had to cling to their companions for support. Soon the Crainnh's chief-to-be was lost in a shouting, back-slapping mob, roaring their praises to the night sky.

She did not stay to listen to the speech; she had heard it often enough in the last week as she made Drwyn recite it over and over again to be sure he knew it by heart. Besides, it would not take much to sway the Crainnh. Drw's face was still fresh in their memories; a few fine words and familiarity would do the rest.

No, the real test would be at the Gathering, when the silver moon next rose new. Then he would have to speak before the other clan chiefs and it would take more than a family resemblance to bring them into line.

Still, that was a way off yet. The silver moon, the one they called the wanderer, had barely begun to wane; they had plenty of time. For now she had to fetch him a woman. Drawing her fur mantle around her, Ytha stepped out into the darkness.

3

TEIA

❖

Teia lifted the boiling kettle off the fire with a forked stick and emptied it into the bucket, careful not to splash herself, then refilled it from the other bucket and set it back to heat.

Mentally she divided the stack of greasy platters

beside her into two. One more bucketful and the dishes would be done, thank the Eldest. Her hands were dishpan-red, the tips of her fingers almost numb from scrubbing at dried gravy.

Dunking a stack of plates into the bucket of hot water, she set to with the sand. She'd lost count of how many she'd washed already and she hadn't even had her supper yet. All the other unmarried girls had had theirs, then drifted away one by one to watch the young warriors wrestle, leaving her, the dutiful one, to finish their chores as well as her own. She sighed and tilted the plate towards the light to check for spots she'd missed, then put it to one side. Complaining about the others' idleness wouldn't get the dishes washed any sooner, but she'd make sure their mothers heard about it in the morning.

When the water was too dirty to be useful, she dipped a finger in the kettle. Barely warm. She had enough time to fetch fresh water. With a bucket in each hand she trudged out of the circle of tents towards the stream.

Gradually the roar of the fire and the war band's raucous laughter faded into the whispery night sounds of the plain. The wandering moon was a little past full, silvering the tall grass so brightly that she could see almost as clearly as in daylight. Habit took her a few yards downstream of the watering place to empty the buckets, then she walked back up the stream-bank to the shallows and refilled them.

The water was deliciously cool on her sore hands. Looking around to see if anyone could observe her shirking her duties, she knelt down and plunged her arms into the stream to the elbows. Wonderful. The sand on the bottom was soft as fine wool. Her hair fell forwards around her face, blocking out all but the faintest glow of moonlight, trapped like fireflies in the rippling water.

She stayed like that for as long as her aching shoulders could bear it, then sat back on the bank and dried her hands on the hem of her dress. No one would miss her for a few minutes more. After the smoke and stink of the camp the plains breeze was refreshing; all she'd been able to smell for two days was elk-grease and ashes.

Teia glanced towards the fire. Poor Drw. Gone now to the Hall of Heroes to sup with his greatfathers. Not for him a glorious death on the field of battle, but his shade would have a tale to tell nonetheless. Carried to Maegern on a woman's sigh.

I'm tired now, Teia. I think I'll sleep.

Tears pricked at her eyes and she blinked them away. *Farewell, my chief.*

Even with the wind behind her she heard the bleat of bagpipes and the throb of a drum; a ragged line of figures was silhouetted against the blaze, men and women with arms linked as they laughed and stumbled their way drunkenly through a dance. Pledges would be exchanged tonight and no doubt maidenheads broken long before any marriage vows were said.

Marriage. That thought left an ache in the pit of her belly more powerful than her grief for Drw. Her mother Ana had been talking to her aunt about the wedding fair again, though she had not realised Teia could hear as she and her sister reckoned up what price they might get for her at the Gathering. Afterwards, Teia had cried herself to sleep. Next morning, she had looked into the water for her future and seen only clouds.

Teia glanced around, biting her lip. She was alone with the soughing grass, the burble of the stream. No one was close enough to see her, even if she was missed. With the Gathering drawing nearer, less than two weeks away now, she had to know what was waiting for her there.

She dragged one of the buckets between her knees. When the water had settled and the silver disc of the wandering moon floated undisturbed in the centre, she

placed both hands on the rim and closed her eyes. Then
she reached down inside herself for the music.

Slow to respond at first, it leapt suddenly into the
forefront of her mind. Quickly she tamed it, narrowed
the flow until it was the merest trickle, then let it out.
Bluish sparks crawled around her fingers, writhing out
over the water. The reflection of the moon shimmered.
It was waning gibbous; not as powerful as a full moon,
but still a good sign for scrying. White light filled the
circle described by the bucket rim then became utterly
still, mirroring a perfect image of her face.

Show me.

The image shivered then cleared. Still her face, but
surrounded now by a cloudy grey sky. Blood smeared
her cheek and her hair was a bramble-thicket of wet
dark curls. Her eyes were dull as a dead bird's.

No matter how many times she saw it, that vision
always dismayed her, hinting as it did of a future no
woman could want. Gripping the bucket's rim, she
took a deep breath to steady herself for the next scrying, in case it was the black warrior again.

Show me.

The image changed to the boy. Dark-haired, blue-
eyed, gazing solemnly out of the water at her, with a
woman's hands resting on his shoulders. Protectively or
proudly? She was never sure. His square, blunt features
and stocky frame left no doubt whose line he sprang
from, even without the glint of gold at the neck of his
shirt.

Show me.

This time she saw a view from a high place, looking
down first on forested mountain slopes, then rolling
silver-beige plains threaded with bright rivers. The landscape resembled the plains south of the camp, near the
an-Archen, but it was not a view she had ever seen during her winters there. Besides, it appeared to be summer,
or at least spring, because the sun shone and there were

flowers amidst the grass. Far off, nearly at the limit of her vision, antlike figures walked away.

'What are you doing, child?'

Ytha! The Speaker was right behind her, moving through the grass as quietly as a huntress. Letting go of the music, Teia swirled her fingers through the water to dispel the image and scrambled to her feet to face her.

'N-nothing, Speaker! I was just fetching water—' She realised she was gabbling and took a deep breath, pressing a hand to her chest as if she could still her racing heart. 'I was daydreaming.'

'Ah. I'm sorry if I startled you,' said Ytha pleasantly. 'I thought for a moment I sensed someone scrying.'

'Scrying?' Teia's heart flung itself against her ribs like a trapped bird. Had the Speaker seen? 'No, not at all. I don't know how.'

'Of course not. Because if you had the gift, you would have come to me, wouldn't you?'

Ytha took a step closer and made a twisting gesture with her hand. A ball of cool blue light appeared, floating above Teia's shoulder. Even though she'd seen the Speaker's lights before, the abrupt manifestation of one so close to her face was unsettling. It gave off no heat, but she felt its radiance prickling her skin like nettle-itch begging to be scratched – or maybe that was just because she was the subject of the Speaker's scrutiny. After half a year of avoiding her eye, it took almost all Teia's courage to stand still and face it.

'My, you are a pretty thing.' Ytha touched Teia's cheek, then tilted her chin towards the light. 'You are fortunate to be blessed with such good skin, my dear. And such lovely eyes, too.' She flicked her fingers at the tangled mane hanging over Teia's shoulders. 'A pity about your hair, but we can fix that. Let me see your hands.'

Teia held them out. Ytha took one in each of hers and turned them over, running her thumbs across the chapped skin and clucking sympathetically.

'Come with me, child. There is much we can do about this.'

'But the dishes,' Teia protested. 'I'm supposed to be washing the dishes!'

'I have already spoken to your mother and sisters,' Ytha assured her with a smile. 'It will all be taken care of. Fetch the water, then come to my tent. Don't drag your heels, mind. I shall be waiting for you.'

Then the Speaker was gone, striding through the long grass back towards the camp. Stunned, Teia followed, lugging the two heavy buckets.

There was no sign of her mother at her family's fireside and the tent was empty. She left the buckets by the hearth, unhooked the now steaming kettle and set it on a rock so it would not boil dry, then made her way through the camp.

Ytha's tent, like the chief's, stood slightly apart from the others. Torches fixed in tall bronze stanchions flanked the entrance and a light glowed within. Teia took several deep breaths to steady herself and scratched at the flap.

'Come,' said Ytha, and she ducked inside.

Speculation was rife amongst the younger girls as to what the interior of the Speaker's tent was like; most of what they speculated was wrong. There were no caged familiars, no reeking smoke-pots or strange totems of feather and bone. Hangings obscured the hide walls and screened off the sleeping quarters. Carpets covered the floor, piled with cushions and ornamented chests. Teia felt the merest twinge of disappointment: it was just like her family's tent.

Only when she stepped further inside did she see that the scenes worked into the hangings depicted birds and beasts she did not recognise, the wools dyed in colours richer than any she had seen, even in Drw's tent. The light too came from a strange lamp hung from the tent's central pole. Instead of a clay dish of oil with a floating wick or Drw's three-armed silver lamps, the flame was encased in a box made of some shiny yellow metal and clear flat panels like the skim of ice from the top of a pond.

She turned around slowly, staring. All at once the tent did not look so ordinary any more.

Ytha pushed back the drapes and stepped through from the private area. Teia jumped. The Speaker had discarded her fur mantle and wore a plain russet-coloured dress with an intricate fish-scale belt. Her thick hair was tied back with a thong and she was smiling.

'I have startled you again, it seems.' She held the drape aside. 'Come in.'

The inner chamber of the tent was similar to the outer in its furnishings, apart from the fur-strewn bed and a large basin of hot water steaming on the floor. Teia eyed it uncertainly. 'Speaker?'

Ytha half-turned, a towel folded over her arm. 'Yes, child?'

'Why am I here?'

'The chief has expressed an interest in you – he has asked that you take supper with him. I will help you prepare yourself.'

Teia's heart renewed its frantic fluttering. It had not been like this when Drw sent for her, two seasons previously. The old chief had spoken to her himself; she had been so honoured that he even knew her name that she had almost burst with pride. Even her father had smiled. Now Ytha was taking a hand, and that unsettled her.

'Come along, child, we haven't got all night.' Ytha handed her the towel and a tablet of soap. 'Get yourself washed whilst I find you something to wear.'

Teia took a deep breath. If the chief had asked for her and the Speaker approved, she could hardly refuse. So while Ytha bustled around the tent in a fashion that was almost motherly she undressed, folding her clothes with care, then knelt beside the basin.

The soap was much finer than the elk-fat stuff she was used to and lathered readily. Rubbing the rich suds between her fingers, she held them to her nose and inhaled the sweet scent of some kind of flower, one she didn't recognise. Had that soap come from beyond the southern mountains? Sometimes pedlars came through the an-Archen for the great fairs, bringing spices and trinkets from afar, but even amongst their wares she'd never seen anything to compare with it.

As if she had heard Teia's thoughts, Ytha popped her head into the inner chamber again. 'Don't stint with it, there's plenty more.'

So Teia soaped and scrubbed, amazed when Ytha brought her fresh water to rinse with, then dried herself on the towel. The Speaker sat her on a stool and gave her a small clay jar with instructions to rub some of the contents on her hands, feet, knees and elbows. Whilst Teia did so, Ytha picked the tangles out of her hair with a whale-ivory comb, then dressed her in a fine lawn shift and a gown of blue wool. Teia fingered the dress. The woollen fabric was almost as soft and supple as the shift, and bright as a bluehawk's tail. Like Ytha's hangings, such stuff could only have come from distant lands. Suddenly she knew what she was being dressed for.

The Speaker held up a bronze mirror so Teia could see herself. She was transformed. The gown fitted her perfectly, showing off her neat hips and rounded breasts. Her hair was still an unruly mane, but now a mane of glossy waves instead of bird's-nest tangles. The thick ointment in the jar had taken most of the redness from her hands and softened the skin so that it was hard to believe she had spent much of the evening up to her elbows in dishwater.

'Fit for a chieftain, I think,' said Ytha, putting the mirror aside. 'Are you ready?'

Was she? 'I don't know. I think so.'

Irritation flickered through the Speaker's expression and was gone so quickly that Teia wouldn't have been sure she'd seen anything at all were it not for the worm of dread gnawing at her insides.

'The chief has asked you to take supper with him. You will stay with him for as long as he wishes you to. He might ask you to dance for him, or sing, if your voice is pleasing. He will tell you what he wants of you.' Ytha fixed her with a steady gaze. 'Remember, child, this is a great honour for you and for your family. It could be a wonderful opportunity for you to better yourself. If you please him, you may be rewarded. If you do not, it could go hard for you.'

Hands clasped tightly together, Teia nodded. 'I understand, Speaker.'

'I'm sure you do. After all, you were chosen as a companion by Drw, were you not?' Again, Teia nodded. Ytha laid a hand on her shoulder. 'Stand up straight, child. A slouch is not becoming. Now, are you ready?'

Making an effort to square her shoulders, Teia decided she was. After all, it would make little difference if she was not. The chief was the chief – even if he wasn't his father. 'I'm ready.'

'Then come with me.'

Ytha led the way from her tent across the camp to the chief's. The new dress had the desired effect: every man who was not too drunk to focus watched Teia pass. Some shouted appreciative comments, or suggestions that brought a furious blush to her cheeks. Lips set in a faint, aloof smile, the Speaker ignored them all.

At the chief's tent, Ytha stepped inside and left Teia waiting between the two guards at the door. The warriors made no attempt to hide their interest in her, their eyes roaming hungrily over her body, tracing her shape beneath the new dress. Cheeks burning, she fixed her gaze on the tent flap ahead. Macha, why didn't they just grab at her bottom and be done with it?

After a moment or two, Ytha reappeared and beckoned to her.

'Now remember,' she said, hand on Teia's shoulder, 'do as you are bid and all will go well for you and your family. If you please the chief, your father could become a very rich man, well able to give your husband a dowry that will make up for your lost innocence. A more pleasant option than the wedding fair, yes?'

Teia swallowed a sudden stab of humiliation and nodded.

'Yes, child, I know it stings, but a woman who cannot go innocent to her marriage bed goes to the wedding fair. It is the way of the clans and always has been.' She squeezed Teia's shoulder. 'Think of what you have to gain here.'

'I will. Thank you, Speaker.'

Ytha smiled, nodded once, then held the tent flap open for her. Teia stepped inside to face her chief.

He shared little of his father's tastes. Gone were the simple rugs woven in traditional clan patterns; the ground-skins were spread with furs, strewn with cushions almost as opulent as the Speaker's, and hangings in dark reds and purplish browns draped the tent sides. All that remained of Drw were the silver oil-lamps that hung from the tent poles, their yellow flames winking on the bronze and leather war gear heaped by the entrance, the chief's sword leaning against the pile lest anyone be in any doubt as to whom the tent belonged.

Drwyn lounged on a cushion in the centre, his shirt unlaced and his muscular legs crossed casually at the ankles. He was much the same height and breadth as Drw had been, and shared his father's dark, blunt features and near-black eyes, even wore the same close-cropped beard framing his mouth. A large gold earring gleamed amongst his thick hair.

'Be welcome, Teia.' He gestured to the cushions beside him. 'Please, join me.'

'My chief.'

Eyes demurely lowered, Teia sat on the adjacent cushion and accepted the cup of wine handed to her. She took a gulp for courage and almost choked as the raw red stuff scraped her throat.

'Would you care for something to eat?' Drwyn gestured to a nearby platter heaped with choice foods.

The savoury smells made her stomach churn, but she did not dare refuse. 'You are very kind.'

He filled a plate for her, his large hands awkward with the fork, and handed it to her. She took it, dismayed by how much he'd served; she made a show of sampling everything, but her mouth was so dry she needed more wine to wash the bread and meat down. All the while Drwyn watched her. His eyes measured the curves of her body, lingered on her breasts and thighs, his gaze as blatant as a touch.

Teia managed another bite of bread, then put the plate aside.

'Does it not please you?' Drwyn asked.

'I'm just not very hungry.'

'Ah.'

He watched her again as she sipped her wine. Teia felt sick. She was too hot and, in spite of the shift underneath, the new woollen dress Ytha had given her was prickling the backs of her legs.

To distract herself from the intensity of his gaze she looked around the tent, pretending to admire the furnishings, but all she felt was queasy. The butcher's-bucket colours of the thick hangings, the furs spread around her feet, made the tent feel like the inside of a crag-cat's den.

A flash of light caught her eye and she stared, startled to see her own reflection looking back at her from an object hanging from the tent pole. 'What's that?' She pointed.

At once Drwyn was on his feet to fetch it for her. 'It's a looking-glass.'

'I've never seen anything like it before.'

The glass was small, not much bigger than the palm of her hand and set in an ornamented metal frame. She peered at her reflection. It was much clearer than in Ytha's bronze mirror. She could see the freckles that dusted her skin, the colour of her eyes – violet-blue, like sunlight on a raven's wing. Her complexion was paler than the norm for her clan, she had always known that, but she had never appreciated just how pale she was. Her reflection in a basin of water – even in a vision – did not compare to this.

'Where did it come from?'

'South of the mountains, I think. I found it amongst my father's things. Do you like it?' he asked. She nodded. 'Then keep it. It's yours.'

She turned to thank him and realised he had sat down on the cushions much closer than before. The arm he leaned on was behind her back and his free hand was resting on his thigh just inches from hers. Though he was barely a hand taller than her, his thick build, his nearness, was intimidating. She fiddled with the glass, trying to appear fascinated by the intricate knotwork pattern on the frame, but she knew what was going to happen – had known it since Ytha had dressed her in fine new clothes, like a doll for a child. Why else would a new chief send for the old chief's bedmate, if not to ensure he could claim any offspring as his own? She knew Drwyn knew that she knew, too. Nonetheless her heart lurched as he took the glass from her and tossed it aside.

'Teia.' He held her hand in his. His breath was hot on her cheek and smelled of wine. 'I can see why my father chose you. You're very beautiful.'

He attempted to kiss her cheek but was foiled by her

hair, so he dropped her hand and turned her face towards him. His dark eyes were even more intent now. Before she could catch her breath he had pulled her against him and his mouth was eagerly exploring hers. At first she tried to drag her head back, but his grip was too strong. She shut her eyes and let her mouth open under the pressure of his tongue.

Once he realised she was pliant, his free hand began to roam over her body. She sat quite still as he ran it along her limbs, as if she were a horse he was buying, then squeezed and kneaded her breasts. His kisses grew no gentler. If anything they became more urgent as he tried to push her dress up. The skirt was too narrow and he growled in frustration.

'Take it off,' he said, tugging impatiently at his own shirt 'Take it off, now!'

Teia bit her lip, then knelt and pulled the dress up over her head, and the shift along with it. There was nothing else for it. She could not run or fight – Drwyn was physically too strong for that. His musculature was clearly defined despite the mat of hair that covered his chest and belly. He could snap her in two if he chose.

Her hair fell forwards, hiding her breasts, but he pushed it back and cupped them in his hands, sucking hungrily at her nipples. Teia shut her eyes tight. His beard prickled her tender skin like the bristles of an animal.

When he released her she opened her eyes again to see him plucking at the fastenings of his trews. He freed his erection and grasped it with one hand, a warrior testing the heft of a spear. His lips drew back from his teeth, somewhere between a grin and a snarl. His other hand twined in her hair and urged her head down.

Teia gagged at the taste and the bulk of him moving in her mouth almost choked her. Drwyn groaned his pleasure, apparently unaware that her stomach heaved with every thrust. Tears spilling down her face, she wrenched her head back, even though the pain of her yanked hair brought more tears to her eyes.

Drwyn stared at her, then without warning back-handed her across the mouth. 'Bitch!'

The force of the blow flung her across the cushions. She tasted salt; when she touched her mouth her hand came away smeared with red.

Drwyn lunged for her, seizing her arms and flipping her over onto her hands and knees. Then he was behind her, kneeling between her legs. One hand grabbed her hair and twisted it into a rope around his fist; she yelled again and was rewarded with another slap, this time across her buttocks. The breath whooshed out of her at the sudden sting. That seemed to excite him, for he struck her again, left and right across her rump. She flinched but stifled her cries, knowing without quite knowing how that if she showed her pain he would only hit her harder.

Eager fingers probed between her thighs, followed by his thick member. Grasping her hips, he pulled her hard against him. Teia squealed, but at least he had released her hair. Pushed face-first into the pillows by his weight, every breath was a struggle. Drwyn's fingers gripped her hips with bruising force, his dense body hair coarse against her skin. Each thrust of his pelvis jabbed pain-fully at her insides.

Eyes screwed shut, Teia clenched her jaw. It would be over soon, Macha willing. The panting and heaving would end, if she could just endure. His movements quickened. Teeth clamped on her shoulder and she bit into the pillow under her face to keep from screaming. Soon now, it had to be soon now. Harsh breaths, harsher words that grew into a bellow of triumph as he strained hard against her buttocks. His breath fanned her ear for a minute and then he rolled off her.

Teia drew her legs up slowly, keeping her face hidden

in her hair as she turned onto her side. It was all she could do not to cry aloud: her shoulder was on fire. Through the strands of her hair she saw him, chest heaving, mouth open in a broad grin of satisfaction. She smelled sweat, stale wine and the bitter realisation that although he echoed Drw physically, there the resemblance ended.

Sometime towards morning Drwyn took her again, with as little tenderness, before falling into a sated sleep. Teia stared up at the tent roof, too exhausted to cry. After a while she dozed, too, but his rasping snores soon woke her again. Birds chattered outside and a finger of pale light edged across the carpet from the door flap.

She sat up, raking her tangled hair back from her face. Between her legs she was abominably sore, but when she touched herself she found no blood, only Drwyn's sticky residue. She looked across at him, sprawling and slack-mouthed. Still asleep, praise Macha.

Slowly she slid out from under the covers and stood up. Her knees refused to support her at first and she almost fell. Taking very small steps, she made her way to her clothes. She put on her dress, rolled up the shift and pushed her feet into her shoes. After a second's thought she stuffed the little looking-glass into the middle of the bundle, then peeked outside.

Nothing stirred around the camp but a few dogs squabbling over discarded bones in the grass. Even the chief's guards had disappeared. The sun was a pale disc in an oyster-grey sky, its light thin and colourless as the smoke rising from the heap of ash that was all that remained of the celebratory fire built on the embers of the old chief's pyre. She thought of Drw, and how different her life had been then, and her throat closed up with tears that wouldn't fall.

Teia stepped outside. Normally the camp would be teeming at this hour; women building fires and kneading bread, men checking their gear and feeding the horses before going hunting. No doubt everyone had celebrated the new chief's anointing so enthusiastically that they were still too drunk to lift their heads.

Clutching the bundled shift, she hurried through the clusters of tents to the stream where she had gone to fetch water the night before, then downstream a little further, to the next shallow place. From there the camp was barely visible; no more than the peaks of the tents to be seen above the tall grass. That would hide her well enough. She crouched down on the sandy bank and took out the looking-glass.

A ghost-white face stared back at her, eyes red from weeping circled with sleepless shadows. Dried blood crusted the corner of her mouth and her lower lip was thick and purpled. She explored the bruise cautiously, pulling her tender lip out to see where her teeth had cut it.

A glimpse of more bruising at the edge of her reflection made her loosen the lacing at the neck of her dress and push it down over her shoulder. Imprinted in her flesh were the marks of Drwyn's teeth. The bruise filled the glass. Fresh tears filled her eyes.

Macha preserve her.

She dropped the glass, clawed the dress off and kicked out of her shoes. The stream was bitingly cold but she couldn't wait to heat water. She had to be rid of him, rid of the juices clotting inside her.

Squatting in the deepest part of the stream, she scrubbed herself as hard as her tender flesh would bear. She scrubbed at his sweat and the memory of his touch, scrubbed until her body shuddered with the cold and her feet and hands had no feeling. Then she fell to her knees in the stream and wept.

❧❧

When she walked back into the camp, people were stirring. Cook-fires had been lit and there were two guards outside the chief's tent again, grey-faced and bleary. She did not go back there. Instead she returned to her parents' tent to change the dress for one of her own. She couldn't be rid of the one Ytha had given her soon enough.

Her father was sitting on a stool at the entrance, mending a bridle. He was a lean, wiry man, tough as rawhide thongs, with salt-and-pepper hair tied back in a horsetail and long moustaches that drooped to either side of his thin lips.

When her shadow fell over his work he stopped, but did not look up.

'Father?'

'Teia,' he said. His tone was flat. Hitching around on the stool, he turned towards the light and continued working, his brown, callused hands deft with the stiff leather.

She waited for something more from him, some acknowledgement that she was still his daughter, but nothing came. Clan law lay between them like a wall of ice, impossible to climb. From now until she wore a wedding tattoo, she did not exist.

Drw had never been so formal. He'd waved the law away, clapped Teir on the shoulder and called for another flask of *uisca* for his old friend. But then Drw had offered for her in the old way, over a cup of water; he and Teir had clasped on a bargain well before it was emptied, all without the Speaker taking a hand. Nothing was the same any more.

So this was how it would be. Sobs thickening in her chest like clouds that grew heavier and darker but never came to rain, she walked past her father into the tent. To her relief, it was empty. Stripped to her skin, she threw the hateful blue wool dress and crumpled shift into the shadows in the far corner, where she wouldn't have to look at them. She was about to hurl the fancy looking-glass after them but hesitated, fingering the ornamented frame. Drwyn had given it to her, but it hadn't truly been his to give. It had been Drw's, and having something of his was . . . comforting. She tugged a clean shift and one of her own familiar dresses from her clothes chest, then hid the glass away at the bottom, under her winter stockings.

She'd just pulled her dress over her head when she heard someone enter the tent behind her and turned to see her mother in the doorway.

'Teia!' Ana exclaimed, rosy face bursting into a smile. She held out her arms and, reluctantly, Teia went to her. When her face came into the light from the entrance, her mother's delighted expression slumped like stale cooking-grease. 'Macha's ears, what's happened to you, child?'

'Didn't the Speaker tell you where I was last night?' Her voice sounded crushed flat, as if she had a great weight on her chest.

'Of course, but—'

'He hurt me, Mama.' Gulping a breath, Teia tugged her unlaced dress down off her shoulder.

Her mother squeaked, hands flying to her mouth, bright black eyes widening. 'Oh, Teisha,' she breathed. She hurried to the tent flap and snatched it aside. 'Teir! Teir, come here!'

Teia's father limped in, the half-mended bridle dangling from his hand.

'Look, just look at her!' Ana seized Teia's arms and pulled her further into the light. 'Look what he's done to her!'

Her father's face was expressionless. 'He is the chief, Ana.'

'That doesn't give him the right to paw over our daughter like an animal!'

'And how am I supposed to stop him?' Teir demanded harshly. 'Am I supposed to march up there and call him out to battle? He is *the chief*! He'll have me staked out for the wolves, woman!'

'Does she mean so little to you?' Ana persisted. 'I told you I did not want her going to him – I knew something like this would happen! He is not his father, Teir, not by a full measure!'

'Mama, please.' Teia tried to shrug off her mother's hands and cover herself, to hide from the storm of raised voices.

'Drw was my friend. I trusted him, and I served him willingly until I couldn't serve any more.' A muscle worked in Teir's jaw and he looked away. 'I owe it to his memory to serve his son.'

'Even after this? She is not a saddle blanket to be traded—'

'Quiet!' Teir snapped. He flung down the bridle and levelled a finger at Ana. She backed away as if he had pointed a spear at her, drawing Teia with her. 'I have heard enough, wife. I have given my word to the Speaker that I will abide by the chief's will in this. Now remember your place.'

Then he turned on his heel and stalked away, making no attempt to hide the stiffness in his gait that he'd carried for as long as Teia could remember, legacy of the Stony River Rebellion. Ana watched him go, then sighed and pulled the tent flap closed.

'I'm sorry,' she said, looking down at her hands. 'I tried to tell him last night, but he would not listen. He thinks he is doing his best for you.' Her shoulders lifted helplessly. 'Your father's a proud man. It hurt him more than he would ever admit to give up the captain's banner and just be a liegeman again. It eats at him.'

'So I'm supposed to feel sorry for him?' The words were thick in Teia's throat. 'What about me, Mama?'

Ana sighed. 'A lame man can't be a war captain,

Teisha. Drw never forgot what Teir did to help put down the rebellion, but now Drw's gone and your father has nothing. If he sees you wedded to the new chief, his name will have high honour in the Crainnh again.'

Teia stared incredulously. 'But first I have to whore for him?'

'Teia!' It was not much of a reproof and still Ana could not look at her. 'He is a good man trying to do the right thing. A Crainnh without honour has no place in the clan and you know that. He is only trying to secure your future. Our future.'

Teia flung up her hands. 'And what if the chief doesn't want me for his wife? Did he think about that? Or will he just auction me off at the Gathering and buy back his honour?'

The clouds broke at last and engulfed her in tears. Jerking her dress straight, she pushed past her mother and out into the weak sunshine, no longer caring who saw her face or pointed at her as she stumbled away. She did not care where she was going either, and blundered straight into the Speaker.

Strong hands caught her, fending her off. 'Wait – wait, child!'

Teia looked up, recognising the voice.

Frowning, Ytha lifted her chin. 'What happened to your face? Did Drwyn do this?'

Mutely, Teia nodded, fresh tears spilling onto her cheeks faster than she could swipe them away.

Ytha harrumphed and released her. 'I thought you would have learned how to please a man by now. You spent long enough with Drw.' The Speaker's voice was flat and chilly as stone and her green eyes just as hard.

Horrified, Teia searched Ytha's face for compassion or even a shred of the brusque kindness of the night before. She found nothing. Her heart sank towards her toes and she could articulate nothing more than a moan.

'Stop snivelling, child! I told you yesterday: do your duty and all will be well. Now wash your face, put on the dress I gave you and attend the chief. He will be expecting to see you beside him when he wakes.' With that, Ytha gathered her mantle around her and strode off.

Teia stared after her through a blur of tears. Maybe the wedding fair would have been a better option after all.

4

SAVIN

✦

The house near the tailors' guildhall in Mesarild to which Savin had tracked Alderan's colours truly was unremarkable: a four-square, sturdy thing of dressed Elethrainian granite, stolid and rosy as a country squire, surrounded by a low wall built more to define the small square of neatly scythed lawn behind which the house sat than for any pretensions to security. To all appearances it was a merchant's residence; someone well-to-do enough to afford a modest garden in the imperial capital, where all the streets sloped steeply away from the Citadel and level ground was at a premium. It was not ostentatious, but possessed of that smug well-keptness that was so dreadfully middle class.

Watching from the shadows of the guildhall's great arched door, Savin wondered what had motivated Alderan to come here. Visiting a friend would be the obvious answer, but Alderan's friends tended to be innkeepers and ships' captains and such – lower sorts who picked up gossip or moved freely around the Empire and could therefore be useful to him. A lace-merchant or mill owner of the type suggested by this house was an unusual choice for the old man.

Another mystery. Another puzzle to be solved.

Light glimmered behind the drapes covering one of the downstairs windows but the upper storey was dark. So the family was at home – at this hour, probably at supper. Good; they'd all be in one place. That would make things easier.

He was about to step out of the shadows and cross the street when the front door opened and a woman appeared, carrying a brass lamp. A housemaid, by her sober gown and white apron. She hung the guest-lamp on a hook by the door to light the way for visitors, then vanished back inside. The door closed behind her with a solid thud.

Savin frowned. How many other servants would there be, for a house that size? A parlour maid and cook, perhaps a housekeeper? Carefully, he reached out with his mind towards the house. Five tight knots of colour clustered in the room with the light behind the drapes, and at the back of the property there was a further dull smear that was most likely the maid, probably in the kitchen or scullery. A scan of the other rooms said they were empty; maybe the householder was not quite as wealthy as he pretended to be.

Something dragged over his senses, as fine and clinging as a cobweb in a darkened room. It was a ward of some kind, one as subtly engineered as any he had ever encountered outside of the Western Isles, and it bound up the entire house – mouse-holes to chimneypots – so delicately that the least touch would tear it.

Impressive.

Savin looked again at the colours he'd found, studying them. Three were children, their nascent gifts as carefree and tangled as a patch of wild flowers, but the other two, now that he looked more closely, were carefully modulated to appear almost nothing at all. The discipline required to conceal a gift so effectively took years of practice.

He almost laughed. Now Alderan's visit made sense, and the weaving he had detected had most likely been him opening a way through the ward. Which meant – oh, and the realisation filled him with such glee – that this self-satisfied little mansion was probably the Order of the Veil's safe house in the capital.

So. Kitchen first to deal with the maid, then, once there was no chance he'd be disturbed, he'd see what the others could tell him about the old man.

Under his senses the Veil was a rippling many-coloured fabric, billowing like a goodwife's laundry line. Holding up his hands, palms out, fingers spread, he stilled it, then slid his will into the spaces between the threads. With a simple gesture, he drew the evening apart and stepped into the Hidden Kingdom, then out into the somnolent warmth of the residence's kitchen.

The maid had her back to him, busy at the table with a bowl of some fruit and custard concoction that she was serving into fine cut-glass dishes. A twist of air around her neck jerked her upright. The serving spoon clattered onto the table, splashing gobs of scarlet fruit across the maid's white apron. She clutched at her throat, found nothing there and began to struggle against the compression of her windpipe. Clawing at her neck, raising welts on her own skin. Savin tightened the garrotte. The maid kicked out, once, twice, and hit the table hard enough to set the dishes rattling against each other. Time to finish it; he couldn't afford any more noise. Another twist and the maid's dance ended with the brittle snap of the horseshoe bone in her throat.

Quietly, he lowered her to the floor and waited a moment to see if anyone had heard anything. No voices, no footsteps approaching. Good.

On the table were desserts for four, and a fifth bowl containing stewed apple. He scooped a fingerful of the dessert from the serving bowl and tasted it: raspberries, and a dash of brandy in the sauce. Delicious. He picked up one of the dishes and a spoon and let himself out into the passage. The gentle *chink* of cutlery and a murmur of conversation, punctuated by the treble interjections of the child who was clearly too young to be eating brandy-laced trifle, led him to the room at the front of the house where the master and mistress were indeed taking their supper.

All conversation ceased when he opened the door. The woman, mousy-haired and prettyish, paused in wiping the mouth of the smallest child whilst the two older ones stared. At the head of the table, a stocky man in a brocade waistcoat was slicing meat from a fragrant pork roast. He looked up at the sound of the door opening and the knife stilled in his hand.

'What the—'

'Good evening,' Savin said, cutting him off with a bright smile.

The man blinked, momentarily thrown by a display of good manners, then his affront came storming back. The carving fork clattered onto the platter, but he kept a firm grip on the knife.

'Explain yourself, sir, or I'll call for the watch.' He had the rolling brogue of the marches and his voice was pitched low and steady, no doubt to avoid alarming his family. *Splendid*, Savin thought. Now he knew exactly where to apply pressure.

'I'm hoping you can help me,' he went on conversationally. He hooked a chair out from beneath the table with his mind and sat down, spooning up some trifle. 'I have some questions about a visitor you received a few days ago. I'd like to know why he was here.'

The little demonstration of his gift did not even make the man blink, confirming the fellow was well acquainted with the Song.

'My visitors are none of your business! You can't—'

Savin sat back in his chair and crossed his legs, bowl of trifle cradled in his lap. 'Actually,' he said, taking another spoonful, 'I think you'll find I can.'

The man's mouth worked as he gathered himself. He exchanged a look with his wife. 'I think you'd best take the children upstairs, dear.'

'Mmph.' Swallowing, Savin gestured with his spoon. 'Please, don't let me interrupt your meal. This shouldn't take very long.'

He looked around the room, feigning interest. As he'd suspected, the furniture was rather too large and dark for the proportions of the space, and the table overdressed with flowers, candelabra and too much gilt-edged plate. 'What a charming room.'

Out of the corner of his eye, he saw the woman lay down her napkin and slowly lift the youngest child into her arms. She shifted in her seat and gave herself away with a panicked glance at the door. A single thought slammed the door shut hard enough to rattle the china in the ugly breakfront cabinet. The woman flinched and the child in her arms began to grizzle.

'I'm afraid I must insist you stay.'

Fear rolling off her, she stared at him with eyes wide as a trapped animal's. The room froze, became so utterly still that Savin could hear the candlewicks hiss as they burned.

'Where's Cally?' Even allowing for the dread weighing it down, the woman's voice was unexpectedly lovely.

'The maid? She's in the kitchen.' He scooped up some more trifle. 'Did she make this? It's really very good.'

'Please tell me you haven't hurt her!'

Savin shot her his most dazzling smile, the one that usually set society ladies' fans fluttering. 'She's in no pain, I assure you. Now, I'd like you to tell me why Alderan was here, and where he was going.'

'Who?' The man was frightened now, judging by the over-firm tone, the white knuckles on the handle of the carving knife. The rise and fall of his waistcoated breast betrayed how fast he was breathing. 'I don't know that name.'

'But you know his face.' A flick of fire-Song sculpted Alderan's likeness from one of the candle flames, bristle-browed and leonine.

'You're mistaken,' the fellow insisted. 'I've never seen him before.'

'Mama, who's that man over there?' asked one of the children, a boy by its clothes, though at that age the piping voices all sounded the same. His mother hugged the brat on her lap closer and fumbled for the other child's hand.

'A . . . friend,' she managed, voice brittle as first frost.

Savin dropped a broad wink for the benefit of the boy.

'Yes, I'm a friend of your father's.'

'Have you come for supper?'

He laughed indulgently. 'Something like that. Why, would you like me to stay?'

At once the hairs on his scalp lifted as someone in the room reached for the Song. He glanced across the table as the couple's carefully muted colours flared into brilliance, all subterfuge abandoned.

'There's no need for that,' he said.

The man flung down the carving knife and bunched his hands into fists. 'Get out of my house,' he growled.

Savin clicked his tongue. 'That'd be a shame, just when we're starting to get to know each other.'

Wrapped in the Song, he felt their weavings begin. The woman snatched her children against her skirts beneath a shield as her husband launched fists of air in Savin's direction. A flick of his own power turned the blows aside; another smashed the man backwards into the breakfront, shattering the glazed doors. Display plates tumbled from their stands and flew into pieces as they hit the floor.

'Egan!' The woman yelped her husband's name. To his credit he recovered quickly, shook broken glass from his hair and lunged for the table. His hand closed around the hilt of the carving knife.

'I'd rather you didn't,' said Savin softly, power thrumming through him. The knife came up, greasy blade glinting, and he exhaled irritably. People never listened.

A thought trapped the knife with his will. The man cursed and threw his weight forward but his hand and arm moved not an inch. Gripping his own wrist, he tried to pull it back, equally fruitlessly. His fingers were locked around the handle as if it was a part of him.

'What are you doing?' The man's shoulder worked as he tried to wrench his hand free by main force. Then the Song surged and blow after blow hammered at Savin's will. Beads of sweat broke on the man's forehead. The two younger children started wailing, too young to understand the forces being wielded around them, and pressed their hands over their ears to try to block out the power's roar.

'Shush now, darlings,' their mother quavered, cuddling them close. Beneath the soap bubble of her shield, her eyes were glassy with tears. 'It's all right, it's all right. Shh.'

'Damn it, let me go!'

Head tilted to one side, Savin watched the man's

efforts grow more and more frantic. 'No,' he said, 'I don't think I shall.'

Slowly, his will bent the man's arm, lifting it up then across his body. Guessing what was about to happen, the fellow tried to jerk his head back but another thread of air-Song held it still.

'Oh, Goddess, just let him go!' his wife moaned. 'Please, we'll tell you anything— *Egan!*'

Without looking, Savin threw a ward for silence around the woman and her keening children. She rained blows on him and on his weaving but she hadn't her husband's strength; they were easily turned aside and ignored. Instead he watched the man staring at the rising blade, his eyes swivelling desperately to keep it in sight as it glided towards his neck.

When it passed out of his field of view, he shut his eyes. Huffing stertorously, he whispered, 'Please . . .'

The knife came to rest against the side of the man's bull-like neck, pressed, stopped. A tiny thread of blood trickled down beneath his collar, staining his white shirt.

Sitting back in his chair, Savin smiled brightly around the table at the bewildered, wobble-lipped children, their mother with her face gone pale as whey. Her mouth formed the empty shapes of what might have been a prayer.

'Now,' he said, spooning up some more dessert, 'shall we start again?'

5

ESCAPE

⚜

Drwyn had given Teia a new horse for the ride to the Gathering. Finn, her old dun gelding, was consigned to the pack-train after aiming a kick at him, and had been replaced with a sweet-faced grey mare. By the fifth day of the journey Teia hated her. She was entirely too biddable.

Not much chance of you aiming a kick at the chief's backside, eh?

Feeling guilty, she patted her mount's neck. It wasn't the grey's fault she wasn't Finn.

She darted a sidelong glance at Drwyn. As a mark of her favoured status, she rode at his side now, whilst her family rode with the rest of the clan. He sat his raw-boned black warhorse with easy arrogance, wrapped in a thick plaid cloak against the chill wind. When he caught her looking, he heeled his horse over and leaned down from the saddle to crush her lips with a kiss.

'Pretty thing,' he murmured, stroking her cheek with his thumb. Then he kissed her again, roughly, his tongue pushing into her mouth. The heat in his eyes told her he would want her that night. She managed a smile, then focused her eyes on the mare's dainty tufted ears and tried not to feel sick.

Eight days, and it felt like a year. She lived in Drwyn's tent, fetched his meals and warmed his bed. She was expected to come at his call and leave when dismissed, in between doing whatever was asked of her. In return, he refrained from hitting her, unless she needed to be taught a lesson. He still liked to bite and slap when he

bedded her, but she had learned not to complain. The
one and only time she had, he had whipped her buttocks
with his belt until they bled, so now she pretended to
enjoy his attentions. It was a small price to pay to avoid
another beating. The journey to the Gathering was long
enough without having to make it on a flayed rump.

Teia pulled her chin down into the fur collar of her
coat. Winter had drawn in fast. The plains were sere
and hard with frost; the wind blew out of the north and
in the mornings tasted of snow. Overhead the dull sky
pressed down like a thick fleece. She could not recall a
summer that had felt so short, or a winter that promised to be so long.

She longed to scry out her future, but Ytha watched
her too closely. Ever since that night by the river, the
Speaker appeared suspicious of her, and having arranged the match with Drwyn she watched its results
closely. Whenever those cat-green eyes lit on her, Teia
wanted to scream.

There was so much she needed to know. She hadn't
yet learned how to focus her scrying and seek specific
answers; she saw only what the waters chose to show
her. Sometimes the visions themselves terrified her –
even apparently simple ones, like the boy with the chief's
torc, for not understanding the significance of even the
most innocuous image frightened her all the more.

The last things she had seen had been that eagle's-eye
view of summer plains and her own bloody face. During the long nights in Drwyn's tent, she had tried to
puzzle out what they might mean, had dredged her
memory for every scrap of lore Ytha had ever uttered
on the subject of interpreting dreams and visions, but
come no closer to the truth. Blood could mean an argument, a difficult decision, damage to one's aspirations
or, more often than not, just blood: someone would be
hurt. That frustrated her; it was not an abstract vision
of blood, but a very specific one. Her blood, on her

face. Something was going to happen to her and she did not know what it was.

⁂

Storm clouds roiled overhead. Rain plastered Savin's shirt to his skin and the wind shrieking around the towers of Renngald's fortress whipped his hair across his face. He shook it free and squinted at the image rendered in miniature in the basin resting on the iron tripod in front of him: a tiny ship on a storm-tossed sea, wavering as the rain lashed the shallow water. One toothpick-slender mast was already broken; surely it couldn't be long before the others followed, yet somehow the ship battled on; climbed each towering wave, survived the dizzying drop into the following trough and did not broach. Spread around it like a fabulous cloak was an intricate tapestry of the Song that bulged and billowed with the force of the storm pummelling it.

The Guardian was the architect of that glittering web. Savin could feel his will in the shaping of it – after so many years, he knew Alderan's work the way he recognised the hand of a master sculptor – but the power that gave each gossamer strand the strength of an anchor chain, that was the boy. Untrained, raw as meat on a butcher's slab, but between his strength and the old man's skill they were deflecting a gale that should by now have smashed the ship to kindling.

His name was Gair, the man in Mesarild had said before he died. Some fatherless wretch the Church had cast out; a nonentity, but for his gift. *They're going to the Isles that's all I know I swear please Goddess it hurts—*

Precious little, and it had taken one of the woman's eyes to get that much, despite her protestations that they would tell him everything. Alderan, it appeared, was as close-mouthed with his own subordinates as he was with everyone else. Still, it had given Savin a direction of travel to pursue; learning the rest had only required a little silver in the right palms. Now he had a chance to be rid of the old meddler for good.

Gripping the rim of the basin so tightly the cold metal bit into his fingertips, he threw more power into his working. It sang over him, through him, and he channelled it into the storm he had wrought.

The winds rose again and slammed into the old man's weaving. The ship staggered, her single topsail straining against its reefs. Point by point, her course veered southwards, closer to the foaming shoals just visible at the edge of the image. Around him the northern storm-winds howled in sympathy and set the Kaldsmirgen Sea thundering against the rocks below the castle walls.

Despite the slap and scour of the storm on his face, his lips stretched into a grin. This Gair boy was strong but Savin knew the Guardian's tricks far too well: he'd had the measure of them for years.

You'll have to try harder than that to beat me, old man!

Already the billowing curtain of the Song that shielded the distant ship was beginning to fray under the strain of wind and water. It could last only minutes longer, then the shoals would have them. The whelp was no threat: without training, with no more discipline than was required to call and hold the power, all the strength in the world was as nothing. If he survived the storm, which was not likely, his own gift would no doubt finish the job before the year's end. Candles that burned brightly were apt to start fires if left unattended.

Time to finish it and be done; Savin had other fish to catch. He wove the strands of his power more closely together, thrusting one hand up towards the sky. Physical gestures were unnecessary in working the Song, but it was late and he was bored; it was all too easy to slip back into the habits of childhood.

Viewed through the basin, the clouds above the Inner Sea convulsed, punctuated by the crack and boom of thunder. In his mind's ear the shrieking wind reached a new pitch and the sea's heaving grew more violent. Waves smashed themselves into spray, clouding his vision, but he no longer needed to see. He could feel the storm thrumming in every sinew, every muscle. He was one with it, and it was his to command.

Fist clenched, Savin brought his hand down hard.

The shield bowed but still did not tear. He blinked in surprise. How? Alderan was wily, and skilled at making the best use of what gift he had – how else could he have taught his students that, in the right hands, a dagger could turn aside a broadsword? – but in a contest of raw strength the old man should have been outmatched. Worse – the blow he'd just been dealt should have crushed him, yet his weaving remained intact, and it was brightening. Threads of new colour shone through it: vivid emerald, bright gold, gleaming clean and new as if polished.

The Church whelp; it had to be. Somehow that untried boy had reached further, deeper into the Song and turned loose his strength to reinforce the weave beyond anything Alderan could have wrought unaided. Now the shield arched high over the beleaguered ship like a steel breastplate and turned the storm's force aside. Not stopping it but diverting it, backing the winds around to the east again. Underneath the shield, tiny figures swarmed over sodden decks and out along the straining main yard. Tightly reefed canvas suddenly bellied to the wind, bringing the ship's head up. In moments she was running before the gale, north and west away from the reefs. The winds he had sent to destroy were instead carrying his old enemy to safety.

What are you doing here, Savin? Alderan's voice floated calmly above the roar of the storm.

It's a pleasure to see you, too. Savin reached back into

his power, twisting thick ropes of air together until the winds screamed. *You have no hold over me, old man. I can come and go as I please.*

More's the pity.

Now, now. No need to talk like that – not when we've known each other so long. Can't we be civil?

We passed the point of civility when you killed Aileann.

Still holding that against me? Savin clicked his tongue impatiently. *Maybe she'd still be alive if she hadn't tried to tell me what to do.*

She was your mother! Alderan snarled. His colours quivered with suppressed emotion, or perhaps the effort of communicating over such a vast distance – Savin didn't know which and didn't particularly care. The old resentment burned anew.

Then she should have known better, he snarled back.

But Alderan was gone, and Savin's storm was drifting for lack of attention, driven northwards by the hot breath of the desert. Mastering it again would require as much effort as raising it in the first place, and by the time he did so the ship would be well away from the point of summoning and moving faster than he could send the storm after it.

Shafts of sunlight pierced the clouds in the basin as the vessel pulled away, gleaming on the yards and wet rigging like sailors' fire. The ship was out of his reach now, and his foe with it.

'Hjussvoten!'

He swept the basin off its tripod with the back of his hand. Water sprayed into the air, quickly lost in the rain, and the shallow bowl clanged onto the stones. Before it had stopping spinning he kicked it clear across the tower-top, where it careened off the far parapet with a sound like a cracked bell. Another kick sent the tripod tumbling after it.

Curse him!

Fury boiling through his blood, Savin cast about for something else on which to vent his frustration, but the storm-weathered tower-top was bare.

Curse the crafty old bastard to the stinking pits of hell – and his new apprentice with him!

Lightning arced from horizon to horizon, filling his nostrils with the dry, bitter smell of scorched air. The clouds seethed in response to his rage, and below the castle walls the Kaldsmirgen thrashed itself to pieces on the rocks, hurling spray up over the crumbling merlons. He tasted its salt in the rain, felt its sting in his eyes and howled, and the storm yelled back twice as loud.

At each corner of the tower, squat stone skaldings leered out of the night. Fists clenched, chest heaving, Savin glowered at them. Hideous things. The superstitious Nordmen carved them as both watchers and warnings, and their sly, knowing faces were all over the islands: above every gate, every fireplace, squatting on every gable end. Picking their noses and whispering in each other's ragged ears. As if life on the Northern Isles wasn't charmless enough, he had to be surrounded by so much *ugliness*.

The Song surged inside him and he thrust his hand out towards the nearest statue. With a crack like thunder its horned head flew apart in a shower of stone chips. Another crack blew off its wings and a third scattered the rest of it into the sea in shards.

It wasn't enough, but he felt better for it. Raking his sodden hair back from his face, Savin stalked to the stairs that spiralled down into the keep. The men in the guardroom below glanced up from their dice-cups as he passed but let him be. Just as well, or they'd likely have met the same fate as the skalding. Down the stairs, along the draughty corridor towards his rooms, too furious either to maintain his ward against the cold or feel its lack, despite the chill that prickled his skin with gooseflesh under his wet shirt. He slammed the door behind him and warded it secure, then flung more of the Song at the lamps.

So the Church brat has a gift after all. A thought stoked up the fire. *And a potent one at that – what a charming surprise that was, eh, Alderan?* Another thought picked logs from the basket at the side of the hearth and hurled them onto the flames one by one, sending gouts of sparks boiling up the chimney.

You wily bastard. Playing your hand as if you held nothing but knaves, and then this!

The fire began to crackle, then to roar.

Heedless of the trail of drips he was leaving across his fine carpets, Savin strode to his bookshelves and hunted along them until he found the broken-spined wreck that had once been a finely gilded *Chronicles of the True Faith: A History of the Founding Wars* by St Saren Amicus, and tossed it onto the table by the sight-glass where it landed with its covers splayed open like the wings of a dead bird.

At the slap of leather on wood somebody gasped, and he looked up. The girl was still in his bed. One of Renngald's innumerable nieces, or some castle functionary's plumply pretty daughter; it was so tedious trying to keep track. He hadn't noticed her amongst the mounded furs but now she was sitting up, staring at him with those mussel-shell-blue eyes. Thick white-gold hair tumbled around her bare shoulders, almost but not quite covering her heavy breasts.

'My lord?'

She didn't speak much of the common tongue but knew enough of the important words to please him. He watched her, his fingers tapping absently on the book. Well, it would be one way to vent his frustration. He flicked the cover closed.

'Up,' he said.

She kicked off the covers and presented herself on her hands and knees, her back arched and her round white buttocks raised towards him. Such a pretty arse; it made up for her lack of a brain. Not that he kept her for her conversation; she did far more interesting things with her mouth than talk.

Stripping off his sodden shirt – linen; he hadn't risked silk in the rain – he walked towards the bed. Despite the chill embrace of his wet trousers he was already hardening, his flesh anticipating the girl's hot cunny.

Peering back at him over her shoulder, she undulated her hips invitingly.

He knelt on the bed behind her, unbuttoning his pants. 'I told you to shave,' he said, and shoved himself into her.

She grunted at the abrupt intrusion, but soon caught the rhythm of his movements and pushed back lustily. One hand took her weight whilst she used the other to stimulate herself, the walls of her cunny flexing around him.

Good girl. She was no *najji*, trained from childhood to please, but she'd learned her lessons faster than the others – just as well, as he quickly tired of repeating himself – and had developed something of a knack: her pelvic muscles worked his cock like velvet-gloved hands. Soon the rhythmic pulsing had his balls up tight against his body, the knot deep in his lower belly clenching hard. Yes. He pushed down between her shoulder blades, pressing her chest into the furs, and thrust harder. She mewled prettily, but not too loudly. She'd definitely learned.

He spread his knees, pulled her hips up against him with his free arm and rode her pillowy arse until the knot loosened and he emptied himself in quick, hot spurts. Sitting breathless on his heels, he watched the girl crawl around to take his still-stiff cock into her mouth and suck him clean, murmuring her appreciation.

That bobbing blond head in his lap was proof that even the dullest pupil could be taught, if properly motivated. Those with a bit of ability could even, one day, outstrip their teacher. He grinned. After all, hadn't he done so himself?

Is that what you want him for, Alderan? To be the good little Guardian that I never was?

The girl's teeth grazed his flesh and he grunted. 'Enough.'

Those mussel-shell eyes looked up through bed-tousled hair as she continued to work her lips up and down the length of him. On another day that hot mouth and fluttering tongue might have roused him again, but now his fury was spent the girl had served her purpose.

'I said enough!' He slapped her away.

With a yelp she scrambled back to the far side of the bed to hide herself under the furs, watching him warily over the edge like a house-dog in fear of a beating. Knowing it would make her flinch, he snarled at her and laughed when she cringed.

Stupid creature, but what else were pets for?

What is your new pet for, Alderan? Will he fetch for you, walk on his hind legs, sing on command? Careful he doesn't bite you – even house-dogs have teeth!

A thought dropped into his mind as clean and cold as a drip of snowmelt. His hands stilled on his trouser buttons. *House-dog, or guard dog?*

That was no reject from the priesthood he'd met in the inn's roof garden – not with that sword across his back, and the spread of shoulder beneath his shirt that said he had the muscle to swing it. A Knight, then – or maybe just a novice; the boy was young enough. And with the potential he'd seen in the waters . . .

Oh, the irony was quite delicious. Savin raked his still-wet hair back from his face and thought of the book on his desk, and of a ship on a blue-green sea. The ship was out of reach for now, but all was not lost, not entirely. After all, sometimes an obstacle was just an opportunity in a dirty coat.

Wondering how much that shabby-proud Church youth might know about what had become of Fellbane's treasure when the battle was done, he started to smile.

⚔

Twelve days after the Crainnh welcomed their new chief, they reached the Gathering place. It was a vast, bowl-shaped hollow surrounded by a ridge of black, glassy rock. A crescent-shaped lake lay within, its arms embracing a wide sward. Smoke rose from dozens of cook-fires in the clan camps strewn along the perimeter of the hollow. Corrals of livestock and picketed horses occupied one end of the flat ground by the lake, and at the other stood an open-sided pavilion decked with fluttering ribbons, where the wedding fair would be held. Traders' pitches chequered the space in between, their wares spread out on blankets. The air smelled of woodsmoke, crushed grass and animal dung, laced with the north wind's icy bite.

Whilst the womenfolk set about rigging the tents and preparing meals, Drwyn and a dozen hand-picked warriors from his war band went to greet the other chiefs. Ytha accompanied them, dressed in her snow-fox mantle and carrying her whitewood staff.

From the tent doorway, Teia watched them leave. Could she find the time to slip away before they returned? She cast an agonised look around, at the chores awaiting her. Two of Drwyn's warriors had erected the tent for her, but she still had to furnish it and start cooking.

An idea came to her. She hurried back inside and feverishly spread the ground-skins, unrolling carpets and arranging cushions. Then she changed out of her dress and into elk-hide trews and a thick jerkin, and dug her bow and quiver out of the baggage. Drwyn did not like her to keep them, but she had managed to distract him enough with kisses that he had never got around to taking them from her.

Fingering the beaded stitching around the neck of the quiver, she remembered her father gifting it for her tenth summer. Every Crainnh should know how to hunt, he'd said, then taught her to shoot, and how to care for the bow-stave and the elk-horn nocks. A fierce little pang shot through her and the blue and green beads blurred a bit. Macha willing, she'd be with her family again before too long.

Tying her hair back, she composed her face. Now she had to be strong. Quiver shouldered, heart thumping so loudly she was sure it could be heard right across the valley, she stepped out of the tent.

The two guards looked around as she emerged. One of them, a stringy-haired fellow with bad skin, eyed the shape of her in the close-fitting trews.

'Fetch my horse,' she ordered, amazed that her voice did not quaver.

The guards exchanged a glance. 'And where would you be going?' one of them asked.

'To catch the chief some supper. A brace of widgeon, I think.'

The lecherous one – Harl, she thought his name was – leered at her. 'Well, he does have a taste for a bird, especially one with a nice plump breast.' He stared directly at the open neck of her jerkin.

Teia snatched an arrow from her quiver and in a heartbeat had it nocked and aimed at his eye. 'Careful your eyes don't fall in,' she said. 'I'd hate to see you lose one.'

Harl blinked, startlement replacing his lustful expression. The other guard stifled a snigger.

'I said, fetch my horse.' She drew a little harder on the string, enough to make the bow creak, and he backed off a pace. 'That's better. Come on, Harl, come on. The afternoon's a-wasting.'

Harl bobbed his head. 'Yes, lady.'

When he'd gone she returned the arrow to the quiver, then wrapped her hands around the bow so the other fellow wouldn't see they were trembling. She needn't have worried. However amused he'd been by what had happened to Harl, the man was now standing at his post and keeping his eyes to himself.

Harl returned with her grey saddled and ready. Teia thanked him coolly, mounted and rode out of the camp. Only when she was well away from the tents did she let herself relax, her sigh of relief trailing off into a giggle at her own audacity.

Treating Drwyn's men as if they were her servants! But it had worked. Whether it would work a second time she couldn't say, but for now it had bought her an hour unobserved. She was determined to make the most of it.

A mile or so north of the Gathering place, a string of smaller lakes nestled like jewels in a silvery web of streamlets. With little solid ground to speak of, she had to leave her horse tethered to a bloodthorn bush and pick her way through the reed beds on foot, but the cover was good and the patter of the bone-white stems in the wind covered any noise she might make.

Within a quarter of an hour Teia had dispatched a pair of widgeon at the largest of the lakes, recovered and cleaned her arrows, and tied the birds by the feet with a bit of twine. Now the rest of the afternoon was hers. She knelt on the shore and scooped water into a dainty bronze bowl she'd filched from Drwyn's tent, small enough to hide in her belt-pouch. Holding it steady on her knees, she summoned a little of her power.

At first the image was smeary and difficult to hold. Her face again, this time with a ragged gash on her temple that was the source of the blood on her cheek. As she watched it knitted up into a tight pale scar; where it disappeared into her hairline, her dark hair turned snowy white. The dead look in her eyes changed, too, becoming instead haunted, as if she carried a dreadful secret buried deep in her heart, like a worm in a blush-berry.

Then the image re-formed, stretching and filling the bowl between her hands until she saw herself, in exqui-site detail, robed in snow-fox fur and carrying a Speak-er's staff.

Teia gasped and dropped the bowl. Cold lake water soaked her knees. She was destined to become a Speaker? How was that possible? If Ytha found out about the Talent, she would know she had been deceived and only exile could follow. Teia would have to join the Lost Ones or die alone on the pitiless plains. But if Ytha did not find out, she would have to continue with the life she had.

She closed her eyes and pressed her face into her hands. So the wedding fair would have been her best choice af-ter all. The chance remained that Drwyn would give her up, but it was diminishing. The more she played his will-ing concubine, the more he tolerated her. In time, he might even make her his next wife, and then Teir would get the bride-price of which Drw's death had cheated him.

Poor Drw. He had been kind to her; vigorous but gentle enough that sharing his blankets had not been a chore. Sometimes, when he had only wanted her to sing or keep him company in silence, he had told her she reminded him of his daughter. Then the old chief had cried for the children he had lost, gone to join their mother in the next life.

Macha keep you, Drw.

Wiping her eyes, she retrieved her little bowl and pushed herself to her feet. The afternoon was waning fast, the lake flat and steely under a heavy sky. Dusk would be falling by the time she reached the tents if she didn't hurry. She shook the bronze dish dry as best she could and stowed it away, then gathered up bow and catch and set off for her horse.

When she reached the camp, the sky had darkened to purple and torches were being lit throughout the hollow. Tall iron braziers flamed on either side of the entrance to Drwyn's tent where the two guards stood, looking tense and uneasy.

As Teia dismounted, the tent flap was flung back and Ytha strode out, her face hard in the flickering light. 'Where have you been?' she demanded.

Heart lurching, Teia held up the brace of fowl. 'Up at the lakes, hunting.'

'Did you see anyone else?'

'No, Speaker. Is something wrong?'

'I sensed someone working the power outside the valley.' The words were bitten off as if by a spring trap. Teia flinched; it was all she could do to meet Ytha's gaze. 'Was it you? Do you have the Talent? Answer me, girl!'

'I saw no one, Speaker.'

'Answer me! Do you have the Talent? You know the penalty for deceit!'

Teia shrugged helplessly. Ytha seized her head between her hands and her awareness swept into Teia's mind on an icy wind.

She shrank from it, pulling her thoughts deep down inside herself, hiding from the storm beneath the covers of her fear. 'Speaker,' she whimpered. 'Please!'

'What happens here?' The deep, rough voice was Drwyn's. He loomed over Ytha's shoulder, massive in the shadows. 'Leave her be. She's naught but a girl.'

Ytha's grip on Teia's skull did not relent. 'She may have the power!'

'So?'

'It is clan law! A girl with the power is surrendered to her Speaker. If she is not, she is exiled. To breach clan law is to be stripped of honour unto the child of the child's generation. This is the word of the law, Drwyn, and even you are bound by it.'

The chief laid a hand on Ytha's shoulder and held it there. None but the chief would dare to lay hands on the Speaker and the flash of cold fury in her eyes showed she resented even that.

'Let her be, Ytha. If you insist that she be tested I will give her to you, but for now, let her be. The rest of the clans will be here tomorrow; I've too much to think on without having to come back to a cold hearth and an empty bed every night of the Gathering. Besides,' he added, 'my supper is bleeding over your robe.'

Ytha recoiled with an exclamation of disgust at the dark blood beading her furs. She shot Teia a look, as if the fault was all hers, then turned a frigid face to the chief.

'I await the day, my chief. She should have been sent to me long ago.'

With a stiff inclination of her head, Ytha stalked away. Drwyn came forward into the firelight and Teia's knees turned to water. With a sob of relief she slumped into his arms, grateful for his rough embrace though he would never know why.

'Did she frighten you?' he asked, in a clumsy attempt at comfort. Teia nodded, scrubbing her hand across her eyes. 'Well, there's no need to be afraid. The Speaker means you no harm.'

About as little harm as a crag-cat means a kid. 'She was inside my head. It hurt.'

'She was just testing you for the power,' Drwyn said. 'Perhaps you should be glad you do not have it. Now what about that supper?'

So much for comfort.

Resigned to her mundane tasks, Teia plucked and cleaned the fowl then rubbed their skins with honey and salt before setting them to roast. As she worked, she contemplated what she had seen in the water. It had not clarified her earlier scrying at all, simply posed more questions she was incapable of answering.

If only she'd had more time. She was certain further scrying would have given her other images, clues to help her puzzle out her future. Had the visions come to her in dreams she might have gone to the Speaker for an interpretation, except she could not be sure Ytha would not see it as evidence that she had the Talent – and once she learned that, Teia would have no choice but to show her all that she'd seen. The boy with chieftain's gold around his neck, all of it.

That night, when Drwyn was fed and bedded and sleeping the sleep of the sated, she thought about running away. The idea daunted her: leaving her family, everything she had ever known, for an uncertain fate. She had no idea where she would go or how she would survive the winter on her own, but she was filled with a dreadful certainty that she would not be able to remain where she was for very much longer.

6

THE GATHERING

❖

After a fitful night filled with fractious dreams, Teia woke on the first day of the Gathering feeling stiff as sun-dried elk-meat. Drwyn looked little better; he choked down a mouthful of bread to break his fast and then paced the tent with a cup of ale in his fist whilst she heated water for washing.

Afterwards he dressed with unusual care in his best

plaid trews and cloak, which he fastened at his shoulder with a large gold pin. His beard was combed, his hair tied back from his face; even the spear that was his badge of rank was polished and gleaming. He looked almost handsome, were it not for the nervous chewing at his moustaches as he prowled back and forth like a hound on a short leash.

Teia sensed that he would need little provocation to lash out at her, so she picked up an armful of clean clothes and took herself into the curtained-off sleeping quarters to put them away. She was folding them into a chest when she heard someone else enter the tent from outside.

'Excellent,' Ytha said. 'That should impress them. Well done.'

Teia, a folded shirt in her hands, froze where she knelt.

'Are the others ready?' Drwyn asked.

'Almost. Every clan is here. They'll be assembled in less than an hour. Do you remember what I told you?'

'Yes, Ytha. Don't fuss.'

'I am the Speaker of the Crainnh. It is my job to *fuss*,' Ytha told him frostily. 'You must make the right impression on the other chiefs. If they are to take you seriously, you must be your father's son and more besides.'

Dropping the shirt, Teia hitched her skirts up and shuffled on her knees as quietly as she could across the floor to the curtain. Hardly daring to breathe, she peered through a moth-hole in the fabric. Ytha was wearing a deep-blue woollen gown under her fur mantle, clasped around the waist with a golden belt of interlinked crescent moons. Another crescent kept her mane of hair back from her brow.

'This is an important day, Drwyn. If you do well today, nothing will stand in your way. You will be Chief of Chiefs inside a year and all of the south will be yours for the taking.'

'I am looking forward to it.'

Teia recognised the hunger in his voice. It was the same throaty growl she heard in the dark, when he told her how he wanted to be pleasured. His back was to her, but she could imagine his expression. She shuddered.

Chief of Chiefs! It had not been done in over a thousand years, not since before the clans had been driven north. The idea tumbled chaotically in her mind, a leaf in a welter of possibilities. And the south? Did Drwyn mean to challenge the Empire itself? Incredible. No, it was ludicrous; they would be cut to pieces. The iron men would be waiting for them. What could he be thinking?

'Ah, Drwyn, one step at a time,' Ytha said. 'If we rush the hunt, the game will fly and we will not be able to set the same trap twice.'

'You speak in riddles, Ytha! Say what you mean.'

The Speaker tsked and her tone grew sharper. 'I mean that our objective is closer now than it has ever been, but we must still be patient. If we try too hard we may ruin everything we have planned for. Now come, the chiefs will be waiting.'

Long after they had left the tent, Teia just sat there, skirts rucked up around her knees. She could scarcely believe what she had heard and yet, whatever else he might be, Drwyn was not insane. He would not contemplate something like this unless he was better than half-sure he could get away with it. She had learned that much in recent weeks. What would the other chiefs say? Drwyn could do nothing without their support, after all. That gave her an idea. Quickly, she finished her chores.

⚜

Amongst the rocks of the valley's rim, she had a good view of the fair spread out below her. There was hardly a hide's span of empty grass to be seen now. Tents crowded cheek by jowl, rival clans rubbing shoulders with all old enmities put aside. That was one piece of clan law that was universally accepted: for the four days of the Gathering and for three days before and after, differences were held in abeyance, even blood feuds suspended. The Gathering was the last great fair before winter, the last chance the clans had to trade, to exchange news, to find new wives before the ice and storms swept in off the northern sea to pen them all in their winter quarters in the mountains.

Smoke thickened the air and the whole valley was loud with bawling babies, barking dogs, braying livestock and babbling chatter. If she squinted, she could make out the badges of every clan, standards planted in front of the chieftains' tents. Not far from each ornamented pole was another tent, a fraction smaller but no less well appointed, which would be the residence of the clan's Speaker. In place of a banner, each sported a bronze representation of the clan's totem animal, decorated with feathers and fur and beaded bone charms that tapped together in the breeze.

She counted them; yes, every Speaker appeared to be present. Including the apprentices, that meant there were at least twenty-five, maybe thirty or more women with the power in this valley. Potentially far more, if she allowed for all those girls whose talents had not yet been discovered. No one should notice one more working in all that blather.

Scrambling back down the slope, she hunted for a secluded spring that she could use. It took her nearly an hour of barked shins and stubbed toes before she found one and even then it was difficult to reach. She had to stretch over a sharp-edged boulder to fill her little basin, then carry it gingerly back to a spot where she could sit down comfortably.

Viewing was a trick she had stumbled across by accident. She had been trying to scry and had lost her concentration. A stray thought about her mother had filled the water with an image of Ana's face and Teia's head with the sound of her mother's voice. After that, she had amused herself more than once eavesdropping on her sisters' conversations and occasionally got her ears burned overhearing something not meant for her, like the talk of the wedding fair.

If she concentrated on Ytha as the focus of her viewing, she was afraid the Speaker would sense her immediately and know that she had been deceived. Even thinking about what might happen then was enough to chill her, so she would have to choose someone else, but she knew very few of the other chiefs well enough by sight to be sure of picking someone out. In the end she opted for Eirdubh, chief of the Amhain, a craggy, tough individual she remembered from the last Scattering, in the spring. He had offered to dice with Drw for her, and the old chief had laughed as if he had caught the Eldests' own joke.

In moments an image of the Amhain warrior filled the basin. He was frowning, rubbing his chin between thumb and forefinger. As she concentrated she heard a voice, gradually becoming clearer. Drwyn was speaking, the rest of the Moot silently hearing him out. '. . . too long. It is time we restored our honour.'

'We were defeated in open battle, Drwyn,' one of the chiefs said. 'The vanquished must accept the victory. Such is the law of battle, clan law.'

'They came here in their ships and settled in our lands,' Drwyn countered. 'They hunted our game, despoiled our holy places, trampled over our traditions. To protect our honour we fought and died as true clan warriors, but they defeated us. That is not in dispute. The settlement, the peace they swore us to, is. It was a sham and I do not hold myself bound by it.'

'Word of honour was given,' put in another chief. Teia did not recognise him, nor the one who had spoken earlier. Unusually for plainspeople, they were both pale-haired with deeply sunburned hawk-like faces; they could have been brothers.

'Word of honour is binding only so long as the line remains. Where is the Black Water Clan now?' Drwyn asked them. 'Its honour was lost seven hundred years ago. It no longer has a place at this Moot.'

The circle of chieftains rumbled their agreement, their Speakers nodding sagely. They remembered the histories of the clans, remembered how Gwlach of the Black Water had been raised to Chief of Chiefs, to lead them to battle and ultimately to defeat.

'None of Gwlach's line survives. His word is no longer binding.' Drwyn spread his arms wide as he implored them to consider his proposal. 'The iron men stole our lands then doled out bits and pieces to us and made us grateful for them. Thankful to be given back part of what was wrongly taken from us.

'The faithless sacrificed their honour that day. They sold it to buy peace and broke a people that had roamed these lands for centuries before the settlers came. It falls to us, my brothers, to right that wrong, or else face the contempt of our children and our children's children for ever. We are twice the numbers we were then; the herds cannot sustain us. Our families will hunger, we will starve and die. Maybe not this winter, nor the next, but soon. The Speaker of the Crainnh has seen portents. Without space to hunt, without our honour and our freedom, we will cease to be. The time has come for us to take back what was ours.'

A pretty speech. Not one of Drwyn's making, though. It had Ytha's hand on it, that was for sure. And who had given him this sudden hunger for land to roam? Certainly Drw had seen no need to go to war for it – despite their numbers, the herds had not failed them yet, and he'd been content to follow them across the plains to the end of his days. Had that notion come from the Speaker, too, along with the carefully chosen words? The thought made Teia shiver.

The chiefs and their Speakers digested what Drwyn

had said. Some nodded and murmured amongst themselves; others stared down at the turf or off towards the lake. One or two, like Eirdubh, gazed straight at Drwyn and dared him to hold their eye.

Drwyn did not fail them. He kept his head high, stance erect and proud. The tilt of his jaw, the way he held himself, were so like how she imagined Drw must have been in his prime that Teia felt a sharp pang of loss. The other chiefs obviously thought much the same. She could see it in their eyes, the way they measured him and found little lacking. It spoke powerfully in his favour.

She remembered what Ytha had said, how he must be his father's son and more, and began to see how the Speaker was manipulating not just the Crainnh, but the other clans as well. Teia followed the path with her mind's eye and saw the spear of the Chief of Chiefs at the end of it.

She dragged her attention back to the present and steadied the viewing, which had begun to waver with her distraction. Eirdubh was speaking. The Amhain chief was on his feet, a sinewy man in leather and fur with a face as worn and weathered as a tor. Silence spread around him as the other chiefs listened.

'A grand plan, Drwyn,' he said in that deep, quiet voice of his. 'Grand indeed. But how do you expect to carry it out? The Empire and its Knights will not have vanished. They will still be there, in their stone forts in the mountains, waiting for us.'

'The forts are empty,' Drwyn said. A hiss of indrawn breath snaked around the Moot. 'My Speaker has shown them to me and, to be certain, I have sent warriors to scout them. There are no iron men in the mountains.'

'Can you prove this, Drwyn?' asked Eirdubh. 'Can your Speaker show us also? We do not doubt her words, for a Speaker can tell no untruth, but we men are not gifted in the way of Speakers and need to be shown plainly.'

'I can show you,' Ytha said, cool and composed. 'Your own Speakers can, if you ask them. The lake is here – use the waters.'

Three of the other Speakers exchanged glances as they conferred. Teia recognised two of them: the White Lake and Stone Crow Clans' lands were close and they wintered in the mountains not far from the Crainnh. As one they nodded.

The middle one stepped forward, her staff clasped before her. 'We know the places of which Chief Drwyn speaks,' she said. 'We will scry.'

Teia felt their power draw in and focus, as if the sky had suddenly taken a deep breath. The waters of the lake rippled and grew still, but the water in her basin trembled as the Speakers' scrying overlapped her viewing for an instant. Then the image in the water steadied. Teia brought her viewing closer, so she could see the scrying more clearly.

The Speakers had conjured an image of the an-Archen, blue-white and sharp, the snowy peaks dazzling to behold. The image drew in, as if seen from a swooping bird's perspective, and focused on a mountain pass with a fortress blocking its narrowest point. Massive walls spanned the pass between heavily fortified towers, in which empty windows stared like the sockets of bleached skulls. Ravens circled overhead and bickered along the battlements, their harsh voices echoing around the pass. Of human habitation there was no sign. No smoke rose from inside the fort, no sound came from behind the walls; the entire pass rang with emptiness. If there were armed men there, they were as still and silent as stones.

'It is true,' breathed one of the Speakers. 'It is empty.'

'Can you go closer? See inside?' her chief asked.

The image focused on the nearer of the two watch-towers and closed in. A window loomed, yawned, swallowed, and the basin was filled with darkness. It lightened gradually, revealing a circular chamber with an arched doorway leading onto a stone staircase that spiralled through the centre of the tower. Upwards it led to the ramparts, affording the watchers a view down into the empty heart of the keep; downwards it led past several more chambers until it deposited them in a room off the central yard. Collapsed roofs and echoing corridors told a tale of long disuse, echoed in cracked stones overgrown with lichens and hearths devoid even of ashes. The fortress was utterly abandoned.

The Speakers drew back, letting the image dissolve. A breeze ruffled the lake waters and all trace of their scrying vanished.

Teia huffed her hair out of her eyes. Her concentration was slipping. The Speakers had almost drawn her into their weave, and keeping her viewing separate from theirs required a great deal of effort. Her temples throbbed; she would not be able to sustain this for much longer.

'I am satisfied,' pronounced the White Lake chief, nodding as his Speaker resumed her place at his side. 'I know that place. If it is empty, the iron men will likely have left the others as well. What do you propose? This is a poor time of year to be beginning a war.'

'I propose we all wait out the winter, arming our war bands and readying ourselves, and in the spring, we join our forces for battle.'

Drwyn's face was resolute, fierce, but Eirdubh shook his head. 'It is dangerous, Drwyn, very dangerous,' he said. 'To resume a war which cost us so many brave warriors, and after so long. Even blood feud does not endure through so many generations. Is it not time to let it lie? I confess I am uneasy.'

'The Eldest will guide us,' Ytha told him. 'I have seen it in a foretelling.'

Murmurs of surprise and anticipation flitted around the Moot and Teia leaned closer to her basin, although that would not let her see any better. Signs and portents were common enough; they guided the clans through everyday life – when to hunt, where to camp, what fortune held for a man – but a true foretelling was rare indeed. No wonder the other Speakers were so interested.

'For three nights,' Ytha began, spreading her arms wide, 'I dreamed of a great wolf walking the plains, hungering for prey. For three days a wolf howled at dawn and at sunset our totem wept tears of blood for our imprisonment. On the fourth night, a raven spoke to me in my dream, saying that Maegern will ride again. She will fall upon our enemies like a storm and drive them from our ancient lands so that we may be free once more.'

A shiver tickled Teia's spine and she instinctively made the sign of protection over her breast. Maegern, Goddess of the Dead. Goddess of war, of ravens and discord, the darkest and bloodiest deity in the clan pantheon, with Her eye-painted shield that saw all and Her Hounds for the hunt. Not a name to invoke lightly, even for a Speaker.

She dragged her attention back to the basin in her hands. The Amhain chief was nodding, lips pursed as if, being a reasonable man, he was prepared to allow for the possibility.

'That may be,' Eirdubh said, 'but I would like to see such a sign for myself. Our gods have been silent for too many years. We asked for their help when the plague came and we saw nothing. I say we wait, and on the last day of the Gathering meet again and ask the Raven to give us Her blessing. If She answers, I shall be the first to offer you my spear, Drwyn. If She does not, I shall have no part in this war. I value the Stone Crow Clan's survival too highly to see it go the way of the Black Water.'

'No one values their clan more highly than I, Eirdubh. I would not endanger it needlessly,' Drwyn said. 'But blood feud is blood feud. I mean to extract a drop of our enemies' blood for every drop shed by our people when they were driven from their lands. A life for every life. I will buy back our honour with the southerners' souls, and I will do it alone if I have to.'

A tense silence gripped the Moot. Ytha broke it, stepping forward to lay a hand on Drwyn's arm. 'The Amhain's suggestion is a shrewd one, my chief,' she said. 'We need time to reflect, to ensure that a decision made in anger is not one we later live to regret. I applaud his wisdom in this.'

Drwyn shook himself and nodded enthusiastically. 'Indeed, indeed. Eirdubh's wisdom is renowned and he is right to counsel us all to caution. Three days, then, my brothers, until we meet again and ask Maegern for Her aid. May She smile kindly on us.'

Teia let the image in the bowl fade; a headache crashed down on her skull like a kick from a baulky horse and she had to sit with her eyes closed for a minute or two before she could think straight again.

Three days. Would the Raven come? She did not know. Along with every other clanswoman, Teia put aside a pinch of food from each meal and threw it into the fire as an offering to Macha the Provider. The ritual had been ingrained in her since childhood, but sometimes she forgot, and so far no lightning had struck her down and no giant ravens had carried her off. She had long since ceased to be afraid that they would, and the ritual offering was mere habit now rather than rooted in belief. Nonetheless, she shuddered as if someone had dumped snow down the back of her neck. Absentminded sacrifices to gods who may or may not exist were one thing, but gods that might one day sit down around the cook-fire and demand to be fed were quite another.

Quickly she emptied out the water and dried the basin roughly with her fingers before stuffing it back into her pouch. The Moot would be breaking up now and she would be missed if Drwyn – or worse, Ytha – came looking for her.

It was dusk before Drwyn returned to his tent. Two of his warriors followed him, carrying his purchases from the fair. They made poor porters, stacking the goods haphazardly in the middle of the tent, but he did not appear to notice. He dismissed them with a flick of his hand and rummaged through the bundles like a puppy at play.

Teia, mending a winter tunic by the light of a lamp, watched him with half an eye. The seal fur was deliciously soft on the skin but stitching it was hard work. Even if she followed the holes of the old seam it was difficult to force the bone needle through; her thumb was raw and all she could concentrate on was finishing it so that it would be over and done. She was only dimly aware of Drwyn sorting through his acquisitions, telling her what he had traded for a saddle cloth, some plaid for a cloak, a new steel knife, until an open hand connected with the side of her face. She flew backwards off her cushion, pain blossoming across her cheek.

Drwyn kicked her mending aside and loomed over her. His new knife was in his hand. 'Pay attention,' he snarled. He snatched her by the upper arm and hauled her to her knees. 'Look at me when I speak to you!'

Another backhanded slap landed across her mouth, just to make sure she understood. Her lip stung and she tasted blood. Drwyn's face was twisted, teeth bared in his beard like the fangs of a bear, his breath sour in her face. Slowly he raised the blade and held it flat against her cheek. The steel was cold as ice; she could not help but flinch.

Drwyn laughed. 'I'm not going to mark you, girl. Not this time, anyway.' He released her and stuck the knife through his belt. 'Clean this place up. It's like a goat pen.'

Then he was gone, back out into the night.

When he returned, he was drunk. Not insensible, but

drunk enough to lash out at her when she tried to avoid his lust and the stench of *uisca* on his breath. Enough to keep on hitting after she had submitted, punctuating the lesson in obedience with a harsh litany of the respect she would owe him when he was Chief of Chiefs and king of the plains. Enough to hit her again, later, when after all the grunting and shoving he could not finish what he'd started.

'Useless *cuinh*.' He stuffed his softening organ back into her, scratching her with his ragged nails. 'Take it!'

Teia pressed her face into the furs to stifle a cry. Her tender parts stung and burned with every lunge of his hips against her. Gritting her teeth, she prayed. *Please, Macha, finish him quickly. Bring the rain, and let him sleep.*

After a few clumsy thrusts, he slipped out of her again. 'Bitch!' he roared, and heaved her away from him. She fell against a brass-bound chest and agony burst through her side. For a few seconds she couldn't breathe properly, could only lie there and whimper with her eyes screwed shut. Something was broken, surely. Only a broken bone could hurt that much.

'Get up.'

If she didn't, he'd hit her again. Breathing in fast, shallow pants, she attempted to roll onto her knees. As soon as she moved the pain returned, white and blinding as lightning. She fell back, clutching her right ribs.

'I can't,' she sobbed. *No no it hurts too much I can't move oh Macha keep me it hurts.* Curled into a ball around her pain, Teia waited for the next blow.

'Now, *cuinh*!'

She flinched from his voice. But the blow never came, and she dared to peer up at him through her tangled hair. He was sitting on his heels, sweat-sticky and sullen, thick *daigh* drooping in the dark thicket between his thighs. Catching her eye, he sneered.

'Look at you.' His gaze raked over her as if she was a

mess one of his dogs had left on the bed. 'Can't even keep a man hard, can you?'

She shrank away from the surly light in his eyes. The *uisca* had robbed him, not her, but the drink had also left him too thick-headed to see it.

'Answer me!'

'No, my chief,' she managed. Her cut lip was beginning to swell; forming the words left blood on her tongue.

'Get over here.'

Keeping her eyes on the furs, she crawled towards him. Every muscle in her side was on fire. His right hand was tugging and twisting his member into a semblance of an erection, its angry red head glowering at her like a bloodshot eye. Dread filled her.

'That's better.' As soon as she was close enough, his left hand seized her hair and forced her head down. 'Now show your chief the proper respect.'

7

SUMMONING

In the chill pearly light of dawn, Teia dropped to her knees in the grass behind the chief's tent and retched. Each spasm of her belly hurt her ribs as much as the blows that had given her the bruises in the first place, and the vomit stung the cut in her lip. Again and again she heaved, until there was nothing left to come up but a little sour bile. Strings of spittle trailing from her mouth, she leaned on her hands until the spasms ceased and then stayed there, too weary and sore to move. Tears leaked from her eyes.

So that was that. She was carrying. Slowly, she wiped her mouth with the back of her hand and sat on her heels. There'd been no blood this past quarter-moon, and she'd hoped it meant nothing: Drw's sudden death, the upheaval after – every woman knew events like that could disrupt the moon-tides. But sicking up the bread and milk she'd forced down to break her fast, that was enough to be sure.

Drying her eyes, she looked around to see if she'd been observed, but the camp was barely stirring. Drwyn's snores from inside the tent said he'd not be waking any time soon, but when he did he'd expect to be fed – or brought a bucket. Either prospect set her stomach surging again, and she willed it to steady. Her belly and side were too sore to stand much more vomiting without sobbing.

It was bound to happen, sooner or later. The simples she'd learned from her mother didn't include a preventative that was effective more than three times out of seven, and Drwyn had an appetite that needed frequent sating. Catching for a child had been as inevitable as the goats catching for kids.

He would have to know, of course. Eventually. She thought of him inside the tent, sprawled on his face, reeking of last night's *uisca* and snoring like a thunderstorm. Then she thought of him holding her head down until she gagged finishing him, and shuddered.

The promise of a son might stop him hitting her, if nothing else. He might even marry her. As his wife she would finally be more certain of her status, which would increase with each son she bore, and in some respects she would have more freedom . . . but in many she would have less. It was difficult to say which was worse – concubinage or the fur-lined cage of wifely duty.

Wincing, she eased herself to her feet and walked

back around the tent. Smoke was rising from some of
the Crainnh cook-fires and from the wider hollow where
the other clans were camped, blue against the iron-
coloured sky. Frost silvered the grasses and had left a
skim of ice on the water bucket by the entrance. Teia
scooped it out and held it up to the thin sunlight, tracing the delicate pattern of leaves and stags-horn moss
the frost had made before it melted in the warmth of
her hands.

She was only delaying the inevitable, she knew, but
she wanted a chance to get her stomach under control
before she had to cook and serve Drwyn's meal. The
thought of food made her nauseous again, but she dared
not throw up in front of the chief. He would know for
sure then and she was not ready to face that. Not yet.

⚔

Two days passed, painfully slowly. Bruises coloured
Teia's shoulders and abdomen as brightly as a jewel-
bug's wings and her broken rib made it difficult to bend
over or stand up straight without pain. Drwyn's savage
wine-head that first morning gave her some bitter pleasure, but after that he stayed more or less sober, spending all his time with Ytha or the other chiefs as they
renewed old alliances sworn in his father's name and
began forging the new ones that would secure his position as Chief of Chiefs. He returned to his tent only to
sleep or change his shirt; to Teia's relief, he left her
alone. A small mercy, but she was thankful for it. It also
meant she could seek out a bidewell plant; a sliver of
the root tucked into her cheek helped keep the sickness
at bay, though she feared it would soon be seen for
what it was.

Thus far, however, Drwyn had not noticed, so preoccupied was he with politicking. Teia had decided that
he was not terribly observant to begin with, but come
the fourth morning of the fair he was too full of ner-

vous excitement to have noticed even if she had sicked up all over his boots. Today the Gathering would end and the clans would ask for Maegern's blessing. Drwyn's mind appeared to be fixed on that with an intensity she had never seen in him before.

Teia watched him pacing the tent as she nibbled on a heel of dry bread. It was the only food she had found that she could keep down first thing in the morning. He was dressed in his best again, combed and oiled, the golden torc of the chief gleaming around his thick neck. He kept fiddling with it, fingering the wolf-head bosses with their emerald eyes that glared at each other across his throat.

She didn't like the torc. The wolves' faces were far too lifelike for her peace of mind. They stared, teeth bared to snap, and the jewels in their eyes sometimes caught a light that was not there. She did not recall the torc looking so menacing around Drw's neck. In fact, she could not recall it being jewelled, either, not before the day when Ytha had held it above Drwyn's bowed head whilst the ashes of his father's pyre smoked behind him.

He gave the heavy gold twist a final tug and sighed. His gaze roamed around the tent, finally coming to rest on Teia. Still nibbling nervously on the bread, she looked up.

'You look pale,' he said abruptly. 'Are you sick?'

'No.' She shook her head a little, dabbing at crumbs on her lip. 'I'm just tired.'

'Have Ytha give you a draught to help you sleep.'

'I'm all right.'

His gaze was unsettling. There was something about it, a heat, a hunger, that made Teia's throat contract and her mouth dry up. She could hardly swallow her mouthful of bread. Putting the crust on her plate and her plate to one side, she got carefully to her feet. Drwyn's gaze followed her as she walked to the tent entrance. She

pushed through the flap to find Ytha standing just outside. Before she could stop herself, Teia squeaked in
surprise.

The Speaker raised an eyebrow, her face impassive.
She was pale from three days of fasting but carried herself rigidly upright, as always, wrapped in her fox-fur
mantle. Her hair was once more swept back behind its
golden crescent, emphasising her gaunt, strong features
and the deeply shadowed sockets of her eyes. Like a
horse skull, lying bleaching in the grass.

'Teia,' she said, tone neutral.

'Speaker.' Teia bowed her head and kept it down,
staring at the turf in front of her boots until she got her
nerves under control.

Drwyn emerged from the tent. 'Is everything ready?'
he asked.

'It is.' Ytha's voice was crisp as new snow. 'The other
chiefs await us at the Moot ground.'

'Then it begins.'

Teia darted a glance up in time to see Drwyn offer his
arm to Ytha. The Speaker hesitated, then accepted with
a gracious inclination of her head. Teia bit her lip. Oh,
Drwyn was bold, bolder than ever his father had been.
Most clansmen would sooner run barefoot across the
ash-fields of the Muiragh Mhor than invite a Speaker's
touch, and Ytha amongst Speakers was an ice-bear
amongst foxes.

The two made a striking pair. Almost of a height,
both powerfully built for their sex, but where Ytha was
pale and chill, Drwyn was dark and hot. Teia was struck
by the contrast, but also by the odd rightness of their
pairing, light and shade, ice and fire, totally unalike and
yet interdependent, like day and night. Together they
made a whole to lead the Crainnh, but either one of
them could snuff her out as easily as pinching the wick
of a lamp.

She watched them walk away into the bustle of the

camp, and as they disappeared from her sight a queer shiver ran through her body, like a cold draught through a warm tent. Her mother called it the touch of the harrow-bird: so the superstition ran, it meant a raven alighting on the place of one's death. Teia shook it off, but she made the sign of protection over her brow and heart, just in case.

As she went carefully about her chores, she could not keep her mind from pondering on the rite the Speaker would perform. She had only seen a summoning once before, six winters ago, when the plague had struck down four clans in as many weeks. Their Speakers had formed a circle around a fire and joined in a desperate prayer to the Goddess of the Dead not to take any more souls. Maegern had not answered them and the plague had raged for three more weeks, taking Drwyn's mother, his second wife and infant son in quick succession. Then, as abruptly as it had come, it had ceased. Those who were already sick had begun either to live or to die and the burnings had stained the skies black well into the new moon.

Had the Raven intervened? Teia did not know. Certainly some of the clanspeople said She had and had given thanks and made sacrifices in Her name. Others said She had not, that the plague had simply spent itself. Now the Speakers would importune Her again, not just on behalf of four clans this time but on behalf of all seventeen, and the outcome would decide the future of all of them.

In her mind's eye, Teia pictured them. Seventeen women, dressed in fox-fur robes and carrying tall staffs, arranged in a circle around a brazier set on a low cairn. She saw them quite clearly as she beat and arranged the cushions on the tent floor. Seventeen still, remote faces, each one different, all somehow the same in their agelessness and intensity.

One of them would lead the weaving and make the

sacrifice. In Teia's mind it was Ytha who stepped forward and drew a knife from her belt. The blade was as long as her forearm, single-edged and glinting. She raised it, resting across her open palms, chanting. The other Speakers lifted their staffs and echoed the chant. In the background bleated a tethered kid that would shortly be offered up to the goddess.

Teia realised she was standing still, bent over the last of the cushions. Knuckling the small of her back, she straightened up and stretched her spine as far as she could with all the bruises. She felt stiff and tired, although she had only been working a little over an hour; some air would refresh her. She stepped outside the tent and stopped dead in astonishment. The camp was gone.

Teia gaped. She could see all the way to the shores of the lake across a sea of silver-beige grass, swaying in the perpetual wind. There were no tents, no cook-fires, no animals. She could smell water and earth, but none of the stink of human occupation. The Gathering might as well never have been.

The only people in sight were the Speakers and their chiefs, in two circles around the cairn. One of the chiefs held a struggling kid between his knees, lifting its head up as Ytha approached with the long knife. Down it flashed. Teia looked away.

Yelling children played tag around the clusters of tents. Cook-fires smouldered. Women gossiped and glanced fearfully at the lowering sky; men mended harness or fashioned arrows and the air rang with noise. Teia swung around, but she could not see the Moot ground through the haze of smoke. She turned back to the guards outside the tent, but they looked as indifferent as men could without actually being asleep. One leaned on his spear and absently picked his nose whilst the other was ambling back from the latrine, fastening his trews.

Confusion clouded Teia's thoughts. What had she

just seen? For a few seconds, the camp had not been there, or else she had not been in the camp. Then she heard the chanting again and realised it was not in her imagination this time.

She could not make out the words, only the feel of it. Rhythmic and insistent, it pulsed in her head with the beat of the blood passing through her brain. She had been aware of the summoning six years ago only as a vague restlessness, like a day when the winds changed and made the children whoop and run like hares. This time it had a quality as urgent as the force of life and its pull was irresistible. Of their own volition, her feet took the first few hesitant steps towards the Moot ground.

Suddenly frightened, Teia groped for the music inside her, hoping to be able to pull herself free. Instead she was snatched up by a sweeping current the like of which she had never before experienced and was carried away.

Images filled her mind. Ytha, bloody to the elbows, casting the kid's heart onto the brazier where it smoked and blackened. Ytha dipping her fingers in a bowl and marking the forehead of each Speaker and her chief with blood. The chant grew stronger, a rhythmic repetition of a single phrase over which Ytha declaimed the summoning. The smoke from the brazier began to twist into strange shapes, influenced by neither heat nor wind. Sparks danced through it, first white, then yellow, then deepest red, forming a cloud that thickened and grew.

Overhead, the sky pressed down, such a deep grey it was almost blue. Abruptly the wind died. The children near Teia fell silent, and mothers glanced around anxiously before shooing them inside. Men exchanged wary looks, then put down their work and went to be with their families. In the pens, horses stamped and whinnied as the weight of the summoning settled on the whole camp.

Teia swallowed hard. The lump in her throat was as

large as a fist; it was hard to inhale past it. Her breath came in tight panicky gasps and her insides felt about to turn to water. Yet still her feet kept carrying her towards the Moot ground, and no matter how hard she fought the pull of the summoning she was as helpless as a fish on a line.

The cloud of sparks glowed fiercely, hotter and brighter than the coals in the brazier. All that remained of the kid's heart was a cinder. Ytha was hacking out the animal's liver now, butchering the beast with casual efficiency. Every Speaker had her staff planted on the earth in front of her as the chant drummed on. As she came closer, Teia realised why they needed such support: the earth was trembling underfoot. With each gobbet of flesh Ytha tossed onto the coals the cloud of sparks grew brighter and the pounding in Teia's head increased.

The Speakers' weaving had caught her up and drawn her in. On the periphery of her vision she saw a handful of other girls, one of them no more than six or seven years old, also stumbling towards the rite. They too must have the Talent. The ritual had sucked in every scrap of it that could be found, in order to give it strength. Surely the child was too young to withstand it? Teia herself could barely think for the beating in her mind. What must it be like for one so small, so much younger than she had been when she first experienced a summoning? But there was nothing she could do. The child was twenty paces away and Teia could not break from the course her feet had set.

Ytha offered up the last shred of liver with a triumphant bark. The cloud of sparks leapt, flaring, and a black rent appeared in the smoke. The other Speakers redoubled their efforts, raising the chant to an even higher pitch, although their voices were already ragged. With an overhand blow of the heavy knife, Ytha clove the kid's skull and tossed its brains onto the brazier.

The noise that followed was a mountain falling, or a thousand thousand voices roaring a name in unison. The earth lurched, spilling Teia from her feet, and the rent in the cloud vomited forth a dark shape.

A figure, curled up like a newborn. Slowly it unfolded itself, stretching and straightening as if waking from a long, long sleep. Its outline was blurry and indistinct, seemingly fashioned from dense black smoke, but it had arms and legs, a long cloak, a spear in one fist and a shield on its arm. Reaching up with its shield arm, it pulled off a grotesquely horned helmet and shook loose a mane of dark hair. On the shield, a painted sigil glimmered dully.

The chant cracked and faltered. A surge of power swept through Teia, draining her as it swelled the chant again. Ytha's voice continued above it all, concluding the summoning in firm, clear tones. She spread her arms wide, basin in one hand, bloody knife in the other. Silence fell.

Teia heaved herself up onto her knees, one hand pressed to her side. The silence was the kind that follows an ear-shattering noise, tense and ringing. The air bulged with it; her eyes felt too large for their sockets.

The creature in the fire heaved a breath, then another, savouring the air. *Who are you?* it rasped.

Moaning, Teia clapped her hands over her ears but it was too late. The voice was already in her head, scraping around the inside of her skull like bloody fingernails.

'I am Ytha, Speaker of the Crainnh, the Wolf Clan of the people of the Broken Land.' Ytha bowed low from the waist with her arms still outstretched. 'I bid you welcome amongst us.'

The creature rested its helm on its hip and tossed back its hair, rendering its face somewhat more distinct though no more detailed. A suggestion of eyes, mouth, teeth. Teia had no doubt that this was Maegern. She knew it as she knew of her own existence, as deeply

and intimately as she knew she was a woman. Dread
rose up inside her and soured her throat.

It has been a long time.

Maegern looked around Her at the ring of Speakers
and frowned, and as one they fell to their knees. The
chiefs behind them were already down, although Drwyn
was making a brave effort to meet the goddess's eye.

'It has been too long, great one. More than a thousand years since we were taken from You,' Ytha said.

Maegern waved a gauntleted hand dismissively. *I neither know nor care how you reckon the passing of
time. I care only that you have woken me. Free me, and
I will reward you.*

'Are You not free? I thought the summoning—' Ytha
faltered.

The goddess laughed harshly, and the sound rolled
around the horizon like thunder.

*This? You imagined this petty magic would be
enough? Not yet, little women! Not yet! You have not a
fraction of a fraction of the power of those who sealed
me away, but you have done well, for all that. If you
can do better, you shall have your reward.*

'What must we do? We would have You walk amongst
us once more. We have need of Your aid.'

To what end?

Ytha straightened her spine, held her head up. On
her knees she might be, but she would not grovel, not
even before a goddess. 'To return us to our home,' she
said. 'To purge it of the usurpers who stole it from us.'

Maegern sneered. *I have no interest in your squabbling for land. If you cannot take what you want by
force of arms, you are not worthy of my aid.* She made
to turn away.

'Please, great one, do not abandon us the way the
faithless abandoned You!' Impassioned, Ytha spread
her arms wide, and emotion throbbed through her

words. 'They turned their backs on the old ways. They gave up their freedom and swore themselves to servitude under the yoke of the same powers who exiled You.' Snarling, the goddess swung to face her again. 'The portents are favourable for Your return to us. If You ride with us, we can retake our ancient lands. Ride with us, and You will have Your revenge.'

A silence spread over the circle as the goddess considered. It was the silence between do and do not, the weight of possibility teetering on a knife's edge, ready to come crashing down and become reality.

Maegern's head tilted slowly to one side. Her posture shifted, a subtle rebalancing of weight and tension, like a serpent's restless coiling as it poised to strike. *Vengeance*, She hissed.

'Yes, great one.' Ytha's voice was pitched low and hungry. One of the Speakers behind her let out a low moan, quickly stifled.

Long have I waited. The goddess curled Her fingers around the shaft of Her spear, lingeringly, almost sensuously, as if taking a lover's hand. *Long have I dreamed of it.*

'Help us throw these usurpers back into the sea they sprang from, and it can be Yours.'

The silence stretched ever thinner. Waiting.

I have a test for you. Prove yourselves worthy and I will aid you.

Something like a sigh raced around the Speakers and their chiefs. No one moved, no one spoke, but there was a palpable easing of tension, like a slow exhalation after a breath long held.

'Name it,' said Ytha, exultant, her eyes shining in the brazier's glow. 'We are Yours to command.'

Find the key that was used to lock my prison. That which it closed, it may also open. Demonstrate your fealty and a bargain will be struck between us.

'We will end Your exile, great one, but what do we seek? Where will we find it?'

You will find it in the city of the seven towers, guarded by seven warriors. It has burned in my dreams all this time, but that is as much as I can feel of it. It has not moved since my prison was sealed. She motioned with Her spear towards the distant mountains, where the moons set. *It lies yonder. I will send my Hounds to guide you, but the rest is up to you.*

Raising Her hand, She put it to Her lips and blew a piercing whistle. It shrieked along Teia's nerves, making her sob aloud and clamp her hands even more tightly over her ears. Deep in the furthest recesses of her mind, she sensed a place of uttermost blackness suddenly stir with hot breath and rank fur.

Your power is fading, little women, Maegern told them scornfully. *You are weak.*

Hectic colour burning in her cheeks, Ytha met the goddess's eye. 'We are strong enough to find Your key, great one. I swear it.'

Maegern's lip curled. *We shall see.*

With a sweep of Her arm, She clapped Her helm back onto Her head and turned away. At once She dissolved into the flaming cloud. The brazier died and Teia's thoughts were extinguished with it.

8

CAT'S PAW

⁂

Two hundred-odd Nordmen feasting was a cacophonous affair. Ale-horns banged on tables and hugely bearded men in furs roared at each other, arguing or telling jokes – in their guttural language it was hard to know which was which. Fires blazed in each of the three great pits at intervals down the hall to add to the stench and the heat, and through it all came battalions of servants with platters of burned-bloody meat that they slammed onto the tables without a care for what they spilled, splashed or spoiled in the process.

It was all giving Savin a headache.

He brushed at a gravy-spot on his garnet silk sleeve and frowned. To think he'd given up the sophistication of a desert court for *this*.

'You're not drinking,' boomed Renngald from the high seat, a skalding-infested oak monstrosity that barely contained the man's fur-trimmed corpulence.

'I'm not thirsty,' Savin said, picking at some bread. He'd eaten his fill an hour ago, but the Nords' appetites in food and drink, as in all things, appeared to be insatiable.

His host frowned and pushed his iron crown back up his forehead from where it had come to rest on his shaggy eyebrows. ''S a feast. Should be drinking, man. Ale!' he yelled, thrusting his horn cup aloft. 'Ale for our guest!'

As if it had been a call for a toast, several dozen other men on the lower tables hoisted their cups into the smoky air and voices roared fit to lift the rafters. Most likely they didn't know or were too drunk to care what they were shouting for.

In his time amongst them he'd concluded that the Nords made up for their dark and cheerless island existence by seizing on the least excuse for feasting. A good harvest meant a feast. Renngald's prize sow farrowing – a feast. The sun coming out after rain – yes, another feast. He avoided as many as he could, but for as long as he was enjoying the castle's hospitality it was politic to endure one now and then.

These prodigiously bearded bears of men lolling around the hall were Renngald's thanes. Good warriors all, according to their lord, and they certainly carried well-worn axes and scarred shields, but as far as Savin could see they were all sots – and lechers to a man. Any serving maid who strayed too close was apt to be dragged onto a rampant cock in full view of the hall, while the other men shouted encouragement or beat time on the table with their fists.

And they were fecund, too: the castle was full of their brats, squalling, fighting, sobbing and hurtling around in packs. After a while their relentless shrilling set Savin's teeth on edge. Then he would retreat to his tower room, which Renngald had thankfully decreed out of bounds to all but servants, and ward the walls for silence. He was not averse to the pleasures of the flesh – far from it; something else a warded room was useful for – but at least he had the good manners to take his relief in private.

A servant plonked a foaming jug of ale down in front of him and disappeared. The sharp, hoppy scent made him feel slightly nauseous. The noise was now so loud, such a tangled mess of sound, that he could hardly think but still the bread and the beer were circulating. A scuffling in the rushes by his feet said even the castle's dogs were busy gorging themselves, scouring the floor for scraps. How long until it was over?

Leaning over the arm of his chair, Renngald squinted at him. 'You're still not drinking.' A cunning glint appeared in his eye that made Savin think he was perhaps not quite as soused as he appeared, and he grinned. 'Perhaps you prefer something sweeter than ale, eh?'

The lord of the Nordmen thumped on the table until he made himself heard over the carousing. 'Bring out the girls,' he cackled. 'It's time for pudding!'

This was met with enthusiastic cheers and broad grins flashed in whiskery faces. Overfilled ale-horns were shoved aloft, spilling foam down beefy arms. Savin shifted in his seat and wondered what depravity he was about to witness next.

The doors at the far end of the hall opened to admit a party of musicians. The thanes quietened down, more or less, and soon the air was filled with the floating strains of flutes over a throbbing drumbeat. Shortly after, a troupe of a dozen acrobats threw themselves along the hall in handsprings to whoops of appreciation from the thanes.

They were all female, lean and supple as stoats, and every single one of them was naked but for paint. Savin blinked. Clad in green leaves, swirling blue waters and leaping flames of yellow and orange, they spun and capered around the crowded tables like elemental spirits. Each girl's hair was drawn back into a multitude of tiny tight braids adorned with beads or fluttering feathers, and their hands sported long lacquered nails that made their fingers resemble the clawed toes of birds.

'Extraordinary,' he breathed.

Renngald leaned over the arm of his chair again, his crown once more askew, and gave Savin a knowing look. 'See? We are not entirely uncivilised, my friend!'

'Who are they?' Savin asked, mesmerised by the eldritch creatures. Even their movements were birdlike: they darted abruptly from motion to stillness, observing their audience with tilted heads and bright dark eyes.

'*Inikuri*. Spirit dancers from the islands out past Aar-ish. They don't speak – leastways not a tongue we can comprehend – but they do love to dance.' His host set-tled himself more comfortably in his chair. 'Amongst other things.'

Back and forth across the hall the spirit dancers strutted and spun. As they passed the fire-pits they spat something into the flames that began to burn with a pungent, almost resinous scent. Bluish smoke spiralled up into the rafters and the drumbeat slowed, becoming sensuous. The thanes' raucous shouting slowed with it as the insistent throb of the music took hold of them, and the air in the hall grew thick and heavy.

The dancers gyrated around the tables, teasing the thanes with provocative poses and undulating move-ments. Their bodies were astonishingly flexible, perform-ing arabesques and pirouettes that would have graced the court of any desert prince, and they were so light on their long, narrow feet that they scarcely made a sound.

It was almost hypnotic. Leaning back in his chair, Savin watched them intently. A creeping, tingling heat was washing through him and he felt himself smile. Perhaps the evening might not be a total waste after all.

Beside him Renngald reached under the table, pre-sumably petting one of his hounds. 'That's it. Good girl,' he murmured fondly.

Fragrant smoke tickled Savin's nose and only then did he associate it with the warming in his blood. Some kind of narcotic, and a subtle one; he should leave before it stupefied him. It was already having an effect on the thanes, now lolling against the tables like bears drunk on windfall fruit. Here and there a hand kneaded languidly at a crotch, but their eyes never left the dancers.

Two of the acrobats, painted like firebirds and wear-ing scarlet feathered masks, vaulted onto the high table. They danced amidst the ale-horns and trenchers, high-stepping, birdlike, their lithe bodies gleaming.

One of them squatted in front of him, her head cocked to one side. Streaks of glittering bronze and purple paint defined her eyes, and tiny gold beads had been glued to her lashes. Her mask's beak was decorated with scraps of silk that fluttered like flames as she breathed. She appeared to be waiting for something.

'Go ahead,' said Renngald. His free hand clenched the arm of his chair, his crown drooping over his ear again. 'It's what she's here for.' Then he laughed, and continued to pet the dog under the table, humming to himself.

Savin studied the girl and she watched him alertly. Gold rings pierced her nipples, each one threaded with an amber bead. Intriguing. The heat had reached his groin now and set him stirring. Somehow the girl noticed, or knew; she sat up straight, still balanced on the balls of her feet, and pushed her pelvis forward. Nestled in the rosy perfection of her womanhood was a third ring, also threaded with a gleaming bead.

On one of the lower tables, a water-sprite writhed to the rhythm of the drums whilst a half-naked thane sucked at her cleft like a man dying of thirst. All around her his companions had their rods in their hands, glistening with their juices. Next to him at the high table Renngald bucked in his chair, crown hanging perilously from his ear as he moaned for his good girl, and Savin realised that what he had assumed was a dog beneath the table was actually his wife, on her knees with her husband sunk to the hilt in her mouth. Overlaying all the smells of smoke and sweat and beer, the air stank of lust.

Pushing back his chair, Savin stood up. Time to go. To either side of her mask, the firebird's painted cheeks swelled with a smile. Oh, she was tempting, squatting there with her hands on her knees and her treasure displayed for him to take if he chose. She blinked her gilded lashes, head cocked expectantly. Reaching down between her thighs, he flicked the amber bead with his fingertip.

'Can you speak?' he whispered.

She made a sound in her throat, somewhere between a trill and a purr, and he grunted, his curiosity piqued.

I wonder if I can make you scream?

He caught the bead between finger and thumb and gave it a gentle tug. The girl shuddered. Heh. Very tempting, but not now: he had things to do.

Someone touched him on the elbow and he looked round. The soberly dressed man at his side had the kind of indeterminately aged, pleasant but nondescript face that was instantly forgettable. His height and build were average, his colouring middling, even his eyes were strangely colourless – or rather, no one ever remembered him for long enough to recall what colour they were. It was one of Tully's greatest strengths, and why he had been Savin's agent for almost a decade.

He raised one eyebrow at the scenes of sensual excess filling the hall but made no comment. 'It's time,' he said.

'Very well.'

Tully slipped out of the rear door of the hall as quietly as he'd arrived, and Savin turned back to the girl. Leaning to her ear, he whispered where he would be in an hour, and what he would give her. The firebird sighed, her silk flames tickling his neck. Grasping his wrist, she pushed his hand between her legs and ground herself on his fingers.

'Later.' He chuckled and patted her hairless mound. 'Later.'

Bringing his fingers to his nose, he inhaled her scent. Sweet and spicy. Lovely. Then he followed his agent out of the hall.

The frigid air of the castle bailey hit him like a bucket of cold water. The fug of narcotic smoke was soon washed away, his synapses blasted clean by the chill tang of the northern ocean. Two deep lungfuls had him awake again, shaking off the close, sultry atmosphere of the hall and its revelry.

His eyes took a moment to adjust to the dark, and the quarter moon's glow off the snow shovelled up against the walls. Then he spotted Tully waiting in the shadows by the postern, a saddled horse tethered nearby, and crunched over the frozen slush to join him.

'I take it you've found a suitable ship?' Savin asked.

Tully nodded, untying a thick cloak from behind the saddle and slinging it around his shoulders. 'A fast merchantman out of the White Havens, taking Renngald's amber back south via Pencruik. The captain's glad of the extra coin a passenger brings, so he won't ask questions.'

That would fit well with his plans. Patience always paid off. 'Good. You have the stone?'

'Of course.' From his pocket, the agent produced a small pouch of the sort favoured by jewellers and held it out in his palm.

Savin took it and emptied the contents into his hand. The jeweller had done a fine job. The cut and faceting were very good; being crystal it had only a fraction of the fire it needed, but that could be fixed.

Opening himself to the Song, he called a thread of air to support the stone, then more air, and fire and a little earth in a complex interlocking pattern that knotted and whorled and wove together like the finest Tylan lace. He pulled it taut, checking it for imperfections, then released it.

With the tiniest chime the weave snapped over the crystal and vanished. A brilliant cut diamond now hung in the air before him, catching Lumiel's silvery light and spitting it back in needles of blue and gold.

'Impressive,' murmured Tully.

Deftly, Savin used air-Song to steer the stone back into the velvet pouch and tied the strings. Even he would not be immune to the working. 'Now remember,' he said, 'don't let it touch your bare skin or you'll never want to part with it.'

His agent made a long-suffering face. 'How many years have I been working for you? I remember.' He took the pouch and stowed it back in his pocket. 'The ship sails in four hours, on the dawn tide. I'll have the stone inside Chapterhouse by the end of the month.' Gathering up his horse's reins, he added, 'Does it matter which one I choose?'

If it could have been the Leahn boy, the irony would have been sublime, but he had already demonstrated a reluctance to fall under the sway of Savin's charm. And after escaping the storm sent to destroy Alderan, he would doubtless be even more mistrustful – especially of strangers bearing gifts.

'As long as it's one of the students, I don't need much to work with,' he said. 'A youngster.' A Master would recognise the glamour as soon as they felt it, but someone without their experience, someone easily won over by a trinket, would have no idea, and their ignorance would let Savin force a chink in the Guardian's armour where not even Alderan would suspect it until it was far too late.

Tully nodded and mounted up. 'I'll signal when it's done,' he said, tugging a pair of gloves from his belt. A sharp whistle between his teeth summoned a bleary man-at-arms from the warmth of the guardhouse to unbar the postern gate, then horse and rider were gone into the frigid night, leaving only pluming breath behind.

And so it begins.

Savin pictured the game pieces arrayed on the board, played out the opening gambit in his mind. Soon he would have his cat's paw, and a toehold behind the sophisticated wards Alderan had strewn around Pencruik and the surrounding islands. Then – he slid another pawn forward – establish control. With a little help from his Hidden Kingdom allies, Chapterhouse would fall.

And then came the endgame. Corlainn's treasure. It was at Chapterhouse, he was certain of it. The Knights who'd survived the Suvaeon purge had fled there; they would have taken it with them, or at least taken the knowledge of where it could be found. Alderan was such a hoarder of knowledge, nursing his scraps of lore like a miser with his coin, counting it up and hugging it to himself as if it had some intrinsic value over and above what it could be used to achieve.

On the far side of the bailey, the watchman thumped the bar back across the gate and trudged to the guardhouse, blowing on his hands. The movement snagged Savin's eye for a second before he dismissed it and settled back into his thoughts.

No, there was something hidden there, at Chapterhouse. A miser didn't mount a guard if the vault was empty. The more precious the contents, the stronger the guard would be, the more subtle and skilful the wards. These were skilful indeed – they had kept Savin from setting foot in his birthplace since he was fifteen years old. He allowed himself a thin, bitter smile. They were some of Alderan's finest work.

And what of that other precious commodity, the Leahn whelp? Sprung from the Church's grasp and travelling west with none other than the Guardian himself – that could not be a coincidence. A new Corlainn Fellbane, perhaps; was that what Alderan had in mind for him? Certainly his gift was strong enough that the magnification offered by the starseed would make him potent enough to become . . . problematic. If only there'd been more time in Mesarild to question him: the truth could eventually have been shucked out of his head like a boiled egg from its shell, whether he was willing to be read or not.

Still, there'd be time enough once Chapterhouse had

fallen, and the Guardians were scattered or dead. Then, once the starseed was in his hands, it all became moot.

Savin studied the chessboard in his mind, seeing the pieces converge on a square he had labelled 'Chapterhouse'. Amused himself envisaging Alderan's face beneath the king's ebony crown and the Leahn's on the knight as they executed their moves. He had always possessed the knack of reading the board, the ability to follow the subtle currents of the game and predict the outcome ten or even twenty moves ahead. It was more than simply knowing the rules or being able to play against himself. It was about understanding his opponent: his attitude to risk over reward, his willingness to make sacrifices in the short term to ensure eventual success.

The smile became a curve of genuine mirth. And what he simply would not do under any circumstances.

Queen's knight to lector, pawn takes lector, rook takes pawn. The knight wheels back in defence and the rook . . . He began to laugh softly. *Rook takes knight.*

Checkmate in three.

9

NO WAY OUT

The dogs were gaining on her. They had no shape, no colour; they existed only as a howl, as a flash of teeth in the dark, but they were gaining on her. No matter how fast Teia ran through the warren of stifling caves, she heard them on her trail and the sound spurred her on.

Her breathing rasped and resonated around the narrow tunnels, punctuated by the baying of the dogs. Each time she heard it, it sounded closer. For each step she took they took two, bounding after her with relentless, terrifying speed.

There was no way out. Every turn she took led only to another. Upslope led only to down, downslope led only to up, twisting and doubling back so abruptly that she cannoned into the rough rock walls and reeled away scraped and bleeding. Each time she lost her footing she heard the dogs gain a little more ground. She ran and ran until her lungs burned in her chest and her throat was raw, somehow maintaining her momentum through the endless dark.

Someone called her name. The voice came faintly from deep inside her head, almost inaudible through the fear that gripped her. It called again and Teia staggered to a halt to listen. Silence, then the bay of a hound catching fresh scent. Moaning with terror, she shambled up to a run again, then heard the voice a third time. While it was not friendly, it was firm and familiar and brooked no disobedience.

She opened her eyes. Ytha's face swam out of the lamp glow and into focus, and Teia screamed. Pain lanced through her side, turning the cry into a gasp and hiccoughing sobs.

'Easy, child,' the Speaker said. Her smile was less than reassuring, cold and predatory. 'No harm will come to you here.'

'The dogs . . .' Teia's voice was thick, her tongue too large for her dry mouth. A flicker disturbed the Speaker's expression, then all was calm again.

'There are no dogs. You were dreaming.'

'I— I heard them. Chasing me.'

'As I said, you were dreaming. There are no dogs. You were caught up in our weaving, that is all.' Ytha stared at her. 'You must have something of the Talent.'

'The Talent? Me?' *Macha protect me, she knows*. Teia's hands clutched the fur cover over her. *Ytha knows!* She had to close her eyes for a few seconds before she lost the feeling that she was spiralling down into a pit.

'All is well, child,' the Speaker said briskly. 'We can talk about it later, when you are rested. The idea can strike some people awry.' She laid a cool hand on Teia's brow. 'At least you are not running a fever like some of the others.'

'The others?'

'There were six of you in all – children, mostly. It takes some girls that way, fever, chills. Nightmares. But such things can be overcome, with time.' A genuine smile twitched the corners of the Speaker's mouth, relieving some of the severity of her features. 'It was a rare day for the clan, finding so many of you at once.'

Teia bit her lip, willing the pain in her side to ebb. For two years she had worried that Ytha might suspect she had a gift. Now the Speaker knew, but she had six new gifts to think about. Perhaps, amongst so many, she would pay less attention to one.

'Speaker, what happened?' she asked timorously. By changing the subject, she might learn something. 'My head aches and I don't remember very much.'

'It was a powerful weaving. We called upon one of the Elder Gods to guide us. You must have been pulled into the web, like the others, and it drew you to its centre. You were found unconscious on the ground, just outside the circle.' She paused. 'What do you remember?'

Teia frowned, trying to make herself look uncertain. 'There was a terrible voice, scraping inside my head, and a shield . . . It stared at me.'

'Did you hear any words?'

'I don't remember any. I was so frightened.' She looked up at Ytha with wide eyes and hoped the Speaker would take the bait.

Ytha stared back, then nodded abruptly. 'You need to rest,' she said. 'I shall fetch you a draught and then you should sleep. We ride south tomorrow, but Drwyn's men will take care of you until you can sit a horse.'

With that she stood and left in a swirl of snow-fox fur. Teia allowed herself a small sigh of relief. Looking up at the roof and the hangings, she realised she was in Drwyn's tent – her tent. The day was well advanced: she smelled woodsmoke and cooking, and heard children at play. She must have been unconscious for hours.

Ytha returned in a few minutes carrying a tea-bowl of warmed milk and honey, which she held out to Teia. 'This will help you sleep,' she said.

Pushing up on one elbow, Teia raised the drink to her lips. She'd had one of Ytha's sleeping draughts before and knew that the Speaker put the juice of the white poppy in it; the honey disguised the taste. It would ease her various discomforts, but it would also make her sleep deeply. How deeply and for how long would depend on the strength of the brew.

About to drink, she hesitated. If she slept, the nightmare might return, throw her back into that desperate race. Suddenly afraid, Teia darted a glance a the Speaker. Ytha was watching her, one eyebrow raised interrogatively, and she made herself take a sip of the drink. There was a good chance the Speaker meant to wait until she had drained the bowl dry. To buy time she blew on the milk to cool it, hoping the older woman would lose patience.

Drwyn himself proved an unlikely benefactor, choosing that moment to put his head around the hanging. Ytha shot him an irritated glance and held up her hand, indicating that he should wait.

'Make sure you drink it all,' she admonished. 'It will do you good.'

Teia dipped her head dutifully. 'Yes, Speaker.'

Ytha's lips pursed momentarily, then she drew her

robe around her and walked into the other half of the tent.

'Is she all right?' Drwyn asked at once.

'She's had a nasty fright and some bad dreams, but that's all. Nothing that sleep won't mend,' Ytha told him. 'Now, what news do you have for me from the chiefs?'

Their footsteps and voices faded outside, soon lost in the general bustle of breaking camp. Everywhere people were shouting and animals complaining. With the Moot over, it was time for the clans to make their way to their winter quarters in the caves and sheltered valleys at the foot of the mountains, to wait out the snows until the spring.

Teia set the still-full bowl down on the floor. So Ytha knew about her gift. It was a wonder she'd managed to conceal it as long as she had, since that day she'd first looked into the waters and seen something other than her own reflection. Then Drw had offered for her and she'd begun to see the boy with the chief's torc, but instead of pleasing her the vision had left her so alarmed she'd gone out of her way to avoid drawing Ytha's eye down on her. The Speaker had ways of rooting out secrets, ways of knowing what a man had told to no one but the wind.

It was only a matter of time before Ytha found out about the child, too. She fingered her still-flat belly. Then, if she was lucky, she'd be wedded to the chief and would live out her life in this tent, warming his bed and taking his blows.

Macha's mercy, that was no kind of luck. Tears filled her eyes. Hugging her knees to her chest, despite the discomfort in her side, she buried her face in her arms.

And what if Drwyn did not wed her, or put her aside as he had his first wife when she bore him only a daughter and proved unable to carry another child to term? What then? Perhaps Ytha would take her for an apprentice, and all she'd seen in the waters would come tumbling out like stillborn kids, staring and ugly – the boy chief, the dark warrior, the hundred other images she'd seen and couldn't explain—

Despite the thick furs covering her, Teia began to shiver. She was at a fork in the trail, with no way back and neither of the forward paths leading anywhere she wanted to go. Whichever she picked, there were storm clouds on the horizon.

Or she could make her own path, and run. Flee the Crainnh and become one of the Maenardh, the Lost Ones. She would never be welcome at a clan fire again, but at least she would be free.

She screwed her eyes shut. Free to be alone, free to starve, free to freeze. She might as well kneel down beside the widow's rock and dash out her own brains. The plains' short autumn was all but over and winter was coming hard on its heels; already the mountains to the south were white-mantled like Speakers. And fleeing would mean leaving the mother who'd raised her, the father who'd taught her to use a bow and a knife – never mind the rest of her family.

Misery twisted up her throat. *Oh, Macha, no.*

Beside her bed, a last thread of steam curling up from its surface, Ytha's sleeping draught waited. Its sweet baby-sick smell promised a few hours' rest, a place to hide. From the dogs, or so she hoped, from Drwyn, from thought itself.

No, she had no real alternatives. She picked up the bowl and, in three big swallows, drained it to the dregs.

⚜

Teia drifted awake to a slow rocking as of a cradle. Opening her eyes, she saw the edge of a blanket and beyond it the roof of a tent. No, not a tent; it was too grey and heavy for leather. Sky? Tiny coldnesses stung her cheeks, her lips, like pinpricks. She frowned. Too cold.

Shutting her eyes again, she burrowed back into the warmth that enveloped her and dreamed of horses. Long lines of them, walking, walking, and in the distance the land's white teeth tore into the belly of the clouds.

When she opened her eyes next, she saw a man's arm and shoulder past the blanket, and beyond that a frosty plain, its grasses bowed by the ceaseless wind. Mountains loured along the horizon, closer now, starkly white against a sky the colour of lead. Now the rocking made sense: the clan was on the move into the snows, and she was being carried on horseback.

Ytha's draught had been potent: it had carried her clean through one day and well into the next. She blinked, trying to shake off the poppy-fog that clung to her thoughts, and peered up at the man with his arm round her. He smelled of greasy furs and sweat, and the stringy, drooping moustache looked familiar. One of Drwyn's warriors. The one who picked his nose on guard duty and liked to find reasons to brush past her as she went about her chores. Harl, she remembered dully, and closed her eyes again. Perhaps he would not notice that she had stirred.

Soon she was dozing, until the drumming of another set of hooves alongside woke her again.

'I'm going ahead a ways,' said Drwyn's voice. 'The Speaker has asked for me. If I'm not back by sunset, take care of her when we camp.'

'Of course, my chief,' Harl answered. Drwyn chirruped and his horse cantered away.

Teia tried to doze off again, but could not. They had begun to climb up into the foothills of the mountains and the stony track made for a jolting ride, jabbing at her broken rib. Nonetheless she kept her eyes closed. She was not in the mood for Harl's attempts at flirtation.

A cold hand stole through her furs and moulded itself around her breast, squeezing it. Then it began un-lacing the front of her jerkin.

'Drwyn will have your fruits for fish-bait,' she said quietly, eyes still closed. The hand stopped.

'Only if you tell him.'

'Why wouldn't I?'

Harl resumed picking at her laces. 'You're a whore. One *daigh* is much the same as another to your kind.' He used the crude name for the male genitals, perhaps to see if she was shocked. 'You spread your legs for the old chief, too, didn't you?'

'So what if I did?' Teia snaked her left arm free of her furs and grabbed his wrist. 'I am Drwyn's woman now. What do you think he'll do when he learns you've had your filthy paws on me?'

He was not deterred. 'He'll not marry you. No chief would take a bride who wasn't a virgin, not to be the mother of his sons. He'll tire of you soon enough. Per-haps then he'll give you to me.'

'Who says this? The Speaker herself sent me to him, you fool!' She ground her fingers into the small bones below Harl's thumb until his hand spasmed and thrust it away from her. His face was satisfyingly pained. 'Think before you go dipping your fingers in another man's mead! Now let me down. I want my own horse.'

Harl jerked the reins, bringing his mount to a sudden stop. He let go of her without warning so that she slith-ered helplessly to the ground. Unable to catch herself, she landed heavily on her ankle and fell, yelping with pain.

Her grey mare was tied to the saddle; Harl pulled free the leading rein and dropped it.

'My lady,' he sneered, then spurred his horse into a trot and left her.

Teia got to her feet slowly. Side throbbing, she limped over to the grey as the rest of the clan filed past up the rocky trail into the rumpled skirts of the mountains.

Most kept their faces blank but some watched her curiously, openly, and she wondered how much had been seen or overheard. More than enough to start gossip at the cook-fires, no doubt.

Righting her clothing, she mounted, wincing at the sharp pain in her ankle, and waited until she saw her family riding past. She urged the mare over to join them, but her father brought his own horse out of the line to block her path.

'Da!' she protested, peering past him. Her sisters had their heads high in spite of the wind. Only Ana looked back, one brief, sorrowful glance over her shoulder.

'You don't belong with us any more,' Teir said. He refused to meet her gaze. 'We are not your family now.'

'But I'm your daughter!' Tears prickled at her eyes. She tried to push past him, but her father's horse was war-trained and blocked her at a twitch of the reins.

'Once you were. Not any more. It is clan law. The Speaker . . .' His voice broke and his lips twisted, as if the words tasted foul in his mouth. Just for a second he glanced down at her and she saw the anguish in his eyes. 'Things are not as they were with Drw. Bear him a son, Teia. Make him wed you. Restore your honour, and mine.'

Then he whirled his horse around and cantered away to join the rest of the family. He did not look back. Teia watched him go, fat tears rolling down her cheeks and the bitter wind lashing her hair around her face. Misery welled up in her chest and pressed on her lungs.

'But I *am* carrying, Da,' she whispered. 'Please come back.'

❖

Teia reined in at the top of the stony track leading up to the caves. She was tired and cold after a week spent sleeping – or rather, not sleeping – on the ground; the land in the foothills was too steep to pitch tents, and even rolled in the chief's blankets with his body at her back for warmth, she'd been unable to rest for long before the cold or the pain in her rib woke her.

In between dark, half-remembered dreams she'd lain watching the slow wheel of moons and stars across the heavens until one by one the constellations dipped out of sight behind the wall of the southern mountains. Then, on the third night, the clouds had rolled in and she was denied even that.

Now it was snowing again. Dry, floating stuff for the most part, it hung in the air like ash, or the feathers from a pigeon taken by a hawk. Drifting, snatched up and scattered again by chance gusts of wind, never able to settle. No matter how she pulled her hood up and fur collar close, flakes found their way behind it and down her neck, tiny biting kisses on her skin. She was too tired and sore to try to keep them out any more.

Through the snow came the last of her kinsfolk, thickly wrapped against winter's bite, leading pack ponies, carrying bundles on their backs. In ones and twos they disappeared into the broad mouth of the mountain. Teia watched them from the far end of the ledge outside the cave. Her own family had already gone inside, and the Speaker before them, all without a backward glance. She'd long since given up hoping someone would catch her eye and acknowledge that she still existed.

She should have been inside well before now, readying the chief's chamber for his return from the hunt – after months of disuse it would need work to be made habitable again: carpets spread and hangings hung to mask the stone's chill – but she couldn't make herself go into the mountain and give up the daylight that was her last reminder of her freedom.

The dark of the caves had never daunted her before. Now she dreaded it: the mere idea of going into the earth felt as if she would be descending to the underworld, where the stories said Noam had gone to rescue the princess. Except she wasn't a princess, and no one was going to come looking for her. So she sat her horse under leaden skies and watched the snowflakes dance around her, and wished she was far, far away.

Winter was the wrong time to run. Every season on the plains had its dangers: spring floods that rendered the rivers too swift and turbulent to cross; the windstorms that came with summer's heat and scoured the earth of every leaf, every blade of grass for miles around. But in the winter, when the days grew short and dark and the great white cold crept down from the mountaintops, then men went outside to die.

Hunting the white stag, they called it, when they'd had enough. Old men, mostly, afraid of infirmity or losing their wits, but young men too sometimes, grown tired before their time, would take up a spear and go out into the night for one last hunt. They never returned. Sometimes their kin would find them come the spring, build a cairn over them and sing their souls to the afterworld, but more often the plain simply swallowed them, bones and all.

The wind picked up and Teia shivered despite the thick beaver fur pulled up to her chin. Probably most of the missing were dead, but surely not every man who went to hunt the white stag was ready to die. Surely some of them survived, maybe joined the Lost Ones. It must be possible to endure. It must – if one were strong.

Taking one last look around at the dark pines stubbling the lower slopes of the mountain, the plains beyond shifting in and out of view through veils of snow, she dismounted and led her horse inside.

10

DUNCAN

✳

'Duncan.'

Kael's voice. Duncan opened his eyes, squinting in the lantern-light. Leaping shadows and Kael's steaming breath gave his face a demonic cast.

'What is it?'

'We have company.' Kael set down the lantern and ghosted back to his watch.

Duncan kicked off his blankets and shivered into the cloak he'd been keeping warm underneath them with his body before stepping out of the cave to follow Kael through the sheeting snow. Blizzards had sprung up in the short, bitter days towards the heel end of the year, one after another, slowing their progress to a crawl and finally penning them in that small cave for the night when the conditions grew too dangerous to push on to the shelter of the fortress. The snowfall had slackened a little with the dawn, but the clouds showed no sign of emptying. They squatted over the mountains that ringed Saardost Keep, smothering the sky with their skirts.

He had barely a glimmer of snowlight to help him pick a path along the ledge above the valley. A black shape against the white mountainside beckoned him forward and he tucked into a notch in the rocks beside Kael. Below them, on the other side of the valley, the keep was a smudge in the snow.

'Tell me where I should be looking,' he said, and Kael pointed towards the vague shape of the easternmost tower of the main keep. Duncan squinted but saw only snow. 'I can't see anything. It's whiter than a virgin's thighs out here.'

'Wait.'

There. The snow billowed and lifted like a curtain over an open window and he saw a smear of orange light before the curtain dropped again. Firelight. Someone was either careless or extremely confident.

'How many?'

'Two for sure,' Kael said. 'There's a pair of saddle horses and a pack pony inside the guardhouse.'

'You've been down there? Slaine's stones, Kael!' Duncan bit back anything more. There was no point reminding Kael that he'd put himself in danger, or what might have happened if he'd been discovered. The sallow-faced seeker went his own way and always had. Trying to change him was about as useful as trying to change the wind.

Shrugging, Kael said, 'We needed to know. They're Nimrothi, by their saddle charms.'

The Nimrothi hadn't crossed the mountains in numbers in a thousand years, not even to trade. Duncan stared at him. 'Are you sure?'

'I'm sure.'

He would be. Kael knew his craft too well to be mistaken about something like that. This could not be good news. Sighing, Duncan swiped clinging snow off his face. 'You'd better fetch Sor.'

Kael's outline faded into the blizzard. Minutes later, footsteps creaked through the snow as he returned with Duncan's brother and they wedged themselves amongst the rocks next to him.

'Two scouts?' Sor said. He peered through the wavering veils of snow at the hulking shape of the fortress. 'There's no cover. If they were even half-awake they should have skewered you before you reached the bridge, Kael.'

'I took a different way down. There's a blind spot where the west wall butts against the mountain.'

Sor grunted. 'And they'd have no reason to expect anyone sneaking up on them from that side.'

'They're probably hiding from the weather, like us,' said Duncan. 'I can't see any tracks – they've not come out recently.'

'There's plenty of game here, even in winter. With staples brought in on the pony, they could have been sitting here for months.' Swearing softly, Sor blinked snow off his eyelashes and studied the fortress as it ducked in and out of view.

'Waiting for something.' Duncan exchanged a long look with his brother and knew he was thinking the same thing. The Hound they'd been tracking.

It had been running on a more easterly course when Kael had lost its trail two days north of Brindling Fall, where they'd met the Gatekeeper. They'd doubled back through the pass and then travelled east along the foothills of the an-Archen towards home, only to have evil prickle across Kael's senses like itchweed ten days later and lead them back north towards Saardost Keep. It could be the same Hound, another or something worse; only Kael could say and only when he got closer.

'Can you still sense it, Kael?' Duncan asked.

'It's not moved since the snow started,' said the scarred clansman. His fingers flexed around his knife-hilt. 'Laying up, most like.'

'If it's another Hound and the clans have summoned it . . .' Sor's blue eyes were hard as stones.

'They wouldn't be so foolish, would they?' Even as he said it, Duncan felt the certainty hardening his gut. *No. They can't have forgotten.*

'We need to know what they know.' Sor was brisk, determined.

'I'll go back down and ask. It needn't be a long conversation.' Kael eased his long knife meaningfully in its sheath.

Straightening up, Sor shook snow off his cloak. 'No. If we go, we go together. Tell Cara to make sure the horses are secure, then join us up here. Where's this alternative route down?'

'Not far. Over there, where the ledge runs out.' Duncan followed Kael's gesture, but all he could see was black rock and snow.

His brother nodded, decision made. 'Then lead on.'

The ledge became progressively narrower and steeper as it followed the flank of the mountain around towards the keep. Kael's old tracks were mere dimples in the snow, already well filled. Duncan kept his hood pulled forward to shield his face and his eyes on the ground. If he missed his footing it was a long way down.

When the ledge finally ran out in a stand of scrubby wind-distorted pine trees, Kael stopped and pointed down into a ravine. 'There.'

Sor peered over the edge. 'A waterfall?' he growled. 'You climbed down a frozen waterfall? At night? In a blizzard?'

Kael shrugged. 'I strung a rope. It's only a furlong or so.'

'Slaine's stones!'

Duncan leaned over the edge and found Kael's rope, which had been knotted at intervals for a sure grip. He shook it clear of snow then gave it a firm tug. 'Seems secure enough,' he said. 'Shall I go first?'

'No, I'll go,' said Sor, slinging his strung bow over his shoulder to leave both hands free. 'Then if I fall off the rest of you will have a soft landing.'

Duncan suppressed a smile. 'Still no head for heights?'

Muttering, his brother climbed over the rocks and gingerly began to walk himself hand-over-hand down the glassy wall of the gorge. Dislodged snow and ice fragments pattered into the dark below him, and in moments he was lost from view. After a few more minutes the rope slackened.

'He's down,' said Duncan, with a sigh of relief. 'Cara, you go next. I'll follow you, then Kael.'

The young clanswoman took only a fraction of Sor's time, vaulting onto the rocks and over the edge as nimbly as a goat. Once her weight was off the rope, Duncan took a firm hold and stepped up to the edge. Feet braced on the rock, he leaned back into space, holding the rope as tightly as his cold-stiffened hands would allow. Beside him, the waterfall groaned like a restless sleeper. Carefully setting his feet on the ice-slick gorge wall, he began to walk himself down.

The rock was rimed with ice but the more confidently he placed his feet, the less his boots seemed to slip. In only a few minutes he felt a hand on his shoulder and there was Cara crouched on a jagged pile of rocks by the foot of the waterfall to steady him as he found his feet. His arms and shoulders burned when he let go of the rope, his heart thudding painfully in his chest.

'That was exhilarating,' he said, hopping down into a deep drift. He peered through the swirling veils of snow for Sor and saw him crouched by the keep wall, his cloak and dark hair already almost white.

Duncan waded through the creaking drifts to join him and his brother flung out a hand. 'Watch the ice!' he hissed. 'You're on the river.'

Duncan stopped in his tracks. Through his boots he felt the faintest vibration and imagined black water rushing under his feet. He made the rest of the journey more cautiously, then crouched down next to Sor as the snow whispered around them.

'Kael was right,' his brother said, voice pitched low. 'Unless you've got sentries along the wall up there, this spot's not overlooked. We're clear to the next watchtower.' The other two joined them and Sor motioned

Kael forward. 'You take the lead, since you've been here before.'

Single file, they followed the scar-faced clansman along the wall. Snow eddied around them, thickening then lifting to reveal the pale rib-bone of the bridge over the river that carried the road from one side of the valley to the other and then up to the keep. The road itself was invisible, barely a dip in the dense white blanket covering the valley bottom.

At the watchtower's bulky footings, Kael held up his hand and they halted. Motioning the other clansmen to stay back, he crept around the buttress, his footfalls almost silent in the deep drifts.

Duncan peered around the snow-crusted stone after him, but Kael's dark shape was already fading into the blizzarded dark. If one of the Nimrothi scouts looked out of the tower window before he got into the lee of the gatehouse turret some two furlongs further along the south wall, he would be seen. Duncan strained to make out the firelight at the window, but at such an acute angle it was hidden from him. Besides, between the night and the snowfall he could barely even make out the shape of the tower. He hoped they would hide him as well as they hid the scouts' fire.

'Is he clear?' whispered Sor.

'I can't see him.'

His brother swore.

'Should we follow?' asked Cara.

'He'll signal when he's safe,' Sor said. 'Duncan?'

Duncan peered around the buttress again, just in time to see a snowball arc out of the dark. It burst harmlessly on his right shoulder, showering his face with chilly crystals. 'That'll be the signal, then,' he spluttered.

Quickly, quietly, they moved around the buttress and along the base of the wall. Snow creaked under their boots, alarmingly loud in the cold mountain air. Then it was done, and they jammed themselves into the lee of the gatehouse tower with Kael.

He held a finger to his lips for silence and led them swiftly under the looming arch to the gatehouse entrance. The door was long rotted away, but some sacking had been rigged up across the arch from inside. Kael eased it aside and vanished into the shadows. Hooves shifted against stone inside, then were still. One by one the remaining clansmen followed him.

Inside the guardhouse the darkness was absolute and Duncan waited for his eyes to adjust before he dared move. He smelled dung and horse, sensed large shapes in a small space. Gradually his eyes found the glow seeping down the stairs from the fire above. As his eyes became accustomed to the dimness, he picked out the edges of curving steps, the silhouette of a horse's ears sharpening against it.

The sound of steel on leather made him twitch. Someone touched his arm, then Kael, knife in hand, padded up the first few steps, silent in his soft boots. Duncan made to follow him and slipped in a fresh horse-apple. He stumbled against the flank of the nearest animal and it whickered, stepping out of his way. Kael froze on the stairs, bared teeth bright, knife winking orange. Heart racing, Duncan stroked the horse's back to soothe it. No sound came from higher in the tower except a snap from the fire. Kael eased up another step and Duncan could breathe again.

His relief did not last. Before his feet had found the second step, Cara gripped his arm. He stopped and looked back at her. She cupped a hand around her ear and jerked her head towards the gatehouse doorway, where Sor had an eye pressed to a gap at the edge of the sacking. They'd heard something.

Listening intently, he picked up the rhythmic creak of saddle harness. The snow muffled the hoofbeats too

well to make an accurate count, but there were at least
two more mounted men outside. As he listened, straining his ears above the singing of his own blood, the
hooves stopped.

More scouts, but how many? *How many?* He grabbed
Cara's shoulder, pointed at Sor and made a beckoning
gesture, but his brother was already crossing the guardhouse floor, silent as a thief, and they climbed the stairs
to join Kael a full turn above, out of sight of the lowest
level. A pitchwood torch had been wedged into the
crumbling mortar between two stones. Sor looked
around, gathering their attention, and held up a hand
with three fingers extended.

Duncan clenched his jaw. If their count was right,
three more made five: one apiece and one for the pot.
He drew his knife and pushed his cloak back off his
shoulders out of the way, then Sor stabbed his finger in
the direction of the upper level. Kael took the stairs two
at a time with Cara on his heels.

From below someone shouted a greeting, his Nimrothi accent too thick to pick out the individual words.
One of the two above answered. Boots scraped on stone
and the light above brightened. A cry of alarm became a
gurgle, then Duncan was running up the stairs as hard
as he could.

He shouldered the swinging door aside and burst
into the tower room in time to see Kael lowering a
kicking Nimrothi warrior to the floor as Cara retrieved
her knives from a body on the far side of the fireplace.
Sor pushed past him and all four turned to face the
doorway as feet pounded up the stairs.

Two Nimrothi clansmen burst through the door with
short-bows drawn, flanking a third man who had a
long knife in each fist. For a heartbeat no one moved,
then the shortbows came up.

'Stand fast!' Sor bellowed, but the bows kept lifting.
One of Cara's knives flashed across the room and

took a bowman in the shoulder, sending him reeling backwards into the wall and his arrow tumbling across the stone floor. Kael charged the other and he misfired, the arrow shattering into splinters against the opposite wall. The third man lunged for Sor. A sweeping leg took the fellow's feet from under him and Sor danced out of the way as the man rolled and was back on his feet as quick as a cat.

Duncan looped his arm around the man's neck from behind and rested his knifepoint on his cheek. 'Don't,' he said in the Nimrothi's ear.

The warrior smelled of sweat and mountain air. He struggled but Duncan had the advantage of height and tightened his arm across the fellow's throat. 'Easy, now.'

The Nimrothi spat an obscenity but lowered his knives. Cara twisted them out of his hands and tucked them through her belt.

Kael wiped his own dagger on the coat of the bowman he'd tackled then sheathed it. On the far side of the doorway, the man Cara had brought down slumped against the wall, blood trickling from his mouth.

'Barely breathing,' Kael said. 'He won't last.' With casual efficiency, he broke the man's neck.

Sor clicked his tongue. 'Now I can't ask him any questions.'

'He was dead anyway. You've got a live one – how many do you need? I'll see to their horses.' Kael trotted down the stairs without a backward glance.

'That man,' Sor muttered. 'Sometimes, I swear—' Raking a hand through his hair, he swung around to face Duncan and his prisoner. 'All right, you can let him go. Cara, watch him.'

She grinned and twirled a knife through her fingers for the Nimrothi's benefit. The man swallowed, looking warily between her and Sor as Duncan released his neck and stepped back. Then Cara frowned, glance flicking from him to the first two to die.

'He's Amhain,' she said, pointing at the small bird tattooed on the man's cheek. 'Those two are Crainnh.'

'Two clans,' Sor said. 'Interesting.' He cast around the small room and found a crude stool that had been overturned in the fight. Righting it, he sat down and folded his arms. 'Tell me how that came about and maybe I'll let you live.'

The Nimrothi gave no sign that he'd understood, even though the words were spoken in a tongue that their two peoples had once shared. A wilful misunderstanding, then. Frowning, Sor repeated his question,

This time the prisoner sneered. 'I'll tell you nothing.'

He pursed his lips to spit and Duncan punched him in the kidney. The man staggered and glowered at him. Duncan held up his dagger. 'Be glad I didn't use this. Now answer the question.'

Still the Nimrothi said nothing.

Sor sighed. 'This could be a long night, brother.'

'At least we're warm and dry.'

'That's true enough.' Stretching out his feet towards the fire, Sor crossed his ankles. 'You saw the face of the fellow who killed your friends, yes?' he said. 'Answer my questions or I'll hand you over to him, see if he can loosen your tongue. Your choice.'

The Nimrothi's glower lost some of its intensity. 'The chief sent us to scout the pass.'

Leaning forward, Duncan jabbed his stiffened fingers at the fellow's bruised kidney. 'Tell us something we don't already know, or you'll be pissing blood for a week.'

The man shied, hurt and hate twisting his face to something murderous. 'Faithless bastard!'

Sor clicked his tongue. 'Answer the question.'

'He wanted to know if the passes were clear, prove there were no iron men in the mountains.' Eyeing Duncan truculently, he added, 'He means to ride the war band south.'

Now that was interesting. 'Whose chief?' Duncan asked. 'Yours?'

'Drwyn of the Crainnh. He'll be sworn Chief of Chiefs at the Scattering.'

'He'll go the way of Gwlach if he tries,' Cara snorted.

'And you'd do a Wolf's bidding? A Stone Crow?' Uncrossing his legs, Sor studied the fellow, blue eyes shrewd as a horse-trader's.

'If it means we take back what was stolen from us by the likes of you, aye, I would, and full willing!'

Over the Amhain's shoulder, Duncan shot a look at his brother, trying to catch his eye. He had that itching, crawling sensation at the base of his spine that meant things were about to get more than simply interesting. He flexed his fingers around the haft of his knife to settle his grip, just in case.

The Nimrothi had found some confidence now and his voice dripped contempt like poison. 'Sold your honour for safety, didn't you?' he sneered. 'Gave up your balls and your freedom for the Empire's leash. Where're your iron men now, eh? These forts are empty and have been for generations – the Wild Hunt will carve up your precious Empire like so much tripe for the dogs!'

Duncan's blood froze. Across the room, his brother's face grew very still. 'The Wild Hunt?' he repeated.

'The Speakers summoned the shade of the Raven and bargained for Her aid – Her Hounds are already running, and there's no one's skirts for you to hide behind this time,' the fellow spat. 'We will take back our home!'

So Kael had been right. The Hound they'd tracked these last few weeks was Maegern's, and loosed a-purpose. *Slaine's stones.*

For a long moment there was no sound in the tower room but the crackle of the fire and the dead weight of the Amhain's words settling into everyone's minds. Then Sor pushed himself to his feet and refolded his arms.

'That's quite a boast, friend,' he said mildly. 'You're sure of this?'

'Sure enough.'

'You saw this summoning with your own eyes?'

'No. Only the Speakers and the chiefs were there, and they told us after.' Pride drew the Nimrothi up to his full height, no longer hunched by the pain in his kidney. 'Eirdubh himself gave me the command to come, and when Eirdubh rides with Drwyn, the Stone Crow clan rides with him.'

Duncan's sense of unease intensified. There was no time to waste; the Warlord had to be warned. 'Sor,' he began, unable to stay silent.

His brother quieted him with a gesture. 'And the other clans? They'll swear to this Drwyn, too?'

'They'll swear.'

'How many?'

'All seventeen.'

'And how many men under arms?'

The Amhain laughed. 'More than you've ever seen, faithless! You're dead men, all of you.'

⁂

Duncan swung up into the saddle and reined his restive horse to a standstill so Sor could buckle his saddlebags' flaps closed over their bulky cargo of provisions.

'You're sure about this?' said Sor, slapping the last strap through its retainer. His breath steamed on the bitter air.

'I'm sure. Aradhrim knows me as well as he knows you.'

Planting his hands on his hips, Sor squinted at him in the early sunshine. The blizzard had moved on overnight; now the sky had cleared, the snowy mountains were dazzling, too bright to look at for long. Even the sky looked polished, so blue it was almost silver.

'It's my duty. I'm the Clansman for the Morennadh.'

'And I'm the Clansman's brother.' Duncan grinned. 'The Warlord won't know Cara, and you need to stay with Kael to rein him in when he figures out where that Hound is going. He listens to you.'

'Sometimes,' Sor muttered, pulling a face.

'More than he ever listens to me, at any rate.' Leaning down from the saddle, Duncan gripped his brother's shoulder. 'Stop fretting. I'm the best person to go and that's that.'

Sor seized his wrist. 'Take care of yourself. If anything happens to you, Mother will kill me.'

'I'll make sure nothing happens, then.'

'Ride straight for Fleet. If what that Amhain said is true, we have to tell Aradhrim as soon as possible. The clans will miss their scouts eventually and send more.'

'It's the wrong time of year to be starting a war.'

'Maybe the right time if you plan to catch your enemy unawares.' Face grim, Sor stepped back. 'Go on. Get a few leagues behind you.'

With a click of his tongue, Duncan set his heels and the horse bounded into the snow, kicking up ice crystals that sparkled in the bright air. It was more than seven hundred miles to Fleet as winter closed in. He hoped the old saw was true and bad news really did travel fastest.

11

BLOOD SCRYING

❖

Thirty-one days. Teia had counted them. A full moon's turning and more since the Crainnh had reached their winter quarters, and still Ytha had not come for her. She'd cleaned the chief's chamber and furnished it as comfortably as ever his tent had been, working doggedly through the pain in her rib. She'd taken her turn at the work in which all the Crainnh's women participated: tending the smoke-room, laying in the stores of food and fuel for the season upon them. And she'd waited, eking out her store of bidewell root to hide her baby-sickness and dreading each new day in case it would be the day when the Speaker came to claim her Talent.

But still Ytha had not come.

She would not be able to conceal her pregnancy for much longer, not in the close quarters of the caves. By Firstmoon her belly would have begun to swell; a month after that and she'd be hard pressed to hide it even with her thick winter skirts. One of the women would surely notice, and then everyone would know. Secrets like that were hard to keep in the clan.

Drwyn was another matter. He paid scant attention to her body except when he wanted to use it, and when he did he liked to mount her from behind the way a stallion mounts a mare, spending so little effort on anything but his own pleasure that she doubted he'd notice her roundness even when she was six moons gone.

Besides, he was away with the hunters most of the

time – more often than not, she saw more of the two warriors who stood guard at the cave than she did of him. One of them was invariably Harl. She'd begun to wonder if he traded duties with the other men, since he appeared to be the one watching over her most frequently. Watching her beat the dust out of the carpets, bend over the cook-fire. He even watched her carry out the night soil each morning, which was particularly unnerving as the task was her opportunity to throw up undisturbed if the bidewell root failed. She didn't think Harl had seen her vomit but couldn't be sure, and that only added to her anxiety.

Thirty-one long days. Domestic tasks kept her hands occupied but did little to stimulate her mind, which trod over the same ground again and again until it had worn a path through her thoughts the way horses going to the river wore a path through the grass. Nothing new could grow there before the same hard hooves trampled it down. Ytha would come for her soon, and then the truth would be out.

A prod in the small of her back jolted her from her fears and back into reality. A queue of soot-streaked clanswomen with their hair up in kerchiefs had formed behind her and Sorya, the wizened old bird in charge of the smoke-room for the day, glared at her over a basket laden with bunched strips of elk-meat ready for the stores.

'Oh! Forgive me, I was away with the wind.' Chastened, she took the basket and hoisted it onto her hip. Her slowly-healing rib throbbed in protest.

Someone behind her snorted. 'Away with the chief, more like.'

'Aye, but which one?' added another, and then the whole flock of them were cackling and hooting.

Cheeks burning, Teia ground her teeth and tried to hurry away, but the basket was heavy and no matter how tightly she gripped, her sweaty hands kept slipping on the handles. Laughter followed her all the way along the passage, its echoes capering and leaping off the walls to poke at her ears like some malign sprite.

It had been the same since the Crainnh had returned to the mountains. The weather had held tolerably fair so the men had been able to hunt almost continuously. They were away before dawn every day and on their return each evening, steaming and raucous as if they'd vanquished their blood enemies in battle, there was butcher-work to be done. After the jointing and flensing, which needed a man's weight behind the blades, the Crainnh women took up their tasks. Hides had to be scraped for the tanning kettles, fat rendered, blood puddings and sausage made.

Being the chief's bed-mate did not grant Teia any special privilege in this work, but apparently it gave the others the right to stare and whisper, to ignore her to her face and then make pointed remarks behind her back. She scowled, lugging the creaking basket into the vaulted cavern of the store-chamber. It was unfair. She worked just as hard as they did, raking the smoke-room ash-pit, stretching hides on frames until her hands were curled like claws from tugging on the thongs. Maybe harder. So why did they feel entitled to treat her so disparagingly?

She thumped her basket down next to the others by the wall, shoved it into line then dealt it a last kick for good measure. After days of this, her back was near to breaking and her temper not much better. At least it was cool in the stores, after the smoke-room: new ice had been piled in the cold larder where the fresh meat was kept until it could be preserved. Teia mopped her face with her sleeve, then flapped her bodice to try to pull in some air to freshen her sticky skin.

Two more women with baskets appeared in the entrance to the stores, nudging each other as they came towards her. They didn't appear to be struggling with their burdens, and as they drew closer she could see why: their baskets were little more than half-full. Teia sighed. Was it envy that drove them to such spite – even women like Sorya, who was old enough to have changed Drwyn's swaddling?

She took the long way around the chamber to avoid crossing their paths, then started back up the passage, kneading her aching back. Near the smoke-room, the gossips' heads were bobbing like chickens around a pile of grain. Someone saw her and smirked, then nudged the woman next to her, and the whole group fell into silent stares.

Head high, Teia walked straight past them.

'Hie!' shouted Sorya, grabbing at her sleeve. 'Where are you going? These still need taking to the stores!' She waved at several full baskets piled by the leather-draped entrance to the smoke-room.

Teia shook her off. 'I have other chores to attend to,' she said, and gestured towards the other women. 'Send them. They've nothing to do but flap their tongues.'

Smutty faces creased into scowls. 'Just because you're in the chief's bed doesn't make you better than us,' spat one. 'We all have to work here!'

'I just have to work harder. Yes?' That shocked them into silence just long enough for Teia to smile sweetly and add, 'I'll be sure to tell the chief why his supper isn't ready.'

Then she turned and walked away.

In the chief's chamber, the discarded shirt on the bed and the open clothes chest said Drwyn had come and gone again, no doubt to celebrate a successful hunt with his men. Raucous laughter echoed back from the meeting place. The *uisca* was flowing freely, by the sounds of it; perhaps enough would be poured down Drwyn's throat to dampen his ardour. After the long hours lugging baskets to the stores, she had no energy to feign enjoyment and avoid a beating.

She eyed the bed. All to herself, it would be cosy and comfortable. A nap would do her good, if only to make up for the sleep she would surely lose later. Drwyn was a grown man with two strong arms, after all. If he returned and wanted anything, he could fetch it himself.

Stiffly Teia stripped off her clothes. Even through her shift she could see her shape was changing. Her belly showed the beginnings of a hard, high dome, and there was a little less room in her bodice. Now when Drwyn took his pleasure her breasts jounced uncomfortably together beneath her, making her feel like an unmilked goat unless she could contrive to have a cushion to rest on. Thick skirts and bulky shawls would only be able to conceal her condition for a little while longer.

⚔

In Teia's dream she was a fish on a line being drawn through a dark river. The hook bit painfully into her cheek and the harder she fought it the worse the pain became. Not that it did any good to struggle; the unseen fisherman drew her in yard by yard. A will as relentless as the march of time itself dragged her towards the surface, and all her thrashing was in vain.

Exhausted at last, she lay limp and let herself be towed to her fate. The choking dread that had consumed her eased away, becoming resignation. In that there was calm of a sort, and the pain eased. Through the water she saw the glow of a lamp overhead – no, a moon, bluish-pale and full in a sky devoid of stars. Distantly, she heard a voice call her name.

Teia opened her eyes and gasped with fright. A ball of pale-blue light the size of her fist hovered above her face. On heels and elbows she scrambled back away from it, her heart thumping in her chest, before she realised it was only one of Ytha's lights. The globe did not move. Smooth and perfectly spherical, it shed a cool, shadowless glow, although something inside it twisted restlessly.

Come to me, said the voice in her head. Ytha.

She looked around for Drwyn. He had returned from drinking with the rest of his men and was now sprawled snoring on his belly in a fug of *uisca* fumes. Just as well the orb wasn't dangerous; she'd have got no help there.

The voice spoke again. *Come to me. Dress warmly.*

It was more insistent now. Teia slid out of bed and the globe of light drifted a few feet away from her, hovering by the curtained entrance. By its light she dressed and pulled on her boots, jerkin and a thick coat, then lifted the curtain. The globe darted out ahead of her and paused in the passageway beyond, waiting for her to catch up. Then it led the way down the passage towards the meeting place.

No one stirred about the caves. Drwyn's guards had been dismissed, and the lateness of the hour had sent the entire clan to their beds. From behind the other curtained doors she passed, Teia heard snoring, a baby's whimper, the soft, urgent sounds of coupling. The bluish light of the globe guided her around smouldering hearths and piles of gear, leading her down the steps to the empty vault of the meeting place and then up the other side. Past more occupied caves, store-chambers, then finally down a side-turning into the older caverns.

This stretch of the mountains held more caves than there were cavities in a bird's bones to make it light enough to fly, and for thousands of years, generations of clan-folk had scratched and scraped their way into adjoining caverns to extend their quarters, but there were no chisel-marks here, no crudely fractured stone. Some long-ago flow of water had sculpted these passages; the walls and floors undulated, as curved and graceful as the chambers inside a heart. Only the footprints leading back and forth through the thick, soft dust said that humans had ever come this far.

Teia swallowed nervously. The passage was eerily quiet, soundless apart from the scuffle of her boots in the dust as she followed the light, which in turn followed the footprints. Ytha's, she guessed; they had the look of a woman's rather than a man's. Some of the prints were small enough to be a child's, and she thought briefly of the other girls who had been drawn into the summoning with her. Especially the youngest; if she'd been drawn up to the lake in this fashion, she must have been terrified.

Occasionally other tunnels joined the one she and the orb were following, bringing gusts of cold and a suggestion of a vast emptiness beyond, or warmer air laced with strange smells from deep underground. If she stopped, so too did the globe, although it soon drifted onwards again so that she had to keep moving to stay within its circle of illumination.

Eventually the tunnel began to climb, slowly at first, then becoming increasingly steep until she needed to lean against the wall to help herself up. She skidded in the loose dust more than once and her thighs burned with effort. The air grew colder, too, making her breath curl into clouds before her face. Then, as she rounded a corner, she smelled the sharp, clean scent of snow. The tunnel levelled off and in a few yards opened abruptly to the outside world once more.

Teia stepped out onto a ledge overlooking a lake in a precipitously steep-sided col. The valley was ringed with sharp ridges, black rock and white snow stark against the night sky. A fitful breeze rippled the water.

The Speaker was waiting for her near the lip of the ledge. Wrapped in her snow-fox mantle, with the gold crescent across her brow to hold her hair back from her face, she looked imposing, the way Teia imagined Queen Etheldren from the stories: a queen of stone and moon and water, brooking no rival.

Despite her thick coat, she shivered with a sudden

unease and the globe of light at her shoulder winked out. 'Join me, child,' said Ytha, without turning.

Cautiously, Teia crossed the ledge to her side, boots crunching on smears of frozen snow. The wind tugged at her clothes and hair.

'I have been waiting for this night, when the wandering moon comes full again,' the Speaker went on. Her breath whitened on the chill air before the breeze dashed it away. 'On a night such as this, we might glimpse our futures.'

She took Teia's arm to draw her alongside and the two of them looked out over their reflections to the far side of the col, where the wandering second moon, silvery white, rode serenely between the horns of the mountains.

'The Talent is drawn to gateways. It seeks out doors, borders, places where two worlds brush against one another. It is drawn to water, for water can pass through the tightest seal, span the world through rivers and oceans. Water gives life and drives it. It powers a seedling's roots down through rock, supports a mighty tree, runs through our veins in our blood. It is everywhere and it is all-powerful. It can show us what we would not otherwise see.' The grip on Teia's arm tightened, pinching just a little. 'But I think you know this already.'

Icy dread slithered down her spine. Ytha suspected, but how much did she know?

'Why have you brought me here, Speaker?' Teia ventured.

Ytha turned, fixing her with those cold green eyes. 'Because the time has come to decide what I must do with you.' She drew a knife from her belt. 'And because you have something that I need.'

Teia saw the blade glint and recoiled. She tried to pull herself from Ytha's grasp, but the Speaker's grip was iron and the knife was rising. Blind panic assailed her and she screamed.

'Quiet, child!' Ytha snapped. 'I need only a drop.'

'What?' Teia's knees turned to water and she almost fell. 'But I—'

'Hold out your hand.' When she did not respond, Ytha seized her left hand, turned it over and deftly cut the palm, not deeply, but enough to set the blood flowing. Then she curled Teia's fingers around it so that the blood did not spill. 'Now wait.'

Tucking the knife back into her belt, the Speaker turned to the lake and held out her hands. Her eyes closed. Badly shaken, Teia watched, as the lake water stilled and became as flat as a mirror, in spite of the breeze gusting around them.

Whatever Ytha was weaving tugged at the music inside her, pulling at her to join in the working. She fought it as best she could, fearful of being sucked into another horror, as she had been at the Gathering. The longer Ytha worked the more effort was required to resist; Teia's ears rang and her spine felt as if it was being drawn out of the top of her head.

Finally the dreadful tugging ceased. The air hummed like a plucked bowstring and the silver moon looked so hard and bright it might shatter the sky. Ytha breathed out slowly and lowered her arms.

'Let your blood fall into the water.'

Teia stepped up to the edge of the rocky shelf and extended her bleeding hand over the lake. A few drops spilled, as black in the moonlight as Maegern's tears. The waters swallowed them without a ripple, leaving the reflection of moon and mountains undisturbed.

A strange pulsing struck up through Teia's feet and into the music inside her, and she gasped aloud. A pause, then it came again. The next pause was shorter, the beating stronger, coming again and again until it acquired a rhythm as steady as her own heartbeat.

This was unlike any scrying she had ever witnessed. A blood scrying – the most powerful of them all. In blood was truth, but only another Talent could unlock it. She felt the beat of Ytha's power in every fibre of her body. The air in her lungs vibrated with it, the air in her ears, and still it grew louder.

Then Ytha spoke inside Teia's mind. *Show me.*

The lake waters shimmered and cleared. Floating in them, larger than any mere reflection could be was an image of Teia's face. Of Ytha's there was no sign.

Thus it begins, the Speaker said. *Show me.*

The image changed. Blood sheeted down Teia's face from a gash on her temple and her eyes stared up out of the lake, dull and flat. She blinked, startled. This was the image from her own scrying. So it had been a true future she had seen!

Show me.

No blood this time, just an ugly red scar and a lock of her hair turned snowy white. Around her shoulders was draped the fox-fur mantle of a Speaker and she held a whitewood staff in her hands, but her eyes still gazed upon the pits of hell.

This was a familiar vision. Teia dared a sideways glance at Ytha. The suggestion of a frown creased the Speaker's brow, but her concentration remained fixed on the images in the water.

Show me.

The Speaker's accoutrements vanished but the scar remained, now white with age. In the lake, an older Teia stood with her hands placed protectively on the shoulders of a boy of about twelve summers – the same boy she had seen before. Her son, it now appeared. As in her previous visions, he wore a chief's torc, wolf-head bosses shining, but this time the torc ran with blood. She gasped. So the boy would be chief, but the torc would be taken in battle. Battle against whom?

Show me.

The boy's image wavered and disappeared, leaving Teia's behind. Now the torc was around her own neck.

Ytha's eyes widened and she shot a look at her, but Teia could only stare back helplessly. She had never seen this before. Herself as chief? That was impossible!

The beating in her blood grew stronger. Ytha was concentrating again, drawing in her powers. Pain lanced through Teia's cut hand; she sobbed and clutched it to her.

Show me.

The shimmering took longer to clear this time. When it did, the image lasted only a few seconds, to Teia's relief. It showed a battle in progress. Spears lunged. Axes hacked. Horses reared as men screamed and died. The image blurred into the battle's aftermath, where not a living soul stirred. Torn and bloody corpses littered the sodden grass and ravens stalked amongst them. Putrefying flesh melted from shattered bones; abandoned gear rusted where it lay.

It changed again, the images flickering faster and faster. A bloody hand clutching a torc. Sunlight on a broken spear. A wolf's mask, snarling – no, a she-wolf, crouched over her litter of mewling pups. A grassy plain, bright with summer flowers. An unknown man, his head wreathed by spreading wings. Utter blackness. Fire. A woman's face, contorted, wailing. Virgin snow under sharp, cold stars.

The images began to change and re-form so fast it was impossible to see what they were, and the beating in her head had grown so loud it seemed to shake the mountains around her. Teia fell to her knees, hands pressed to her skull—

And it stopped. Panting, her ears ringing, she dared to look up. Ytha's eyes were closed and she swayed as she leaned on her staff. Then the Speaker took a deep breath and straightened, shaking her hair back over her shoulders.

'Remarkable,' she said at last. The faintest tremor weakened her voice. She turned to Teia and studied her for a long moment. 'Scrying does not show what will be, only what is most likely. Where two futures are so finely balanced that neither is more likely than the other, the scrying will show both. Never before have I seen so many images. Your future hangs in the gods' own scales, child.' She paused and her eyes hardened. 'You ought to have told me about the baby.'

Tears stung Teia's eyes. Now Ytha knew. Now there could be no more pretending, no more hiding. The Speaker *knew*. How could she ever have imagined she could keep it to herself?

Her shoulders sagged and she howled, all the pent-up misery of the last two months boiling out of her like a storm. 'I was frightened!' she wailed. Her chest heaved and she sobbed so hard it distorted the words. 'I was s-so f-frightened!'

Ytha's hand came down on her shoulder, but gently.

'Hush now, Teia,' she said. 'Don't be afraid. There is no greater honour for a woman than to bear her man a son. The first one will be hard, but there are herbs to lessen the pain.'

Gradually Teia's tears spent themselves, though her shoulders continued to shake with dry sobs. Ytha's words sank in. Was it possible that the Speaker had misunderstood the reason for her fear? That it wasn't the pains of childbirth she had been dreading, but the revelation of the futures she had glimpsed? A tiny spark of hope kindled inside her.

'I'm sorry, Speaker,' she managed.

Ytha patted her shoulder. 'Rest easy, what's done is done. Now tell me, when was your last bleed?'

Teia thought back. It was difficult to remember; the chance that she might yet escape the worst of Ytha's wrath was as intoxicating as aged mead. 'Three moons ago. A little more.' Not too long before Drw's death.

'A son before summer's end.' Ytha smiled, tight and self-congratulatory. 'A good omen for the clan. Come now, up off the cold stone. We must tell your husband.'

Dread curdled in Teia's belly. Had this actually been Ytha's plan all along, not just to put her in Drwyn's bed but to see her wedded to him? Wiping her eyes, she followed the older woman back through the mazy passageways to the inhabited caves. With each step, her anxiety grew.

⁂

When they arrived at the chief's chamber Drwyn was in a fine temper, striding about in just his trews, ordering his warriors to form search parties. He fell silent when he saw Teia approach, accompanied by the Speaker with a hand on her shoulder. The war band milling about the passageway, many sleepy and still only half-dressed themselves, fell back to make way for them.

'Where in all hells have you been?' Drwyn demanded, seizing Teia by the arm as his other hand drew back.

'Hold, Drwyn,' Ytha said sharply. 'Not here, in front of your people.'

He lowered his hand, but his bloodshot eyes remained murderous. He jerked his head towards the curtained entrance to the cave. 'Inside.'

Teia hurried in, followed by Ytha at a more stately pace. Drwyn came last, yanking the curtain closed behind him.

'I will teach you what it means to run from me, wench,' he snarled, advancing on Teia, who shrank back against the wall.

Ytha rolled her eyes. 'Macha's ears, boy! I summoned her for a blood scrying.'

That halted him. He swung around to stare at the Speaker. 'You did? What did it foretell?'

Ytha smiled. 'I think that is for your wife to tell you,' she said.

Teia swallowed hard. Her palms were damp with

sweat that stung in the cut from Ytha's knife, but in spite of her coat and the cave's warmth, she was shivering. Even with the Speaker there, she feared the glint in Drwyn's eye.

'I'm carrying,' she said in a tiny voice. She could not look him in the face, already flinching from his reaction.

He simply stood with his jaw hanging, dumbstruck.

'A son, Drwyn,' Ytha put in. 'An heir for the chief.'

'A son?' he echoed. A huge grin split his beard and he held out his arms. 'A son!'

Scooping Teia up, he swung her around and kissed her soundly on both cheeks. He even forgot himself enough to try to plant a peck on Ytha, but she ducked out of the way.

'When?' he demanded. 'When will he be born?'

'Around midsummer,' said Ytha, 'but if you cease mauling the girl about I'll make certain. Lie down, child, and draw up your knees.'

Teia did as instructed. As Drwyn watched eagerly, Ytha knelt and parted Teia's thighs, pushing two cold fingers inside her. With her other hand, she pressed low on her belly, there and there.

After a moment, Ytha nodded, satisfied, and stood up, wiping her fingers on Drwyn's discarded shirt. 'The birth will be in the summer. Six full moons from now.'

'Under the trinity,' said Drwyn, and grinned. 'You're sure it will be a son?'

'It is too soon to know for certain,' Ytha told him, 'but I am confident. In a little while, perhaps we will find out. There will be plenty of time then for a wedding.'

Teia sat up, adjusting her skirts. A wedding, if she bore a son. A dark-eyed boy, with the stamp of his sire and grandsire in his stocky build and sturdy, well-made features. This future, at least, would come about as she had foreseen. Thoughts whirling, she touched her cheek where the wolf-head tattoo would soon go, and realised with a sudden chill that in none of her visions of her older self had she seen such a mark. Her thoughts churned even faster.

'Um, Speaker?' she said diffidently. 'I have the Talent. What will that mean?'

Ytha frowned. 'By clan law, as the chief's wife you cannot be a Speaker amongst the Crainnh, but I will not risk the chief's child by burning out your gift. Perhaps some lessons should be arranged for now, then when we know whether the vision I saw is indeed the child you carry, I will decide. Now I shall leave you in peace.'

With an inclination of her head to each of them, she glided out. Drwyn was away hard on the Speaker's heels, sparing Teia only a rough hug in his eagerness to share the news with his men.

She watched the heavy hanging swing back into place after him. So it was all arranged. No longer just the chief's bed-mate, but now his bride-to-be. The prospect should have pleased her, she supposed; it would certainly please her father. As greatfather to the next chief, his position in the clan would be secure. As for hers, well, if Ytha was to be believed, a great honour had befallen her, though the prospect of bearing a child and losing her Talent did not feel like much of an honour.

She ran her hands down over her belly, smoothing her dress and shift flat with her palm. Would it be a boy? Tomorrow she would make an offering to Macha the Mother in the hope that it would, if only because it would bring a rare smile to her father's face.

Turning down the wick on the lamp thickened the shadows in the chamber, hiding Drwyn's scattered clothes. There would be time enough for her chores later. She was still so very tired and all twisted up inside, like a dishcloth wrung out and left to dry in the sun. All she wanted to do was burrow down into the bed and pull the coverings over her head.

But even Drwyn's lingering warmth in the furs was not enough to lull her to sleep. Her mind would not rest: too many secrets had been revealed – that she had the gift of the sight, and carried the chief's child – and Ytha's reactions had been so far from what she had feared that now she could not help but fear some worse censure to come. She had seen the lightning flare, and now lay awake dreading the thunder that would surely follow.

Then there was the matter of the visions' contents: the bloody torc as a portent of war, the other fragmentary images now spiralling out of reach of her recollection like so many leaves on an autumn gale. In time, the Speaker would want to pick them over, unravel their tangled truths, but it might all be for nothing if the apocalypse she had seen so many times in the waters came first.

If only she had some way to determine the order in which events would occur; a way to grasp the meaning of these glimpses of the yet-to-be. Too often under-standing came only in the aftermath, when it was far too late to do anything but weep.

Lying on her side, she cradled her cut palm in her other hand. It throbbed faintly, though Ytha's knife had not gone deep. In a day or two the cut would have closed. In a week it would hardly be visible, though what it had unleashed would be with her to the end of her days.

A blood scrying was used when there were pressing questions to answer. Only another woman with the Tal-ent could unlock the secrets in someone's blood; did that mean that Teia was a pressing question to Ytha in some way? Why else would the Speaker go to the trou-ble, when she surely had enough to ponder on with Drwyn's ambitions to make war on the Empire?

More chilling thoughts occurred: did it mean Ytha considered her a threat to those ambitions – and did the child she was carrying make her more dangerous to them, or less? And what about the blood scrying and the images the waters had shown?

Teia shuddered and wrapped her arms about her knees beneath the furs. She'd tried not to think about what she had seen in the lake, but she should have known that not thinking about something was the surest way to have it consume her thoughts. Now, in the dimness with nothing else to occupy her attention, the images rose up again and filled her in a flood.

Horrors stalked across her mind's eye, no less vivid for being viewed a second time. Blasted landscapes, bloodless faces. Battles fought and lost, and fought and won, though she was hard pressed to tell the difference. All was slaughter and only the crows were sated by it. Teia screwed her eyes shut, though it made no difference. Blood and death and darkness come again, the Wild Hunt sweeping across the plains. A sob thickened her throat, then another. Fire-eyed Hounds that bayed in tones to curdle her soul, waved on by a dark hunter. Nothing but ruin behind them and the harsh clatter of the gallows-birds.

More sobs shook her, though the tears would not come, nothing but a hot prickle behind her eyes. She pressed the heels of her hands into them as if to blot the visions out, but they marched on. Nightmare after nightmare, one after another. Teia sobbed and sobbed and sobbed.

Finally, exhausted, she lay staring at the oil-lamp in its niche in the wall. Its tiny flame danced on the merest breath of air, bright and brave against the thronging shadows. The Wild Hunt. Now her visions made sense. The Hounds in her dreams, the dark hunter – oh, Macha preserve her, she recognised him now. Or rather, Her. Maegern the Raven, Keeper of the Dead. And Ytha had summoned Her.

If Teia had been standing, she would have fallen to her knees. Her bones could not have supported the weight of the realisation crashing down on her. Ytha and the other Speakers had summoned the Raven to aid them, but Teia had seen Her Hounds scouring the plains like a firestorm. Already the goddess's bloody hand was reaching out from Her exile. Her powers would only grow now, and She would not be satisfied with just the plains. Devastation would follow the prints of Her Hounds all across the world.

Teia's fingers spasmed closed over her wounded palm. Dread clawed at her stomach. *Oh, Speaker, what have you done?*

12

WINTER

As the year waned, winter tightened its grip on the mountains. In the caves, far below ground, the clanspeople did not feel the deadly chill of the storms that howled above them. Hunting had been good and the larders were full, with plenty of fodder for the animals. Provided confinement did not drive folk mad, it was a comfortable enough way to wait out the snows.

But for Teia, winter also reigned inside. The Wild Hunt would be freed. She could not escape that knowledge, no matter what she did, and it left a ball of icy dread in her stomach that no amount of hot broth or mead could thaw. As the days in the caves turned into weeks, chilly fingers of premonition stroked her spine at unexpected moments as she did her chores, or skittered over her thoughts as she lay shivering in the chief's bed. When she managed to sleep, she heard the Hounds in her dreams, but now they were accompanied by a dark hunter bearing a shield that stared and a helm wreathed in battle-smoke.

The Wild Hunt would be freed, and it would scour the world with fire.

To her surprise, Drwyn became more solicitous of her now that her womb was filling, curbing some of his desires in bed and indulging her if she complained of an aching back. On one memorable occasion, he even sent Harl in her stead to fetch fuel and snow for water, which left the blond warrior so sour-faced he did no more guard duties than his own from then on.

She also began to receive gifts. Lengths of woollen cloth and pieces of the softest sealskin appeared at the door. Some of the women smiled at her as she went about her chores through the caves. Others still curled their lips, or spoke behind their hands as she passed by, but it did not sting quite so much now. Her greatest relief came when her mother ventured a shy greeting whilst Teir looked on, still grim but a little kinder around the eyes.

Yet even that could not outweigh the dread gnawing at the edges of her awareness. The Hounds were running. Sometimes they chased her through the caves, snapping at her heels; sometimes they were nothing more than a howl in the distance that intruded on the landscape of some other dream and made her shiver in her sleep. Each time she heard it, it sounded a little closer.

If the Hounds were running, the Hunt would follow. With every day that passed the certainty grew stronger, like watching thunderheads massing over the mountains and knowing that, inevitably, the lightning-storm would come.

Each day, as all the women did when a child was due, she made a simple offering of food to Macha, to ask the Mother to look kindly on the birthing. After the meal, when Drwyn wasn't looking, she also implored Lord Aedon to shelter her family when the storm broke.

A scrying might have shed more light on her future, but she dared not draw on her power with Ytha so close by. There was nowhere in the caves that she could go without being observed, not even the lake nestled amongst the peaks above; there was nowhere she could be sure the Speaker would not find her. Besides, she remembered too well what had happened when last she had been to the lake. She feared the waters would remember, and speak.

As the winter deepened, Teia cut and stitched infant's clothes whilst her belly grew larger. Her growing roundness delighted Drwyn. He would put his hand over her belly and laugh aloud to feel its changing shape, talk and even sing to the son he imagined inside. He finally noticed the marked fullness of her breasts, too, which delighted him all the more.

Another full moon passed and at the dark of the year Ytha came to examine her again. This time she did not feel inside her, but simply laid hands on her rounded abdomen and closed her eyes. Something tugged at the music inside, and Teia hoped with all her heart that the child was a boy. It would please the chief, and if the chief was happy, everyone's lot in the clan improved. Not least of all her own.

The tickling, pulling sensation faded and Ytha opened her eyes, studying Teia for a long, long moment. Teia's heart raced. She had a sudden, dreadful fear that whatever future son her scrying had shown her, the unborn inside her now was a girl.

Drwyn, pacing the cave in a fever of impatience, suddenly loomed over the two of them. 'Well?' he demanded.

Lips pursed, Ytha got to her feet. 'It is still too soon. In another month I will come again, to be sure.'

She turned to leave and Drwyn followed her to the door. 'You said you would know by now,' he hissed.

Ytha's gaze flickered to Teia. 'Not here,' she said and led him outside.

Teia could hear no more than a murmur of their conversation; it was impossible to make out the words, but she knew they were talking about her. Discussing her fate, what would happen if her child was a girl. She stood up, pulling her coat around her. Whatever it was, it could not be any worse than what she had seen.

As she stepped out into the passageway, the Speaker hissed a warning and Drwyn fell silent. Teia felt their eyes on her back as she walked away from them, up the slope towards the outside. They made no attempt to stop her.

It grew colder the higher she climbed, and brighter as the thin winter light seeped in from outside. Blown snow crusted the rock underfoot, and she carefully crunched and slid her way up the passage to where it widened like a great yawning mouth. Snow lay more thickly there, sculpted into troughs and pillows by the wind, reflecting what little light there was from outside so that the cave looked almost bright after the gloom of the passageway.

From the ledge at the cave's entrance, Teia looked down on a trackless white wilderness. The blizzards that had kept the hunters inside for four days had blown on, leaving the landscape changed in their wake. Familiar landmarks were smothered, the trees on the slopes so bent and stooped by snow they resembled a crowd of old women mantled against the cold. The iron-coloured sky spat flurries of fine snow, but it was clear the storm was spent.

Wrapping her fur collar close around her neck, she stared out over the foothills. She did not really feel the chill or the prickle of snowflakes on her skin; she was already numb. Numb from the inside out, cold as a stone.

Some time later, she had no idea how long, she heard feet crunching through the snow behind her, drawing closer. Only when a hand touched her arm did she glance around.

Her father stood behind her, dark eyes anxious. 'You should come inside,' he said.

'Not just yet, Dada.' She hadn't called him that in years, not since she was tiny. 'I wanted to see outside again.'

With heavy cloud masking the sun, the only light came from the snow itself, the ghostly glow of a fresh fall, shadowless and pure. A few tiny flakes whirled away on the breeze. Deep beneath their snowy blanket the plains slept, waiting to be reborn.

'Beautiful, isn't it?' said her father, stepping up beside her. 'Beautiful but cold.'

He did not say that he was pleased she would soon be wed, that one day he could count the new chieftain of the Crainnh amongst his grandchildren. He did not have to. Just being there said so much more than Teir's few words ever could.

He laid a tentative arm around her waist. Teia let her head rest on his shoulder and he hugged her. 'Come inside, sweetling. This chill is not good for you.'

'I know. It's just the days are so short now, and in the caves . . .' She trailed off with a helpless shrug. 'I wish the winter was over.'

'Soon, Teisha, I promise.' He kissed the top of her head and Teia smiled.

'You used to call me that when I was a little girl.'

'You are still my little girl. No matter how tall you get, you'll always be my Teisha.'

Tears threatened and she was too tired to try to blink them away. They spilled over her lashes, became a flood. 'I missed you so much, Dada.'

Teir pulled her into his arms and held her tight. She buried her face in the front of his jerkin and let herself weep, wrapped in his warmth and the strong, steady beat of his heart.

It had always been her father who banished the monsters of childhood, never her mother. If she had woken from a bad dream to find Ana there, she had wailed all the louder until Teir came and made her world safe again. How she wished he could save her now.

'Ytha has done something terrible.' The words were out almost before she knew they were forming and once they had escaped she could not call them back, or stop the ones that followed. 'She has made a terrible mistake and she doesn't even know it.'

'What do you mean?'

'At the Gathering, when she summoned the shade of Maegern, I was pulled into the weaving. I saw Ytha perform the sacrifice and heard her make bargain with the Raven: Her freedom in exchange for Her aid.' Teia took a ragged breath, scrubbed her eyes with the back of her hand. 'She's going to unleash the Wild Hunt, Dada, and she doesn't realise that she'll never be able to control it.'

Teir swore under his breath. 'Are you sure? How do you know this?'

'I've seen it in my dreams, over and over. I hear the Hounds in my sleep.'

'You have the foretelling?' he asked, and she spread her hands helplessly.

'I don't know. All I know is that sometimes I see things and some of them have come true.'

'And the rest?'

She could only shrug. 'I don't think they've happened yet.'

A grim frown drew his brows down, mimicking the lines of his moustaches. He had worn a similar expression to do battle with the kelpies and kobolds that had stalked her as a girl. She knew these new demons would not be banished by a war cry as the drapes were swept aside. It would take more than a cook-pot-lid buckler to defend her, even one wielded on Teir's doughty arm. But she did not know where else to turn.

'When Ytha told me you had the gift, I could scarce believe it,' he said. 'There have been no Speakers in our line in near three hundred years. You are certain of what you saw?'

'I'm sure.' Of that she had no doubt at all. 'I saw Her when the Speakers summoned Her; I heard Her speak. She called them little women and mocked them for their weakness.'

That awful voice grated around inside her skull again and she flinched at the memory.

'The Speaker has powers beyond our comprehension, Teisha,' Teir said dubiously.

'Enough to best one of the Eldest? I have powers too, Dada, and seeing Maegern appear in the circle near made me soil myself.' Teia half-laughed, incredulous at Ytha's audacity, her towering arrogance, terrified of what it meant for her people. Hysteria tickled the edges of her mind. 'How does she imagine she can ever bend the Raven to her will? She might as well try to compel the wind to blow westerly.'

'Then you must warn her.'

'She already knows. She saw the blood scrying. The images were there in the water, clear as day, but I think she saw them as a sign of victory. It was only after that I realised what I'd seen was the Hunt turned on our own people. On all people, even the Empire.'

Her father frowned. 'We were sent here by the Empire, Teisha. I doubt many in the clan would grieve to see it gone.'

'That means nothing to the Hunt,' she said. 'Blood feud, history – it doesn't matter. To the Hunt we are all prey.'

Though it was barely dawn, the day had become gloomy as dusk, without a bird call or any sound but the low moan of the wind. Blown snow crystals stung Teia's face and the chill suddenly pinched her so hard it hurt. Inside, she wanted to curl up and weep.

'Does anyone else know what you have seen?' her father asked at last.

She shook her head. 'Who could I tell? Who would believe me, even if I did tell them?'

Teir's teeth flashed suddenly, whitely in the murky light. 'I believe you.'

'It's my word against hers, Dada. What is my word worth against the Speaker of the Crainnh?'

'More than you think, my daughter. To me, anyway –' he squeezed her shoulders '– and my word still counts for a little amongst the men. Some of them, anyway. If this weather holds, we'll hunt again soon. I'll speak to them then, quietly.' Blowing out his moustaches, Teir raked his fingers back through his hair. 'I'm not sure what else I can do, but I believe you.'

'Ytha cannot find out what I know, or know I have shared it. Not yet.' She didn't dare voice her fears of what would happen to her then.

'I'll be careful, I promise.'

'Thank you.'

She pulled her coat tighter around her. The cold had struck into her bones and she was suddenly so very tired.

'Let's go inside,' Teir said, putting his arm around her. 'Come visit us on Firstmoon, stay for supper. Ana misses you.'

'But clan law—' She broke off. According to clan law, her father shouldn't even be standing there, and there he was, with his arm protectively around her. The rush of fierce affection that followed that thought was as warming as a bowl of soup. Being promised bride to the chief had to count for something, didn't it?

She leaned into his embrace. 'I miss her, too. I'll come if I can.'

With her head on her father's shoulder, she walked back into the maw of the mountain.

⚓

That night, Teia dreamed a new dream. Ytha stood proud in her snow-fox robe, whitewood staff in one hand, the other hand pushed deep into the ruff of a massive Hound that sat on its haunches at her side. Another lay at her feet. Bigger than plains wolves, larger even than the timber wolves that lived on the slopes of the mountains, they had a wolf's deep chest and plumed tail but the massive jaws of a mastiff. As she watched, the Hound at Ytha's feet yawned lazily, exposing teeth as sharp as icicles and a tongue so red it was almost purple. Then it looked right at Teia with its fiery eyes and grinned.

She came awake with a start, her heart racing. Beside her Drwyn stirred, asking what was wrong, his voice thick with sleep.

'I had a bad dream,' she told him. 'Go back to sleep.'

Pushing her sweaty hair out of her eyes, she got up and poured herself a beaker of water. It tasted flat from standing in the jug, but it gave her mouth some moisture and swallowing it relaxed the knot of tension in her chest.

The beast's eyes had been frighteningly aware, as if an intelligence greater than its own had been looking through them and laughing at her. She shuddered. Water finished, she climbed back into bed and pulled the still-warm furs around her.

At the summoning, Maegern had said She would send Hounds to guide them. Teia pictured those massive forms running through the snow, true as arrows, towards their destination. According to the legends they would run for ever, day or night, through stormy

weather or fair, and they would not stop. Ever. When
their quarry was brought to ground, they would feast.

She winced, sick from her premonition. Whatever
they would feast on, it did not bear contemplation.

⁂

For three nights after she'd confessed her fears to her
father, Teia saw more Hounds in her dreams. Sometimes
a single animal, sometimes a whole pack, spreading
across the plains like a great yellow tide, always with
the smoke-and-shadow figure of Maegern behind, urging them on.

Each morning she woke filled with a heightened sense
of dread about the days to come. The weight of the
mountains above grew more oppressive and she felt
ever smaller and more helpless in the face of it. As the
wandering moon waxed towards Firstmoon, her appetite deserted her and even the clearing skies, bright with
the promise of spring to come, did nothing to cheer her.

The break in the storms had sent the Crainnh out
hunting again, every man who could lift a spear – her
father included. The smoke-room was raked out and
fresh fire kindled, ready to preserve their catch. Though
her baby-sickness was diminishing, Teia pleaded a tender stomach to excuse herself; she had boiled enough
elk-fat soap to last her years. Nothing could help her
escape the stink, though, even up at the mouth of the
caves. It clung to her clothes and her hair like smoke,
and not even the sharp mountain breeze could blow it
away.

On the fourth day, Ytha gave a perfunctory scratch
at the door-curtain.

'It is time to begin your instruction,' she said when
Teia greeted her. Then the Speaker looked her up and
down, noting the shadows around her eyes, and her lips
formed themselves into a dissatisfied quirk.

'Perhaps I should come another time.'

'Not at all, Speaker. Please, come in.' Teia stood aside to let the older woman enter.

'Are you sick?'

'I didn't sleep very well, that's all.'

'More dreams?'

Ytha's agate-green eyes were cool, incisive, but Teia met them squarely. She could lie to them now; she knew she could. She had to. Ytha could not know the truth of her visions, not until she was sure what to do about them. The Speaker had been in her head more than once and she had kept her Talent hidden from her. In comparison, not speaking the truth to her face should be easy.

'Something I ate, I think.'

Ytha sniffed. 'You must have a care for your diet, girl. Remember you are feeding your chief's heir, not just yourself.'

'It was only a sour stomach, but I will be more careful in future, I promise.' Lowering her eyes, dipping her head, Teia was every inch the chastened girl before her clan Speaker. It seemed to work.

'So. Are you ready for your first lesson?'

From the ashes in her mind, a green leaf of hope unfolded. If she learned to shape and control her foretellings, maybe she could understand them better, learn what to do, even if it was only to find a way to warn Ytha of the dangers in treating with the Eldest. Yet she had to be careful and show the proper deference, or surely the Speaker would suspect that she knew far more than she ought.

She controlled her expression but could not prevent a tremble in her voice. 'I think so.'

'You must be sure!' Ytha's tone cracked like a breaking spear. 'You have a rare Talent, a strong Talent, and I will not see it wasted through uncertainty or doubt. I may yet have a use for your abilities after your child is born, if the other Talents I found with you prove not to be strong enough to train as apprentices.'

For a moment Teia was more afraid of that particular statement than if Ytha had said she was to burn her out the next day. After what she had seen in her dreams and in the blood scrying, she dared not let her imagination dwell on what she might be called upon to do. But she needed to learn how to tame her Talent, make it work for her instead of tossing her about like a toy in the hands of a petulant child. If she was to have any chance at all of understanding what lay ahead and how best to steer herself through it, she had to learn. The Speaker was the only one who could teach her.

Deep breaths, Teia. Remember the manners your mother taught you. With a gesture, she indicated the embroidered cushions arranged on the floor. 'Then will you not be seated, Speaker?'

The look Ytha flashed her way was unreadable, but the older woman sat, arranging her skirts around her. Teia sat facing her, hands on her knees.

Immediately, a bluish globe formed in the air between the two women at eye height. As it came into existence Teia felt a little tug inside, in the place where she reached when she wanted to scry. Ah. So that was what it felt like to be aware of another woman working the power. She had felt that tug before but never known what it was. Now all was clear.

'Can you hear it?' Ytha asked.

Teia listened, but her ears heard nothing. Then she opened herself to the music and found it shimmering and thrumming in response to the Speaker's weaving. 'I hear *something*.'

The little globe changed colour from blue to violet. As it did so, the note in the music changed tone, becoming richer and more rounded somehow. There was a texture, too, almost a warp and a weft. Teia could see the weave clearly now and was amazed that she had never thought to study it before. After all, Ytha's lights were no new thing to her.

Underneath the soft chiming of the Speaker's power, Teia heard her own Talent echoing every shade and inflection as if urging her to copy the weave. The ball of light was all but showing her how it was made.

Excitement thrilled through her. Could wielding power really be this simple? Could she learn just by studying what another woman did and letting the music – was it magic? – form itself like soap poured into a mould?

'May I try?'

Ytha's eyebrows twitched up a fraction. 'We have barely begun, child. Do you think you are ready?'

'I can see it, how it is woven. I know I can do this.'

The globe was now coppery-pink and paling like a sunrise.

'Very well.' Ytha's tone was grudging.

She expects me to fail. But I won't.

Holding out her hand, Teia concentrated. The power rose eagerly and sang along her nerves as she spun it into a perfect sphere hovering above her palm. She had just enough time to notice Ytha's expression shift from doubt through startlement to being quite satisfyingly impressed when a black vault opened in her mind and a Hound leapt through it. Shock ripped the power from her grasp and the globe winked out. Teia gasped, but the Hound was gone as swiftly as it had arrived. Gone as if it had never been.

Her thoughts reeled. A waking vision? She had never experienced that before. She had only seen things in dreams or when scrying.

Dragging her attention back, Teia focused on the Speaker, who was, she noted, nonplussed. It did not last long. One breath and Ytha was herself again, chill and deep as the mountain lake.

'Remarkable.' A knife-cut smile. 'I congratulate you.

It is rare that an apprentice manages so much from so little instruction. Can you repeat what you did?'

Power rose up the instant Teia thought of reaching for it, in spite of her weariness. Once more a little globe blushed into existence over her outstretched palm; she frowned, concentrating, and its colour paled to match the cool blue of Ytha's. She tensed, waiting for the reappearance of the Hound, but nothing happened. The globe remained, gently rotating to the rhythm of the song inside her. She relaxed, even dared a small smile of achievement.

'Remarkable,' Ytha said again. She examined Teia's globe carefully, then with a twitch of her hand snuffed it out.

The severing of her contact with the power stung Teia like the snap of a herdmaster's quirt. She yelped, more from surprise than pain.

'Again.'

A test, then. So be it. Another globe, quicker and more assured than the others. Again Ytha struck and extinguished it. It stung fiercely this time, but she did not flinch.

'Again!'

Now she could spin the globe almost without thinking. She had sensed the Speaker weaving something before she struck; she saw it now and as the other woman's fingers flickered, she raised a fist of power.

Ytha's weaving struck it and flew into fragments. 'How did you do that?'

That agate-green glare demanded an explanation. How *had* she done it? Teia was not sure; she had simply known. Instinctively.

'I saw the shape of your weaving and copied it. But I made a shield instead of a knife.'

'How impressive.'

Something in the Speaker's tone fair screamed a warning. It was the flat-eyed look of a cat before it scratched, the rattle in the long grass that said tread with care. Had she gone too far? Perhaps. But she was not a child any more and she was tired of being spanked like one.

'Forgive me, Speaker. Have I done wrong?'

'No, not wrong. You run headlong where you should barely be walking, perhaps, but nothing wrong.' The older woman rose, drawing her robe around her. Her globe rose into the air to hover at her shoulder. 'I think that is enough for one day, though. You do not want to overtire yourself.'

'Of course.' Teia stood, folding her hands meekly in front of her. 'Thank you for your instruction, Speaker. I am sure I will learn a great deal under your guidance.'

Ytha favoured her with a long look. Teia had seen it before, knew the Speaker used it to create the kind of silence that ached to be filled and usually resulted in unwise words. She faced it with a mildness of expression that drew its sting completely, like milk-weed after nettles. Drwyn's temper had taught her that, though the skill had not been acquired without a price. Another moment's consideration, a stiff little nod and the Speaker was gone.

Alone, Teia wondered whether it was a mistake letting Ytha see how apt a pupil she could be. Would it make for more trust, or less? More lessons, or fewer? She even let herself wonder whether it made her more likely to be burned out or safer, if she sat at the Speaker's right hand as her apprentice.

She touched the firm curve of her belly speculatively. As long as she carried Drwyn's child she would be safe. It even gave her power, of a sort. Not even Ytha would risk harm to her until after the birth, not unless provoked. So she had some time, at least, in which to learn as much as she could.

Very gently she let a thread of her magic reach down through the layers of skin and muscle under her hand, let it slip into the warm darkness of her womb and caress the child. Sleeping. The infant mind was wrapped in a somnolent fug in which colours shifted slowly, a skyful of sunset clouds.

Teia touched it, no more substantial than a breath. Colours swirled and rose. Deep blue, rich amber, other colours for which she had no names, opulent as jewels. Startled, she withdrew, not daring to linger, for if there was one thing she did know about her Talent it was how little she knew. Fading to the muted glow of lamplight through a thick curtain, the colours subsided. But Teia still sensed them, long after she let the music sink back into quiescence.

For the first time, she felt aware of her child as more than just the source of backache and indigestion. Did that mean the child would be gifted, too?

That thought struck an unexpected spark of fear in her. She had never heard of a male with the Talent. It followed the female line, though it did not always breed true and sometimes died out or appeared in families that had never produced an apprentice for as long as anyone could remember. But it was always a girl who went fearfully to the Speaker's tent a month or two after her first bleed – sometimes even before, for those with the strongest gifts, when boys were still deciding whether to be warriors or herdsmen. If her child was gifted, didn't that mean she would give birth to a girl?

Teia chewed at her lower lip, then made herself stop. If she had a daughter, she had a daughter; no amount of fretting would change it. She would not be so favoured as if she bore a son, but it would prove she was fertile enough for sons in the future, unlike Drwyn's first wife, and he did not appear to be displeased with her, so perhaps things would not change all that much.

Her standing with Ytha, though . . . that was another kettle of soup entirely. Would the Speaker view a source of gifted children as an asset to her plans, or would she feel threatened by it, by Teia herself? That was a question with no easy answer.

And what of the Hound? What had triggered that brief, startling vision? For a fraction of a second her mind had been filled with rank fur, hot breath and a . . . presence, and then it was gone. Lacking in detail yet extraordinarily vivid, the way a few charcoal strokes and a smudge of ochre on the cave wall could depict a buck elk brought to bay by spears. Not so much a Hound as the essence of one, the core and root, the hunter of which all others were mere reflections in a bronze mirror, hazy and dim. It had consumed her entirely.

That must be how the hare felt when confronted by the fox, or the sparrow under the talons of the hawk. Nothing to see or hear or feel but the predator, and the certain knowledge that she was nothing but prey.

13

FIRSTMOON

After that first lesson, Ytha came every day. For an hour or so, she drilled Teia in the making of lights and the summoning of the wind. Her praise was grudging and her rebukes swift, but Teia accepted such chiding as came and considered it the price of knowledge.

For the first time she truly felt she had control of the power inside her. Only in small ways, to be sure, but she could command it to do her will, reliably, repeatably.

After ten such lessons she could summon three globes at once and, like a juggler at the fair, make them dance between her hands.

Ytha raised her eyebrows at such frivolity, of course, but let her play for a minute or so, then cleared her throat. Teia brought the whirling spheres back into a line and lowered her eyes.

'Forgive me. I let myself be carried away.'

'Though there is joy in it, the Talent is not for games,' Ytha said severely. 'If you lose your focus, it can become dangerous. Remember that.'

'Yes, Speaker.' She bit her lip. 'I was wondering, might I be allowed to practise between lessons?'

'Absolutely not.'

'I thought it might improve my concentration—'

'No!' Ytha cut the air with her hand, and the draught sent Teia's globes tumbling in the air. 'You are too impatient, too undisciplined. You should not even be spinning simultaneous weaves this soon – always you are reaching for more, more, more.' She glared at Teia, snapped her fingers and, one by one, extinguished the bobbing lights. 'Your gift is strong, but if you overreach yourself, power alone will not save you.'

If she could not touch her power unsupervised, she could not scry. If she could not scry, she could not learn her future. Before she could stop herself, Teia began, 'But—'

'*It – is – forbidden!*'

Teia's hopes fizzled out like her lights. Trying to hide the disappointment she was sure must be written on her face, she bowed her head. 'Yes, Speaker.'

The next few lessons saw Ytha more strict than ever, repeating simple exercises and allowing Teia no freedom to stretch her growing control. She schooled herself to obedience, and was finally rewarded a week later with an opportunity to practise multiple weavings. She did not ask about unsupervised practice again, though the desire to do it anyway was enough to keep her awake some nights. It was too soon to try pressing Ytha's indulgence again just yet.

Three weeks into the new year, the silver moon rose full again, and Teia celebrated Firstmoon with her parents in their family chamber on the far side of the meeting place. Ana had baked mooncakes for the feast day, and fussed so over Teia's comfort that Teir exclaimed she was only their daughter, not Queen Etheldren herself stepped down out of legend. At that, Ana gave a sniff that said she would not spare this much effort for the Queen and all her court, then proffered another pillow for Teia's back.

Conversation was stiff at first; they had forgotten how to be at ease with one another. Her elder sisters did not seem to know how to treat her. She was no longer a girl, but not yet a wife; no longer a maiden, but not yet a mother; Talented, but not yet a Speaker. She was Teia-in-waiting and they had no cues to follow, so fell back on a guarded formality that fair broke her heart.

But Teir was generous with his store of mead and soon tongues loosened and smiles came more freely. Ailis had titbits of the choicest gossip to share, then Tevira told a story so salacious that her father clapped his hands over his ears to spare himself whilst the women drummed their heels on the floor and hooted with laughter.

For a time Teia put aside all that troubled her and wrapped herself up in the warmth of family, but eventually the evening had to end. Tevira had a pair of sleepy-eyed boys to take home and Ailis a young husband to attend. Whilst Ana busied herself with clearing bowls and cups, Teir took up a pitchwood torch to light her way back to Drwyn.

'I don't need a light, Da,' Teia said, settling her coat around her shoulders. 'I can make my own now.'

A thread of power was all she needed to spin a globe of pale yellow and set it hovering above her shoulder. Ytha would no doubt have words to say about that come the morning, but with a spike of defiance she decided that was for the morning to worry about. Its gentle glow chased a look of consternation across Teir's face. 'Macha's ears, girl, give me some warning!'

Teia stifled a giggle. 'Sorry. I told you I have powers.'

'Yes, you did.' Teir blew out his moustaches, thumping the torch back into its ring on the wall. 'I just did not expect to see them in my own home.'

He reached out one long finger and cautiously stroked the surface of the globe. It swung around his fingertip and over the back of his hand, clinging like a soap bubble, slick as a fish. It reflected in his dark eyes like a miniature sun.

'My own daughter,' he murmured. 'I never imagined this fate for you, Teisha. A home, a husband, children to gladden your heart, but not this. Gifted with powers I cannot begin to comprehend.' He scrubbed his hand on his trews. 'It tingles.'

Teia picked up the rest of her things. Tevira had given her some sturdy winter clothes her sons had outgrown, which made quite a bundle, and there were a few of Ana's sweet mooncakes wrapped up in a cloth.

Arms full, she watched her father staring at the little yellow globe between them. Its light was not kind to the lines on his face, and he had more grey in his hair now, too, she noticed. When had that happened? In the space of a season her father had become an old man, his hair the colour of burned bones.

Premonition yawned its black maw in the rear of her mind, threatening to swallow her completely. Clutching her thread of power she flung herself away from the abyss. The yellow orb flared painfully bright for a moment, then resumed its steady glow. Behind her eyes, the void closed again.

Teia let out a shaky breath. Sunk in the bundle of children's clothes, her fingers unclenched. Relief flooded her like the blood coming back to her cramped fingers. Just for a moment she had imagined some terrible future lay ahead for her family and she could not bear to see it. Not tonight. She would behold it eventually, of that there was no doubt, but please by all the stars, not tonight.

'Does he still hurt you, Teisha?'

'No, Da.'

He did not look at her. 'I will never forgive him for that. He is the chief and I am his liegeman as I was his father's, for whatever that is worth, but I cannot forgive him.'

'He knows no other way,' she said softly. '"When you must bed down in the same cave as an ice-bear, you learn how not to wake him."'

Her mother had used that old proverb many a time about her father. Recognition brought a ghost of a smile to lift the ends of Teir's moustaches. 'So wise, little Teisha.'

Finally he dragged his eyes away from the globe and fixed them on her face. He pitched his voice low, though there was no one but Ana to hear and she was singing to herself over the dishes.

'I spoke to some of the men, on the hunt. They are uneasy about Drwyn's ambitions, for much the same reasons as you. But they think they are too few and that Ytha has so filled his ears with promises of glory that he could not hear them, even if he wanted to listen. I dare not bring them all together to strengthen their voices.' Teir rested his hands on her shoulders and squeezed them. 'I tried, sweetling, but they are too fearful of the Speaker to say a word against her.'

She dipped her head to press her cheek against his hand. She had known as soon as she saw his expression that he had no good news. It had been a small hope to begin with, so it was no great disappointment to see it wither and die. She had always known that in the end, it would come down to her. She simply wished she knew what she was supposed to do. Her dreams had shown her nothing new for a week or more, though the Hound had leaped silently through her mind twice more since that first lesson with Ytha. Each time she saw it, she was convinced it was gaining ground.

'I'll think of something, Da. Don't worry.'

'Now who seeks to pit her powers against the Elder Gods?' He chuckled and tweaked her chin to make her smile, the way he used to when she was small.

'There's a long way to go before I'm ready for that.'

'Is she giving you lessons?'

'Every day. Simple things, like these lights – she doesn't share her secrets freely, but I'm learning everything she shows me.'

'Is it difficult? Doing this?' He gestured at the globe.

'No. Once she's shown me how to do something, it's as if I've always known the trick of it and only needed to be reminded. The hardest part is not letting her know how easy it is.'

Teir leaned forward to press a kiss to her brow. His eyes were grave; the creases in his leathery face looked deeper, or maybe that was just the light. 'Have a care, Teisha. I mistrust what she has planned for you.'

'So do I.'

She kissed her father's cheek, called farewell to her mother. Ana scurried out to hug her with wet hands, apologised for them and then hugged her again regardless. With many smiles and promises to visit again as soon as she could, Teia walked away from her parents and into the dark.

⊹

The falcon shape fluttered apart and the Leahn youth stretched back into human form, sprawled panting in the snow. Blood from a wound to his neck had soaked his shirt collar; the salt-sweet metallic smell tickled the snow leopard's nostrils. Savin felt its hunger leap, the claws tighten, even without him willing it.

Another day he would have let himself relax and ride the great cat's will as it tore into its prey, but he was here for answers, not appetite. He had to learn what this shivering pup knew, and neither of them had the time to waste with questions. The cat bared its teeth, lips curling back with resentment at being reined in – always a risk with predator species, that concentration would slip and allow the hot red tide of instinct to take over – and the boy gagged, trying to turn his head away from the beast's foul breath.

Savin lifted one huge silvery paw and placed it carefully just below Gair's throat, leaned in a little to make the point that the cat had more than enough speed and strength to overpower a wounded human. Through the animal's pads he felt the boy's heartbeat race.

'What do you want, Savin?' Gair gasped.

Such a happy accident, running into him here, well outside the span of the Western Isles' wards, alone and unprepared. It was almost too easy.

You.

He reached for the Leahn's thoughts. Saw the frantic shapes skittering beneath the shifting colours, and met no resistance. Still only half-trained – what were the Guardians teaching their apprentices these days?

This.

The boy scrambled for the Song to throw up some kind of defence, but Savin shouldered through it as easily as one of those Arkadian paper screens. A gasp of indrawn breath. Eyes flying wide with the sudden cold shock of violation – grey, Savin noted, fringed with those extravagant lashes some young men had that women spent hours with cosmetics and combs trying to achieve.

Colours enfolded him, a hundred shifting shades of them in a gauzy tangle. Shoals of thought eddied through them and flashed their silver sides, like yellowtails fleeing a shark. Pleased by the imagery he chuckled to himself, and with a hooked claw of will sliced his way into Gair's memories.

The boy screamed.

A variation on the ward for silence muted the noise before it could grate on Savin's nerves too badly. He paid no attention to the gaping mouth, the corded neck; his attention was bent inwards, on the trove of curiosities he had exposed.

First, a place to start. He twisted the claw into the memories and pulled. They spilled out in a great colourful mess, each one glinting and glittering like sunlight refracting off a thick hoar frost, like the dust from a trapped moth's wings. Thousands of tiny instants of colour and sound and taste, constantly turning; quite beautiful, really, in the scattering, maddening way of a kaleidoscope. Sifting through them, he found the heart of a pattern, touched it.

A boy, nine or ten summers old, lay on his back on a flat rock warmed by summer sunshine. The drowsy drone of bees wafted to and fro on the upland breeze. He had a hand raised above his face to shield it from the sun's glare as he studied something far overhead.

Savin traced the slow turn of the pattern outwards. An eagle in flight, hanging motionless in the blue up-turned bowl of a northern sky; an idle murmur of music becoming a full-throated cry; another eagle perched on the rock, flapping red-gold wings like a fledgling trying his strength on the edge of the nest.

Interesting.

The earth fell away and the pattern branched apart into a riot of others, clustering like flowers on a dog rose. Savin flicked through them faster now, disregarding the failures, the shapes that wouldn't hold, until he came to another efflorescence, each bright whorl a subtly different shade. New shapes. Spotted owl. Finch. Eagle. Wolf. Eagle again. Back to the wolf, and there the memories tangled, twining together, woven around a single scintillant point.

He touched it, and felt the warm summer-raindrop burst of a kiss. Sudden confusion, shot through with pleasure: a first kiss, then. How sweet. A trawl of the myriad branches of the pattern brought him the woman's face. Startlingly blue eyes, short, silky hair, skin the colour of cinnamon. Archly pretty in the clever, confident way of a cat. Even more interesting.

Arrested by a sudden adolescent prurience, Savin lingered there in the roil of the boy's recollections. Wanting to see where that kiss led, to lift the veil on the boy's fevered dreams and know his most intimate secrets. It led to another kiss, this one burning with the red heat of desire long banked now erupting into flame. Dizzying, falling. Savin shivered as remembered sensation washed over him. Skin and curve and wet silk enfolding, lifting and crashing over and down into peace, and then, only then—

Bowed shins. Twisted ankles. The blurry brown-yellow thumb-prints of old bruises. The coiling urgency in his own belly stilled.

Really? He waved away the ward; he had to know.

You have feelings for her? A cripple?

'Please . . .' The boy found his voice, a rasping wreck of a thing. He twisted weakly under the snow leopard's paw, fresh scarlet seeping into the churned snow around him.

Apparently he did have feelings for her. How bizarre.

Move on. Discard the woman for now, return to the start of this particular branch of the pattern. Lessons. Masters, some familiar, some not. Sift their words for meaning, hints. Nothing. Alderan, then; a new pattern. Skip back to the start of it. Snatches of conversation echoed in the vault of the boy's head.

—have tremendous potential, Gair, but there is work to do to unlock it—

Wasn't there just? His gift was rough as unplaned timber.

—all that preserves the Veil between the worlds—

Yes, yes, so you keep saying.

—what you showed me on the Kittiwake *I have absolutely no doubt that you're up to the task—*

What task would that be? Savin followed the threads, fast as thought; tried to piece together the tumbled fragments but found nothing. His stretched concentration began to fray.

What has he told you? he demanded. *What?*

No answer. The boy's face had drained of all colour with shock, or maybe just the cold. His eyelids fluttered, lips stretched wide in a rictus of pain. A frown stitched itself across Savin's forehead and the cat hissed, perplexed by alien emotion. He'd best finish this, whilst there was still time.

Deeper into the patterns, then. Seek out what was buried. Perhaps Alderan had some new trick, or a long-held skill he'd kept secret; something that would enable him to hide who knew what in the folds of a living mind. Savin knew him well, better than almost anyone, but that didn't mean the old bastard hadn't concealed something from him.

Old grievances stung anew. Renewed fury began to lap around his mind like a sea of flames. It would be just typical. The Guardian had always tried to thwart him, to control him; Savin's earliest memories were of *no* and *can't* and *must not*. From his parents, from his teachers, always trying to make him into something he was not and never allowing him to be what he was.

Back he raced through the boy's memory, tracing the twists and turns down, down into the very heart of the web. The images were less complex there, surrounded by simpler emotions. Pleasure at learning to sail a dinghy along a craggy, crumpled coastline. Sleepy satisfaction after a long day in the sun and sea air. Still nothing. Further back, skimming through childish joys: an eagle feather, a pebble with a hole in it, becoming progressively simpler as the spiral narrowed, funnelling down to a first startled breath, to sleep, back to a blessed darkness and the all-consuming rhythm of a mother's pulse.

Nothing at all.

Not a word, not the smallest crumb of knowledge of the starseed. Impossible.

Swearing foully, Savin swam back up through the foggy layers of childhood, into the crystalline sharpness of the present.

Where is the key? You cannot hide it from me, boy!

He clawed the living mind pinned under his will, left bright welts of agony across its surface.

Where is it?

Another swipe of his claws, and another. Colours flared and dimmed. The boy knew something; he had to. The Church, his gift, there was a connection – there had to be! All that careful planning . . .

You must know! Tell me! TELL ME! he roared in frustration. *TELL ME!*

Again no answer. Only soft, helpless sobbing. Pathetic. This was Alderan's great hope for the Order of the Veil?

This puling excuse for an apprentice is what you choose, old man?

Rage flared, white-hot behind Savin's eyes, sour in his gut. By all the Seven Kingdoms, he would not be made a fool of in this way. He reached into his power, the dark and twisted undercroft of the Song that the

Hidden Kingdom had shown him how to unlock, and wove its leathery strands together.

If Alderan thought this clod-footed northman's brat was the future of his withered rump of an Order, he would be deeply disappointed.

The daemon seed took shape under his will. The instructions for its making crackled through his mind like hoar frost over dead leaves, all spiky eldritch syllables in voices colder than a winter's night. Good, good. Almost done.

Around him the leopard-shape convulsed. He was losing his hold on it, but he didn't care. It had served its purpose for now, so he let its Song go and felt the uneasy sliding of muscle and sinew and bone back into a human configuration.

The seed was sown. Even dormant it exuded a malign self-awareness, as if that dull-as-pitch carapace would at any moment crack and its two halves lever apart like the lids of an eye. Which, in a way, they would. Once the daemon was fully grown, Savin would be able to observe everything its host observed.

As lightly as if tossing a flower into a grave, he dropped the daemon into the boy's ravaged mind.

And when your precious Order collapses in flames, Alderan, I will watch it happen and laugh.

⊰⊱

The Cold Stars Gaze was hove-to in the deeper waters off the northernmost of the Five Sisters, with her head turned into the wind. Canvas flapped and banged sullenly, and her dragon-carved prow tossed up and down on the swell as if in frustration. Plaid-and-fur-wrapped warriors stood about on her afterdeck, half of them watching the sailors at their make-work and errands, whilst the other half stared south across the leaden rollers towards the inhabited islands and fidgeted with their axes.

Eager for the raid, no doubt – but then Nordmen were always eager for a raid. In fact, fighting, fornicating and feasting was about all they were fit for. No cultured pursuits to speak of: their music consisted of drinking songs, their poetry of turgid, leaden-footed sagas about hacking and hewing. As for their theatre, they had none worthy of the name, unless you counted feast-day mummery to entertain their litters of brats.

As he flew, Savin's mind wandered somewhat wistfully back to the sun-baked garden city of Aqqad with its courtyard fountains, the urbane discourses on philosophy and civics – not forgetting the kohl-lined athleticism of the *najjir*, who made northern women look as pale and lumpen as tallow. He tried not to shudder. No point dwelling on it. Once he found the starseed and united the Kingdoms, he could retire to Aqqad and spend the rest of his days in a cloud of *mezzin* smoke, but until then he had to remain here, where the Veil was so permeable, and cultivate the primitives who controlled this region – however distasteful a task that might be.

Flying a tight circle around the masthead, he shrieked until someone on the afterdeck looked up, pointed. Other faces turned skywards, including the brooding cliff in human clothing that was Jaldur, who commanded the war party. The hulking Nordman barked a few guttural words and waved the rest of his men back to make room. Savin folded the peregrine's wings and dropped like a stone, flaring them out at the very last second to arrest the dive. Then he let the Song go and stepped out of the blurring air onto the scrubbed planking as casually as if he'd just returned from a stroll.

Jaldur inclined the ruddy thicket of braids and tangles that passed for his head. 'My lord.'

His pale-blue eyes were carefully impassive, but behind him a couple of the more superstitious sworn men made signs of protection. Savin gave them a flat-eyed glance, just long enough to let them know he'd seen them. It didn't hurt to keep them fearful.

'You need to leave these waters,' he said, in common. 'Have the captain set a course to rendezvous with the others.'

'We go?' Jaldur's expression clouded. 'But we raid, yes?'

Savin nodded. 'Soon.'

'Hah!' Jaldur beamed and threw some words at his men in his own tongue. A forest of weapons was thrust aloft on a raucous cheer. The shaggy thane grinned, shaking his fists in the air. Then he frowned and waved a hairy paw at Savin's arm.

'You bleed.'

Savin looked down. His golden shirt was salt-spotted and splashed with blood across the sleeves. It was ruined.

'Your hands, see?' Jaldur rumbled on, but Savin barely heard him, paid even less attention to the deep scratches that laced his hands and wrists, black with congealed blood. One of his favourite shirts was *ruined*.

He walked away from the Nordman's clumsy concern, heading for the ladder to the lower deck. Stalked aft to the stern cabin that only Nordships of *The Cold Stars Gaze*'s size and prestige possessed. Slammed the storm door behind him, flicked fire at the lamps swinging from the overhead beams.

Intolerable.

Savin ground his teeth. Finest Sardauki mugatine, which cost more gold to the bale than that useless Leahn guttersnipe could even *imagine*, and it was utterly spoiled. Gah.

Quite, quite intolerable. He wrenched the shirt off over his head, unable to bear it against his skin any longer.

'By the Seven Kingdoms, I should have made a new

shirt out of his hide,' he snarled, balling up the silk in his hands. He hurled it across the cabin, but instead of smacking into the ship's side it ballooned open in flight and fluttered down to the deck as lightly as a bird.

From where he stood the marks were invisible, but he knew they were there. Even if there'd been a way to clean the fabric and restore its lustre, in his mind the shirt would forever be stained. Soiled, imperfect. He levelled his finger at it and called fire. The silk burned with a quick, almost smokeless flame, and in less than a minute had been reduced to a handful of blackened buttons in a smear of soot on the planking. Another thought crushed the ivory to powder, then scattered it with a breath of wind.

The scratches on his hands and wrists began to itch and he held them up to the light. None of them was deep enough to scar: the boy had been panicked, more intent on escape than making a fight of it. Tsking, he fetched a damp washcloth from the basin mounted on gimbals on the bulkhead and began to dab away the drying blood.

And on top of it all, he'd learned nothing. Oh, there had been a few amusing titbits, like the crippled woman, but no useful information about Corlainn's treasure or where it might be hidden. Either Alderan had indeed told the boy nothing at all, or . . .

Abruptly Savin stopped sponging his cuts. He frowned, water dripping unheeded from his hands.

. . . or the whelp had known something and kept it hidden.

For a second he considered it, then dismissed the idea with a quick shake of his head. It was impossible. The discipline required simply to withstand a reiving would take years of study to perfect, and this Leahn boy was a barely trained brute: all muscle and no control. Impressively strong, to be sure, but still with less skill than

Savin had possessed at the age of five. No real challenge, and certainly not a threat.

He thought of the broken, bloody shape he'd left mewling in the snow on the island and finished cleaning his hands, lips curved into a smile. *Not any more, anyway.*

No, Chapterhouse was where the answers lay. He dropped the red-streaked cloth back into the basin, then hauled his clothes chest out from underneath the bunk to find a fresh shirt. In all his searching, the length and breadth of the Empire and beyond, he had found no clues that led him anywhere else.

Well. That wasn't *entirely* true, but the remaining trail was faint and less likely to reap him a reward than Chapterhouse, so that was where he needed to direct his efforts. Pluck the lowest-hanging fruit first, as it were.

As he buttoned his shirt, he eyed the rail-edged table bolted to the deck on the opposite side of the cabin. In the centre stood the velvet-shrouded oval of the sight-glass. Silent, since he had set sail. Just as well. It irked him to have to carry the wretched thing wherever he went, but not as much as being dressed down like an errant schoolboy afterwards if he was not there to answer when *they* stirred.

The Hiddens' aid had been useful thus far, but they needed him much more than he needed them, and their meddling, the constant questions and petulant admonitions were . . . wearing. Still, he'd not have to tolerate them much longer. Come the trinity moon he'd have their fealty, and then no one would dare tell him what to do ever again.

⚜

Duncan leaned back in the chair and tried not to let the fire's warmth lull him to sleep. After so many weeks in the saddle the simple hide chair felt as comfortable as a feather bed, but he had to stay awake to deliver his message. He could only hope the chieftain's steward hadn't decided to go back to bed and leave him sitting there. He'd tried to impress urgency on the man, but still. It was well into the small hours of a bitter winter's night and no one would be keen to rouse their chief after feasting unless the whole longhouse was afire.

He yawned. Slaine's stones, it felt good to be warm again. Riding the plains in winter was part of a captain's lot so he shouldn't complain, but there was a lot to be said for a cosy fireside at the end of a long journey, for heat that wrapped itself around him like the thickest, softest blanket. He yawned again, shook his head to clear it. Tried to sit up straight, because it wouldn't do for his chief to find him dozing by the hearth like an old man. Yawned again, even longer than the last one, and blinked eyelids that felt as heavy as tent curtains. Ended up leaning his elbow on the table when his weary back just didn't want to hold him upright any more.

His eyes drifted closed and his drooping chin fell off his hand, jerking him awake again. Footsteps sounded outside and the double doors at the end of the hall swung open. Between them strode a tall figure wearing what looked like yesterday's shirt, hanging loose over buckskin trews and bare feet. Sleep-tousled brown hair gave the chief of the Durannadh and Lord of the Plains the appearance of a hastily roused lion. 'Duncan,' he said by way of greeting.

Duncan pushed himself to his feet. 'Forgive me for disturbing you like this, my lord.'

'If it's as important as my steward implied I won't hold it against you, Firstmoon or no.' Aradhrim came into the light from the fire-pit. 'Slaine's stones, man! Sit down. When did you last sleep?'

He rooted through the feast's debris on the long tables until he found a *uisca* flask still with something in it and two cups, and pushed a generous measure into Duncan's hand. The spirit scorched down his throat and set his stomach aglow.

'Better?' Aradhrim asked. Duncan nodded. The chieftain threw more fuel onto the dying fire and dropped into another chair opposite. 'Your face says this is bad news. Spill it out.'

'It's bad, my lord. I think the Nimrothi mean to come down through the passes again. In force.'

Aradhrim's cup stopped halfway to his mouth. 'You wouldn't say something like that lightly.'

'No, my lord. Sor and I were scouting near the border forts and surprised some Nimrothi warriors at Saardost Keep, watching the pass. One of them was persuaded to talk and confirmed the rumours we heard after the Gathering last year. The Crainnh's new chief is to be made Chief of Chiefs, and he means to bring a combined war band south to retake the lands lost in the Founding.'

The *uisca* went down the chief's throat in a single swallow. 'I'd ask if you were joking except I don't think you are.' He looked away, into the glowing embers in the fire-pit. 'How many clans?'

'We saw two for sure, but the Nimrothi we questioned was certain it would be all seventeen, and that they'd swear to this Drwyn's spear at the Scattering. There hasn't been a battle chief in a thousand years, my lord. This cannot bode well.'

'Another Gwlach.' Aradhrim shook his head. 'And you're sure?'

'I don't know how I could be more sure,' said Duncan.

'And what were you doing so far west at this time of year?'

'You heard from the Eldannar rangers?' A nod. 'We were tracking the beast that tore into the herds. It almost killed one of our men, but he survived and fol-

lowed it into Whistler's Pass. It was headed east of
north when Kael lost track of it. We were coming back
to Fleet when he picked up another trail near Saardost.'
Duncan swallowed the last of the spirit for courage.
'Kael's a seeker, my lord. He says the beasts are Maegern's Hounds. Two of them, headed north into the
Broken Land.'

Frowning, Aradhrim rolled his empty cup back and
forth between his hands. 'Brindling Fall?'

'The keep was empty both times we passed it. They're
not likely to come down through Whistler's Pass – not
willingly, anyway. Too many ghosts for them.'

'What about King's Gate?'

'Snowbound. We couldn't have checked it even if
we'd wanted to. It's always the last to thaw.'

The chief sucked his teeth. 'Not much evidence,' he
said, 'but it's compelling.'

'I don't think we can ignore it, my lord.' Duncan sat
forward. 'If they're summoning the Hunt again—'

'I agree. I'll have to re-garrison all three forts until
we know which way the Nimrothi will jump. There's a
full legion here in Fleet which is enough to make a start.
I'll send south for reinforcements, but it'll be a hard
march for them in winter.'

'Will the Emperor agree?'

Aradhrim shrugged. 'Theodegrance appointed me
Warlord so he didn't have to make these decisions. He
doesn't really have to agree, though it helps.' He stood
up and tossed Duncan the half-empty flask. 'Here –
you've more than earned it. I'll have my steward find a
bed for you.'

'There's one more thing,' Duncan said. 'At the beginning of winter, we met a Guardian called Masen at
Brindling Fall. He said he was Gatekeeper to the Order
of the Veil.'

'I've heard of him.'

'He told us that the Veil is weakening. Take that with

the Hounds and what the Nimrothi told us . . .' Duncan spread his hands and saw the high chief's face harden, the shadows sharpening his features until he resembled one of the stone warriors that flanked Endirion's Gate.

'It makes this news all the more troubling.' Aradhrim cocked his fists on his hips and stared down at the floor between his feet. 'I need to speak to Maera,' he muttered, then scrubbed a hand across his face, palm rasping over his stubbled chin. 'This is a bad business, Duncan. A thousand years ago, the Founding divided the clans. We made our peace with the new Empire rather than fight on. The Nimrothi have never forgiven us.'

'If they come south, Arennor will bear the first blood.'

'Exactly. And we have no passes to choke them, no forts to block their path, only leagues of empty plains between the mountains and Mesarild.'

Arms folded, the chief began to pace the width of the fire-pit. Duncan watched him, his dragging exhaustion replaced by an awful tension. The silver cup in his fist gave suddenly and he looked down to see his grip had crushed it to an oval.

All at once the chief swung to face him. 'Rouse that steward of mine, cousin. We must raise the clans for war.'

14

PLANS

❦

Like most men, Drwyn was hard on clothes. Teia's pile of mending never seemed to grow any smaller; there were always buttons to be replaced, burst seams to be closed. When the men's heads had cleared from their Firstmoon celebrations and they rode out to hunt again a few days later – with Drwyn at their head; the chief enjoyed the chase far too much only to stand his turn – she was glad of the opportunity to catch up on her needlework.

The week's tally of mending consisted of a couple of shirts, a fur-lined jerkin that the moths had got to during the summer's storage and a pair of trews that would have had years of wear left in them were it not for the long tear down the side of one knee. Incredulous, Teia poked her hand through the rent. How under heaven had he managed that?

The shirts were easily repaired, needing only a frayed seam stitched and a loose button re-attached. When she was done and the mended garments had been returned to Drwyn's clothes chest, she picked up the trews again to assess the tear.

Even if she stitched it up, a rent at the knee would likely give again in short order, but the woollen cloth was far too good to throw away. Maybe she could make something for the baby from it later, when her other chores were done. She shook the garment straight and held it against herself to fold, and was reminded again that her legs were only a little shorter than Drwyn's.

Her heart lurched. Could she . . . ?

Carefully, she arranged the trews with the band where her waist used to be and kicked out the legs. Close enough. Better, if she took them in to suit her more slender limbs, re-making the seam would cut out the tear and yield enough fabric that she could gusset the trunk, let out the waist . . . And that jerkin, whilst cut for a man and far too broad in the shoulder, would still be perfectly warm and more than roomy enough to accommodate a swelling belly.

A feeling that was one part excitement to two parts naked fear crashed over her. Her skin turned cold, her stomach dropping down to her toes whilst her heart began to race. This was possible. She could make it work. The larders were well stocked; she could secrete provisions, hide extra winter clothes in readiness – clothes like these, Drwyn's cast-offs that he wouldn't even notice were missing. If she could convince Ytha of the folly of her pact with the Eldest, all well and good, but if not . . . she could leave.

Macha. The very idea was dizzying. She tried not to think about leaving her family or the anguish would paralyse her into inaction, too afraid to stand up to Ytha, and then the whole clan would suffer. And then other clans, maybe all of them, when the Hunt was unleashed. Images of an ashen plain filled her thoughts and she shuddered.

No. There was no time to dwell on that, either.

She focused on the good woollen cloth in her hands. Pins. She needed pins. Quickly, she hunted through her sewing bag for the roll of felt that held the good steel pins she'd traded for at the Scattering last year. Then she hiked up her skirt, stepped into Drwyn's trews and began to mark up the lines of new seams.

⚙

For the rest of the day she cut and stitched, working feverishly fast to be sure she was done by the time the hunters – and her chief – returned. At the finish her fingertips were numb, but it was done. She slipped out the last pins and stowed them away carefully in her sewing bag. Then, her hands trembling with more than just the effort of all the stitching, she tried them on.

They fitted. There was give at the knees and seat for riding, and two hands'-worth of room at the waist into which her baby belly could grow.

Yes. I can do this.

The enormity of what she was planning struck her anew, and she had to sit down before her knees folded underneath her. Her thoughts bolted in all directions like panicked rabbits. Dear Macha preserve her. Leaving the clan, leaving her family, in the heart of winter . . . surely her wits had deserted her. She shut her eyes, pressed the heels of her hands into them. She might as well take up a spear and go and hunt the white stag – she had as much chance of success.

Teia raked her fingers through her hair and squeezed her palms against the back of her skull, as if she could press some order into her whirling thoughts. She had little time, and none to spare for uncertainty. If a job was to be done, it was best done with a whole heart.

Near drunk with elation and anxiety in equal measure, she slipped off the trews and hid them with the jerkin at the bottom of a basket, covering them with a sack. If she carried it down to the stores and came back with some provisions, no one who saw her would be any the wiser. As long as she was careful where she hid everything, and didn't take too much of anything that might be missed . . .

I can do this. I know I can.

Before her courage could desert her, she hoisted the basket onto her hip and headed down to the stores. On the way she had to pass the smoke-room, where a handful of women were cleaning and preparing it for the hunters' catch. They paused as she approached and leaned on their brooms, their sweating faces smudged with ash. The flickering lamplight was unkind, flattening the contours of their features and emphasising the lines and creases, so women who would have been comely in daylight had instead the pinched look of kobolds, their eyes colourless and glittering like glass.

Teia felt their stares from yards away and her steps faltered. When word had spread throughout the caves that she was carrying the chief's child, it had softened the attitudes of many of the women, but some had hardened against her completely: younger women, mostly, those who'd hoped to catch Drwyn's eye themselves – or those who'd shared his bed before her.

Throat suddenly dry, Teia hitched her basket onto her other hip so that it was away from the watching women. She had to pass them; there was no other way through to the stores. Taking a deep breath, she tilted her head up. Let them stare.

I can do this.

Walking briskly, but not fast enough to let on that she was anxious, she passed the smoke-room. A hard stare or two followed her; though nothing was said, the sheer intensity of their gazes was enough to set her magic to prickling. When a bend in the passage finally took her out of their sight she sighed with relief, and only then realised that her hands were shaking.

The stores were rarely empty, even when they weren't being replenished, so Teia took her time selecting this and that for her basket until the other women left. In the gloom at the back of the cavern, behind the sacks and bushels, there were hiding places aplenty where some long-ago water had scoured odd scoops and whorls into the stone. Ears straining for the sound of approaching footsteps, she stuffed two pounds of pur-loined meal and some dried meat and fruit into her sack with the jerkin and trews, and pushed the lot into one of the cyst-like apertures.

There. It was well out of sight at the back, and even if the stores became so depleted over the winter that it was exposed, it would look like any other sack of sup-plies. By the time that happened, her fate would have been decided. Either she would have left the clan – she flinched at the thought of her parents' faces – or she would be past the point at which anyone would care about a stolen bag of meal.

Hefting her fresh-laden basket onto her hip again, she turned to leave. She'd walked barely ten paces up the passageway towards the smoke-room when she heard a susurrus of voices ahead, distorted by the water-worn rock walls. Teia quickened her steps, straining to make out more words than the *what is it what's happening* buzz of confusion.

The women were gone from the smoke-room entrance, their abandoned rakes and brooms scattered about. A basket of cinders had been tipped up and its contents left strewn across the passage amongst the tools. Whatever they'd heard had sent them running.

The hunters, it had to be. She hurried on. Now the timbre of the voices was one of alarm; ahead women were streaming up the passage towards the great arching cavern of the meeting place, and amongst the jumbled shouts and anxious pleas to know what was happening, Teia heard a man moaning in pain.

She dropped her basket and ran. Despite the close warmth of underground, her skin grew cold. Heart drumming, she wormed her way through the crowd of women milling at the passage mouth, not caring who tutted at her. She had to know who was hurt. In her haste she trod on someone's toes and got a curse and a shove for it, but she made it through to the front of the group.

Flickering torches lit the cavern, wedged in wall-cracks and held aloft by hunters in snow-dusted furs. Two of them were carrying a rough litter fashioned from saplings on which lay a young man. Teia hardly recognised him as Joren, the youngest of Drwyn's war band. His eyes were black pits of pain in a waxy-pale face and his bloody hands shone wetly in the sooty light as they clutched at his belly.

'Please,' he sobbed. 'It hurts!'

His head rolled from side to side on the blanket and her stomach turned over when she saw the gleam of bone through his torn scalp. Even Ytha might be hard-pressed to save him.

On the far side of the cavern, a commotion in the

crowd of clansfolk dragged her eyes away. Someone cried, 'Make way! Make way for the Speaker!' and Ytha swept out of the shadows with her fur mantle billowing after her.

The other hunters fell back, exchanging anxious looks. With a snap of her fingers, the Speaker summoned one of her pearly lights and gestured it close to the young man's face, then over his ripped scalp.

'Wolf?' she asked.

One of the hunters holding the litter nodded.

Ytha lifted the boy's hands away from the glistening mess that had been his abdomen and clicked her tongue. Teia couldn't see the extent of the wound from where she stood, but the change in the Speaker's expression told her Joren would be lucky to see another hunt.

'Bring him,' Ytha said tersely, and strode away, her light bobbing after her. The two men followed with the litter, trailed by an ashen-faced woman with tears on her cheeks.

The clanspeople surged together in the Speaker's wake, Joren and his weeping mother quickly forgotten as they searched for loved ones amongst the returned hunters, desperate to assure themselves that their own menfolk were unhurt. Teia scanned the sea of faces for Teir but there were too many people moving around, their features rendered strangely unfamiliar by the torchlight.

'Da?' she called. A glance or two was flung her way, but none lingered. Panic edged into her voice. 'Da!'

More commotion, up by the entrance with its long sloping ledge that all but circled the cavern. More torches, more leaping shadows in the tunnel leading up to the air, and voices, but the shouts this time were of jubilation. The rest of the hunting party had returned, and they were shouting Drwyn's name.

Teia began pushing her way through the crowd towards the noise. 'Da!'

She had to find him, had to make sure he was all right. It was early in the season for a wolf attack; there was still too much game at hand for hunger to have driven a pack out of the forest. Why now? Why here?

'*Da!*'

Face after face loomed before her, but none of them belonged to Teir. Too old or too young, she stumbled past them, searching, hoping, snatching sleeves and tugging elbows of returning hunters until she blundered into something so solid she nearly fell.

Looking up, she found herself face to face with a brindled timber wolf, its jaws agape, and squealed with fright. Only then did she realise the beast was dead and slung over a hunter's shoulder with the broken-off head of a spear protruding from its breast. Not the beast from her dreams, then. Pressing her hand to her chest, she looked up further and saw that the hunter was Drwyn.

His furs were daubed with blood and caked in snow, now starting to melt and drip around his boots. One arm was looped over the carcass of the wolf to steady it; his other sleeve hung empty.

'Teia,' he said and grinned, clearly pleased with himself, and that she'd apparently come looking for him. 'I have brought you a gift.' He slapped the beast's shaggy side and his coat gaped, revealing his left arm crudely bound up with sodden red rags.

'You're bleeding,' she said.

He glanced at his arm. 'A scratch, no more. The beast bit me.'

If the wound became infected, he'd be as sour-tempered with the pain as a bear with a broken tooth. Teia could guess who he'd take it out on.

'Dog bites are apt to go foul,' she said carefully, reaching for his injured arm. 'At least let me clean it.'

He snatched it away. 'I said it's naught but a scratch! Hold your fussing, woman.'

Two of his chosen men came up behind him and clapped him on the back. 'A fine kill, my chief!' crowed one, tweaking the wolf's tail and making its head loll.

'Aye, if you hadn't grabbed that spear and spitted the beast, Joren would be dead now. You're a hero – he'll name his firstborn after you!'

Quite suddenly, Teia's temper snapped. She had no idea if her father was safe, she was tired and frightened and had no patience left for the posturing of men.

'When you're done playing hero, I'll bind your arm,' she said tartly and turned on her heel.

'Hark at that one,' said one of the men.

'Not even wearing your mark yet and already styling herself as the chief's wife!'

The men's laughter only stoked her temper. Stupid oafs. It would serve them all right if the chief's arm rotted away to the bones for want of attention.

'Enough!' Drwyn snapped, and she heard a meaty thud that could only be the wolf's carcass hitting the ground. 'Get that skinned.'

Footsteps came after Teia. She picked up her pace, hurrying through the thinning crowd, but before she'd reached the far side of the cavern a hand closed on her elbow and jerked her around.

Drwyn was scowling like a thunderhead. 'Don't walk away from me, wench,' he growled. His hand came up, open-palmed.

That was simply the last straw.

Grabbing his wounded forearm, she squeezed it hard. Fresh blood welled through the rags and he cursed.

Teia flung his arm away from her. 'Serves you right! If you won't heed what a wiser voice tells you, I've a good mind to let it blow up with pus and teach you a lesson!'

A shocked silence hung between them, tense and expectant, like the moment between the slap and the sting. Somewhere at the back of her mind it occurred to her that he'd likely not heard a woman speak back to him since his mother died. None except the Speaker and – Macha preserve her – she had not a fraction of Ytha's authority.

Any moment, she thought, her heartbeat drumming in her ears. *Any moment now.*

Drwyn glared at her. His jaw worked – in surprise or fury she couldn't tell – and then he jerked his head towards the curtained doorway to their sleeping quarters. 'Get inside.'

Tears burning at the back of her eyes but determined not to let them fall, she climbed the rough-hewn steps towards the curtain. Drwyn's presence loomed behind her all the way, and she was unable to prevent her shoulders rounding in anticipation of a blow. For defying him like that, he'd strap her with his belt for sure – or else ride her raw to remind her of her place, pregnant or not. Either prospect was enough to cleave her tongue to the roof of her mouth with dread.

He snatched the curtain closed after them, plunging the chamber into shadow save for the glowing eyes of the lamps around the walls. Teia waited in the near-dark, listening to the sounds of him fumbling with his clothes, waiting to be shoved to her knees.

'Get some light in here, woman.'

She shut her eyes, hands bunched in her skirts. 'Why? So you can see better to hit me?'

Something soft and bulky flew past her towards the bed. His coat, she realised.

'Can you dress a wound in the dark?'

Macha be praised. Weak with relief, Teia made her way to the nearest lamp and fumbled for the screws to adjust the three wicks. Her fingers shook so much the flames danced, but she wound all the lamps up one by one until the chamber was filled with golden light.

'Well? A man could bleed to death waiting,' he grumbled, and she turned around. Sitting on a stool in the middle of the chamber, he held out his blood-soaked left arm.

'Just a scratch, eh?' she said, then bit her lip when he glowered at her.

Without another word she fetched a basin of water and some clean rags, and the leather bag of simples her mother had taught her how to prepare. A generous pinch of bittermint went into the water to cleanse the wounds; whilst it infused she knelt at Drwyn's feet to untie the rough bandage, but the knot was swollen too tight to unpick. It would have to be cut off him.

She sawed through the knot with her belt-knife, unwrapped the bloody cloth and threw it aside for burning later. The wolf's teeth had left deep gouges in the meat of Drwyn's forearm, laced with smaller scratches as if there had been a struggle and its jaws had slipped. Wolves had a fearsome grip; he was lucky not to have a broken arm.

Carefully, she bathed his wounds with the bittermint-infused water. He endured it without flinching, though the herb must surely have stung, and watched her hands as she worked.

His scrutiny made her nervous; Drwyn had never shown much curiosity about what she did before, and for some reason it was more disconcerting than anger. It gave her no clues to predict what might come next.

'The wolf came while we were sleeping,' he said suddenly. 'It took Joren by the head and dragged him out of his blankets. He woke the camp with his yelling and kicking – we thought a whole pack was coming down on us.'

Patting his arm dry with a clean rag, Teia glanced up, wondering if she should say something.

'It was gone moonset and the fire was out, everyone crashing around in the dark. Joren must have pulled free and then tripped. We found him hung up on a broken branch.'

She flinched. Wood splinters in a deep wound rarely ended well. Corruption was quick to set in, and in the belly . . . Forcing her tone to be optimistic, she said, 'If anyone can save him, Ytha can.'

He grunted. 'It was his first season on the hunt. He was no more use than a warped arrow, but still.'

Noticing her bag of simples, Drwyn reached down with his free hand and poked amongst the jars and pouches inside. 'You know healing,' he said. It sounded almost like an accusation.

Her hands faltered. 'Just what my mother taught me, household remedies and such.'

He lifted a pouch stitched with a leaf design and sniffed it cautiously. 'What's in this?'

'White nettle.'

'What's that for?'

'Disorders of the bladder. You brew a tea with it.' Making conversation with her, showing an interest in her skills beyond the bed and the cook-pot, was unlike him. She began to dread where it was leading.

He returned the pouch to the bag, selected another and peered at the beads she'd worked into the design on the front. 'And this?'

'Firethorn bark, for the drawing of boils.'

Back into the bag it went. 'And what will you use on me?'

'I'll not stitch it – dog bites are best left open to drain – so I'll use that ointment, in the red jar.' She pointed at the pot of pennywort salve, made to Ana's grandmother's recipe.

Silently Drwyn handed it to her and watched her dab the salve onto his wounds, then bind them up with a clean bandage. 'There'll be a scar,' she said, tying off the ends, 'but it should heal well enough. If it burns hot or starts to stink, tell me.'

He examined the bandage as if looking for fault, though she was confident he'd find none; with the benefit of Ana's teaching she'd made a neat job of it. Jar sealed again, she tucked it away in her bag and began tidying up.

'You have some skill,' he said. She looked up. He'd stripped off his ruined shirt and was pulling on a clean one. 'But don't ever think it gives you the right to up-braid me in front of my men.'

Black eyes fixed her, hard as stones. She lowered her gaze.

'Yes, my chief.' She hadn't expected gratitude; it wasn't in his nature. At least she knew how to react to a scolding. 'Forgive me, I misspoke. With all the com-motion . . . I was worried.' At the last second, she stopped herself from adding who she'd been worried about.

He grunted, apparently satisfied with her explana-tion.

Keeping her tone meek, she ventured, 'My father? He wasn't hurt?'

'Teir's well – he's bringing the horses in. Now see that you remember your place.'

With that, he left the cave.

Teia watched the curtain settle behind him, the rod chiming gently on its hooks, and blew out a long breath of relief. If she didn't guard her tongue, she'd not be so lucky a second time. She'd caught the rough side of his temper often enough to know that.

Her gaze fell on the basin in her hands, the bloody water in it nearly the colour of blushberry wine. Wolves preying on men was rare. They were shy creatures for the most part; the hunters usually saw no more of them than a few tracks in the snow, a pair of glowing eyes in the darkness. For one to come right into a camp like that . . .

Winter was the wrong time for her to run. Snows that could bury a tent in a night; wolves in the hills. Or she could stay, and face the rest of her days as the Speaker's pet, or the chief's.

Her earlier determination drained away like water from a holed kettle and she quailed. Winter was the wrong time to run, but what else could she do?

<hr/>

'If you've got more bad news, Aradhrim, I'd rather not know. There's enough trouble in these to last me 'til next Saint Simeon's.'

Theodegrance thumped a sheaf of papers down onto his desk and himself into an overstuffed leather chair, which groaned in protest. His broad, weather-beaten features were creased with a frown.

The Warlord unfastened his cloak and waited until the Emperor's steward had closed the doors behind him before he spoke. 'I'm afraid it's bad,' he said.

'Thought as much,' grunted Theodegrance. 'You've come a long way in foul weather. Sit down by the fire and get warm – you too, young man. I won't hold you long.'

Duncan followed his liege lord to one of a pair of couches that flanked a carved marble fireplace and perched nervously on the edge of the seat, very conscious that his snowy boots were dripping onto a thick *qilim* carpet large enough for his entire family to sleep on. Aradhrim appeared to have no such concerns, lounging at his ease with his feet extended towards the hearth.

Of course, as Warlord he was no doubt accustomed to being in the imperial palace, in the Emperor's private study, whilst the man himself sat at his desk in his shirt-sleeves, frowning over his papers. For Duncan, who had never even crossed the borders of Arennor in his life before this trip, it felt unforgivably informal.

He dared a look around. The room, like its occupant, was generously proportioned and ruggedly, unashamedly masculine. Broad-backed, sturdy furniture was thickly cushioned in earthen colours that matched their owner's ruddy complexion. Every surface bore the scuffs and scars of daily use; it was a working room, not one for diplomatic niceties. A room where the real business of Empire took place.

At the desk, the Emperor leafed through his documents, initialling here, scrawling a comment there. Within a few minutes he was done and tossed down his pen. 'Very well,' he declared, hoisting himself to his feet and taking a seat on the opposite couch. 'Let's hear it.'

Without preamble, Aradhrim said, 'I have reason to believe the Nimrothi clans will come down through the mountains before the spring is out.'

If he had expected a great show from the Emperor, Duncan was disappointed. Theodegrance merely pursed his lips and sat back in his seat. 'Go on,' he said.

Duncan listened as the Warlord laid out the bones of it. Every night on the week-long journey from Fleet his chief had questioned and prompted him, teasing out what he actually knew to be facts from the speculative conclusions wrought in his roiling gut. Now he set it all out neatly as a pedlar displaying his wares.

The Emperor listened impassively, thick fingers laced together on his belly, and barely blinked at the mention of the Hunt. Only when the Warlord stated his intention to re-garrison the an-Archen forts did Theodegrance's expression change. 'Out of the question,' he said. His wide mouth cut off the words like the jaws of a trap. 'I can't commit two thousand men or more on this evidence.'

Aradhrim spread his hands and shrugged. 'How much more do you need? We caught Crainnh and Amhain warriors together at Saardost Keep and questioned one of them at length. Unless Drwyn's deceiving his own men, his intentions are clear.'

Theodegrance shook his head. 'Not clear enough.

Where do you place your troops? How do we even know that this Drwyn will be raised Chief of Chiefs? If just one clan refuses to recognise him his position will be greatly weakened.'

'He'd still be able to bring a sizeable force down on Arennor – more than she can contain with her own warriors. The Nimrothi have not forgiven our forefathers for breaking spears and joining the Empire, Theo.'

Theo? Duncan swallowed, impressed.

'It's not enough,' the Emperor said again. 'I can't commit thousands of men in the north on a hunch, not when Gimrael's simmering like a pan of milk about to boil over. The Suvaeon Preceptor sent me a report corroborating the intelligence, returned by my own agents, that the Cult is making a nuisance of itself. Brushfires so far, but I dare say it won't take them long to start something larger.'

His tone sharpened. 'I know you think I'm dismissing your concerns, Aradhrim, but trust me – the rest of the Council won't be so sympathetic. To them, you clansfolk are more than a little strange. They don't understand your history with the Nimrothi and they'd see talk of Maegern's Hounds and the Veil as campfire storytelling.'

'I thought they were imperial legions, not feudal levies,' Aradhrim returned tartly. 'The soldiers took your shilling, Theo. They follow your standard and they answer to you, not to Belistha or Syfria or Leah or Tylos.'

Theodegrance grinned, crow's feet crinkling around his brown eyes, but it was humourless, feral. 'Aye, they do. But who do I answer to, eh? The Council. I need something more solid than this to convince them. The Founding Wars were fought a thousand years ago. Few people remember the truth of what happened.'

'They should not have forgotten. *We* have not forgotten.'

Aradhrim's voice was dangerously soft. Duncan shifted in his seat, uncomfortable with the sudden tension in the air.

'Memory fades, my friend,' the Emperor said. 'Most folk live their lives from birth to death without wondering what lies beyond the Veil. They worry about whether there'll be enough rain to sprout their crops, or that there'll be too much and it'll spoil the harvest. That's the beginning and the end of it for them.' He spread his hands. 'I'm sorry, Aradhrim, but there it is.'

Even Duncan, who had no familiarity with the man, could see that Theodegrance would not be moved. Though to all appearances the Emperor was a twinkling, affable soul, the sort that could be pictured dandling grandchildren on his knee or wrestling on the floor with his favourite hounds, there was a steely edge to the sparkle in his eye, a sense of solid muscle beneath the unbuttoned shirt and wine-spotted breeches.

Aradhrim obviously knew it, too, pushing himself to his feet. 'Then I think there is nothing further to discuss,' he said. 'Arennor must secure her borders as she sees fit.'

'Indeed.' Just as swiftly the Emperor was on his feet, too. For a large-framed man, he moved like a cat. He extended a square hand. 'I know you will do the right thing for your people, Aradhrim. I trust your judgement, as I know you will respect mine.'

He isn't going to help us. Duncan stood up. 'But you remember!' he burst out. 'You understand. If the clans come through the passes it will fall to Arennor to turn them back. Sire, we are brave people and we will fight to the last man, but we cannot defend an Empire alone. Not with the Hunt ranged against us as well.'

'Duncan,' Aradhrim warned.

Theodegrance held up his hand. 'No, let the lad speak. You have my attention, young man. Say your piece.'

Except now that the Emperor's eye was fixed on him and the room was silent but for the sleepy murmur of the fire, Duncan couldn't find any more words. The expectant emptiness of the air was too great to fill with one voice. Embarrassment scorching his cheeks, he dropped his gaze. 'Forgive me, sire. I spoke in haste.'

'What is your name?'

'Duncan, sire, of Clan Morennadh.'

'My cousin,' Aradhrim supplied. The relationship was several times removed, but from the Warlord's chagrined expression, not far enough.

'I see.' The Emperor spread his legs and folded his arms across his chest. 'You were at Saardost Keep when these scouts were captured.'

'I was, sire. I helped to question one of them.'

'So you believe, as your cousin does, that this threat from the Nimrothi clans is real? That these Hounds are real?'

Taking a deep breath, Duncan looked him in the eye again. 'Aye, I do.'

'They couldn't just be wolves, say, or mountain cats?'

'I have ridden the plains all my life, sire. I have seen what wolves and cats can do to a herd and they do not kill for sport the way these Hounds do. If Kael was here, he could tell you.'

'And Kael is . . . ?'

'One of my men. He has seen a Hound up close – it killed his horse under him and tore open his face.'

That gave Theodegrance pause, but only for a moment. 'Creatures from myth. Children's stories. Excitable clansmen. That's all the Council will see. Even if your friend Kael were here and I could bring him before them . . .' He shook his head. 'My decision stands.'

'My lord—' Duncan began, then fell silent when Aradhrim laid a hand on his arm.

'I'm sorry to shatter your illusions, Duncan of Clan

Morennadh, but this Empire works, and has worked for eight hundred years now, because my predecessors and I do not act as if we are in sole charge. Consensus,' the Emperor boomed. 'Compromise. The wagon rolls much more smoothly when all the oxen pull in the same direction.'

He dropped a wink, his soft-footed steward materialised from somewhere in the shadows to open the door and the audience was over.

As the door to Theodegrance's private apartments closed behind Duncan and Aradhrim, two armed sentries in imperial green snapped to attention in the presence of their Warlord. He barely glanced at them, setting off down the panelled corridor with long, loping strides. Duncan had to hurry to keep up.

'Forgive me if I shamed you, cousin,' he said, when the guards were out of earshot. 'I spoke out of turn. We've come all this way and to have nothing to show for it—'

'Don't trouble yourself with it.' Aradhrim's tone was offhand but he did not look Duncan's way. *More angry than he wants to let on. Slaine's stones, I should have held my tongue.*

His cousin's strides grew quicker and at the end of the corridor he descended the stairs two at a time, boot-heels rapping on the polished marble. Clerks and servants scuttled out of his path.

'So what now?' Duncan asked.

'Get some sleep – I have quarters here you can use. In the morning you ride back to Fleet. The chiefs will be assembled in a day or two – you know what to tell them.'

'And you?'

'I'll follow you with another legion as soon as I can.'

'You're taking the troops anyway? But—'

Aradhrim rounded on him, face hard enough to crack stone, the silver-frosted hair over his ears fit to bristle. 'Don't "but" me, Duncan! Theodegrance told me to protect Arennor and by Slaine's hairy stones that's what I intend to do. I will not put the safety of my birthland in jeopardy for the sake of a thrice-cursed *committee*.'

'It's the imperial Council!'

'I don't care!'

A liveried maid with an armful of linens squeaked and pressed her back to the wall as the storm-faced clansman strode past her.

'I'll send a rider down to Yelda tomorrow and bring up one of the Syfrian legions in reserve. It will take time to muster the supplies and equipment, especially in winter, so until I arrive you'll have to make the best shift you can. The Fleet garrison commander, Brandt, knows what he's about – let him worry about the troops while you take care of the clans. Post scouts at every pass, every goat trail across the Archen Mountains. I want to know where Drwyn pisses before the first drop hits the ground!'

15

GONE

Aysha knelt above Gair on the disordered bed. She straddled his thighs, tawny as a tiger in the glim-light. He watched her hands move over her breasts, teasing, tweaking, and she watched him want her. Dark nipples ripened to peaks under her fingers, but when he reached for her she leaned away.

Not yet. Not until I say.

I want you.

I know.

But you're still going to make me wait?

I enjoy seeing you like this, in thrall to me.

I always have been. You know that.

Eyes sparkling, she rocked forwards onto her hands and kissed him, then pulled back before he could capture her in his arms. Fingertips trailed down his chest, his belly, dancing past the part of him that ached for her caress. His hips bucked.

Witch!

Laughter shivered through his thoughts. *Is that what you think I am?*

She made another circuit of his belly, close enough this time to brush the length of him with the back of her hand, making him bob and twitch with desire. He bunched the sheets in his fists to keep his promise not to touch.

Goddess, you're killing me!

She smiled, slow and sultry as the last days of summer. Her eyes never leaving his, she reached into the shadow between her legs. His pulse hammered. It should be his fingers sliding between those silky folds, dipping into the heat of her. His touch that made her breathing quicken. Her pelvis rocked rhythmically, pressing her sex onto her circling fingers, and the drums in his blood beat louder.

His own arousal was a physical pain. He wrapped his hand around himself; a few strokes would finish him, but release alone was not enough. What he craved was her. To be inside her, deep inside, when she reached her orgasm and her Song folded around him and bore them both into flight.

Grasping her waist, he pulled her to him. *I can't wait any longer.*

She was slick and ready; he plunged into her, needing

her too much to be patient. Yes. Oh, saints, yes! He withdrew, thrust again and she gasped.

Don't stop.

Her thoughts tumbled into his, wordless, joyous, and he knew that she wanted this, wanted him, as much as he did her. Colours swirled around him, white and blue and a red dark as wine, sweet like the sweat shining on her breasts, twice as intoxicating.

She gripped his shoulders hard; her fingernails bit into his skin but he welcomed the pain – it meant she was close to what she sought. Maybe this time she would find it. Maybe this time she would come in his arms and afterwards everything would be different.

But the dream ended as it always did, with the click of a closing door. Sweating, breathless, Gair stared up at the filmy drapes, pale as ghosts clustered around the bedposts. He'd lost her. He shut his eyes. Goddess, he'd lost her. Pressing the pillow in his arms to his face, he tried to conjure up the scent of her skin, but all he smelled was stale linens and dusty feathers that tickled his nose. Not a breath of her perfume remained.

Opening his eyes again, he let the pillow fall onto his chest. He should have been able to remember her as she had been. After their time together, first as teacher and pupil, then as lovers, she had become almost a part of him, but without something tangible with which to conjure her, all he could see was how she had been at the end, broken and bleeding in his arms.

A sob clawed its way up through his chest. All teeth and talons, it trampled on his lungs, scrabbled for purchase in his throat on its way up to the air. He gritted his teeth against it. His shoulders shook, but he would not, could not, let it draw breath. Instead he smothered it with the pillow crushed between his hands, held it tight until the jerking and struggling ceased and the sob died.

Only when he was sure it was gone did he push the

pillow aside and lie staring up into the dark. He was exhausted. His body ached for rest but he couldn't sleep for more than a couple of hours – he hadn't been able to sleep the night through for almost a month. There were always too many dreams, too many memories waiting for him. Things that should have been sweet turned sour, things that should have lived turned cold and empty and grey.

Unbidden, an image rose up of the vaulted crypt beneath the chapel, lit by chains of clean white glims, and the goodwives of Pencruik with their sleeves rolled up and kerchiefs covering their hair, washing the dead.

Let me through, Saaron!

No, lad. Leave this work to those who are used to it.

I should be taking care of her, not strangers!

I understand. I know it hurts, but if you do this you'll never see her whole again, and you'll never be able to put it out of your mind. Trust me – it's better this way.

Better? Bitterness twisted Gair's lips into a snarl. This was supposed to be better? He couldn't imagine anything worse.

Sudden, scorching fury ignited inside him. Sitting up, he hurled the pillow across the room. It thumped into the carved closet doors hard enough to rattle the latch in its keeper, then slumped to the floor. One door slowly swung open.

Savin. Just thinking the name balled Gair's hands into fists. Savin, with his tricks and his theatre, the games he played with others' lives. Like poor Darin, a pawn sacrificed to lure the king into check, as if he was nothing. As if he didn't *matter*.

'I should have killed him,' he muttered.

You gave it your best, out at the Five Sisters.

She stood in the shadows, watching him, leaning against the open closet door. His heart lurched painfully.

My best wasn't enough. It had been nowhere near enough. He had to be faster, stronger, and then he'd make Savin pay the butcher's bill for the attack on Chapterhouse, right down to the last ha'penny.

Don't be so hard on yourself, Leahn. You might as well blame Alderan, or Godril, or the others who were there the last time.

But I should have stopped him when I had the chance. If I had, you'd still be here. I failed you, Aysha!

He blinked and she vanished, leaving nothing but the moonlight on her favourite wrap, hanging from a peg inside the closet door. A fold in the fabric, some shadows and loss had done the rest. He buried his face in his arms.

Saints, he was so tired. His eyes were scratchy and sore, and there was a dull pain behind them that never eased no matter what he did. He was so tired he was talking to a ghost.

Eyes screwed shut, he pressed his head between his hands. 'I miss you, *carianh*.'

Aysha didn't answer. There was no one there but him, and a nightwatchman wind outside that gently shook the long windows leading onto the balcony, found them secure and blew on.

Aysha was gone.

⚔

It was almost Ninth when Sorchal ambled along the covered walk at the side of the practice yard, his coat over his shoulder and his shirt untucked. Gair turned from first position and propped his sword point-down in the dust in front of him, leaning on the pommel. This was the third time this week the Elethrainian had let him down.

'Good afternoon,' he said dryly.

Grinning, Sorchal swept him a florid bow. 'Good morrow, sir Knight! Goddess's blessings to you on this fine morning.' He staggered as he straightened up, which rather spoiled the effect.

'Are you still drunk?'

'Very probably.'

Gair sighed. 'I thought we were practising at half-Prime today.'

'Ah, yes, about that.' This time Sorchal looked genuinely contrite, ducking his head and scrubbing his fingers through his uncombed hair. A shadow of beard on cheeks and chin said he'd been out all night. Green eyes flashed and the grin returned, then he shrugged, as if that made everything all right. 'I got . . . side-tracked.'

'I see.' Hefting his sword again, Gair squinted along the blade to the point, trying to keep his irritation reined in. 'What was her name?'

'Molly, I think. Or it might have been Maisie. Blue eyes and freckles – so wholesome I just wanted to eat her up. So I did.' Sorchal dropped his coat over the rail and leaned on it. 'If you ask me, that's what *you* need.'

'What?'

'You need a woman.'

Gair stared at him. 'Excuse me?'

'A woman, to suck some of that intensity out of you.'

Once, a turn of phrase like that would have made his ears burn. Now he felt faintly insulted that anyone – even a rake like Sorchal – could imagine he was done with grieving so quickly.

'I didn't ask you,' he said. 'It's too soon.'

The Elethrainian clicked his tongue. 'Look, I know it's only been a month—'

'Less.'

'—but there's a house in Threepenny Yard, very discreet, with fine feather beds and a good breakfast after.' He dug a gold Imperial from his pocket and flicked it into the air. 'Here. A gift from a friend to a friend.'

At the height of its arc, the coin caught the early-morning light and blazed, bright as a fire-eagle's crown. Squinting against the sky, Gair tracked it as it tumbled towards him.

Twenty-four days, nineteen hours and thirty-some minutes. It wasn't precise; it didn't need to be. He no longer counted them as days lost – he had the rest of his life to count those – but as days elapsed until he could exact his revenge. No other measure made sense.

He swept the blade up. Metal chimed on metal and Sorchal had to duck as the coin went spinning over his head to bounce off the wall behind him.

'Bloody hell, these aren't dockside grunters, you know,' he grumbled, trudging over the dusty boards to the corner of the walk to retrieve the coin. He rubbed his thumb over the edge where the longsword's steel had bitten a deep notch in the gold. 'They're nice girls, very clean, and I can attest to their talents. There's a redhead alone could bring a dead man to the salute—'

'Holy saints, Sorchal!' Gair stared at him. The girls' quality or otherwise wasn't the point. 'No!'

'Because money changes hands?'

'That's one good reason.'

A slave-trader had left his sigil on the nape of Aysha's neck: a tattoo of a crescent moon with stars between the horns. *Just ink*, she'd said, but he'd thought of it like a cattle-brand and loathed the idea of a man marking her as property. That someone kept a stable of women and hired them out by the hour or the night was only a little different.

'It's simple economics, my friend. They provide an essential service and charge for it accordingly. What's the problem with that?' Sorchal gave a lazy, just-bedded smile. 'Long live the spirit of enterprise, say I.'

A woman wasn't what Gair needed. Not by a mile. He flexed his hands on the grip of the longsword, already dark with his sweat from two hours' practice at the solo forms, and imagined swinging the blade hard at a gaudy silk shirt.

'No thanks, Sorchal.'

'Those Knightly principles of yours again,' the Ele-thrainian said sourly. 'You know, you'd be a lot more pleasant to be around if you bent them once in a while.'

Gair ground his teeth. 'You don't understand.'

'Don't I? And whose fault is that? I'm your friend, Gair – or I thought I was – but you won't talk to me. I can't even persuade you to keep me company in my cups.' The words burst out of him like flood waters breaching a dam. 'I come down here every day and practise swordplay with you until you could take that great blade and cut the flame from a candlewick, but that's all you do. You don't talk, you don't laugh. You only want to kill.'

Reversing his grip on the longsword, Gair drove the point into the ground. 'And you think the quickest way to get over a woman is to tumble a new one! I'm not like you, and that's not what she was to me.'

Sorchal would never understand. He changed girls the way other men changed their shirts, and the funny thing was, they seemed to like it. They ate out of his hand like cage-birds, and fluttered and sighed when he moved on without ever a harsh word spoken. He behaved appallingly, and they loved him for it.

Lips pursed, Sorchal studied him for a long moment. 'So it would appear,' he said at last, and sighed. 'All right. Let me soak up the last of the wine with some breakfast and I'll meet you back here in half an hour.'

Gair shook his head. 'It's not worth fighting if you're not at your best. Get some sleep.'

'Tomorrow, then?'

'Tomorrow.' He jerked the longsword out of the ground and wiped the dirt off the blade on the leg of his whites. 'Half-Prime, if you can.'

Slinging his coat back over his shoulder, the Elethrai-nian turned to go. 'You need another way to spend your time, my friend.'

He walked away. Before he was out of the yard complex he was whistling a jaunty tune, something with the rhythm of a dance to it that said his evening had comprised more than merely drinking and wenching, and for a moment Gair wondered if an hour in the hop-scented fug of the Red Dragon would be such an ordeal. Maybe not – but maybe next week, or the week after. Not today.

Standing still had allowed his muscles to cool; he worked his shoulders to loosen them, tossing the sword from hand to hand as he walked to the midline of the yard and set himself to begin the forms again.

A figure moved in the shadows of the eastern walk. Even shading his eyes he couldn't make out who it was after the glare of the morning sun, but it had the height and breadth of a man.

'Now what?' he muttered, lowering his sword. Louder, he asked, 'Yes?'

'Sorchal was only trying to help, you know.' It was Alderan.

He hadn't seen much of the Guardian over the past few weeks. A few words in a corridor, a nod from across the refectory. A little distance had suited him, and still did – it was one less distraction from the task at hand.

Gair gripped the earth with his toes and focused on his breathing, slowly bringing the longsword up in salute.

'Sorchal's never loved a woman for longer than it took to get inside her bodice,' he said, directing the words as much to the steel in his hands as to the man at the far end of the yard. 'He doesn't understand.'

'Still no reason to be rude to him.' Alderan came around to the steps leading down into the yard and sat on the topmost one, leaning his forearms on his knees. 'What are you doing to yourself, Gair?'

'Is it not obvious?'

'You've already got the beating of Haral three times out of five. Arlin won't practise with you any more. Only Sorchal will put up with you, and I'll be surprised if he continues much longer. You're running out of friends.'

Balance. Breathe. Feel the tension drain from the muscles, relaxed but ready. 'Arlin was never a friend of mine.' *And begin.*

Step by step, feint becoming lunge, a high guard becoming a sweep of steel like a striking falcon, then back and away, turning, blocking, dancing through the forms against an invisible opponent with only the gasp and sigh of air over blade for accompaniment. He felt Alderan watching him, tracing each move he made down the yard, but inside his perfect sphere of concentration the old man's scrutiny ran off him like rain off a windowpane. Like the sweat down the channel of his spine as the sun warmed the day and his longsword flew.

Down the yard and back again, his feet scuffling on the earth. Faster now, more fluid; he didn't feel the fabric of his whites tugging at his legs, the growing dampness of sweat around his waist. He was approaching that time-stretching place where hand and wrist and arm moved faster than serpents, faster than thought . . . Then Alderan spoke again and shattered it.

'Come south with me.'

Gair mistimed the next move and the tip of the blade scored a line through the dust perilously close to his toes. 'What?'

'Come to Gimrael. I think I know where we might find the location of Corlainn's starseed, and I could use your help.'

Gair straightened up, breathing a little hard. Back home in Leah the snowbells would hardly have begun to poke their noses above the drifts, but on the Western Isles spring was well advanced and warm as a northern summer. 'I have work to do, Alderan.'

'I don't think the faculty has seen you in the lecture halls in a month,' said the old man mildly. 'You're either here or off Goddess knows where shape-shifting.'

'You know what I mean.'

'Yes, and that's what concerns me. You're working so hard to turn yourself into the perfect weapon that you're not giving yourself time to heal.' Alderan stood up and walked down the three creaky steps to the yard. 'Are you still having nightmares?'

His rhythm broken, Gair lowered the sword and let the tip chop into the dirt. 'Sometimes,' he hedged. Chop, chop went the blade, cutting little grooves in the packed earth like marks on a tally-stick. 'Mostly they're just confused – memories all mixed up and spliced together. Tanith said it would take time for them to settle down.'

'You need to get away from here, let yourself breathe again.'

Gair watched the blade counting out the other dreams, barely feeling his hand contract and relax, nor the weight of the steel dragging at the muscles of his forearm. The other dreams were the ones that hurt the most and left him sweating tears, with a weight in his chest as if his lungs were made of cold, dark iron.

'You know I can't go back to the mainland – the Church saw to that.'

'So come with me. The desert has its own dangers, true enough, but it's far away from here.' Alderan's tone became gentler. 'Not all memories should be clung to, lad.'

'And you think Gimrael will help me forget?' said Gair bitterly. 'A place where every face I see will remind me of her?' Another chop into the dirt, harder than the others; he leaned on the blade, driving it deeper, and didn't look up. 'No.'

The idea of leaving Aysha behind, even though she was long gone to ash, filled him with something close to panic. Not to be amongst the objects she had touched, not exist in the space they'd shared . . . No. He couldn't – wouldn't – do that.

As he worked the sword's point deeper into the earth, fine brown dust dulled the shine on the blade. He'd dulled the edge, too, but nothing a few minutes' work with an oilstone wouldn't put right. Gouging the earth was strangely satisfying; it reminded him of poking a stick into the smooth wet sand below Drumcarrick Head on summer evenings, in the hopes of digging up razor-shell clams to bake on the embers of a driftwood fire.

'Haral told me something he'd learned in the desert wars, at Samarak,' Alderan said absently. 'He said that picking the best ground is halfway to winning the battle.'

'It's one of the things they taught us at the Mother-house.' Finally Gair set the sword's point on the ground between his feet and folded his hands on the pommel, looking Alderan squarely in the eye. 'They also taught us that sometimes we don't have a choice. Sometimes we have to take the battle to our enemy.'

The old man didn't blink. 'I won't let you go north after him, Gair.'

Gair scowled. 'You can't stop me.'

Scratching at his beard, Alderan said, 'Actually, I can, but I'd rather you simply saw sense. When you can't defeat a man with main strength, you have to do it with guile. There's no shame in that. Have patience.'

Pulse thumping dangerously hard, the blood loud in his ears, Gair glared at the Guardian of the Veil. 'You said *when*, not *if*. You don't think I'd beat him.'

'Right now?' The old man's lips twisted ruminatively. 'No, I don't. In a fair fight, maybe you would, but Savin's never been interested in fair. In Gimrael we might find a way to clip his wings without him even feeling it.' He showed his teeth. 'It's not as direct as your approach, but it might be more effective, at least until you're fully recovered.'

Stung, Gair began to protest. 'I don't need to be coddled, Alderan. I'm fine—'

'Are you? Are you really?' Blue eyes fixed him, cold

as glacial ice beneath those tangled brows, and he had to turn his head away before they saw too much. 'Do you remember: last year you gave me your word that one day I could ask you to do something for me, and you'd do it?'

The inn in Dremen. Sudden anxiety fluttered inside Gair, thrashing against his ribs. Dismayed, he stared at the dusty ground. If the old man called in that favour, he would have no choice but to go with him.

Alderan grunted, satisfied. 'I see that you do remember. This is that day, and this is me asking. Come to El Maqqam with me, and maybe we can bring this wretched business to an end.'

Every face a reflection of Aysha, every voice an echo. *Don't ask me to do this.* 'I can't.'

The resolute lines of the old man's face did not relent. If anything they hardened. 'You can and you will, Gair,' he said harshly. 'On your honour: this one thing, and we're done.'

'Oh, we're done all right.' Gair turned on his heel and strode over to his scabbard. Slamming the sword home, he glared back at Alderan. 'I will make him pay. As the Goddess is my witness, I will put Savin in the ground.'

'And once you've done that, what then?' the old man demanded. 'Once you've filled the hole in your heart with hate so there's no room in it for anything else, how will you let it go when you've nothing left to hate any more?'

'*I don't know!*' Gair threw down the sword. 'I don't know, Alderan! I can't see past what I have to do – I'll deal with what comes after that when it comes!'

He'd looked to the future, and it ended at Savin's death. The road unrolled to a corpse; there was nothing beyond it but blackness, as if the significance of it was so enormous that it blotted out all light from a world beyond that point.

Alderan reached out to him, perhaps intending a

sympathetic touch, but Gair shied from the contact as if it would sting.

'I've got things to do,' he said and scooped up his sword, slinging the baldric over his shoulder.

The old man's gaze followed him across the yard, heavy on the back of his neck with things unsaid. When he reached the opposite steps and began to ascend them, Alderan called after him. 'I will hold you to your word, Gair. Three days, then we embark for Gimrael.'

Three days, then we embark on a colossal waste of time. But he'd given his word, damn it. He couldn't take it back now.

※

The boy's rage blundered about in Savin's head like a bumblebee on a windowpane, butting its head against the glass over and over as if sheer persistence would wear it down. It was almost funny. To think he'd had such high hopes for the lad and his potential.

'Strong but oh so stupid,' Savin murmured. *Don't you realise I can hear you?*

'Hear' was too strong a word, of course; he couldn't actually pick out any words, but when emotions ran high and especially when strong feelings were channelled against him, he could sense it in much the same way a man sensed he was being stared at. And these emotions were certainly strong. Hate. Fear. A seething morass of pain-death-vengeance that sucked at him the way a bog sucked at a boot.

'My, you are a very unhappy boy, aren't you?' he said to the air, pouring more wine into his glass. 'You'll rupture something if you're not careful.'

He'd hoped for a stronger hold on Gair's thoughts than this, but that Healer had been good – very good, and fast as a knife. She'd recognised what he'd done and thrown a shield around the boy's mind, then used the Leahn's own strength as a weapon to weed out his influence before it was fully rooted. Now instead of a window into Gair's head he had only a crude shadow play on the curtain of the shield: all impression, no fine detail. Amusing as it was to watch, so far it was completely unproductive.

He settled back in his chair, feet outstretched towards the fire. Much as his failure irked him, he couldn't help but be impressed by the girl's skill. Idly, sipping at his wine, he wondered if she was as pretty in real life as she had been in Gair's head.

From her iron cage in the corner, the firebird watched him unblinkingly. Her painted feathers were smeared and smudged now, and even from across the room he could smell her: the sharp note of sweat, the rich reek of her plundered cunny. The animal odour was repellent and at the same time intensely arousing – it appealed directly to his hindbrain, where desires dwelt that he couldn't afford to unleash, not just yet. Finding a way to make her scream would have to wait for another day.

16

THE USES OF POWER

❧

In the water, another Teia was learning to work with fire.

She saw herself sitting cross-legged, wrapped in the warm golden glow of a clay lamp on the floor. Around her was a suggestion of carpets and cushions, enough to imply that she sat in the chief's chamber, as she did now.

At first the image was cloudy, like her reflection in Ytha's bronze mirror. As it began to clear, details emerged: folds in other-Teia's clothing, the glint and shimmer of a bead necklace. The lamp flame reflected in other-Teia's eyes, and as she watched, it stretched up as tall as her hand was long then dwindled to a bluish glow about the blackened wick before returning to its former size. She could almost hear the thin, whispery music that made the flame dance.

Careful, Teia told herself, recalling Ytha's instructions. To scry was to observe; it was dangerous to allow herself to be drawn into the image in the water, the Speaker had admonished, or to attempt to change it. She could only watch, whatever she might see.

Nonetheless, a little thrill of triumph turned her stomach over. At last she was learning to control her gift: the water was showing her a glimpse of the future she had chosen instead of bewildering fragments with no sense of time or scope.

Just as she felt her lips curving into a smile, white fangs flashed past her face as a Hound's jaws snapped closed on the image and snatched it away.

Teia recoiled. Her eyes flew open, her heart racing, but there was no Hound in front of her, only Ytha, cross-legged on a cushion as she had been every day for a month now, since just before Firstmoon. Between them, the water in the wide bronze basin shimmered and cleared.

'You almost had it, child,' Ytha said. 'Come, try again.' She reached for Teia's hands to place them on the rim of the basin once more.

'I saw a Hound.' The words came out small and timid, like mice. 'As soon as I saw the image clearly, a Hound bit it.'

'It bit you?'

'No, the scrying. The Hound snapped at it and the image disappeared.'

She struggled to remember details; the Hound had leapt through her thoughts in a heartbeat. Each time was the same: the creature present only long enough for her to recognise it for what it was then gone again, leaving nothing but a cold foreboding in the pit of her stomach.

She rubbed her forehead and screwed up her eyes, but there was nothing more to tell. Besides, learning to guide her scrying was too precious a gift to waste. 'I'm sorry, Speaker. Can we try again?'

'Of course.'

Grasping the Speaker's outstretched hands, Teia let her wrists rest on the rim of the bronze basin and closed her eyes once more. No sooner had she reached for a strand of that glorious music to begin to scry than massive paws thumped into her chest.

She felt herself driven backwards into the cushions by the impact. The huge beast crouched over her, its weight crushing her chest, and all her breath left her in a *whoosh*. The Hound's jaws lunged towards her, ready to crush her head like a bird's egg, then stopped just inches from her face. Eyes as red as madness fixed her. Lips curled back from jagged teeth, and it gave a coughing growl that sounded disturbingly like laughter, its rank breath fanning her face. Teia struggled to breathe with its weight bearing down on her. Her lungs began to burn; panicked, she tried to thrash her way out from underneath the beast. Its mask contorted into a warning snarl, saliva dripping on her dress. It could kill her with a snap, and it wanted her to know it.

A scream clawed its way up Teia's throat but she had no breath for it and it emerged as little more than a moan. Then the weight lifted and the Hound was gone.

Her eyes snapped open and she sucked in a huge breath, as if she'd just emerged from underwater. Let it out, took another, and the burning in her lungs began to fade. Only then did she realise she was still sitting upright, and the feeling of being knocked over and half-suffocated had all been illusion.

The Speaker frowned at her.

'What did you see?'

This time, Teia would have to tell her all of it. Ytha had chosen to teach her scrying today and she had no way of knowing how much of the vision the other woman had seen in the water.

'I concentrated on tomorrow, like you said, and I saw the two of us with a lamp. You were teaching me to work with fire. As soon as the image was complete, a Hound leapt out at me. When I tried again, the Hound knocked me over and crouched on top of me as if it was going to tear out my throat.'

'A Hound?'

'One of Maegern's Hounds,' she said, hating the taste of the words.

Ytha's expression cooled. 'What do you know of that?'

'At the Gathering, Maegern promised She would send two of Her Hounds, didn't She? I think . . . I *know* it was one of them that I saw.' She heard the Raven's voice again, scraping around the inside of her head like claws, and shivered. 'It threatened me.'

The Speaker sniffed. 'I think perhaps you have let fireside stories go to your head,' she said. 'The Hounds mean you no harm.'

So why had it felt so much like a warning when the beast hulked over her? A demonstration of its power, of what would happen if she stood in its path. 'I can only remember fragments from the summoning, but I see images of Maegern in my dreams, all the time. Her Hounds chasing me, and destruction everywhere I look.'

'You saw our victory, that is all,' Ytha scoffed. 'You saw our enemies driven before us, as She promised us they would be. You are imagining monsters in the shadows, girl.'

I'm not. I know I'm not. Teia took a deep breath for

courage. 'I'm afraid, Speaker. I'm afraid of what She might do once She is freed.'

Ytha straightened up, drew herself in. Teia watched her wrap herself in her authority as clan Speaker the way another woman would pull on a coat. 'She will help us, in return for our aid.'

'What help could one of the Elder Gods possibly need from us?'

A crease appeared between Ytha's brows. 'You ask many questions.'

Ducking her head, Teia mustered herself. 'Forgive me, Speaker, but these dreams trouble me. I have . . . misgivings.'

A bony hand gripped her jaw and forced her to look up. Green-flame eyes stared into hers, icy and remote as Finndail's Banner unfurling across the midnight sky. 'Do you doubt the goddess's word, child? She vouchsafed us Her aid – would you call Her a liar?'

'N-no,' Teia managed. Rising panic shook her voice, but she pressed on. Ytha had to be made to see, for all their sakes. 'I don't know what She told you, but I think you heard what She wanted you to hear. Once She's free She doesn't need you any more. She'll do what She's always done and turn the Hunt loose.'

If she'd slapped the Speaker across the mouth, she doubted she could have made her look more stunned. Sandy brows rose; for just a second the mask slipped and Teia saw the face of the woman behind it. A woman who must once have been a considerable beauty, before the plains wind stripped the softness of youth from her skin and stitched lines into the leather that remained. In a blink those lines contorted into a snarl.

'Blasphemer!'

Inside her, Teia's power jangled a warning. She opened her mouth to speak but Ytha's magic was building, throbbing through the grip of her fingers, and her voice wouldn't come.

'You dare to speak ill of one of the Eldest? Dare to speak ill of *me?* I am Speaker of the Crainnh.' The words hissed like vipers. 'It was I who summoned Maegern, who bargained with Her for the benefit of the clans. No other could do it – none *dared* to do it without me to lead the way. Our victory against the usurpers will be sung throughout the ages, and it proceeds according to *my* plan. Remember that!'

Her eyes narrowed. Teia saw her own face reflected in them, bloodless with fear, and for one terrifying instant thought Ytha was about to burn her out on the spot.

'And what of you, Teia? No obvious Talent until my weaving caught you and now you learn quickly – too quickly! To be newly come into your gift yet be this strong is a rare thing. The power is like a muscle; it needs work to make it grow. How long have you been working it in secret? How long have you known?' Hard fingers ground into Teia's cheeks. 'Answer me, child!'

A rush of compulsion deluged Teia's mind. It seized her, shook her, bent her to its will. She would answer; she had to. She had known of her gift since Macha brought her first blood; why had she ever thought she could keep that a secret? There was nothing Ytha could not know, nothing she could not find out. It would be better by far to volunteer the information than wait for the Speaker to enter her mind and take it by force. Surrender was the only choice.

'Answer me!'

Wave after wave of Ytha's will bore down until Teia thought she would break under their weight. Her mouth shaped to say the words and, in desperation, she flung herself open to the music within.

'No.'

Ytha recoiled as her compulsion broke apart. 'What is this? You will not defy me!'

This time it came like a rockslide, hammering Teia

with blow after blow. She drew deeply on her power and raised it as a shield. Ytha threw her will against it but was turned aside.

Amazed, Teia tried to study what she had done. If she closed her eyes, she could see and feel the strands of her magic gyring around her, around a still place in the centre where she stood. Walls of sweet, potent music surrounded her, laced with lambent colour; beyond them, the Speaker's fury broke apart in discord. She could set her feet here, in this calm. From this place she could not be moved.

'No,' she said again. With one hand she gripped Ytha's wrist and squeezed. The Speaker's fingers spasmed and Teia firmly pulled the hand from her face.

'I have seen it, Speaker,' she went on, climbing to her feet. 'If you fulfil your side of the bargain and free Her, Maegern will unleash Her Hunt on the plains, and you will be powerless to stop it. She will destroy us all.'

'Liar! You cannot know this!'

'I can. What I see in my dreams is the truth. I may not always understand them until the events play out, but they have never been wrong.'

'You're nothing but a jumped-up apprentice!' Ytha snarled. 'What can you know of foretelling?'

'More than you, I think.'

Spitting curses, Ytha struggled to rise. Teia released her hand and took a half-step back to give her room. At once the other woman raised a fist to strike at her. With a small gesture Teia trapped the fist in a knot of air and held it there. She had no idea how; she simply reached for the power and it was done.

'How do you know this?' Ytha tugged at her arm. 'Release me!'

'Not until you listen to me. I'm trying to warn you!' The magic sang as Ytha's power struck Teia's weaving and skittered aside, again and again. Though the weave held firm, she couldn't stop herself flinching. 'Please, for the good of all our people, don't go through with this plan. Maegern cares nothing for you, nor the other Speakers – you are only tools. All She wants is Her freedom. Once you've served your purpose She will abandon you.'

Teeth bared, the older woman clawed with her power at the nothingness imprisoning her. Her free hand bunched into a fist, starseed ring glittering. 'You know nothing of our plans. Now release me!'

'Please, Ytha, listen—'

'*Release me!*' the Speaker howled, flinging back her head. Cords stood out in her neck with fury.

Outside Teia heard running feet, excited voices. Quickly she unravelled the knot and let the power go.

Fighting something that was suddenly no longer there, Ytha staggered backwards, caught her heel on a cushion and sat down hard. A startled gasp was followed by the foulest curse Teia had ever heard, then the Speaker climbed slowly back to her feet with murder in her eyes.

'I should have ripped the Talent from you months ago.' Her voice was low in her throat. 'How dare you lay hands on me? Remember your place, bitch!'

Teia swallowed hard. She had never seen the Speaker in such a rage. But she had cast the bones now; there was no going back.

'My place is where you put me, Speaker. I am Drwyn's betrothed and the mother of his heir.'

'Do you presume to lecture me? You are *nothing*!'

'I am what I am. I have seen what will be and, Macha as my witness, I have spoken the truth of it. Ytha, I beg of you, listen to me.'

Several warriors spilled in past the door-curtain, dirks at the ready. Finding no foe, they stared at the women in confusion until Drwyn pushed his way through them.

'Aedon's balls, can a man not have some peace in his own home?' he boomed, fists cocked on his hips. 'What happens here? With all that shrieking, I thought a viper had found its way into the cave.'

His glower swung from one woman to the other. In the time it took his gaze to cross the chamber, Ytha had drawn herself up to her full height, tucking her disordered hair back behind her ears. Her face could have been carved from ice, but for all that lack of expression, Teia felt fury boiling off her.

'We must speak privately, Drwyn.' Even the Speaker's tone was frosty. 'I have grave news.'

'News of what?' Drwyn frowned. 'Tell me what's amiss.'

'In private.' One glance speared Teia where she stood, then Ytha stalked out with the chief, regal as any storied queen. Drwyn's warriors put up their weapons and followed after.

As the curtain fell behind the last man, Teia's knees finally failed her and she had to sit down on the cushions. Every part of her was trembling. Her heart raced as if she'd just outrun a rock-wolf and her lungs ached for air.

Oh, Macha preserve her, she'd looked the Speaker in the eye and told her she was wrong.

She pressed her hand to her aching chest to steady herself. Once she'd sooner have crossed the Muiragh Mhor barefoot than cross Ytha, but fear of what was to come if the Hunt was loosed had spurred her to an audacity of which she'd never dreamed herself capable. She tried not to imagine what might have happened had Ytha managed to work free of the weaving before Drwyn appeared.

Under her hand she felt damp spots on the front of her dress and looked down. Dark patches splotched her bodice as if she'd been splashed with something. *The Hound.* It had only been a vision, not actually present in the chamber, but somehow the vision had been real enough to spray her with its spittle.

With mounting dread, she unlaced the neck of her

gown and pulled it open. The ache in her chest had been more than anxiety. Red marks the shape of splayed paws spread across the tops of her breasts, tipped with purple indentations where the claws had dug into her flesh.

Her stomach fell head over heels down to her feet. Maegern's Hound had been in her dreams. Now it had come out of the otherworld and marked her.

The legends said that once the Hunt was set after its quarry, it never stopped. There was no barrier to it, neither mountains nor rivers nor the great gulfs of the ocean. The Hounds kept coming. In the old tales, Finndail had kept one step ahead of them for forty years and gone to his bed one day thinking he was finally safe, only to find a Hound on his pillow beside him the next morning.

Teia let her hands fall. Were the Hounds now hunting her? Was that why she saw them so often? Macha's mercy, what had Ytha unleashed?

Someone scratched at the door and at once she feared the worst. Her heart galloping again, she jumped to her feet, quickly refastening her laces. Then she realised that no one who felt they had to ask permission to enter would have the power to do her harm. Nonetheless her voice was unsteady as she called them in.

Ana's homely face appeared around the curtain, eyes wide. 'The Speaker looks like a crag-cat with her tail afire,' she exclaimed in a scandalized voice. 'Teisha, what did you say to her?'

'I told her the truth and she didn't like it.' Teia aimed a kick at the cushion Ytha had tripped on and sent it tumbling across the rug. 'I think she's made a mistake, Mama.'

'Teir told me what you had seen.' Ana came closer, laid a hand on her arm. 'Is the clan really in danger?'

Teia nodded. 'Last time Maegern walked the earth our people were broken and four clan-names lost before the iron men sealed Her away. She's had a thousand years to brew Her vengeance – it should be at a fine boil by now.'

Worry lines furrowed Ana's brow. 'But I'm sure the Speaker knows—'

'She's wrong!' Teia's child squirmed. Instinctively she put her hand to her belly and for an instant sensed those colours again. 'I've tried to warn her, but she doesn't believe me – or she chooses not to because it puts a crick in her plans. Clan law means she can't be chief herself, so I think she means to have the Chief of Chiefs in her pocket instead. Drwyn may lead us back to the lands of our ancestors with the Raven at his side, but it'll be Ytha's hand on the reins.'

'Macha's mercy!' Hastily Ana made the sign to ward off evil intent.

'Now she's gone to tell him what I told her and how I know it. I hid the Talent from everyone for more than two years, Mama. I could seek out parts of my future long before she ever came to teach me.' Dark clouds of despair rolled through her soul. 'Promise me you'll leave. As soon as the clan rides for the Scattering, take Ailis and Tevira and the boys and go, as far away as you can. I don't know if you'll be safe anywhere, but it might give you a chance.'

'Oh, Teisha—'

'Please, Mama. Promise me you'll go. There's nothing but blood for the Crainnh once it begins.'

Ana hugged her fiercely. 'But what about you? You've made a dangerous enemy in the Speaker, I think.'

Teia lifted her shoulders, spread her hands helplessly. 'I tried reasoning with her and I failed, so I'll have to stop her somehow. She's damned us all if I don't.'

'But how? She's the Speaker and you're only an apprentice!'

'I don't know, Mama. Perhaps I could seek out the iron men – they turned the Hunt back once before, after all.'

'But the Speaker said their forts are empty. How will you find them?'

She hadn't thought that far ahead and scrubbed her hands over her face. 'I'll have to go where they are, then. Go south.'

'Into the Empire?' Her mother was horrified. 'They'll never help us. Teisha, please, think about what you're suggesting!'

'They might help if they know the Hunt is a threat to them, too.'

But her mother was shaking her head. 'No. There must be another way – will Drwyn not speak up for you?'

'He's Ytha's creature, always was. He likes to tug on the leash from time to time, but he knows who holds it.' Tears threatened. Quickly Teia knuckled them away before her mother could see them. 'I'll be all right, Mama, don't worry.'

'You're carrying his child. Does that count for nothing?' Plump, sparrow-like Ana with her bright button eyes, trying hard to look aggrieved. Teia's heart ached. *I'll miss you, Mama.*

'It might count for more if it were a son,' she said, forcing her voice to be light, 'but I think I'm carrying a girl.'

'What makes you say that?'

'I'm the youngest of three sisters. You're the middle one of five.' She laid a hand on her belly. 'And I think she has the Talent, like me.'

Her mother looked disbelieving. 'You can tell this, before the child's born? Not even the Speaker can delve a babe in the womb!'

'When I look at her with the power, she responds to it. I see colours in her mind.' Teia cradled her belly with both hands, feeling the solidity, the weight of it through her woollen dress, though she still had four moons to wait.

'Teisha, there's been no Speaker in our family in a

hundred generations,' her mother said, 'and none in Teir's for almost as long. There's been barely a handful of girls apprenticed between us. Your Talent is the first since my greatmother's days.'

'So?' Gods, she was tired. Now that the exhilaration of confronting Ytha had faded, she felt as drained as a punctured water-skin. All she wanted to do was sleep. Except she couldn't: there were preparations still to make, more clothes and provisions to secure in case worse came to worst as she now feared it must. There was little chance Ytha would teach her any more about scrying. She'd be lucky if the Speaker didn't simply burn her out for spite, and the chief's child be damned.

'So is it not a sign?' Ana spread her hands. 'Are you not meant for great things, you and your child?'

Teia thought of the vision of herself and her sometime-future son, her hands protectively on his shoulders and the torc of a clan chief around his still-beardless neck. And her lightless eyes, bleak as the Muiragh Mhor. Great things that could ruin a woman's gaze so completely must be great indeed.

'If I am, I haven't seen them. Mama, please promise me you'll go once the spring comes. Get as far away from Ytha as you can. If something were to happen to you and Da, I couldn't bear it.'

'And let you go into the south alone?'

Teia bit her lip. Her mother had guessed – she should have realised Ana was sharp-witted enough to deduce Teia would not be leaving with the rest of her family in the spring.

'I don't think I'll still be here by then.' Dead or exiled, it made no difference; the Speaker's word was law. In the heart of winter, there was little to choose between the two anyway.

'Hmm.' Ana pursed her lips and Teia tried one more time.

'It's for the best.'

'I will speak to your father. It will be his decision, after all.'

'Mama—'

'Teir is the head of the family, Daughter,' her mother chided gently. 'I know he believes you, as do I. He will know what to do for the best, when the time comes.'

That was the closest to a promise from Ana as she would get, so she nodded and tried to smile. Lifting the corners of her mouth felt as hard as lifting the Archen Mountains themselves.

'You'd better go,' she said. 'I have my chief's supper to prepare and he will be displeased if it is not ready on his return.'

Her mother borrowed one of the Speaker's long looks. It was not nearly so stern; Ana's complexion was too dimpled and rosy to manage much better than mildly reproachful, but Teia read the question in it nonetheless.

'He won't raise a hand to me, don't worry. I think he's even a little fond of me now he thinks I'm going to give him an heir.'

Ana's sniff was as eloquent as a thousand words, but she kissed her daughter farewell and went to the door. One hand on the curtain, she paused. 'Take care of yourself, Teisha. You cannot best clan law with your powers, even if you can best Ytha with them.'

'I know. But I have to try – it's too important not to.'

Her mother dropped her gaze, sighed and nodded. She understood. Then she lifted the curtain and left.

⬦

Ytha swung on her heel at the sound of footsteps behind her, her skirts dragging in the deep snow. Drwyn emerged onto the ledge overlooking the lake and before he could take three steps she levelled a finger at him. 'She could be the ruination of everything, Drwyn!'

'She's naught but a girl.' He lounged against the

rocks, one foot up, as if he could not see her plans crumbling. 'Why so anxious?'

She flung up her hands – how could he not understand? – then counted off the hated girl's crimes on her fingers. 'She has a Talent that she hid from me for years. She has a child inside her whose aura I cannot read – I cannot even tell if it will be boy or girl. She has the gift of foretelling – true foretelling, like the Banfaíth of old. That's a skill not heard of in four hundred years and more.'

'Is that what's soured your porridge? That she sees what is to come? Surely that's an asset to us, to know what is to be before it comes to pass.'

Lackwit! By all the stars, what possessed me to think I could mould this dolt into a Chief of Chiefs fit to burn our names into the histories?

Controlling herself with an effort of will, Ytha stalked over to him.

'What if the other chiefs come to hear of what she has seen? What if they believe her? You cannot become Chief of Chiefs without the acclamation of the other clans. They are as good as sworn to you now, but if even one falls away we will have much work to do to bring him back at the Scattering. If more than one falters, well, we might as well return to our tents and be content with our exile!'

Her final shout echoed back to her from the peaks around them, distorted and shrill. In the corner of her vision, she saw the waters shiver. Drwyn merely folded his arms and gave her a measuring look.

Insolence!

'What has she seen that irks you so?' he asked.

'She sees all our planning come to naught and disaster for the clans. She sees the Wild Hunt turned against us. She questions the word of Maegern Herself.' Ytha spat out the words as if they were coated with bile.

'And when I questioned her, she used her powers against me!'

A dark brow quirked upwards; his beard twitched to hide a smile.

Grinding her teeth, she schooled her own face to stillness. 'She is a mystery, Drwyn. Things I cannot know, I cannot counter. Things I cannot counter may be a threat to us.'

'So what do you propose?'

'She must be silenced. Immediately.'

'She is the mother of my child, Ytha.'

The steadiness of his tone should have warned her, but rage had boiled away her finer instincts.

'Who knows whose whelp it is? I tell you, I cannot read the child! Either she has some power at work to hide it from me – in which case, what other powers does she possess? – or the child itself is prodigiously gifted, even more so than its deceitful wretch of a dam!'

He thumbed his lower lip, black eyes considering. 'Then we wait until the child is born. You can delve it then, find out the truth.'

'By then it will be too late!'

Whirling about, she prowled to the edge of the rocky outcrop. By the Eldest! First the girl, playing her for a fool and putting all her careful plans in danger. Now Drwyn, the man she had moulded to be what his father would not, laughing at her! How dare they? She was the *Speaker*! She kicked out and scattered clods of snow into the waters below.

'She should have been given to me long since. The law dictates that a gifted girl be surrendered to the Speaker of her clan without question.'

'Her kin did not know. You said yourself she had concealed her Talent.'

Insufferable. The man was speaking sense when she was supposed to be leading *him*! Who was the king-maker here – had he forgotten?

She bit off her next words crisply, each one as sharp and clear as a shard of ice. 'She must be silenced.'

'Can you not command her? Is she not under your authority as one of your apprentices?'

'She is, but I suspect she chooses when to obey. She does not fear me, unlike the others. Since she manifested her gift –' *and what a gift!* '– I cannot cow her any more.'

It was easier to admit whilst facing out over the valley, when she did not have to look at him and watch him enjoy her failure, however small, which he most assuredly would, gods rot him. But the power of the girl! How had a gift so strong come to fruition without her knowing? *How?*

'Either her powers are greater than I can assay, or there is iron in that girl's backbone that I never expected. I cannot allow her to put our plans at risk.' *I will take back the plains, and that girl will not stand in my way.*

She heard the scrape of his boots as he came to his feet behind her.

'Speak plainly, Ytha. What do you intend?'

A sacrifice to Maegern, to assure me of victory. She held that thought close and silent. Drwyn would never countenance it if she suggested it, but perhaps she could plant the notion in his mind, arrange matters so that his temper would do the rest.

It would be tricky, though; the thought of an heir to come in a few short months had stayed his hand of late, and he had not even sought an outlet for his lust now that the girl's belly was growing larger. He was not known for such restraint, even with his wives. Ytha's lip curled. Had he actually become *fond* of the wench?

Composing her features, she turned to face him. 'This requires careful handling. She must be stripped of all honour, robbed of any shred of credibility that might make the other chiefs heed her words, should they reach their ears. They must have no reason to trust her. Then when the child is born, I will burn that wench out.'

Drwyn's eyes widened and he took half a step towards her. He stopped when she raised her hand.

'Peace, Drwyn. You will still have her in your blankets and she will bear you many fine children, I'm sure, but I intend to see to it that she cannot so much as light a lamp with her powers. The loss of her foretelling will be a sore one, true enough, but we never knew of it when we drew up our plans, so the absence of it cannot set them awry.'

His hands flexed restlessly at his sides, clenching and releasing a bunch of his thick plaid cloak. A muscle worked in his jaw in time with it.

'I cannot say I like this plan, Ytha,' he grated. 'She's done nothing to hurt us.'

'How do you know? I am certain she spied on us at the Gathering – who knows what she overheard and what she intends to do with that knowledge? She is a snagged thread in the tapestry we are weaving, you and I, and she must be snipped from it.'

'No.'

Had her ears deceived her? After what the girl had done, it was inconceivable that he would defy her, too. Incredulous, she stared at him. 'What did you say?'

'I think you're starting at shadows.' Drwyn refolded his arms across his broad chest, giving her a level look from beneath his brows. 'Do nothing. We wait until the child is born. Women in her way are often given to strange fancies; anything she says can be dismissed as such, and no chief will give it credence. But I will not permit anything that risks harm to my son.' She started to protest and he raised his hand. 'Hear me on this, Ytha. I am the chief.'

And I am the Speaker of the Crainnh! You would not even wear that torc were it not for me, you ungrateful pup!

Oh, it was so hard to keep the words behind her teeth, but she had to, had to. She could not risk losing his compliance, not after all those years, all those plans. But the girl had shaken her – more than she cared to admit, even in the privacy of her own mind. A mere chit had bound her in air and shrugged off her compulsion like rain off oiled leather. How had she learned that trick? How had she become so strong?

'Very well.' Ytha gathered her skirts and dipped the smallest of curtsies. 'It shall be as you say, my chief. But once she whelps, you will give her over to me.'

A curt nod. He was not happy. Well, let him be un-happy. She had more important matters on which to spend herself for the moment, like that child.

17

STRANGE DAYS

❧

After eleven days at sea, the desert heat struck Gair's skull like a hammer as he stepped from the shadows of the *Skimmer*'s stern deck. The steel-blue sky was as hot as a forge, striking white sparks from the waves tossing beyond the harbour mouth. Barefoot sailors swarmed aloft, darting past him as he walked to the railing and squinted against the sun to watch their approach to Zhimandar.

It was not the most prepossessing of places. Sand-coloured buildings girdled a crescent-shaped bay, squat and square as a child's wooden blocks. Behind the city, shimmering in the haze, was a range of low hills of the same sun-dried ochre colour. Nothing green, nothing growing that he could see. Even the ships in the harbour looked dusty and dried out beneath their dead-tree thicket of masts.

And the heat! Not even mid-morning and already he had a headache with it. It didn't help that he had slept even less than usual; the air below decks had been too close and breathless for much more than catnaps, punctuated by the kind of dreams that brought him thrashing awake with his sheet in a tangle. Shading his eyes with his hands, he peered at the approaching city. Once they were ashore, it would doubtless get worse.

If only he'd kept his mouth shut. He'd been so bewildered by the outcome of his trial, so grateful to have been offered a way out of the Holy City, that he hadn't thought through the consequences of what Alderan had asked of him. If he had, he wouldn't be in this predicament, spending who knew how long in this Goddess-forsaken place, dissolving in his own sweat.

Gair mopped his forehead with his shirtsleeve, then wished he hadn't as the least movement made the linen cling uncomfortably across his back. He pulled the shirt away from his skin and flapped it, but even standing at the railing there was barely enough of a breeze to fill the sails. Saints, the heat was brutal.

As the *Skimmer* edged closer to the harbour, shapes began to resolve themselves from the glare. Long stone wharves jutted into the water, backed by tall warehouses and chandleries. Gulls wheeled and shrieked through the forest of masts. Small craft plied the narrow water between the rows of wharves, darting amongst the heavier merchantmen like pond-skaters.

'Welcome to Gimrael,' said Alderan, stepping up to the railing beside him. 'Abode of sun, sand and fundamentalism.'

'I thought the city would be bigger.'

'It doesn't look like much from here, but it's one of the oldest cities in the desert. Only Abu Nidar is older.'

Gair had no patience for a history lesson. 'How long are we staying?'

'A day or two, no more. Long enough to see which way the wind's blowing and obtain some supplies.'

'And then?'

'And then we shall see.'

He bit back further questions. Two days into their journey from the Isles he had realised that Alderan was not going to tell him any more than he already knew, and that was precious little. South to Gimrael was all the old man would say.

South be damned. At least tell me what you're dragging me into!

Alderan glanced sideways as if he'd heard him. 'All in good time, my lad. You'll know when you need to.'

His face must have given his thoughts away – or else the old man simply knew him too well.

'I'll get my things,' he said and headed aft.

As he'd predicted, the heat was worse once they stepped off the pilot boat and climbed the stone steps to the quay. Any breeze off the land was blocked by buildings; in the lee of the dockside warehouses the pale stone underfoot threw the afternoon sun back like a mirror. In seconds Gair's headache had worsened; his skull felt as if it was wedged in a carpenter's vice, and this was just the docks. Saints only knew how hot it would get further into the city. Shifting his bundle to his other shoulder, cursing the sun and the jostle and most especially Alderan, he followed the old man along the waterfront.

Zhiman-dar was unlike any other city he had seen. Instead of the more varied architecture of Mesarild or Yelda, all the buildings looked the same: squarish, rarely more than three or four storeys in height and covered with thick, gritty plaster the colour of pale sand. They piled into and on top of each other in a haphazard

fashion, threaded with narrow alleys. Doors were plain
painted wood, the paint cracked and sun-faded to inde-
terminate shades of brown or grey. There were few
windows, none at street level, and all were narrow and
shuttered. It did not look welcoming.

Even the people thronging the streets had a sameness
about them. They were not tall, and all the men dressed
in loose white or black robes over striped baggy trousers. Gold jewellery on fingers and pierced ears con-
trasted with skins as dark as leather, and black eyes in
closed faces watched the passage of the northerners
without expression.

Occasional stares made the back of Gair's neck
prickle. Every Gimraeli who jostled him or caught his
eye as he stepped out of their path looked more hostile
than the last, though never was a hand raised nor a
frown given. Those who spoke a word or two of common were unfailingly polite, but their heavily accented
speech was hard to follow. He quickened his pace to
keep up with Alderan, who wove through the press of
figures with the confidence of a native. This was no
place to be caught out by a wrong turn.

Rounding a corner, Gair stepped into bedlam. Awnings made from faded blankets and a web of ropes
strung from building to building gave shade of a sort
without offering any relief from the heat, and beneath
them stalls lined both sides of the street in a mosaic of
colour. Between the rows of stalls were more people in
one place than he had ever seen, with scarcely a scrap
of space between them. Dark heads, white robes, colourful veils, all loudly engaged in what was presumably commerce but more closely resembled theatre: he
was surrounded by earnest entreaties and exaggerated
gestures of disappointment or outrage. It was chaos,
and Alderan plunged into it with barely a break in his
stride.

Gair hurried after him. If he lost the old man in the

souq he might never find him again. The awnings appeared to trap the heat and noise of the crowd, turning the screw on his headache ever tighter. Spices and perfumes tickled his nose. Small boys flicking fly-whisks over trays of candies stared as he passed, before their masters cuffed them back to work. Where Alderan found a way through the throng with a nod and a smile, Gair found himself waylaid every yard or two by out-thrust bolts of silk or intricately worked leather goods. Merely waving his indifference was not enough; often he had to physically push past the importunate stallholder and each tiny delay let Alderan get further ahead. Only the old man's distinctive blue shirt distinguished him in the throng.

When a merchant and his customer broke into heated, finger-waving argument, everyone within earshot stopped to watch, forcing Gair to pick his way around them. Except he couldn't: the street was choked with citizens enjoying the spectacle of the two men, now almost nose to nose over a heaped display of fruit, determined to discover who could shout the loudest.

He squeezed through the press into a narrow gap between two stalls but almost at once found his way forward blocked by a broad-hipped, gaudily veiled merchant. She rattled off a volley of Gimraeli and flapped her hands at him as if shooing chickens. No way through there. Over her shoulder he could just see Alderan stopped at the next corner, looking around for him. Turning back the way he had come, trying to keep one eye on the old man at the same time, he stumbled over something and jostled a bearded fellow in the crowd.

'Sorry—' Gair fumbled for the Gimraeli words. 'Your pardon, *sayyar*.'

The man gave him a hard look and grunted something he didn't catch before pushing past. Another robed figure followed close behind him – a woman, judging by the demurely covered head and the burnt orange silks peeping out from beneath the plain white outer robe.

'*Sayyan.*' He stepped back to let her pass, and as she did so she glanced up at him. Perhaps it was to acknowledge his courtesy, or perhaps she had heard him speak to her companion and was curious about this northerner in her city, but all he saw was the colour of her eyes.

She wasn't Aysha. She couldn't be: her nose was too narrow, her plucked and painted brows too perfect, but that glimpse of blue eyes in smooth cinnamon skin was enough to make him believe, for an instant, that she was. Then she walked on, a stranger again, and Gair was left staring after her until her white robe vanished into the sea of other white robes, anonymous as a single snowflake in a blizzard.

Aysha was gone.

A sharp jab at his hip jolted him back to the present. He swung around, ready to snap, but it was the chicken-shooing woman again, firing words at him like arrows.

'I'm sorry, I don't speak much—' Gair frowned, trying to make sense of her rapid chatter with his limited Gimraeli vocabulary, most of it pushed clean out of his head by the appearance of the blue-eyed girl. Finally, the woman sighed impatiently and tugged at his sleeve to indicate that he should move.

'All right, I'm sorry!' Hands held up in appeasement, he shuffled aside to let her through. With more rapid Gimraeli and a series of further prods to press her point home, she heaved her bulk past him and joined the throng of the souq.

Gair looked up the crowded street one more time for the girl, but she was long gone. Part of him wanted to go after her, but what would he say if he caught up with her? What would he do? She didn't even resemble Aysha very much, and besides, the bearded man was probably her husband or father and likely to offer a knife in the belly to an inarticulate northerner who came blundering up. It was a stupid idea, but oh, Goddess, he couldn't shake it.

He raked a hand through his hair. This journey, coming to Gimrael, was a colossal mistake. He should never have come. If only Alderan hadn't— Blood and stones!

Swearing in frustration, he cast around quickly for the old man but couldn't see him at the next corner. He'd been sidetracked only for a minute or two, but it had been long enough for Alderan to pass out of sight. Now he was lost.

Pushing through the crowd, Gair hurried towards the spot where he had last seen his companion, muttering *your pardon* for each jogged elbow on the way. Fresh sweat broke on his chest and back, and under the pack slung on his shoulder his shirt stuck to his skin like a mustard plaster. The deeper he ventured into the souq, the slower his progress became: the Gimraelis, all smiles and bows, simply would not get out of his way.

Eventually he reached the junction with the next street and had to stop. The souq stretched away in all directions, each alley as cluttered and clamorous as the next. His head throbbed. Which way had Alderan gone – straight ahead or left? Gair was tall enough to see over the heads of almost everyone else, even without standing on his toes, but the sagging awnings overhead and the shadows they cast obscured much of his view.

Damn, damn, damn.

He chewed his lip, looking both ways again, then plunged back into the press to follow the busiest street. It was all he could think to do since he didn't dare use the Song – even in Gimrael, where they had little love for the Church, there could be a witchfinder, and he had enough problems without tangling with another one of them.

Up ahead, at the entrance to another cross-alley, he

caught sight of a distinctive mane of iron-grey hair and headed for it, but in a couple of strides he had lost sight of it again. He continued to make for that point, hoping the press might thin a little, but when he had fought his way to the corner, Alderan – if it had been him – was gone.

Four streets converged here, the market stretching away in each direction. Gair turned around slowly, scanning the bobbing heads in the crowd. Dark heads, white robes, no sign of a blue shirt. Round again, standing on tiptoes this time, though it didn't help much as the throng ebbed and flowed around him. There – a flash of colour, disappearing between two stalls off to his left. Weaving through the market-goers as fast as he could, treading on some toes in the process, he followed the elusive scrap of blue down another side alley.

The crowd was thinner here, with fewer stalls, and he was finally able to run a pace or two. Another turn, left then right again, and he dodged around a handcart from which two men were unloading bales of cloth. Nothing else lay beyond it. In this street the stalls had come to an end and there were barely a half-dozen people ahead of him, flickering through the stripes of shadow cast by the scattered awnings, only their white robes visible in the deep shade. Apart from them, nothing moved.

Gair swore again, louder this time. One of the labourers at the handcart glanced at him and said something to his companion, then the pair of them stared, the last bale still slung between their hands. After a second or two, they carried it through a nearby doorway. One slammed the door and shot the bolts after him whilst the other fellow picked up the shafts of the cart and trundled it away.

The street was suddenly very quiet. Gair could still hear the sounds of the souq, but faintly, as if it was several streets away instead of just around the corner. The high sun beat down on his exposed head and shoulders like fists. A sick, heavy pain sat behind his eyes and his feet throbbed in his boots. This was not good.

He peeled his sticky shirt away from his skin and muttered a curse at his own foolishness. Then he shrugged his belongings onto his other shoulder and turned to make his way back towards the market to try to find some trace of Alderan. Maybe he could find a stall-holder who spoke enough common to ask after him. It was the best plan he could come up with.

Before he had taken three paces, he heard a noise behind him that sent a prickling down his spine: the sound of swords being drawn. Gair stopped. That was not good at all. Slowly he turned around.

There were three Gimraelis in the alley with him. They wore the familiar loose white outer robes over their long divided tunics, but also the elaborately twisted head-dresses and sand-veils of men from the inner desert. Two held drawn *qatans*; the one in the middle had his arms folded across his chest and his sword still through his sash, but his stance said he could have steel in his hands in a heartbeat.

Gair's chest constricted. His own sword was thrust through the bundle on his shoulder – Alderan's suggestion, to avoid attracting unfriendly attention. Too late for that – worse, now that he needed a weapon he was unable to draw it cleanly.

'You are a long way from home, my friend,' said the Gimraeli in the middle, his common speech accented but clear. 'Zhiman-dar is no place for *ammanai*.'

Politely translated it meant 'outlanders', Alderan had said, what the desertmen, particularly the deep desert-men, called pale-skinned imperial citizens. He'd declined to give the other interpretation, but it was safe to say it was not a compliment.

'I'm just travelling through,' Gair said. 'I'll be gone in a day or two.'

'Nevertheless.'

'What do you want?'

'You to be gone.' A different speaker this time, the Gimraeli on the left. He took a half-pace forward. The naked blade of his *qatan* flashed blue, reflecting the sky overhead.

Gair held his hands away from his sides, palms down. 'I'm going,' he said, stepping back.

'I think not.'

He froze. He'd let himself lose track of the third Gimraeli. Now a *qatan* was laid flat against his right arm, ice-cold in spite of the heat. Sunlight ran down the edge like quicksilver. A little more pressure, a twist of the wrist and it would take off his hand.

Slowly, he lowered his arms. Careless. If he'd been paying attention he might have avoided this. Now there was no way out that wouldn't leave blood on the ground. His, theirs, it didn't matter. Blood was blood and all things end.

Take a breath, deep and slow. Weight onto the balls of his feet. It was time to dance.

Behind him, an unfamiliar voice murmured, 'I'll take the one on the right.'

Gair resisted the urge to look around. He didn't need to know who was behind him. As the Gimraeli ahead of him darted forward, he tossed his pack off his shoulder and threw himself into a roll. A hot thread of pain scored the point of his shoulder as a *qatan* swung at him and almost missed, but he kept hold of his pack and snatched out his own sword as soon as he regained his feet. The pack itself he flung after the swordsman who had marked him.

The desertman fended off the pack with his free arm, *qatan* flashing in an arc. It met Gair's longsword and glanced off with a fat spark. Across the street, his unexpected ally danced between two flickering blades, his own singing through fluid curves as it blocked and slashed.

Gair had only a second in which to settle his grip before the desertman attacked again. He parried quickly and was almost caught out when the Gimraeli rolled his wrists and brought the curved blade slashing upwards at his belly. Leaping back, he ducked the follow-through and then had to duck again as his opponent whirled and nearly separated his head from his neck.

He thrust himself back upright in time to catch the next slash on his sword. The *qatan* shrieked half the length of the blade and jarred against the longsword's heavy quillon. Black eyes glared at him; Gair threw his weight forwards, slamming his right elbow into the desertman's face. Bone crunched, and as the Gimraeli staggered backwards, sand-veil bloody, Gair swung. A grunt, and the *qatan* clattered to the ground.

The dance went on, but he had the rhythm of it now. It was in his head, in his blood; his sword carved the air into a web of silver around him. Crimson drops glittered like glass beads on a mandala, turning and tumbling through shape after shape before spiralling finally, gracefully, to rest.

Gair blinked and the illusion was broken. Dust and heat filled the alley and the air smelled sticky-sweet as a butcher's shop. Over the thudding of his heart, he heard the hubbub of the souq a street away, but the music to which he had been dancing was gone. Even his headache had dulled, at least for now.

Slowly, he straightened up. He held his sword cautiously at the guard in case the threat was not over, but nothing moved in the alley save his unexpected ally, busy wiping his *qatan* on the shirt of a corpse at his feet. Two other bloody bundles that had once been men lay on the ground nearby, dark stains spreading beneath them. The first time he'd drawn steel against another man with real intent he'd felt a rush of nausea after. This time, he felt nothing at all.

When the desert-robed man was done, he scabbarded his sword and stood up, lowering his sand-veil.

'That was neatly done,' he said. 'A straight blade rarely does so well against a soul-sword. I am N'ril al-Feqqin.'

Gair lowered his own weapon. N'ril was a few years older than him, with lively black eyes and a crescent-shaped scar across his right cheek. He pushed back his headdress, revealing long hair as dark and glossy as a raven's wing held in a tail with a green and gold enamelled *zirin*.

Inclining his head, Gair gave his name. 'The sun smiles on our meeting.'

N'ril grinned, clearly pleased. 'You know the proper response.'

'A friend taught me a little about Gimrael. I owe you my thanks.'

'You owe me your life, I think, but we can discuss a bloodprice later.'

Stooping, N'ril ripped open the other two desertmen's shirts. Each had a tattoo over his heart in the shape of a many-rayed sun. 'Cultists, like the other one,' he said. 'I had not thought to see them this far from the inner desert. Alderan will be interested to learn of this.'

'You know Alderan?' Gair asked, cleaning his own sword.

N'ril flashed him a dazzling smile. 'But of course. He asked me to find you.'

And that explained that. Gair slid his sword into its scabbard and slung his belongings back over his shoulder. 'This is becoming a very strange day.'

'It will get stranger before the sun sets, I think,' said N'ril. 'Strange days usually do. Shall we go?'

'What about them?' Gair jerked his head in the direction of the corpses in the dust.

'Do not trouble yourself – they will be dealt with, and probably feeding yellowtails in the harbour by morning, I would think.' The desertman showed his teeth. 'But we should move, in case they have friends.'

With N'ril leading the way, it took only a few minutes to reach their destination. The house was no different from any other in the street: a wooden door set deep in the wall of a blocky, thickly rendered four-storey building on the corner of a narrow alley. The lower storeys had no windows at all, and those on the upper two were narrow and well shuttered. The blistered paintwork had once been green.

'Protection against the heat, and the storms,' said N'ril, following the direction of Gair's gaze. 'Like a woman, a home wears its true beauty inside.'

He unlocked the door and pulled it wide, revealing a passageway so deeply shaded that Gair was blinded after the intensity of the sunlight in the street. The passageway led into a square courtyard where fragrant herbs and bright flowers spilled from terracotta pots and a fountain burbled in a mosaic-tiled basin, providing an illusion of coolness. Around the sides ran cloister-like walks, the arches picked out with glazed tiles, a different colour for each of the four storeys. Shrieking swallows quartered the brilliant sky above.

In the cool of the shadiest walk stood a long carved table set for a meal. Alderan was taking his ease on a bench beside it, his back against the wall and a cup in his hand. He looked up as they entered.

'All safely gathered in, N'ril?'

'There was a little trouble,' the Gimraeli said. 'Cultists. Three of them.'

'You're sure?'

N'ril nodded. 'They had the mark.'

Alderan grimaced into his cup. 'Something tells me they didn't open their shirts and show you because you asked them nicely.'

'Indeed no! We were quite impolite about it, although they were most rude first.'

N'ril gestured that Gair should take a seat, the sweep of his arm encompassing the bowls and covered dishes arrayed on the table. 'Please, Gair, be at ease in my house.'

'No one saw anything? There was nothing that could connect them to you?' Alderan reached for a tall pitcher on the table and filled two more cups.

'The alley was empty apart from us and them,' said N'ril. 'They had cornered Gair – it would never have ended without bloodshed.'

'We could have done without it, though. I was hoping to slip in and out of Zhiman-dar without attracting any attention.'

N'ril dropped into a chair and tugged off his headdress, tossing it onto the table. 'The Cult is not well liked here. The city has prospered lately through trade with the Empire, and the Zhimandari merchants worship at the altar of commerce. They will not take kindly to any who disturb their devotions. No one will grieve much over those three, except perhaps their brothers-in-arms.'

Now that he was out of the sun, Gair found his headache easing further, enough to feel a little hungry. He explored the dishes in front of him and found sticky boiled rice in one, an aromatic stew with raisins in it in another. A third dish contained some kind of vegetables in a sharp-sweet yellow sauce. A basket held doughy flatbreads wrapped in a cloth. His stomach growled.

N'ril smiled at him as he filled his bowl. 'Sword-work gives you an appetite, yes? Eat your fill, my friend.'

The food was strangely spiced to Gair's northern palate, but for all its savour he might as well have had ashes in his mouth. Nothing tasted good any more. Nonetheless he needed sustenance, so he worked his way through a goodly helping, chewing and swallowing mechanically, washing it down with wine until his stomach was full.

Afterwards he pushed his chair back from the table and stretched out his legs, trying to relax. But his muscles felt tight and twitchy, ready at any second to have him up and pacing, and even when he unfastened the silver *zirin* and shook out his hair the headache wouldn't budge completely.

The quicker this errand to Gimrael was over the better he'd like it. It felt too much like sitting still when what he wanted – what he needed – was to be moving, to be taking the battle to the enemy, not wasting time in some library. He kneaded his temples and sighed.

'So, Alderan, what do you need?' said N'ril, when they had finished eating. 'I can arrange horses, provisions for your journey. Is there anything else?'

'Desert clothing and temporary adoption into your house.' Alderan topped up their cups. 'And news from the capital, if you have any.'

'Not much that is new; still less that is good. When the Cult's Emissary speaks, more and more people are listening. The peace holds, but increasingly only at the end of an imperial lance. Theodegrance has had to strengthen the garrison in El Maqqam and I do not think it will be long before he has to send troops to the other cities as well, maybe even here now that the Cult is bold enough to assault travellers on the street in daylight. When that happens, he will exhaust his desert legions and I fear sending in heavily armed *ammanai* – forgive me – will only inflame the situation.' N'ril spread his hands. 'It is only going to end one way, I think.'

Frowning, Alderan tapped his cup against his chin. 'What's Kierim's position?'

'My princely cousin has a *lyrran* by the tail: he cannot hold on and dare not let go. If he clamps down on the Cult's activities he will offend the tribes who are sympathetic to the Emissary, which will make his rule even more uncomfortable than it already is. But neither can he allow the Emissary and his followers to become so powerful that they have influence enough to force him to cede from the Empire. When the Cult's sway was confined to a handful of deep-desert settlements, they were little more than a nuisance. Now that they are gaining a presence in the cities, especially those which have forged strong links with the Empire, well . . .' Leaning on his elbow, N'ril raised his cup to his lips. 'I would not be in his boots for all the horses in his herd.'

'The Emissary?' Gair asked. 'I thought the Suvaeon executed him after the war?'

N'ril smiled thinly. 'I think perhaps they executed a wild-haired zealot who claimed to be the Emissary, but only he and God know the truth of it.'

Gair blinked. 'You mean they beheaded an innocent man?'

'There's no such thing as an entirely innocent man, Gair,' said Alderan, frowning into his cup. 'Not in a time of war – and there certainly wasn't in that one.'

'But—'

'Does it matter?' The old man's lips twisted as if the wine he was drinking had turned sour in his mouth. 'The Knights exacted their retribution, and justice was seen to be done. Does it really matter whether the man who died twenty-odd years ago, after a failed uprising, was the actual Emissary or not?'

Somewhat shocked that Alderan could be so callous, it took Gair a moment to find his voice. 'It should.'

'In a perfect world, I'd agree with you,' Alderan said, 'but we have to live in the world that is, not in the one we might wish it to be.'

'You must understand, my friend,' N'ril put in before Gair could retort, 'the Cult believes Lord God Himself chooses the Bearer of the Word. Any one of their initiates would gladly sacrifice their own life to protect his – to die in the Emissary's service is to walk the path to heaven.'

Behind Gair's eyes the headache was intensifying again, beating time with his pulse. He rubbed his temples harder, wishing he could will it away. 'Maybe if the Church had executed the right man, we wouldn't be having all this trouble now.'

'If they had, the Cult would merely have heralded a new Emissary. This is not a snake that can be killed by simply cutting off its head.' The Gimraeli broke off a piece of flatbread and sopped it in one of the dishes. 'The Voice of Heaven is eternal, for he speaks the Word of God,' he intoned, and popped the sauce-laden bread into his mouth.

So it really didn't matter, in practical terms, who had died that day. 'Is it likely to be the same man, though?'

N'ril chewed, considering. 'Probably, but I cannot be certain. They say he speaks from behind a curtain to spare him from the sins of the world. Nobody sees him but his chosen preachers, who translate the Voice of Heaven's commandments for the masses.'

'Most of which can be interpreted as "Death to the unbeliever!",' said Alderan sourly. 'An impossible situation indeed. Still, Kierim's an able politician – he'll thread a path through it if anyone can.' He drained his cup and looked over at Gair. 'We should do something about your shoulder.'

Gair glanced at the bloody rip in his shirt. 'It's just a scratch.'

'Even a scratch can turn rotten overnight here, in the heat.'

'I said it's nothing.'

Anger sparked in the old man's eyes again, sudden as summer lightning, gone just as quickly. 'Come and see me when you've got cleaned up. I've a salve that will help.'

Standing up, Gair turned to their host. 'N'ril, is there a bathhouse I can use?'

'Of course.'

The Gimraeli gave him directions to it and where to find his room after. Shouldering his belongings, Gair excused himself and left. He had a feeling he knew what they would talk about next, and he did not want to hear it.

❖

The door into the house swung closed quietly behind Gair, but Alderan rather suspected that if they hadn't been guests, the Leahn would have slammed it. He was coiled up inside like an over-wound clock and had been for the last two weeks, ever since he'd realised he had to come to Gimrael or break his word of honour.

If only the boy could see that this was the best way to stop Savin. But he was young, and all tangled up in the bramble-thicket of his own hurt. Who could blame him for wanting – needing – to lash out, after what he'd been through? Staring into the dregs of his wine, Alderan sighed. *I wish you'd trust me more, lad. I'd tell you all of it if I could.*

From the corner of his eye he saw N'ril reach for the wine jug, and after only a brief hesitation set his cup down firmly and slid it across the table to be refilled. Goddess help him, he needed a drink.

N'ril topped up both cups. Leaning his elbows on the table, he began picking at the last flatbread. Out in the courtyard, half a dozen brown and black birds no bigger than sparrows swooped down to the rim of the fountain's basin, to drink and splash and chatter amongst themselves. From time to time they cocked an eye towards the two men in the shade, watching.

'He has a true gift with a blade,' the Gimraeli said at last. He threw a few crumbs out into the sunshine and watched the birds squabble over them.

'Gair? I should think so, after a decade at the Motherhouse. Whatever else I may think of the Suvaeon, they turn out fine swordsmen.'

'That is not quite what I meant.' N'ril tore off another piece of bread and ate it. 'He did not need my help today, Alderan. He could have stood his ground against those Cultists, all three of them. The way he fights – not reckless, but . . . We call it *qalen al jinn*. I do not know the word for it in your tongue.'

The phrase was unfamiliar, so Alderan translated it literally, word by word. 'Heart of the dragon?'

'Close enough. It means to put one's whole self into a task, to commit to it absolutely, holding nothing back.' The desertman paused. 'Or perhaps with nothing left to lose?'

In a practice yard in Alderan's memory, bright blades rang together, over and over, and sweat pocked the earth floor like tears. 'You have a shrewd eye for a situation, N'ril.'

'Ah. Much now becomes clear.' N'ril helped himself to some of the darkly spiced mutton *tajani*, scooped up on another piece of flatbread. 'Someone close?'

'He won't thank me for telling you, but yes.' Alderan swirled a mouthful of wine around his teeth, remembering, then let it trickle down his throat. The memories were not so easily swallowed. 'Chapterhouse lost some good people to Savin's creatures that day.'

'Mmm. He needs to grieve, I think.'

'We don't mourn the way your people do, with blood,' said Alderan. 'Gair just needs some time.'

In all his visits to the desert, he had seen the grieving ritual only once. He'd climbed a stony hill and found a kneeling woman on the far side, rocking at the foot of a freshly filled grave. Seeing her slice open her own arm and daub the blood on her face, watching it drip from her chin with her tears . . . he'd had to walk away.

N'ril shook his head. 'Let a wound fester for too long

and it will need to be drained. Better to cleanse it now, though it is painful, before the infection takes hold.'

'He just needs time,' Alderan said again. He hoped with all his heart that was true, and tried to ignore the voice at the back of his mind insisting he was wrong. 'He'll heal or else he'll learn to live with the hurt, like the rest of us.'

18

A BARGAIN

❦

Gair turned his shoulder towards the looking-glass. The cut was as neat as a surgical incision, oozing a little bloody fluid and stinging from the soap he had washed with. He dabbed it carefully with a washcloth. It was shallow enough that it should heal without stitching, unlike his shirt, which was only fit for rags. He eyed the bloody clothes by his feet, then abruptly kicked them across the tiled floor out of his sight.

Leaning on the washstand, he closed his eyes. Saints, he was exhausted. Once the battle-blood had cooled, the heat and food had done their work and left him ready to crawl into his bed. Not that it helped these days. It didn't matter how much or how little he slept, he always felt the same: hollowed out, like old bones.

I miss you, carianh.

'You've lost some weight.' Alderan's voice sounded from the doorway.

Gair glanced up, then looked away. 'Food's too good at Chapterhouse. I was getting fat.'

'Gair,' the old man said gently, 'if I rendered you down for lard right now there wouldn't be enough to grease a skillet. Saaron could use you as an illustration to teach first-year anatomy.'

'So?'

'Sit down and I'll see to your shoulder.'

'It's fine.'

Alderan said nothing, just shrugged off his scrip and nodded to the stool beside the washstand.

'I said it's *fine*. Leave me alone, Alderan.'

The old man hooked the stool with his foot, dragged it over to where the light was best and pointed. Gair's jaw tightened, but he wrapped the towel more tightly around his waist and sat down. Maybe if he submitted to the unwelcome ministrations he would be left in peace.

Alderan took his time setting out jars from his scrip on the edge of the washstand, carefully scrubbing and drying his hands. A brief tug at the Song summoned a glim to supplement the light from the oil-lamps on the wall whilst he examined the wound.

'It could use stitching,' he mused.

'Just put some salve on it, it'll close overnight.'

'And as soon as you lift your arm over your head to put your shirt on it'll open right up again.' Eyebrows raised, the old man peered at him as if over the top of spectacles. 'I've been patching folk up for a long time, lad. I know what I'm doing.'

'Fine, stitch it, then.' Gair didn't even try to keep the irritation from his voice.

He felt Alderan's gaze linger on him but didn't turn his head to meet it. Instead he stared at the tiled floor, plucking at the thin gold ring piercing his left earlobe. Something else that irked him: the stupid thing snagged his comb and collected soap when he shaved – he still hadn't become accustomed to it, and in his present mood he didn't want to.

Behind him he heard Alderan moving about, the

plink of a needle into a saucer, the gurgle of liquid being poured. Then the old man said, 'I know you don't want to be here, Gair.'

That was an understatement. 'So why did you make me come?'

'It was necessary.'

Gair snorted. 'But you won't even tell me what I'm supposed to be doing! All I know is that you told me to pack my things and go and see Saaron to get my ear pierced – the reason for which still escapes me, by the way.' Gair winced as the needle penetrated his skin. 'Damn it, warn me first!'

'That ring is a sign of a Gimraeli male's passage into manhood.' Alderan tied off the stitch and snipped the thread with scissors. 'There's deep desertmen with paler skin and lighter eyes than most Gimraelis and some of them married into the Feqqin, so we'll pass you off as a distant cousin. N'ril's going to provide us with house colours, but we might have to dye your hair.'

Now Gair looked around. 'Dye my— Blood and stones!' Another stitch had caught him off guard. '*Dye my hair?* Why are we going to such lengths to pass as desertmen, Alderan? How long are we going to be here?'

'I don't know, exactly,' the old man said calmly. 'Maybe weeks, maybe longer. It depends what I find in El Maqqam, so until I do know, it's best we stay as unobtrusive as possible. Now sit still, I don't want to stitch you crooked.'

'Why can't you just Heal it?'

'I've told you, that's not my gift.'

'Neither is sharing information,' Gair muttered.

Curved needle poised for the next stitch, Alderan frowned at him. 'You gave me your word freely, remember? Rather unseemly now to complain about having to keep it.'

'That was before I knew what you would ask of me in return!' Gair snapped back.

'It's for your own good.' The needle bit into his skin again.

'That's why Goran wanted to burn me, as I recall.'

The scissors clattered into the washbasin. Leaving the needle bedded in Gair's shoulder, Alderan cocked his fists on his hips and glared at him, blue eyes glinting beneath the rampart of a ferocious scowl. 'Would you rather I'd let you go north? When it would almost certainly have killed you?'

'Yes!' Gair thrust himself to his feet and began prowling the small room. 'At least then I would have felt I was doing something useful instead of dragging my arse around here.'

'I know you won't believe me, but I understand what you're feeling.' Given Alderan's expression, the words were unexpectedly soft. 'I understand better than you will ever know. But it's too soon.'

'It's never too soon for justice.'

'Is that what you think you'd be doing? Seeing justice served? For the love of the saints, lad, think with your head instead of your pain. If you go after Savin now you'll lose, and then your life will have been wasted just as surely as Darin's or Donata's or anyone else who died that day. Is that what you want?'

'I want him to pay for what he did.' Gair's voice trembled with the rage baying inside him. It leapt and slavered like a hound at a gate and it was all he could do to hold on to its chain.

'I want that too, believe me, and my vengeance has been brewing for a lot longer than yours,' said Alderan. 'But there's nothing to be gained by rushing into it and far too much to lose. If you want to be useful, come with me to El Maqqam. Help me in the archive. If we find what we're looking for and it leads us to the starseed, we can pull Savin's teeth for good.'

'I won't rest until he's cold in the ground, Alderan. I swear it.'

'And I'd like to be there to see you finish him, but what's more important? Killing one man, or saving the thousands of others who'll die when the Veil comes down?'

'But if Savin's dead, the Veil remains intact and we can save ourselves all this sneaking around!'

'Maybe,' the old man said, reaching for his scissors. 'But if you take him on and fail, he will tear the Veil apart and open up the Hidden Kingdom. Then there'll be even more work to do, one fewer Guardian to help me do it and Savin will still be here.' He spread his hands. 'Remember what happened the last time you faced him, at the Five Sisters? Do you really want to go through that again?'

Yes! the rage roared. *I'd do it a hundred times, a thousand, if it meant he paid his debt!*

Vengeance was beating its drums, pounding in Gair's ears with the rush of his blood, and he could hardly think for the din. His hands clenched into fists. The muscles knotted in his arms, his shoulders, until the sword-cut began to throb around the needle.

When Alderan touched his arm, he all but flinched.

'Come on, lad – sit down,' the old man said. 'There're still a couple more stitches to do and I can't reach all the way up there.'

Gair stared at him. *When I think of something you can do for me, I'll ask, and then we'll be square,* the old man had said, in the inn in Dremen. And he had agreed, given his word. Now his honour shackled him as surely as forged steel.

Alderan's head tilted, eyes twinkling. 'Or shall I fetch a stepladder?'

The gentle humour had an effect, allowing some of the tension to drain out of Gair's limbs. Raking his hands through his hair, he returned to the stool, then sat in silence whilst Alderan finished stitching his shoulder. He barely flinched at each stab of the needle, the odd tugging sensation of silk thread drawn through flesh. But the rage still chewed at his gut and he had to grind his teeth together to keep it from bursting out.

Finally the old man snipped the thread on the last stitch and dropped his scissors back into his scrip and the needle into its saucer. Then he dabbed some salve from a small jar onto the cut.

'How long?' Gair asked.

'Hmm? The stitches can come out in about a week. Leave your shirt off for an hour or so if you can – let that salve soak in.'

He should have been clearer. 'How long have you been waiting?'

'Oh. About twenty years, give or take.'

It was almost as long as Gair had been alive. He flinched, eyes fluttering closed. Only six weeks, and he was burning up inside. 'Does it get any better?'

'It gets easier with time,' Alderan said, wiping his hands. 'Whether it gets better is up to you.'

❊

Six stalls were arranged around two sides of the yard at the back of N'ril's house. The sound of Gair's boots on the cobbles was enough to bring five heads out over the stable doors, five pairs of ears flicking inquisitively. He walked slowly from stall to stall, scratching whiskery chins and tugging satiny ears through his fingers as the horses nudged his pockets for treats.

He had always loved horses, the warm sweet reek of the stable-yard. They made such easy companions, both trusting and trustworthy. They didn't care what he said as long as his tone was kindly, and if he said nothing at all they didn't sulk or flounce away. They judged a man by his actions alone. He could think of worse creatures with which to spend his time.

The sixth stall appeared to be empty. Certainly there was no response when he clicked his tongue. He leaned on the door to peer into the gloom and a shadow surged towards him. Ivory teeth snapped at him, then the horse whirled and crashed two steel-shod hooves into the stable door hard enough to bounce it on its hinges.

Gair ducked to one side. 'Whoa there!'

The seething shadow in the stall glared back at him and stamped a warning.

'It's all right, I'm not here to hurt you.' He held out his hand.

The horse did not approach. Its feet shifted restlessly in the straw and its head tossed again and again, but it came no closer. Maybe he should have brought an apple from the kitchen. This animal would not easily be won over.

'Are you always such an early riser?' called N'ril.

Gair looked around as his host crossed the yard towards him. 'It's a habit I can't seem to break,' he said.

'The early hours are the best part of the day here, before the worst of the heat.' Leaning on the wall by the door, N'ril tipped his head towards the stall's occupant. 'I see you have met the she-demon.'

'I went to say hello and she tried to kick the door down.'

N'ril grinned. 'That is how Shahe says good morning. Would you like to see her?'

When Gair nodded, he shot the bolts on the stall door and swung it wide. The mare leapt out into the sunshine with a furious whinny, kicking and bucking her way around the yard. She was a shard of midnight, with the dancing feet and wide, dished face of a purebred *sulqa*. Fragments of straw flew from her wavy mane as she tossed her head.

'Is she not magnificent?' N'ril demanded. 'Like a thunderstorm made flesh!'

'She's superb.'

Gair took a cautious step towards the horse. Shahe

backed away, watchful. One ear fixed on him whilst the other swivelled back and forth and she blew gruff warnings through her nostrils.

'Shahe,' he crooned. 'Shahe.'

Both ears snapped upright, the tips curving to attention. Gair took another half-step, holding out his hand, alternating calling her name and clicking his tongue.

She snorted, and that was all the notice he got. Her head snaked towards him and he had to snatch his fingers away as her teeth clacked together barely a hair's breadth from them.

'Perhaps I should have warned you,' said N'ril. 'She was sired by Lord Kierim's warhorse.'

'Is she yours?'

'She is now. She belonged to my brother.' Something in the desertman's tone made Gair look his way. 'My brother is dead.'

Goddess. 'I'm sorry for your loss, *sayyar.*'

N'ril smiled and dipped his head but his eyes remained sad. 'You honour me, and my brother's name,' he said. 'Shahe was the pride of his stable.'

As if she had heard him, the mare threw up her head, lips curled back from her teeth. Gair took another careful step towards her, hand extended again. She arched her neck, restless feet scraping on the cobbles.

Only a few more inches and he could touch that satin-black hide. She really was stunning. Anxiety twitched and skittered over her shoulder and she tossed her head again, huffing hard.

'Easy, girl,' he murmured. 'Easy now.'

Her ears slashed back and forth. She lifted her chin, staring down her nose at him as his fingertips drew closer. An inch more and he was able to put his palm on her neck.

'There. Not so bad, is it? Not so bad. Good girl.'

He patted her, ran his hand down her high-crested neck. She snorted and feigned a nip at his arm, then stood more quietly as he walked slowly around her to admire her conformation, always keeping one hand in contact with her so she knew where he was.

The mare was a fine example of her breed, straight-backed and deep-chested, and carried herself as if she knew it, too. When he came around to her head again, she fixed him with fiercely intelligent eyes and dared him to find fault with her. And he couldn't.

He scratched under her jaw, utterly captivated. She tried to bite him again, but he was half-expecting it from her now and pulled his hand away in time. 'Is she saddle-broken?'

'She is,' N'ril said. 'Do you think you can ride her?'

'With your permission, I'd love to try.'

'She was mild as milk for my brother, but I am unsure how she will take to another hand on the rein.'

Gair tried to keep the disappointment from his face, stroking Shahe over and over. 'Of course. Forgive me, I shouldn't have asked.'

'I think you misunderstand, my friend. I intended my words as a warning!' Now there was laughter in N'ril's voice. He lifted a bridle down from its hook outside Shahe's stall and brought it to Gair. 'Try not to hurt yourself when she throws you.'

Gair grinned back. 'I'll try not to hurt your pride when she doesn't.'

Holding the bridle down by his side with his right hand, he murmured soothingly to Shahe. She stared along her nose at him but stood firm. He brought his left palm slowly towards her muzzle and held it steady whilst she sniffed then lipped at his fingers.

'Good girl,' he told her.

He offered his hand again, this time with the bit flat across it. Shahe dipped her nose and in a smooth movement he slipped the bit between her teeth and the crown of the bridle over her ears. She tossed her head, mouthing at the bit, but let him fasten the throat-strap and

lead her back to N'ril, who waited with a saddle over
his arm. It was elaborately finished in the desert style,
with silk tassels and silverwork across the high saddle
horn and cantle, all red and black to match the bridle.

When Gair set it on her back Shahe aimed a lazy
cow-kick at him, then sucked air in as he fastened the
girths. He prodded his fingers into her ribs. 'Stop that.'

She grunted and blew out, letting him tighten the
girth a couple more notches. Moving around to hold
the opposite stirrup, N'ril chuckled. 'That trick is not
new to you, I think.'

'My first pony used to do the same thing. He dumped
me on the ground regularly until I worked out why the
girth kept slackening.'

Reins gathered loosely, he grasped the saddle horn
and set his foot in the stirrup. He mounted slowly, carefully, but the mare still took exception to his weight on
her back. She reared and whinnied as soon as his rump
touched the saddle, then crabbed her way across the
yard, jerking at the reins. Gair didn't try to stop her. He
kept a light rein and let his body move with hers until
she settled and allowed him to walk her around the
yard.

'You know horses,' N'ril said, sounding impressed.

'I grew up around them, and when I joined the
Knights I worked with them almost every day.'

Gair stroked the mare's neck to soothe her as she
danced sideways. Powerful muscles bunched and flowed
under him; she was strong, and restive from being sta-
bled too long. He let her work out the kinks for a minute or two then nudged her back towards her stall with
a squeeze of his calves.

N'ril smiled his approval. 'A daughter of the sands
responds best to a gentle hand,' he said. 'But you knew
that already, yes?'

Gair's fine mood evaporated like dew. 'What do you
mean?'

'Your *zirin* – it is inscribed in Gimraeli, but the other pattern is Leahn, is it not? I assumed it signified the union of two houses, that your wife—'

'She wasn't my wife.' Pain knotted itself around his heart, made it hard to speak, hard even to breathe. He fixed his eyes on a fragment of chaff in the mare's mane, willing it not to blur. 'What did Alderan tell you?'

'That you were mourning, nothing more.' N'ril rubbed Shahe's nose. 'Forgive me. I did not think before I spoke.'

Gair blinked the sting from his eyes. It wasn't N'ril's fault. 'There's nothing to forgive. It's still a little raw, that's all.'

'I understand. My brother went to the God over a year ago and my heart remains broken.' Folding his arms, N'ril stepped back a pace or two and looked Gair and Shahe over, from crown to hooves. 'You look well on her,' he pronounced, with a firm nod. 'I have no heart to ride her myself, and it is cruel to keep her in a stable. She belongs out in the wind.'

'I'd love to try her paces,' Gair said. Impulsively, he added, 'And I'm going to need a mount.'

The desertman tilted his head, considering. 'You know something of horseflesh,' he said. 'What do you say she is worth?'

There was still a goodly amount of silver in Gair's purse. 'Twenty marks.'

'Twenty? If we were not friends, I would be insulted. A hundred talents and not a copper less.'

'Twenty-five,' Gair countered and N'ril threw up his hands.

'Outrageous! I cannot take less than seventy, in gold.'

'Then you'd beggar me.'

'She is pure-bred! Her lineage is better documented than the Emperor's.'

'That's not difficult. Men take more care with their

bloodstock than they do with their own seed. Thirty, in silver.'

'Bah! Sixty-five.'

'Thirty-five.' Gair tugged one of the oakmarks from his pocket and tossed it to him.

'These? No money changer in the city would take them.'

'Holy City marks are the least-adulterated coins in the Empire. Almost pure silver.'

'Too many here remember the wars, my friend.' The desert-man scrutinised the Lector of Dremen's face and the Oak stamped into the obverse, then sighed. 'Fifty, though it will break my mother's heart.'

'Forty, and you can throw in the tack.'

There the price hung, for a long, long moment. Ears pricked alertly, Shahe seemed to be waiting, too. Then N'ril asked, 'Have you travelled the sands before, Gair?'

'Never. Why?'

'Because you haggle like an Isfahan carpet-seller.' A brilliant smile lighting his face, the desertman flipped the coin back. 'Forty.'

He held out his hand to seal the contract. Gair reached to take it and a monstrous concussion shook the morning air. Shahe shied, snatching their hands apart as dozens of smaller, sharper detonations punctuated the rolling boom. Above the rooftops, thick black smoke stained the sky, spangled with blue and silver sparks.

'What the hell was that?' Gair had his work cut out not to be unseated as the horse reared and plunged. Another barrage of explosions sent more sparks showering down. 'Are those *fireworks?*'

'I think so,' said N'ril, shading his eyes to study the drifting smoke. 'Coming from the docks.'

With gentle pressure from heels and hands, Gair gathered Shahe up and reined her in circles around the yard, though her laid-back ears and jinking gait told him she remained deeply unhappy.

Behind N'ril the houseboys crowded into the yard to chatter and point. A shirtless Alderan pushed through them, a towel around his neck. A shrill whistle made him look up just in time to see a scarlet flower blossom across the deeply blue sky.

'Fireworks?' he exclaimed.

A small face craned over the edge of the roof of the main house, shouting in Gimraeli. The speech went far beyond Gair's store of simple phrases, so he looked to N'ril.

'A warehouse at the east dock is on fire,' he translated.

Alderan mopped his dripping face and frowned. 'The east dock is the northern merchants' enclave,' he said. 'And barely a day after three Cultists ambush a lone *ammanai* in the souq. They're escalating.'

Unease prickled down Gair's spine. 'Are we in danger?'

'Not immediately, but I'd say we're less safe than we were yesterday. N'ril, how quickly can you get those supplies ready?'

'A few hours. Tomorrow at the latest.'

Clicking his tongue against his teeth, Alderan tugged at the towel around his neck. 'Sooner would be better.'

'I will see what can be done.' With a quick bow, N'ril hurried out of the yard.

'Maybe I can help.' Gair made to dismount, but Alderan shook his head.

'N'ril has enough to do without watching your back as well.'

'They jumped me – it wasn't my fault, Alderan!'

'Not for what you did, no, but for what you are.'

'Ammanai.'

'And with your height you stand out like the maypole on a village green. Even if you hadn't killed those men, you draw attention.' Alderan shook his head. 'I'm sorry, Gair, but there it is. Until we can make you look more like a desertman, it's best if you stay out of sight.' He stroked Shahe's velvety nose. 'I see you've found yourself a horse. I suggest you spend some time getting to know her. Once we're out of the city your life might depend on her.'

19

ASTOLAR

❖

Tanith slid open the screens and stepped onto the slate-flagged terrace behind her house. The day was barely begun, skeins of mist still drifting across the face of the Mere, the hills beyond pale shapes in the haze. On the silver water, tightly furled lily buds stood ready for the day like spears above shields of leaves. Far out on the lake, a grebe dipped something from the water and shook its head, scattering pearly droplets in the air.

Astolar. She had missed this place. She had grown up listening to the sigh of the birches, the gentle thunder of Belaleithne Falls, and throughout her five years on the Isles she had filled her room each evening with memories of her homeland. Deep moss beneath her feet instead of carpets, arching trees above her head instead of beams and stone, all had eased the pain of separation.

Yet five weeks ago, when she'd stepped off the jetty onto the earth of her people, there'd been no jolt of connection. On the long ride inland from the port to

Carantuil she'd recognised the deep lakes, the wide-hipped roofs and layered towers rising above the trees, but all at a remove, as if seen through thick glass. Even there, standing on the terrace of her own house on a sweet spring morning, she felt more like a stranger than one of the White Court's daughters come home.

A breath of a breeze ruffled the lake and she shivered, pulling her silk robe more closely around her. Five years she had spent amongst humans, learning to be a Healer. She had become accustomed to the world of men; perhaps too much so. Perhaps that explained why Astolar's touch on her soul still felt so cool, so distant. They would have to learn to love each other again.

Behind her, she heard the careful tread of her housekeeper, the chink of porcelain on the glass-topped table as her breakfast was laid out, but she didn't turn. She had no appetite. Next week she would stand before the Ten as House Elindorien's heir and the butterflies that had been multiplying in her stomach since she took ship from the Isles left no room for food.

Without a sound, a sleek head broke the surface of the lake. Smaller than a child's and covered in dark fur, the creature had a broad snub muzzle and tiny ears towards the back of its skull, almost hidden in its pelt. Wide black eyes watched her.

Lady? enquired a voice in her mind.

'Good morning,' she said.

Lady! The head disappeared and re-emerged moments later, close to the edge of the terrace. *Lady has returned!* Several more heads popped out of the water and crowded around the first. *Pretties? Did you bring pretties, lady? We like pretties! We like you. We missed you!*

'You saw me yesterday. That wasn't very long ago.'

We still missed you.

Tanith couldn't help but smile. The saelkies had no more sense of time than small children: to them an hour was as long as a week, and a year as short as a day.

Kneeling on the dew-damp stone, she held out her hands to them. 'Then I missed you too, little ones.' The saelkies jostled each other to be the first to be petted, pushing their heads into her hands like kittens and chirring happily. 'No pretties today. Another time, eh? But I have something that's even better than pretties. Do you know what it is?'

Sweets! they chorused, bobbing up and down in the water.

She pushed herself back to her feet and went to the table that had been so carefully set for her to break her fast. On her plate was a sweet cinnamon roll which she broke into pieces, one for each saelkie, and threw them out into the lake. Sleek dark bodies dived after the scraps, supple as otters.

'You should not encourage them.'

Ailric's voice was rich and liquid as a cup of buttered rum, warming her from the inside out. In the three years since she'd last heard it, it had lost none of its power to intoxicate. Willing herself to stay clear-headed, she turned to look at him.

The high collar and nipped-in waist of his long coat accentuated his lithe frame, and House Vairene's cool jade green suited his golden Astolan skin. His pale-blond hair was still long, but swept back from his face and barbered into neatness. The unkempt, heart-stoppingly beautiful boy-poet was gone. The man framed by her screen doors was as polished and perfectly sculpted as one of the statues in the palace gardens.

Only his eyes were unchanged. The colour of fire, they danced and sparked and promised to burn her again if she got too close.

'I like the saelkies,' she said, amazed at the steadiness of her voice. 'I find them diverting.'

'I find them a nuisance.'

She smiled. 'Perhaps you shouldn't scold them, and then they wouldn't leave dead fish in your shoes.'

'If they did not leave dead fish in my shoes, there would be no need for scolding.' He came towards her, holding out his hands to take hers. 'I am pleased to find you amongst us once more. Astolar has felt empty without you.'

'It's good to be home.' Tanith tilted her cheek for his kiss. 'You look well.'

'And you are even more lovely than I remember,' he said, squeezing her fingers. 'Please forgive me for not being here to greet you when you arrived. I had business on our estates in the north that could not be postponed.' He leaned to kiss her other cheek and his face lingered next to hers. 'I have waited so long for your return,' he whispered. His breath caressed her ear, sending a familiar tingle skittering up her arms.

'Events conspired to delay me, I'm afraid.' Tanith stepped back, increasing the distance between them.

In the corner of her eye the soft-footed housekeeper reappeared to set an additional place at the table before vanishing into the house, discreetly closing the screens after her.

'Ah yes. Your father told me about the one who was riven.' Ailric drew out a chair for her and saw her comfortably seated before taking a seat for himself, folding his long coat carefully around his elegant frame. 'A human.' He made it sound like *peasant*.

'A patient,' Tanith corrected him gently. 'To be a Healer is to treat all as equals, without fear or favour, regardless of race. Tea?'

'Thank you.'

She busied herself with cups and teapot, aware of his gaze on her, moulding the robe to her body like rain, or as if his long-fingered lutenist's hands were on her. *No.* That was in the past now. It was pointless to breathe new life into ashes best left cold. But her body remembered his touch and ached for its loss.

She settled back in her chair, teacup cradled in her lap. 'So, what brings you out this early in the day?'

He picked up his own cup but did not drink. 'I wanted to see you as soon as I returned to Carantuil. I was hoping to escort you to the Hall for your presentation to the Court next week.'

Keeping her voice light to mask her sudden unease, she said, 'You think the Ten are so daunting that I need an escort? I used to play with dolls in the Great Hall as a child. Berec carved a wooden horse for me with his own hands when I was four.' She sipped her tea.

'But you are not four any more, with your mother still beside you and the Succession as distant as the moons. Your mother is gone, and you are House Elindorien's only heir.' Amber eyes watched her through a wreath of steam rising from his cup. 'Would you not welcome the company of a friend?'

If she walked into the Great Hall on his arm he would appear to be her consort, and the Ten would expect her to give him her troth. She could not allow that.

'Friends are always welcome, but I must face the Ten alone. As High Seat of House Elindorien I cannot appear to be leaning on anyone.'

'Not even a friend?'

'Not even a friend.'

Ailric lowered his cup to its saucer untouched and looked out across the lake. 'I spoke with your father before I left for the north. He gave me his blessing to ask for your hand.'

Tanith's tea suddenly tasted bitter; when she swallowed it left her mouth dry. 'It's too soon for me to think about marriage.'

'I will wait.' Putting his cup aside on the table he leaned towards her, reaching for her hand. 'Only let me love you, the way I have loved you since I first saw you, swimming in the Mere.'

Memories assailed her like a storm of flower petals, each one bright and tender. Hours lost in music, lost in each other. Kisses that felt as if they would never end; fingers twining together as if they would never let go.

Swallowing another pang, she said carefully, 'That was a long time ago.'

'Not so long! My feelings are unchanged.'

Oh, spirits keep me. 'We were little more than children then. It was wrong of us to let things develop as they did – we both knew it.'

Her words struck home like arrows plunging into his flesh, crumpling his earnest expression. It *had* been wrong – she'd simply been too young, too drunk on each kiss to heed the words of caution wiser heads had given her at the time. Leaving him behind to go to the Isles to pursue her dream of becoming a Healer had almost broken her heart, but she'd promised to return whenever her studies permitted, and he'd promised to wait for her. But each time she'd come home, full of stories of the people she'd met and the things she'd learned, the more selfish and impatient he'd become.

Why do you waste your time and talent on those humans? You belong here in Astolar, with me.

In the end, it had been that more than the distance that drove them apart. Now there could be no going back for either of them.

She stood and walked to the edge of the terrace to stare across the Mere to the distant hills, outlined in thread-of-gold by the dawn. A step sounded behind her. His hands came to rest on her shoulders, then caressed them.

'I love you, Tanith. I always have.'

She shut her eyes, drew a deep breath for strength.

'I told you three years ago that it was over between us. In truth, it should never have begun.'

Opening her eyes again, she watched the first sun burning through the mist, the saelkies leaping into the light as they chased each other through an endless game.

'You know that is not true.' The caress moved down her arms to her waist, his embrace folding around her. His body pressed against her back, his lips against her hair. 'Let me love you again and you will remember.'

He kissed her neck. His breath stirred the tiniest hairs on her skin, his Song stroking over her just as delicately. Desire yawned and stretched in the depths of her belly and she had to stiffen her knees or surrender herself into his arms again.

'Please. Don't.'

'Who else can touch you like this?' he whispered. 'Who else knows your body as I know it?'

Kisses roamed down her neck to her shoulder; his Song curled around hers and left it thrumming. Tanith's teacup fell from her hands and smashed on the flagstones at her feet.

'Let me love you. Be my bride and we can rule Astolar together.'

To lean back into Ailric's embrace would be so easy. To let his caresses steal under her guard and disarm her, let him fulfil her promise to her father that Astolan seed would bear fruit on Astolan soil. Except in growing up they'd grown apart, and the boy she'd once loved had become a man she didn't recognise, all polished court manners and cool disdain, and her heart was filled with longing for someone else.

With a gasp she twisted out of his arms. Shards of porcelain crunched under her bare feet, sharply painful.

Ailric stared at her, face gilded by the new sun, hands open towards her in appeal. 'Tanith—'

'There's no future in this,' she said, ashamed that her voice quavered. 'What we had . . . it ran its course years ago. It's over.'

He lowered his hands, eyes still fixed on her. 'Your body says something different.'

With every quick, shallow breath Tanith was conscious of the treacherous points of her nipples beneath her silk robe. She straightened it uncomfortably and refastened the sash. 'I think you should leave.'

Flame-coloured eyes slid over her as intimately as any caress, knowing her as surely as his lips or his hands had ever done. 'Is that really what you want?' he asked softly.

'Go, Ailric! Please.'

He smiled. 'Of course. Forgive me – I have overwhelmed you. This is an important time for House Elindorien, and for you. I cannot expect you to give your answer now.' Gathering her unresisting hands in his, he raised them to his lips. 'Until later, my love.'

Then he bowed and left her alone on the terrace.

Tanith stared at the carved screens long after they had snicked closed behind him. Had Ailric heard a word she'd said to him? Or had he simply chosen to ignore her? She could never marry him – she would never – yet he'd brushed her refusal aside as if he knew better than she what she thought and felt.

How dare he?

As soon as she moved towards the house pain stabbed through her foot. The broken teacup. She hobbled to a chair and sat to lift her foot onto her other knee. A shard of porcelain, curved like a claw, had been driven into her flesh. Gritting her teeth, she pulled it out; scarlet welled from the wound and she fumbled for a napkin to staunch it.

Blood shed on a parting made a poor omen. Division. Estrangement. Loss. Tanith winced and applied more pressure as the pale fabric turned crimson between her fingers. Spirits forfend that it was not an omen for her presentation to the White Court.

20

ONE THROW
OF THE BONES

❧

Ytha watched impassively as Teia summoned a flame above her outstretched palm. The music of it was insubstantial as a whisper yet she could feel its heat on her skin. That always amazed her, no matter how many times she practised it. She let the flame grow until it was as long as her finger, then held it steady. Perfect.

With a snap of her fingers, the Speaker snuffed it out. 'Again.'

Dipping into her magic, Teia brought forth another flame. Again Ytha extinguished it and Teia winced as the power snapped back at her.

'Again.'

This had been the pattern for the entire lesson. Ytha demanded that she complete the simplest tasks over and over again and taught her nothing new. And nothing satisfied her. Teia was either too slow or too sloppy; the flame was too small, too large or else had some other flaw only the Speaker could see. The one time she had dared to speak up and ask what she had done wrong, she had earned an open hand across her cheek hard enough to make the stars spin. Her lip still felt fat and bruised.

She summoned a new flame and held it until she felt Ytha's magic draw in, then let go of her own accord to spare herself the sting as it was severed.

One sandy brow rose. 'Do not defy me, child. Again!'

Teia dipped her head, misery thick in her throat. She should never have tried to dissuade Ytha from her pact with Maegern. She had learned nothing new from her in the two weeks since then. She had simply been made to repeat the same trivial exercises, over and over like a slow-learning child, and been punished arbitrarily for her trouble.

Once, she had tried to complain to Drwyn, but he had barely even heard her. With the snows too deep now for hunting and more falling every day, he was interested only in the growing roundness of her belly, which he loved to stroke and talk to as if the child within could hear him. He remained convinced she would bear him a son, whereas she had grown more and more certain it would be a daughter. She saw colours in the baby's sleeping mind every time she so much as thought of it, and they responded to her touch the way the power inside her rose up to her call. It would be a girl. It would be the end of her, by summer's trinity moon.

'Attend, Teia!' Ytha snapped.

With a start Teia realised the flame over her hand had blazed up high enough to threaten the hangings on the wall. Macha's ears, she had to concentrate! Quickly she drew it down to a more modest size. Her palm stung from the heat.

'I'm sorry, Speaker. My concentration slipped. I will do better next time.'

'See that you do.' Ytha's lip curled. 'I agreed to teach you, not sit weaving my thumbs whilst you daydream.'

Another fire took hold, this time inside. 'Perhaps I would pay closer attention if you were actually teaching me something!' Teia flung the flame aside and it winked out. The Speaker blinked.

'I have sat here for an hour every day for two weeks since I tried to warn you about treating with the Raven and you have shown me *nothing*! You make me repeat exercises I mastered a month ago, reprimand me for no good reason, and I've had my fill of it.'

She had barely a flicker of warning before Ytha's magic lashed out and caught her around the throat. It was not tight enough to choke her, but she certainly could not swallow. Teia felt as if she was about to be lifted off the cushion, bloated belly and all. A shiver of fear chased over her skin.

Ytha's cat-green eyes narrowed. 'I think you forget your place, child,' she said. 'You are my apprentice and you will study as I direct you. If that means you sit here and call flames until the heavens crack and the stars fall down, you will do so. I will not tolerate disobedience.'

'Yes, Speaker,' Teia managed. The band of air around her neck unwound and she sagged.

'Now, a flame.'

Resigned, she called on the power again. The new flame flickered and jumped like a lamp in a draught and she had neither the will nor the energy to steady it. There was no point. No matter how perfect she made it, Ytha would only slice through her magic and send it back into the dark.

One of Drwyn's warriors scratched at the door-curtain then pushed his head inside. It was Harl, and he looked uneasy. 'Forgive me intruding, Speaker,' he said diffidently.

'Yes, man, what is it?'

He swallowed and dropped his gaze from the Speaker's ire then looked back at her, and Teia realised it was the first time she had ever seen him afraid.

'They are coming.' He stepped back, holding the curtain aside.

Ytha rose, straightening her skirts. Green eyes glinted. 'How far?'

'The other side of the valley and running fast. Less than an hour away.'

A cold, cold smile lifted the corners of Ytha's mouth. 'I see.'

She picked up her staff and settled her snow-fox robe across her shoulders. 'Ask the chief to attend me at the lookout to receive our guests, then assemble the clan at the meeting place. We must give our guests a fitting welcome.'

'Yes, Speaker.'

Harl ducked out and Ytha followed him. She paused on the threshold, one raw-boned hand holding the curtain as she looked back at Teia, still cross-legged on the floor. 'We are not done, you and I,' she said. 'You will obey me, or I will snuff you out.'

Then she was gone.

Teia waited until she could no longer hear footsteps, then pushed herself to her feet as fast as her belly would allow. She had hoped to be long gone by now, but between tending to her chief and her lessons from the Speaker, there had been so little time to make things ready. Now it might be too late. The Hounds were nearly here.

In the sleeping chamber, hidden under the bed-furs, she had concealed the last few pieces of clothing she needed. Her sealskin jerkin. A leather tunic lined with fur, somewhat moth-eaten but still serviceable. An old shirt of Drwyn's that she had carefully altered. Good boots, which she changed into from her kidskin house-shoes – her skirts were long enough that no one should notice – and a few other things.

Hastily she pushed everything into a basket and tucked a provisions sack over the top. There. She'd used this subterfuge a dozen times now, and never been challenged; women with baskets on their hips walked to the stores so often each day it was unremarkable, yet each time she was afraid the hammering of her heart would give her away before she got halfway across the meeting place.

She took a deep breath, but it did nothing to calm the frantic knocking on her ribs. Time had finally run out. She couldn't even spare a few minutes to say goodbye to her parents. She had to be well away before Ytha came back.

※

Ytha's skirts whipped about her ankles on the raw wind, but the icicles that bearded the cave entrance were dripping in the sunshine. No new snow had fallen for several days and between the sunlit skies and the heavy feet of the hunting parties, the ledge was almost clear of snow and ice. She stepped out to the edge and shaded her eyes against the sun as she looked down the valley.

Two shapes loped from the foothills. She could hardly make them out, but the track they cut through the deep snow ran arrow-straight towards where she stood. Neither rocks nor ridges nor the thousand streams that criss-crossed the ground were enough to divert them and they ran as if they would not miss a stride until they reached their destination.

Yes. Maegern had kept Her word, despite everything that wretched girl had said.

A smile tugged at Ytha's cheeks. This would hand her the hearts of all the chiefs. When they saw this demonstration of her power they would have no room for doubt, no stomach for scepticism. They would swear to Drwyn at the Scattering, all of them. She glanced at the sky, where the thinnest crescent of the second moon lingered above the pale ghost of the third. *And under a trinity moon* . . . the first victory would be *hers*.

Boots scraped on the stone behind her and she looked around. Drwyn stepped out to join her, squinting against the brightness.

'So the Hounds come,' he said.

'Yes, my chief.' Ytha dipped him the merest bob of a

curtsey and could not keep her smile from widening into a grin.

'Teia's prediction came to naught, then.'

'Apparently so.' By the Eldest, she would rub the girl's face in this and enjoy every moment of it.

'If this weather holds, we should be able to start moving north soon.'

'You will not wait for the thaw?' The Speaker schooled her face to composure, but it was a struggle to suppress the fierce excitement that boiled up in her breast.

Drwyn shook his head. 'No. My father used to tell me: if a job is to be done, it is best done quickly. I've already sent out more scouts. It'll be hard travelling at first, but the sooner we move, the sooner we can call the clans' war captains together. I have some ideas about our strategy to put to them before the Scattering.'

Do you indeed? You'll not deviate from the strategy I gave you last winter, my wolf-cub, or you risk repeating Gwlach's mistakes. But I'll be interested to see if you hit upon anything I have missed. You might even surprise me. 'Very wise,' Ytha said.

She studied the Hounds again. They were closer now, and she could make out their lolling tongues, see the plumes of snow they raised as they breasted drift after drift. How much ground they had covered in just a few minutes! Each bounding stride consumed six or eight spans of snow-covered earth. She could almost hear their paws breaking the frost crust.

'You will be the greatest chief the Broken Land has ever seen, Drwyn,' she said, pulling her snow-fox robe close around her. 'Your name will sing loud in the histories.'

'Louder than Gwlach's?' he asked.

'Of course. Gwlach lacked the battle-craft to match the breadth of his ambition. You have seasoned warriors in Eirdubh and the others; if you heed their counsel and strike bravely, I think you will have little to fear.'

He chuckled, dark eyes snapping. 'And I owe it all to my clan Speaker, Ytha the wise,' he said.

With the effrontery she had come to expect from the man, he slipped his arm around her waist and pressed a whiskery kiss to her cheek. But not even that could cast much of a shadow over her mood. The Hounds were coming and she would be triumphant. The clans would have a Chief of Chiefs to lead them back to the lands of their ancestors, and she would sit at his right hand. Nothing could prevent that now, no matter what that cursed girl said or saw. Once she'd dropped her calf, Ytha would take great pleasure in burning her out, and if Teia happened to be left mute or drooling in the process, well, so much the better.

A small, tight smile curved her lips. The important thing was that Drwyn knew to whom he owed his coming glories.

She would make sure he did not forget it.

⚜

No one spoke to Teia as she made her way to the stores. She had to skirt the meeting place to get there and it was already filling up with people, talking anxiously amongst themselves about the sudden call to attend.

The few who hailed her she acknowledged with a smile and a wave and a harried nod towards the basket on her hip. She had chores to do, it said, or she would be happy to stop. They returned her wave with nods of their own that said they understood, she had a chief to attend, so she could hurry on without worrying about hiding her nervousness from their eyes.

By the time she reached the store-caves and ducked into the shadows to catch her breath, her heart was stumbling like a three-legged deer. Anxiety pressed down so hard on her breastbone that she could barely fill her lungs. Under her clothes, her skin prickled with sweat.

Please let everything still be there. The child kicked sullenly. *Macha look kindly upon me, mother to mother.*

She had hidden saddlebags in the furthest store-chamber, transporting them by the same ruse she had just used. Quickly she emptied her things from the basket and carried them through to where – praise Macha! – the saddlebags were still tucked out of sight behind the dung-sacks. She had been desperately afraid that some-one would stumble across them when they came seek-ing fuel, but the stores had lasted well. Teia dragged the bags out and stuffed her last few things into them wher-ever she could. The buckles had to be forced closed when she was done.

She had been secreting stores for weeks, things that would keep, like salt fish and dried berries, oatmeal and flour, as well as her warmest clothes; the bags were so bulky she could scarcely carry them. Only with some puffing and cursing did she manage to get her shoulder under them. Now she would have to be quick. She had to fetch her horse from the corral, saddle him up, then make her way outside.

It sounded simple enough, but there was one prob-lem she had been trying not to think about until the time came because it made her bowels turn to water. There was only one way out of the caves: to reach it she would have to cross the meeting place under the eyes of the whole clan.

When she reached the horse-pen her back was near to breaking from the weight of the saddlebags and her own swollen belly. Panting, taking short, quick strides so she could keep herself moving smoothly, she turned towards the saddle rails and there was her horse, already tied up and waiting. Not the pretty grey mare Drwyn had given her, but her own slab-shouldered dun gelding Finn, with a saddle blanket already over his back.

She almost swallowed her tongue when she saw her father with Finn's saddle on his hip.

'What are you doing here, Da?'

His pepper and salt moustaches twitched. 'I could ask the same of you, my Daughter, but I already know.' He heaved the saddle onto the horse's back and cinched it tight. 'I know what Ytha's about, Teisha. I saw her go up to the lookout and went straight to warn you but you'd already left your quarters. I guessed I'd either find Finn gone, or you here.'

He lifted the bulging saddlebags from her shoulder and slung them behind the saddle, tying them on securely. Finn bared his teeth at him, but without any real malice.

'I have to go,' she said miserably. Tears stung her eyes and she held out her arms to him.

He gathered her up as if she were still a small child and held her close. 'I know, Teisha. I wish I could have done more to help you.' He kissed her forehead and wiped her eyes with his hard thumbs. 'There now, don't cry, sweetling.'

'She knows, Da, I'm sure of it. She's treated me with nothing but contempt since I tried to warn her.'

'I heard you used your powers against her,' he said.

'Only to stop her when she turned hers against me.' She hugged her father tight one last time and stepped back. 'I have to go now, Da. It's the only chance I'll have. While she has the whole clan watching her, she'll be too drunk on her triumph to notice me.'

Her father looked doubtful. 'It's risky, Teisha. You're wagering it all on one throw of the bones.'

She shrugged. 'It's all I can do.'

He squeezed her shoulders fiercely and kissed her on both cheeks.

'Then go quickly and may Macha watch over you.' His voice was even gruffer than usual as he pushed Finn's reins into her hands.

'Da, please get away if you can, before it's too late. Promise me.'

'My word on it. Now go!'

Clansfolk crowded the meeting place when she reached it. Every one of them, from the smallest child in its mother's arms to the most grizzled ancient, faced the raised platform near the entrance where Ytha stood with Drwyn. The Speaker held herself upright, her cheeks flushed from the cold outside. Her right hand rested on the waist-high shoulder of one of two massive Hounds. The other lay at her feet.

'Mother preserve us,' Teia breathed.

She felt herself falling, tumbling headlong into a whirling vortex of light and darkness. This was her dream, her vision, exactly as she had seen it.

Blindly she put out a hand to support herself, but Teir was not there. He had returned to the war band lest he was missed, and there was only the cold stone of the cave wall to keep her upright. She clutched at it, sure she was about to fall.

'People of the Crainnh!' Ytha spoke clearly, distinctly. The acoustics of the chamber amplified her voice so all could hear her. Triumph throbbed in every word.

'As you can see, Maegern the Eldest has favoured us with two of Her Hounds, Her aid, just as She promised. They stand here before you as proof of Her word. With the Wild Hunt at our side, we can be assured of victory. We will succeed where Gwlach failed and sweep the invaders from our lands once and for all. We will buy back the honour of our people with the southerners' blood!'

The war band roared their approbation. Spears drummed on the floor in time with the cheering.

Still dizzy, Teia pushed herself away from the wall. She had to move, take advantage of the diversion whilst it lasted. She would only have one chance at this. With a quick tug on Finn's reins she began to circle the meeting place to the side furthest from the platform.

It was slow going. The chamber was so crowded that

there was little room for her laden horse to pass; she had to nudge elbows and press backs to clear a way for him. Most of the clansfolk moved without a backward glance, too enthralled by Ytha's speech and her hulking companions to pay attention to people moving behind them, but Teia felt one or two curious gazes latch on to her as she passed. Her heart leapt in her throat. Her hands were sweating but her mouth was so dry she had no spit to swallow.

Closer now, the crowd a little thinner. Everyone watched the Speaker and her monstrous allies as she spoke of the glory to come, exhorting them to still wilder cheering. Finn's hoofbeats would surely be smothered in all that din.

Beneath her boots she felt the first rise in the floor. She had made it to the ramp; now came the most dangerous part. In order to reach the passage she needed she would have to ascend until she was at the same height as the Speaker and clearly visible to everyone in the crowd. Surely someone would call out and give her away.

Finn's head rose clear of the crowd; she ducked in front of him to walk on the other side and let his bulk hide her. Now his neck, followed by the saddle horn. Sick with fear, Teia kept walking. As the ramp rose it began to curve around behind Ytha, so that the more exposed she became the further the Speaker would have to look around in order to see her. Not far now. Just a few more yards and she would be safe.

Someone in the crowd gasped and Teia felt a terrible crawling on the back of her neck, as if fire ants had been tipped down her dress. Ytha's presence blasted into her thoughts like an ice-storm.

I see you, Teia.

She stopped, her feet suddenly too heavy to lift. Peering under Finn's whiskery chin she met Ytha's gaze. The Hound at the Speaker's side cast baleful eyes in her direction and grinned.

'Come out where we can see you, child.'

Slowly she stepped past the horse to face her Speaker. Now that she was caught she felt calm, resigned. This was it, the endgame. She had a fair idea how it would play out. Teir had told her she was gambling on a single throw of the bones, but truthfully she had laid her bet against an even fainter hope than that. Now there was nothing left to lose.

She dipped into the music of power and spun an orb of cool pale light above her head. 'Can you see me now, Ytha?' she asked. Her voice was steady.

'Where are you going?'

'I'm leaving the clan.'

At Ytha's shoulder she saw Drwyn frown and reach as if to touch the Speaker's arm. Ytha tilted her chin a fraction and his hand fell back to his side.

'I see. And where do you propose to go?'

'As far from you and your folly as possible. I'm only sorry that I can't take everyone with me to spare them what is to come.'

'And what is that? The Hounds are already here, Teia. Our victory awaits us.'

Teia took a deep breath. She could keep silent no longer; she had to speak what she had seen and hope someone heeded her. Maybe even Drwyn could be persuaded to listen to reason. But then she met his gaze and realised that the Hounds' arrival had crushed that fragile hope like a warhorse trampling new grass. He might be more tolerant of her now, even respect her a little, but he had eyes only for glory.

'If you ride out with the Hunt, Ytha, it will turn on you.'

The Hound lying at Ytha's feet hoisted itself onto its paws and turned to face her, holding itself utterly still. From deep in two throats came growls like a mountain yawning.

'You know I have seen it. You saw the truth of it for yourself, when you took me for a blood scrying.'

Ytha's lip curled. 'I saw a child's imaginings, that was all. You have played me false for years, girl, hiding your Talent from me in defiance of clan law. Why should I give credence to any words spoken by a proven liar?'

A sigh rippled through the crowd assembled below the platform. A thousand eyes turned on Teia, but she was wrapped in her magic and the weight of their gaze slid off her like water.

'It was a foretelling. In your heart of hearts you know it to be true. The Raven is not to be trusted. She has given you Her word, but no proof that She means to keep it.'

'These Hounds are Her proof!'

'Those Hounds do Her bidding, Ytha, not yours.'

'Teisha, what are you doing?'

Teia looked down. Her mother was pushing through the crowd, scything folk aside with her plump elbows. Her face was crumpled with worry.

'I'm doing what I have to do, Mama. Someone has to point out her folly whilst there is still time to undo it.'

Mocking laughter echoed around the chamber.

'Listen to the child!' Ytha scoffed. 'She dares talk to her clan Speaker of folly. You are the one being foolish here, Teia. Heed your mother and return to your home. Your chief will be expecting his woman at his hearth-side.'

Teia lifted her head. 'No.'

Ytha's sandy brows arched. 'This will be the last time you defy me.'

Anticipating the whip-crack of compulsion, Teia threw her magic into a shield around herself before it struck. A clanging, discordant note sounded in the song inside her as power met power and was shattered. Ytha flinched.

'And that will be the last time you try to compel me. I am not afraid of you any more.'

With a snarl the Speaker snatched for her magic again but thanks to her lessons Teia was quicker. A hand of solid air slapped Ytha across the mouth and sent her staggering backwards.

'Wretch!' she shrieked. A drop of blood trickled from her lip, black in the pearly light. On her hand, the starseed winked.

Hammer-blows struck Teia's shield and rebounded harmlessly, though every one made the shield quiver like a drum-skin. Even Finn appeared to sense it, whickering and tossing his head against the reins in her hand.

Over and over Ytha lashed out. Each weaving was wilder than the one before, less refined, then finally the Speaker clenched her fists at her sides and threw back her head. 'Kill her! Kill the traitor!'

Drwyn grabbed her shoulder. 'No! She carries my son, Ytha!'

'Take your hands off me!' Ytha snatched at his hand, raking the back of it with her fingernails when he would not relax his grip.

'I command you as your chief.' His dark eyes glinted dangerously.

She rounded on him and jerked herself out from under his hand. 'And I am your Speaker,' she raged. 'Hounds, kill her! Eat your fill!'

The two yellow-grey beasts exchanged the briefest glance and then dropped their rumps to the stone.

Ytha glared at them. 'Up! Up, I say!'

'You cannot command them, Ytha,' Teia said. 'I told you. They answer to no one but the Raven Herself. Now I am going and you will not try to stop me. Our ways part here. May the Mother take pity on the Crainnh.'

Chirruping to Finn, she walked the last few yards up the ramp. The heaviness was gone from her feet; nothing Ytha could do would stop her now. Nonetheless the space between her shoulder blades itched in anticipation of an arrow from one of Drwyn's men.

'Go, then,' the Speaker spat after her. 'Go to the Lost Ones and see what welcome awaits you, if the winter does not finish you first!'

'What of my son, Ytha?' cried Drwyn. 'Stop her!'

Teia turned her feet towards the passage that led up to the open air and kept walking. She had tried her best. There was nothing more she could do now except leave.

Distorted shouts echoed up the sloping tunnel from the meeting place, soon drowned out by the hollow *clop* of Finn's hooves as he plodded along beside her. She tried not to think about the enormity of the task she had set herself, which rolled and boomed around inside her head like a plains thunderstorm. Instead she clung tight to her belief that she was doing what she had to do as if it was a coal in a fire-pot that would give her a warm fire one day, if she could just keep it alight through the storm.

Finn snorted and shook his head as he caught the scent of outside. She patted his sturdy dun shoulder affectionately. 'At least I have one friend left, eh?' she murmured. Running footfalls sounded behind her. A hard hand snatched her arm and spun her around to face Drwyn. He had a long knife in his fist.

'I cannot let you go, Teia,' he said. 'One wife bore me naught but a daughter. The plague robbed me of the next and took my boy along with her. I will not lose another son.'

'No, Drwyn.' She shook her head. 'You'll have to find yourself another brood-mare. You'll get no sons from me.'

He pulled her towards him, the knife level with her throat. 'I will have my heir, if Ytha has to cut him from your womb.'

The knifepoint pricked the tender skin at the base of

her neck. Teia wrapped his hand in air and pushed it away from her. In his face, consternation warred with rage as she overpowered muscle and bone with only her will.

'I carry a daughter, my chief. I am of no value to you.'

'You lie!'

Teeth gritted, he tried to press the knife home again but his effort succeeded only in making his boots skid backwards on the wet rock. He crashed to his knees and the knife skittered away down the slope.

'I speak nothing but the truth,' Teia said. 'I know what I have seen and I know the truth of it.'

Her light drifting at her shoulder, she turned her back on him and with Finn at her side continued her climb out of the caves. Behind her, Drwyn howled.

Teia closed her ears to it, concentrated on setting one foot infront of another as she walked away from everything she had ever known. There could be no going back now. She had tried to warn Ytha, tried to make her see reason, and she had failed. She had tried to show her clansfolk the truth, and she had failed. She would have to find another way to avert disaster.

Only one force had turned back the massed war bands before and that lay to the south. She prayed that the iron men of the Empire would listen to her when her own Speaker had not.

21

YTHA

❧

By Aedon's swinging balls, the girl had struck her. How *dare* she?

Ytha dabbed at her mouth with the back of her hand and tasted blood. Her lip stung as if a physical blow had landed instead of mere air; she explored it with her tongue and felt torn skin where it had been cut by her teeth. The girl had *struck* her.

Fury boiled through her veins, heating her face, roaring in her ears. The temptation to go after the girl and deal back what she had been dealt was almost overwhelming. No one defied a Speaker like that – no one! And to do it with the Talent, in front of the clan . . .

Her fists knotted in her mantle, crushing the snow-fox fur. *I am the Speaker of the Crainnh, you insolent cuinh!*

With deep breaths she mastered herself again. As Speaker, she must always be in control of herself, even more so as the Speaker to a Chief of Chiefs. Layer by layer, she rebuilt the composure she had lost whilst the temptation to lay about her with her fists, to smash and rend, capered around the edges of her awareness. She could not afford to surrender to it, not before her people, or she would lose them for ever.

Below the water-formed terrace on which she stood, the clans-people milled uncertainly. Whispers scurried around the meeting place like rodents, furtive and anxious. Glances darted between her and the passageway, from which the fading *clop* of hooves could still be heard.

She had to rescue the situation, and quickly.

'People of the Crainnh!' Her voice snapped their attention back to her again. 'Do not be deceived by a frightened child. Our course holds true, and we will be victorious. Put your trust in the Eldest and your chief, and no harm will come to you.'

The crowd stared at her. They weren't convinced; they needed something more.

'Was it true what she said?' someone asked. 'Will the Hunt turn on us?'

'Whose word do you trust?' Ytha scoffed. 'A foolish girl's, or Maegern's?'

Mutters flitted through the crowd at her casual invocation of the Raven. Let them mutter; she was not afraid.

A plump, homely woman pushed to the front and stood with her hands on her round hips, frowning. Teia's mother – what was her name? Ana? 'My daughter is no fool, Speaker. If she says she has seen this, I believe her.'

There must be no room for doubt. Ytha lifted her chin, cooled her voice. 'I am sure you do. As her mother, I would be surprised if you did else. But I have seen her so-called foretellings too, and she is wrong.'

Now the cavern fell silent.

'I made bargain with one of the Eldest, and She promised us Her aid if we give Her ours. She sent these Hounds –' she let her hands rest on their massive necks '– as proof of Her intent. What has Teia given us for proof? Only words. Only her fears.'

She paused to let that sink into their minds. Her timing here was key – possibly even more important than the speech itself. With the right cadence, the right inflection, the people would convince themselves that hers was the only logical conclusion to draw. Already she could see the doubts forming, in the way they looked at their neighbours, the lift of a shoulder here, a nod there. Yes. They would be wholly hers again.

'I took Teia's fears seriously. I cast her blood into the waters and read there what she had seen. She saw our victory. She saw the Wild Hunt unleashed, sweeping us to freedom, and the restoration of what was taken from us so long ago.'

'That's not true!' Ana burst out. Her husband caught at her arm, trying to quiet her, but she shrugged him off. 'Teia told me you refused to believe her visions!'

'She misinterpreted what she saw.' With a shrug, Ytha added, 'Teia is a child. When the truth would make us think poorly of them, children lie.'

'A child?' the girl's mother repeated, incredulous. 'You thought she was old enough to warm his bed!' Face pale with anger, she thrust out her arm to point across the cavern.

Drwyn was emerging from the passage leading up to the air, wiping his long dagger on his sleeve. For one giddy instant Ytha thought he'd used it, until the wet on the blade proved to be only water. A pity he hadn't silenced the little bitch once and for all, but no matter. The winter would do it for them.

This was her moment. She could feel it, the moment in which all would be won or lost, tingling over her skin like a weaving. Now.

'Your daughter was shown great honour by the chief. He gave her gifts as a sign of his esteem and made her his intended bride. And what has she repaid him with? Betrayal.' The entire assembly caught its breath. A little fury crept into Ytha's voice. 'Yes, betrayal! She has flouted clan law, thrown the chief's generosity back in his face, and now she rides south to warn the faithless that their doom is come upon them.'

'But leaving in winter?' exclaimed one of Drwyn's captains, a grizzled knot of a man with a face that was more scars than whole skin. 'She'll never survive the snows – or the wolves will take her. You all saw what happened to Joren.'

Fresh voices murmured their agreement. They were almost hers again.

Ytha leaned on her staff, gathering the crowd up with a look. 'If she cares so little for us, why should we care for her? I name her outcast. If any of you would mourn her, you have until the sun's rise. After that, her name is not to be spoken. Teia is no longer a daughter of the Crainnh.'

Drwyn came to stand next to her, sheathing his dagger with a *snick*. In a lower voice, pitched so that only Ytha would hear, he said, 'Speaker? A word.'

After the crowd dispersed to speculate amongst themselves, she joined him in his chamber. He had his shirtsleeve rolled up and was bathing the bloody scratches She had left across the back of his hand in a basin of water. Ytha let the curtain fall closed behind her, rings tinkling.

He glanced up and scowled. 'I mean to go after her,' he said. 'I'll take ten men, and have her back before dawn.'

By the Eldest, the man had barely the sense he was born with. 'And make a liar of me in front of the whole clan? A clever move, my chief.'

'I want my son!' He threw the sodden washcloth back into the water so forcefully it splashed all over the carpet.

'You don't know what she's carrying – it could be a girl, or a two-headed goat for all I know! I couldn't delve the child. She masked its aura somehow – if I hadn't been able to feel the fullness of her womb I'd barely have discerned she was in pup!' That still grated, jagged as sawgrass. How had the girl known how to do that? Though it pained her to admit it, even in the privacy of her own mind, Ytha wasn't sure she could do it herself. *What other skills had the deceitful little bitch acquired? What else could I have learned from her?*

Grunting, Drwyn snatched up a towel and dried his hands. 'She told me it was a girl, but I don't believe her. I think she said that to make me leave off pursuing her.'

Yes, that was a likely deception. Ytha studied her chief with slightly less scorn. *You're not entirely as stupid as you look, are you, Drwyn?*

'Her belly seems full for her progress, but I never saw her naked. How did she look?'

Drwyn blinked. 'She looked pregnant.'

Men! 'Did she carry it low, like this,' curving her hands in front of her to illustrate, 'or was it all out front, or up high?'

He considered, rolling down his sleeve. 'Round,' he said at last. 'She looked round, like a fruit.' His hands began to make a shape in front of his own stomach, then he caught himself and stopped, embarrassed. 'Her hair was softer, too.'

Ytha pursed her lips. The signs were too mixed to be sure, plus it was always difficult to predict the first time, when the woman's muscles were still firm and strong. She sighed. 'Then I cannot say for certain. But you had best let her go, my chief.'

His fingers stilled on his shirt-laces and his expression hardened. 'Why?'

'For one, we are too close to the Scattering for you to take your eye from your goal,' she said, irked that she was having to explain this to him yet again. After Teia's defiance, daring to strike her like that, she would not stomach more of it from him. 'And for two, you will not undermine me in front of the clan if you expect to be named Chief of Chiefs at the next full moon!'

Eyebrows raised, he stared at her. 'I am still chief of the Crainnh.'

'Only because I made you so!' she fired back. 'Don't ever forget who put that torc around your neck!'

'How can I, when you remind me of it every hour of the day?' He reached for his coat and pulled it on with quick, angry jerks. 'I am not your lapdog, Ytha, to roll over on command.'

'Ingrate!' In a heartbeat her power was in her hand and she flung out a fist of air that hit him squarely below the arch of his ribs. Whooping for breath, his knees weakened, then failed, and he crashed to the floor. She seized his chin and lifted his head.

'Without me, you would still be waiting for your father to die,' she snarled. Her fingers ground into his cheeks. 'Without me, you are *nothing*. Remember that.'

He gurgled something unintelligible, leaking spittle over her hand.

'The girl is gone, and good riddance. I will not see all my planning go for naught because of her. If an heir is so important to you, I'm sure you can find another willing *cuinh* to plough.'

She released him and he slumped onto his arm, coughing and gasping.

'We go on. Tomorrow I will read the sky and if the weather will hold fair, we make preparations to ride for the Scattering.' Picking up the discarded towel, she wiped her hand. 'Clan law says I cannot lead the Crainnh home again because I am a woman, and a woman cannot be chief. For that I need a man.' She dropped the towel in front of him. 'I am not fussy who that man is.'

22

TRIAL-AT-ARMS

❧

A stiff breeze whipped across the moors from the distant Laraig Anor, snapping the banners out from their poles behind the exhibition lists so they shone like painted metal in the pale spring sunshine. Ladies clutched their coifs as they made their way to their seats, whilst their men shouted greetings to folk in the opposite stands. Ansel wondered how many of those shining faces were due to blue skies and good humour and how many to the servers busy amongst the throng with their trays of refreshments.

'A good day for it,' Danilar said.

A gust of wind made the canvas awning boom overhead. Ansel grunted. 'Aye. It's rare to be so warm this early in the year.'

The steady southwesterly that had melted the snow on the shady side of the tors and thawed the greening turf enough to allow the tourney to go ahead had given him some relief from his killing cough, and made the pains in his joints a mite easier to bear, although he still required a number of thick down pillows to shield his hips from the hard wood of his seat in the pavilion. He shifted irritably, and the Chaplain shot him a concerned look.

'Are you well, Ansel?'

'Well enough, for a spavined old nag who should have been put out to pasture years ago.'

Danilar's lips twitched as he hid a smile. 'And how is our beloved Elder Goran?'

'Frankly, I couldn't care less – he's the Lord Provost's responsibility now. I just want to enjoy the day.'

Down in the lists, a herald appeared in white and gold livery, a large Oak worked in gold thread on the front of his tunic. The last few spectators scrambled to find their seats and a couple of latecomers in Curial scarlet hurried up the steps to the benches below Ansel just as the herald removed the ribbon from his scroll and began to read.

'My Lord Preceptor, Elders, ladies and gentlemen, it is my great pleasure to welcome you all to the third and final day of the Grand Tourney, on which we shall see contested the final trials-at-arms for those novices of our Order now seeking to advance to Knighthood in the glory of our Goddess Eador.'

In the same clear voice, pitched to carry over the crack and snap of the banners, he announced the day's programme of events. Ansel paid him scant attention, busy punching his pillows into a more comfortable arrangement. Not that it would last long; no matter what he did, in five minutes he'd have to do it again. Damn his age! Too many years in the saddle, and too few of them left. Anxiety didn't help, nipping at him like lice in his drawers with no way to scratch until the tourney was over. Chewing on curses he didn't dare utter, he shifted again.

Danilar chuckled. 'Saints, you're more anxious than Selsen is!'

'I can't help it,' Ansel growled, then smiled benignly and nodded to acknowledge the polite smattering of applause that followed the herald's announcement.

'He'll do fine, I'm sure of it. He's top of his group for mounted sword and second for sword afoot. Even the grand mêlée didn't faze him.'

'But the joust is where the glory lies.' Ansel thumped his pillows again.

'Despite being the least useful of the Knightly disciplines,' Danilar remarked, then patted Ansel's arm. 'Relax. I saw him in the novices' tent this morning and he was cool as you please.'

'Easy enough for you to say "relax",' Ansel muttered. 'I haven't been this nervous at a Grand Tourney since I was competing for my own spurs.'

In the lists the tilt-marshals were setting up the targets. Bright brass rings were hung from hooks on wooden carousels at either end of the lists for each pair of novices to tilt at, with the first to collect five rings on his spear and return to the start line declared the winner of the round.

In the first draw, Selsen competed in the sixth heat of eight, winning easily and brandishing the five rings on the start line before the other novice had collected his fourth. The citizens gathered on the lower slopes of Templemount roared their approval, whilst the more gently born in the banner-decked pavilions applauded – including those Elders who were actually paying attention to the contest. Most of them, however, appeared to be talking amongst themselves, with a degree of head-shaking and gesticulation that set Ansel's ears to burning.

It was impossible to hear anything above the thunder of hooves and the panting of horses as pair after pair of novices strove to progress to the next round, and with the Elders' backs to him he couldn't even attempt to read their words from the shapes of their mouths. He fidgeted in his seat, frowning.

Danilar leaned over, voice pitched low. 'What's wrong?'

'There's too much talk.' Ansel nodded at the rows of scarlet robes below him, from which came only scattered applause at the end of the next heat.

'They're still buzzing over what happened last month,' said the Chaplain. 'Don't pay it any mind.'

Last month. Well, that had been enough to keep even

a House of Eador in gossip. He had almost died, right there in the Rede-hall in front of those same scarlet robes, facing down Goran's attempted coup and defeating it by the narrowest of margins. Despite the unseasonable sunshine, Ansel shivered. *Defeating it with the chill hand of death already on my shoulder.*

There was so little time left and so much still to accomplish. He – or more accurately, the young librarian, Alquist – still had to find Malthus's missing journal and uncover the real reason Gwlach was defeated. If his suspicions proved true it would be a bitter pill for the Order to swallow, but if they could not face their own sins, what right did they have to castigate others for theirs?

With some effort, he forced his thoughts away from the journal. Vorgis was already suspicious; Ansel didn't dare antagonise the Keeper of the Archives any further by intensifying the search or commandeering more staff. That precious book would come to light in its own time. Right at this moment he had to concentrate on the tourney. By the end of the day he would know whether or not all his careful planning had been in vain.

More applause snagged his attention as it rippled from the lower pavilions, punctuated with a few cheers as the good burghers of Dremen felt the effects of their refreshments. A grinning novice was galloping the length of the arena with five rings nestled on the neck of his spear; across the lists, his opponent flung his own weapon to the ground in a temper as the trumpeters blew a flourish to signal the end of the round.

Ansel peered over the heads of the Curia to watch the Master of Swords, Master of Horse and Master of Arms conferring at the judges' table.

'Come on, come on,' he muttered. A page appeared at his elbow to offer him a goblet of wine, but he waved the boy away. At last the three Masters completed the draw for the next round and handed the sheet of paper to the herald to announce. 'Finally!'

He dismissed most of the names until he heard the one he was listening for. Selsen had been drawn against the boy who had won the final heat, and they would compete last.

More agony for his nerves. Waiting. Hoping. Knowing Selsen would do well, having observed the preceding two days' events, but worrying nonetheless. Worrying most of all that his concern would show on his face, for it would never do for the Preceptor of the Order to display favouritism. He could not afford to, not at any cost.

In the end, he needn't have fretted. Selsen survived that round and the next two and recovered from a heartstopping stumble in the final, when the horse lost its footing in the churned turf at the third turn, to win the event by a nose.

Relieved, Ansel sat back in his chair to watch the victor's parade around the lists. Spear-butt propped on toes and the five brass rings chiming to the rhythm of the horse's trot, Selsen nodded graciously to the applause whilst the other novices clustered at the paddock rail whistled and punched the air.

Ansel couldn't help but smile. Selsen's easy grin had won more than a few friends at the Motherhouse. The lack of a voice had proved no barrier; in fact several of the novices had asked to be taught some thieftalk, much to the consternation of the novice-master who could not find a way to punish them for speaking in the refectory when they hadn't actually made a sound. As Preceptor he'd had to take a hand to enforce the silent contemplation of the Goddess's bounty on the table, but he'd been hard pressed not to laugh.

'See, Ansel?' Danilar prodded his knee. 'Didn't I say the boy would do well? The Daughterhouse at Caer Amon can be proud of that one.'

'Aye, and his mother too, I reckon.' *Selsen owes it all to you, Jenara. You had the raising of that splendid child. How I wish you could be here today!*

In the lists the tilt-marshals prepared the ground for the final event, trundling heavy rollers up and down the hoof-marked turf and moving racks of blunted ash lances into position, but Ansel didn't see them. All he could see was a sunlit cobbled courtyard with wild roses on the wall, and a little girl in a yellow dress hanging daisy chains around his neck.

Jenara. He hadn't let himself say her name, hadn't let himself even think it, in so long. It still sounded like music, even in his mind.

'Will she be here to see him take his spurs, d'you think?' Elder Festan, in the row below, had twisted around in his seat.

'The Superior at Caer Amon tells me Selsen's mother took holy orders some years ago,' said Ansel. 'The Tamasians, I believe, on Sanctuary Isle.'

'The leper colony?' Festan made the sign of blessing. 'I suppose she won't, then.'

'Did you know her well, Preceptor?' asked Ceinan, from further along the row. A hint of a smile played around his lean features. 'You appear keen to see her son succeed today.'

Just what do you think you know? 'I am keen to see any gifted novice do well, Elder,' he said casually. 'Selsen will be an asset to our Order.'

'I'm sure he will.' Ceinan's voice was smooth as buttered silk. He looked down at his sleeve and brushed away a speck of something too small to see. 'I thought perhaps you had some connection to the boy.'

The day's sunshine lost all its warmth.

'Connection?' Ansel asked.

'That he was a relative.' When Ceinan looked up again, his pale-blue eyes were veiled with innocence. 'A son, perhaps.'

And there it is.

Several shocked Elders stared back over their shoulders, openmouthed and glassy-eyed as fish on a slab.

Danilar recovered fastest. 'Elder Ceinan, that is an outrageous suggestion! How dare you imply—'

Ansel reached out a hand and gripped the Chaplain's shoulder, silencing him. 'No, Elder. That novice is no son of mine.' He spoke clearly, calmly, but couldn't resist adding, 'Although his mother has seen me naked.'

'Preceptor?' Festan spluttered.

Ansel forged on, as more and more Elders turned to watch. 'Yes, and more than once. She ran a hospital for the Order during the desert wars. I had a broken arm, badly set by the field surgeon. She rebroke it and set it straight for me. Thanks to her I could still couch a lance at Samarak, so in a way she saved my life. When Selsen was of an age to join the novitiate, the least I could do was find a place for the child.'

He stared at Ceinan, waiting for a reaction, but the Dremenirian's mastery of his expression was absolute. Not so much as an eyebrow twitched.

'It appears I am misinformed,' he said and inclined his head. Politeness, not apology.

'Apparently you are.'

Ansel turned back to face the lists, giving a quick shake of his head in answer to Danilar's anxious frown. He would not take this further, though the Elder was straying perilously close to a charge of Curial misconduct. Best to let it lie for now, and allow the tourney to play out. There was too much at stake to permit himself to be goaded, too much that could still go wrong. Soon enough, Goddess willing, it would cease to matter.

Nonetheless it worried him that Ceinan had tried to trip him so blatantly, so publicly. It must have been misdirection, a colourful lure to hook his eye whilst the assassin's blade slid home from the other side. The executioner's stroke – when would that come? Or had

Goran's arrest deprived Ceinan of his cat's paw and driven him to act in the open instead of at one remove?

Goddess, his brain was as twisted up and useless as his arthritic hands. He couldn't think it through. His heart raced to keep pace with his thoughts as he stared unseeing at the advancing herald, the two trumpeters raising their instruments for the fanfare that would signal the final event.

Ceinan had always been the one to watch. Ansel should never have allowed himself to become so focused on Goran. However lofty the man's ambitions or how heinous his sins, that fat deviant had never been a real threat to the Preceptorship. Ceinan, now – he was another kettle of herring entirely. *What does he know?*

The silvery flourish of the trumpets jolted him from his brooding and he dropped the thread of his thoughts. Whatever the Dremenirian fox had planned, it was too late to worry about it now. The joust was about to begin.

At the end of the lists to the left waited the Order's first champion, anonymous in a white and gold surcoat over unadorned plate, his shield plain, his visor down. Traditionally, the novices never knew who they would face in the lists on this day. Their opponent was drawn by lot from the ranks of full Knights present at the Motherhouse; in times past, even the Preceptor could be drawn for this duty, when the incumbent was still hale enough for tilting. Some were betrayed by their height or breadth, their manner of sitting a horse, but in most cases all the young Knight-to-be knew was that they faced one of the best the Suvaeon could field, and he had to measure himself against that standard.

From the right came the first challenger, already helmed, reining his restive horse into position. Around his right upper arm was tied a coloured ribbon to identify him to the judges and the eager spectators. Liveried tilt-marshals did duty as squires, checking the combatants' gear was properly secured and handing each man a lance before scuttling to safety behind the Oak-painted hoardings.

Even though the rider was not Selsen, Ansel couldn't help but lean forward in his seat as he waited for the signal. The crowd had fallen silent, only the snapping banners giving the lie to the feeling that the world was holding its breath.

Grinning fit to burst, the Order's master farrier brought his hammer down on the anvil across the lists from the judges' table with a mighty clang, and the two combatants surged forward.

In a handful of strides the horses were at a rolling canter. Two lances swept down to the couch. Two shoulders tensed and blunt coronals crashed into shields to a chorus of cheers from the crowd. Both combatants swayed but retained their seats, trotting back into position to receive a fresh lance from the marshals.

Clang! The second pass jolted the novice hard in the saddle, the boy mistiming his thrust so his lance-head glanced off the Knight's shield in a shower of paint-flecks. The third all but unseated him; he had to drop his lance and hold tight to the saddle bow to keep his seat.

On it went into the afternoon, clangs and crashes and thundering hooves, roars of appreciation and gasps of dismay. Ansel saw four novices unhorsed, including one youth helped to the hospital tent with a badly broken arm, before the youngsters got their own back with a decisive unhorsing of their own.

'Who was that?' he asked, applauding vigorously as the discomfited Knight collected the reins of his mount and the victor took the acclamation of the crowd with a florid bow from the saddle.

Danilar squinted at the youth's green ribbon. 'Berengir,' he said. 'Top of the group for sword afoot, and young Selsen's greatest rival for the oak leaves.'

The cluster of oak leaves was awarded to the most

promising young Knight in the final year of the novitiate. Many recipients went on to be First Knight, in time. Ansel tried not to let himself hope too hard that Selsen might be one of them.

'He's good. That's a seasoned Knight he just dumped on his arse.'

Danilar snorted. 'He knows it, too. A little more humility wouldn't go amiss there.'

'His vigil tonight might teach him some. Sunset to sunrise is a long time to spend caught between the Goddess and your own thoughts.'

The crowd sucked in a collective breath as the next novice to tilt was all but unhorsed by an impact that shattered both lances into cartwheeling fragments. His reprieve was brief; the subsequent exchange ended with the Knight victorious and an unconscious novice carried off to the physicians.

'This waiting is thirsty work,' Ansel muttered, looking around for the hovering page. The liveried youth brought goblets and wine and the Preceptor shifted yet again on his pillows to find relief from the constant nagging in his joints.

Danilar eyed him over the rim of his own goblet. 'Painful?'

'It's been a long day, and I'm a day older than I was yesterday.'

Ansel paused. A new novice had entered the lists, even before the tilt-marshals had finished clearing up the splinters from the previous bout. Stockily built, cramming a helm over sandy hair with an arm tied with a blue ribbon and a white.

You should be here now, Jenara. You would burst with pride.

'See?' Danilar murmured. 'Cool as you please.'

Ansel's mouth was dry. He wanted to swallow but he had no spit, and he couldn't move his arm to raise the wine to his lips. He could only stare.

Selsen looked every inch a Knight, sitting the horse easily, sighting down the lance the marshal handed up to ascertain whether it was as true as fourteen feet of tapered ash pole could be. The novice paid no attention to the crowd, by now so well refreshed they happily cheered anyone who entered the lists, whoever they were. Once the customary courtesies had been given, Selsen took position and waited as if there was no one else on the field.

'Goddess keep you,' Ansel breathed, then the farrier's hammer came down.

Selsen's bay horse leapt forward, quickly hitting its stride as the Knight raced up from the far end of the lists. With the crowd now silent, Ansel heard the drumming hooves, the creak of harness, and timed the run in his head as if he had the horse between his own knees. *Kick him on now.* The bay stretched into a gallop. *Fifteen yards and couch.* Smoothly the lance swept down, butt tucked beneath Selsen's arm. *Now brace!*

Selsen shifted forward to meet the charging Knight. Blunted spear-heads crashed into waiting shields and with whip-crack reports the two lances shattered. The crowd roared like some wounded beast, spectators surging to their feet. Whistles shrilled from the watching novices in the paddock and Ansel exhaled noisily. He hadn't even been aware he was holding his breath.

Both challenger and champion discarded the useless truncheons and collected new lances from the marshals as they reined their mounts around for the second pass. On both shields the painted Oak was scored and dimpled, testament to the force with which the four-pronged coronals had struck.

'He takes it well, eh, Preceptor?' said Festan, twisting in his seat. 'Oh to be that age again.'

'Thirty years younger and a hundred pounds lighter!' chortled another Elder, patting his ample belly, and set the whole row to cackling.

Ansel gripped the arm of his seat with his free hand as the marshals cleared the field and the farrier raised his hammer. Knight and novice waited, separated by less than a furlong of hoof-pocked turf. Hammer met anvil, spurs touched hide and the second charge began.

Again Ansel watched Selsen time the run perfectly and strike true. So too did the Knight, and the impact rocked them both in their saddles. Lances shivered but did not break, to gasps from the spectators that quickly became a cheer. Both combatants took new lances and reined their blowing horses into position for the final course.

Danilar gripped Ansel's arm. 'Don't look so anxious, old friend. He'll do fine.'

'Does it show?' he asked.

'Just a little.'

Ansel took a swig of wine to steady himself. 'I'm proud of this one, Danilar. Truly.' Out of the corner of his eye he saw Ceinan's head turn to listen and did not care. *Let him think what he wishes.*

The ringing note of hammer on anvil was quickly lost in the drum of hooves and the snorting of horses. Lances wavered, swung down to the couch, arms curled tightly around behind the flared vamplate, and then struck. Both shattered on impact. Selsen pulled the broken shaft of the lance clear but the whirling tip, almost a yard of unpainted ash pole, struck the oncoming Knight on the helm and whipped his head to one side.

He's lost line of sight. Ansel surged to his feet, heedless of the stabbing in his hip-joints. 'Cast up!' he shouted. '*Cast up!*'

Too late. There was no way for the Knight to hear him and recover. His horse surged into another stride and the jagged-ended truncheon of his lance struck Selsen's shield, skidded off and punched into the overlapping lamés of his pauldron before the horse's next stride wrenched it free.

Selsen's own truncheon tumbled to the ground. Scarlet stained the surcoat's white fabric and somewhere in the crowd a woman screamed. Tilt-marshals ran to catch the horse as its wounded rider slumped in the saddle; voices shouted for the surgeons. Even the Knight who had struck the blow dismounted and ran to help, tossing his helm onto the turf as he went.

No. Slowly Ansel subsided into his seat, his heart thumping so loud in his chest it deafened him. He didn't hear Danilar's reassurances, the anxious chatter of the Elders in the next row. All he heard was splintering wood and his own voice barking an order. *Cast up!*

Through the throng of figures at the end of the lists he saw Selsen helped down, armour hastily unbuckled and thrown aside. Hengfors' lanky figure appeared, and the physician stooped to examine the wound. Then a litter was brought to carry the youth to the hospital tent, out of sight behind the far pavilion. It carried Ansel's attention with it.

The tilt-marshals cleared the field for the event to continue, the crowd settling back into their seats. Ansel stared at them, unseeing. Injuries were not uncommon at a tourney; they were to be expected in a Knight's life – if not in the tilt-yard then on the battlefield. It was a risk each man accepted with his spurs. How could it be any different for a novice seeking to gain them?

'Ansel.'

Danilar's patient tone said he'd been speaking for some time but hadn't been heard. Ansel turned towards him and realised he had a death grip on an empty goblet. Wine stains marred the sleeve of his formal robes. Scarlet on white; blood on a surcoat. *Goddess watch over you, Selsen.*

'Forgive me, Danilar,' he said, setting the goblet down. 'I'm afraid I missed that.'

'I said he's in good hands. Hengfors is a fine physician.'

'Oh, I know. I know. It just came as a bit of a shock.'

Blood on a surcoat. *Oh, holy saints, how do I tell her?* 'I'm sure Selsen will be fine.' *Fine? What in hell's name does that mean?*

All Selsen had ever wanted was to be a Knight and ride to arms, Jenara had written. It had been the child's dream from the age of three, playing with carved wooden figures in that dusty courtyard. If the shoulder had been shattered there would always be a weakness there. Selsen would never be able to shield adequately, would never swing a sword two-handed.

How do I break the news that would crush that dream for ever?

The final four novices to compete rode unseen by Ansel. He barely heard the farrier's signal, the applause for their achievements. Even the fanfare to signal the conclusion of the event did not stir him.

'The judges will read Selsen's name,' he muttered. 'They must, surely.'

'I should think they'll award him the oak leaves,' put in Festan. 'By the Goddess, I'd say he's earned them!'

I only hope the price wasn't too high.

Minutes passed. The judges conferred for a nerve-shredding length of time before handing the list of names to the herald.

From the centre of the lists where all could see him, he began to read. 'My Lord Preceptor, Elders, ladies and gentlemen. On this day, in the presence of Holy Eador and before divers witnesses, the following individuals have demonstrated sufficient feats of arms to earn their elevation to Knighthood. If they are so able, we require and command these Knights to present themselves in our sight to receive their rank and assume the privileges pertaining thereto.' A ripple of applause. 'Berengir of Dun Riordain, come forth.'

Smiling broadly, the young man who had worn the green ribbon took his place before the judges' table.

Gone were the plate and mail, replaced by the plain white tunic and surcoat in which he would spend his vigil. Young man after young man followed him in alphabetical order, some sporting slings and bandages, and Ansel found his fingers gripping his chair-arms more and more tightly as the list went on.

They have to name Selsen. They have to.

'Selsen of Caer Amon, come forth.'

Goddess be praised!

But Selsen did not appear. Not from the paddock, not from behind the pavilion opposite, where the physicians' tent was located.

'Selsen of Caer Amon, come forth.'

If a novice was called a third time and still did not attend, nor send a representative to explain his absence, his Knighthood would be forfeit for a further year. The herald paused, then issued the final call to a new Knight to present himself.

Some kind of commotion broke out at the entrance to the hospital tent, people pushing, others falling back. Then a figure in white came striding forward, one tunic sleeve flapping empty. As the figure drew closer, Ansel saw the shape of the left arm immobile beneath the tunic, presumably strapped across the chest to immobilise the shoulder joint. The edge of a thick dressing poked out of the tunic's neck.

Pale-faced, sandy hair clinging to a sweaty brow, Selsen was quickly outpacing the robed physician hurrying along behind. At last, all the named novices stood in a line in front of the judges, and the final ceremony could take place.

More relieved than he had ever thought he could be, Ansel pushed himself to his feet. Down the pavilion steps he walked and out through the gate to the judges' table, where Endirion's sword lay before them on a white velvet cushion.

Blunt now and pocked with age spots of rust no amount of polishing could remove, it was nonetheless a fearsome-looking weapon, longer even than Ansel's own greatsword. Biting the inside of his cheek to keep from wincing at the pains accompanying every movement of his legs, he lifted the sword across his palms and turned to face the young Knights. Together, they dropped to one knee.

'Over three days you have proven yourselves worthy in body to carry the honour of Knighthood,' he said. 'You shall go forth from this place to be bathed and purified, thence to the Sacristy to spend the hours until dawn in contemplation, that your spirit may also be found worthy in the eyes of Eador.' Both hands wrapped around the hilt, he raised the sword to the salute. 'For the Oak and the Goddess, to your last breath.'

It was done.

'Stop!' Hengfors' shout was all but lost in the chorus of twenty-three voices repeating the oath, but there was no ignoring the heron-like physician himself as he strode up to the table, somewhat out of breath.

'Hengfors?' Ansel asked, lowering the sword to rest point-down on the turf. The blade was too heavy for his crippled hands to hold aloft for long.

'The novice Selsen is disqualified,' the physician said. Selsen flashed an anxious glance at the judges.

'On what grounds? Selsen has already taken the oath.' Amazingly, Ansel's voice remained steady. Inside he felt like a small boy again, hoping that if he wished it hard enough, something he dreaded would not come to pass.

The physician pointed a wiry, startlingly hirsute arm, his sleeves still rolled to his elbows and spattered with water. 'This person is not eligible for Knighthood.'

Ansel turned to the judges. 'Tourney marshals? Has this novice performed in any way counter to the tenets of our Order?'

The three men behind the table shook their heads. Selenas, the Master of Swords, sat back with his hands laced across his stomach and said, 'On the contrary – Selsen is one of the most capable novices I have seen in years. Unless the Goddess strikes him down in chapel tonight, we can see no reason why he should not receive his spurs.'

The physician's pale eyes bulged, with fury or outrage Ansel could not determine.

'Well, Hengfors?' he said. 'Why is he ineligible? Because he is mute?'

'Because Selsen is female!'

23

FLY BY NIGHT

❊

'So I find you at last in the women's garden,' said N'ril.

Gair put up his sword and looked around. The desertman was lounging on a stone bench by the parapet, dressed only in baggy trousers and soft boots with a *qatan* thrust through his emerald sash. A reddish-purple scar gleamed across the meat of his left forearm. Beside him on the bench lay a long, flat box.

'Should I not be here?' Gair asked, breathing hard. Overhead, canvas awnings flapped and cracked in the onshore breeze, tugging at their iron supports like badly set sails. 'Forgive me. There was nowhere on the ship I could work the sword and I needed to practise.'

'Please, you are a guest in my house. Use it as you will.'

N'ril poured a cup of water from the jug Gair had brought up from the kitchen and held it out to him. He propped his sword against the wall and drank. Despite the breeze and the shade from the awnings, the day's heat and his exertion had left sweat coursing over his chest and down the furrow of his spine.

'This is a garden?' he asked, gesturing around at the rooftop. It was empty but for a few benches and some glazed urns that looked as if they should contain flowers or shrubs.

'It does not resemble one now but one day, God willing, my wife will sit here with her mother and her sisters to watch our children play. Then you would see it bloom.' He smiled at Gair's expression. 'In Gimrael, men and women do not sit together.'

'I see,' said Gair, although he didn't.

'Your face betrays you, my friend. But it has always been thus, for thousands of years. When men converse, they discuss horse-racing and money, smoke *chaba* and pick their teeth in a most unseemly manner, and so the women have their garden, where they may be spared such things.' He grinned. 'I do not know what women converse about, but I suspect it involves the unseemly habits of men.'

Gair drained the cup and refilled it. 'You're not married, then, I take it.'

'I would have been,' N'ril said, 'but it is considered unlucky to bring a new bride into a house in mourning. I was patient; her mother, alas, was not.'

'I'm sorry to hear that.'

'My mother was more disappointed than I, I can assure you. As a minor scion of House Feqqin, and a younger son at that, I am not much of a prize.' N'ril shrugged and changed the subject. 'Alderan told me you were raised by the Suvaeon Knights. That is where you learned the sword, yes?'

He flipped open the box on the bench beside him.

Nestled in crimson velvet inside was a *qatan*. The black scabbard was scuffed but the hilt had been recently refurbished, its black and red whipping fresh and bright. 'Have you used one of these?'

'Never.'

He held it out across his palms. 'Try it.'

Gair took the sword and drew it from its scabbard. It weighed maybe two pounds, perhaps a little less – half the weight of his longsword. The curving single-edged blade was mirror-bright and perfectly plain, apart from a short Gimraeli inscription below the fuller. Experimenting with the grip, he slashed it this way and that to get the heft of it.

'The balance is perfect,' he said, rolling his wrists. Steel hissed through the air like a razor on a strop.

'The soul-sword is traditional in Gimrael. If you are to pass as Gimraeli, and from the ruling house in particular, you will need to carry one.' N'ril stood and drew his own blade. 'And to look like you know how to use it.'

He walked out to the centre of the roof and set himself, balanced on spread feet, with the sword winking in his right hand like the flickering tongue of a serpent.

Gair followed him and copied his stance. It was not too dissimilar to the opening positions he had learned in the Motherhouse. He brought his blade up to mirror N'ril's, the tips a handspan apart.

'Good.' The desertman smiled. 'Now we begin.'

N'ril was an excellent tutor, both encouraging and thorough. After an hour, Gair's arms ached to the bone. By the time the sun had dropped low enough to set the awnings ablaze with orange light he was a-drip with sweat and gasping for breath, whilst the desertman's mahogany torso was barely damp.

'Was making me work this hard your bloodprice?' he panted, leaning on his knees. The cut on his shoulder burned.

'I am honoured that you value my humble teaching

so highly, but no.' The desertman bowed and sheathed his sword with a flourish. 'A blade sings in your hands. If skill-at-arms is all that is required, I cannot understand why you were not Knighted.'

Gair uncurled his cramped hands from the *qatan*'s hilt. Dark sweat-lines crossed his palms and the scar throbbed from the unfamiliar grip.

'There's more to it than that. I have other gifts,' he said. 'Ones the Church doesn't care for.'

'Ah.'

'Does that disturb you?'

'I have known Alderan for a long time. My soul is at peace.' N'ril tilted his head to one side. 'May I ask, are you a man of faith?'

Helping himself to more water, Gair considered his response. Once, he would not have had to think before answering a question like that. 'I was raised by Goddess-fearing folk, if that's what you mean.'

The desertman flashed a smile. 'It is close enough.'

'And you? What do you believe in?'

'I believe my father sired me, my mother birthed me and my land sustains me. The sun rises and the rains fall whether I will it or no. That is enough for me.' Gair offered him the borrowed *qatan*, but he shook his head. 'Keep it for now. Like Shahe, it has no master.'

Of course. Red and black, like Shahe's harness. Now he realised the significance of the scar on N'ril's arm. 'It belonged to your brother.'

'Once. He has no further use for it now.' N'ril sketched a bow. 'Sleep well and rise happy, my friend,' he said, and walked away into the gathering dusk.

※

A hand on Gair's shoulder dragged him out of his dreams. He scrubbed sleep from his eyes and sat up, peering into the dark to see who had woken him.

A pearly glim popped into being, making him shield his eyes with his hand. 'Time to go,' said Alderan.

'What time is it?'

'Later than I would have liked. As near Third as makes no difference.' The old man enlarged the glim until the whole room was bright as day. He was dressed in the loose trousers, long divided tunic and voluminous *barouk* of the inner desert. 'There's desert clothes for you on the chair. Get dressed and meet me in the stable-yard with your gear.'

A distant shriek, abruptly cut off, galvanised Gair out of the low bed and onto his feet. 'What was that?'

Alderan looked grim. 'There's been trouble,' was all he would say. 'You'd best hurry.'

Gair washed and dressed as quickly as he could. A ruddy glow around the edge of the shutters proved, when he looked outside, to be a fire elsewhere in the city; either the warehouse was still burning or another building in the same district had been fired. The cool night air tasted charred.

N'ril arrived when he was almost done dressing with a pot of strong tea and some pastries. He quickly demonstrated how Gair should secure the *qatan* in his sash and fasten the complicated loops and twists of the *kaif* headdress, securing it with a circular enamelled pin in the Feqqin house colours of green and gold. Then, with two cups of tea scalding his stomach and his pack over his shoulder, Gair hurried out to the stables.

Alderan had the horses already saddled, an elegant grey for himself and Shahe for Gair, who was visible in the darkness only by the silver ornaments on her tack.

'Do you know your horse bites?' the old man said, rubbing his arm. 'Mount up. I want to be well away from the city before dawn. It's no longer safe here for northerners.'

Gair swung into the saddle. 'What's happened?'

'Apparently warehouses are not enough for the Cult. Two imperial merchants' houses have been put to the torch, and some people have been killed,' said N'ril, securing Gair's pack and a bedroll behind his saddle. He wrapped the longsword's baldric around its scabbard. 'You should leave this here. It betrays you even more than your height.'

'Will you keep it for me until I can come back for it?' Gair rested his hand on the hilt of the borrowed *qatan*. 'A blade for a blade?'

'With pleasure.'

Then the desertman loped across the yard to the gates and swung them wide. The alley outside was empty but for a stray dog nosing through some refuse, but the breeze brought distant shouting.

Alderan paused at the gate and leaned down from his saddle to grip N'ril's shoulder. 'Thank you,' he said. 'Keep yourself safe. Your mother's buried enough sons.'

White teeth shone in the dark. 'I will be careful.'

To Gair, N'ril said, 'May it please God that you have no need of what I taught you yesterday, but if you do, make it tell, and honour my brother's memory.'

'I'll try.' Gair clasped his hand. 'I hope we meet again.'

'We will, I am sure of it. We have swords to exchange. Now go!'

The moon-silvered streets of Zhiman-dar were quiet but strangely watchful, as if the people inside the shuttered houses were wide-eyed and uneasy, waiting for the mob to move on to another part of the city. Alderan led them the length of the alley then paused where it joined a main street, looking around carefully before urging his horse across the thoroughfare. The jumbled roofs of the houses opposite stood silhouetted against flickering orange light. A dull rumble as of a discontented hive came from a few streets away.

'We'll have to be quick,' Alderan muttered. 'I think it'll get worse before it gets better.'

'N'ril said the Cult is not well liked here.'

'Even a desertman can be wrong about his own people sometimes.'

Another cross-street, then down another alley, black as pitch with the moon hidden by the city's buildings. Gair's pulse quickened as he rode. It was all he could do to keep Shahe to a fast walk; the mare was eager to be gone as well and burst into a bouncing trot at the least touch of his heels. In the dusty alleys she made little sound, but on the stone-flagged wider streets her steel shoes rang shockingly loud.

A pale tower loomed over the buildings ahead. The square shape looked familiar. 'Is that a church?' Gair whispered.

Alderan nodded, then swore as the bell began to ring. Cheering erupted from the next street and Gair smelled the tang of burning paper. Quick as a man half his age, Alderan swung down from his horse and ran ahead to the next intersection to peer around the corner. Firelight gilded his face, making him duck back into the shadows. Gair grabbed the grey's reins and walked Shahe over to him.

'What's happening?'

Alderan was scowling. 'I thought men had outgrown book-burning,' he growled. 'Look for yourself.'

Gair dismounted and edged his head around the corner of the building. The church stood on the far side of a square, its splintered doors hanging askew like broken teeth in a beaten man's mouth. White-robed figures hurried in and out, carrying armloads of books to a bonfire blazing at the foot of the steps. In its leaping yellow light another figure, massively tall and bearded, exhorted a whooping, cheering crowd of two hundred or more citizens clustered around the fire.

The man's arms were spread wide, his head jerking as he delivered a torrent of Gimraeli in a booming voice. Gair could barely recognise a word of it but the anger and hatred needed no translation. He watched, horrified, as two figures emerged from the church carrying a single large book between them. The Cultist zealot swung around, pointing, and the two men held up the book, open at a gorgeously illuminated page for all to see.

'That's the Book of Eador!' Gair exclaimed.

With the crowd roaring its approbation, the zealot strode to his two helpers and began to wrench pages from the book, flinging them into the flames. Then the three men hurled the entire book onto the bonfire in a gout of sparks and smoke. The zealot's voice rose in pitch and he jabbed his finger at the curling pages, spittle flying from his lips.

Gair felt sick. 'They're burning holy books, Alderan! How dare they? How—'

Alderan dragged him away from the square and pushed Shahe's reins into his hands. 'We have to leave now. Quickly, before they realise we don't belong here and we go the same way as those books.'

Gair mounted, still reeling from what he had witnessed. 'Which way?'

'Across the square, then hard left and south as fast as you can.'

The old man dug in his heels, sending the grey leaping forwards. Shahe needed no encouragement to follow. A few shouts of surprise rang out from the church steps. Even over the sound of the horses' hooves Gair heard the tattoo of running feet and imagined the mob surging after him. He bent low on the mare's neck and pushed her to a gallop.

Street after street flew past with no sign of another human being. Here and there shutters squeaked or a door banged closed as the two horsemen clattered by, hoofbeats echoing down the moon-shadowed thoroughfares. Sounds of pursuit quickly fell behind, but Gair could still hear the Cultist zealot's voice, his hate harsh as acid; could still see the hand-lettered pages of the Book crinkling into ash.

The plaza before the south gate stood silver in the moonlight. Torches burned on the squat gatehouse and the gates themselves were closed. At the sound of horses, four men spilled from the gatehouse doorway with more torches – city guards in boiled-leather cuirasses with scimitars at their hips. Hastily Gair pulled his sand-veil up over his face.

'Who goes there?' The guard captain held his torch aloft, squinting into the night.

Alderan cantered his horse across the plaza, dust swirling around the grey's hooves. 'Open the gates!' he barked. He used the common speech but had adopted a heavy Gimraeli accent. 'Courier coming through!'

'Hold!' The captain of the guard came forward with his torch high. 'I said *hold*, curse you!'

Alderan had to rein back or run the man down. Behind him Gair pulled Shahe up with some difficulty, the mare dancing from foot to foot. Under his robe, he gripped the hilt of the *qatan*.

'Stand aside! Messenger for his Highness,' said Alderan.

'On whose orders?' the captain asked. His men glanced uncertainly from the distant glow of flames to the two horsemen in front of them and fingered their weapons.

'Imbecile! Do you see his colours? You will answer to Lord Kierim if his personal courier is delayed!'

'The city is under curfew. No one goes in or out and I don't care who—'

A squeeze of Gair's calves and a tug on the reins were all it took to bring Shahe into an impressive rear. Tassels swinging, long mane floating on the night air, she

pawed her hooves just inches from the captain's face,
forcing him and his squad to back off a pace. The instant her feet touched the ground, Gair had his *qatan*
levelled at the captain's neck, burnished gold in the
torchlight.

The man gulped. 'Your pardon, *sayyar*. I did not see
your colours in the dark.' He pushed his men towards
the gatehouse. 'Quickly, there! Open the gates!'

A windlass groaned and chains clanked as the thick
gates swung open, revealing the pale ribbon of the
road. Gair sheathed his sword and followed Alderan as
he spurred his grey out into the night.

The old man set a brisk pace, alternating cantering
and walking to keep the horses fresh. Outside the city
the chill of a desert night enfolded them, crisping the
stars like frost. Lumiel was halfway to setting in the
black sky, silvering the road ahead, with Simiel already
creeping up behind her.

Orchards of date palms rustled in the restless breeze.
Goat pens and dusty fields webbed with irrigation ca-
nals gave way to thorn scrub and dry gullies, with here
and there a gleam of moonlight reflected in the river.
Then all signs of habitation fell behind and they had
only the road and whirling sand-devils for company.

Alderan finally called a halt beside a straggle of flat-
topped trees. Overhead, the eastern horizon was brightening, the last skeins of stars beginning to fade. Gair
dismounted and took a drink from his canteen to rinse
the dust from his throat. Then he filled a leather bucket
from a water-skin for the horses, though Shahe was
more interested in looking around her than drinking,
her ears pricking at every cricket-chirp and lizard-
scuttle.

'That was quick thinking back there,' Alderan said,
and drank from his own flask. He wiped his mouth
with the back of his hand. 'We should push on further
whilst it's still cool. It's about three days to El Maqqam.'

'Will it be the same there? Book-burning, mobs in the streets?'

'Possibly.' The old man sighed and slapped the stopper back into the flask. 'Probably worse. The capital stands right on the edge of the inner desert and the Cult is strongest amongst the remote tribes. We will have to be careful.'

'What are you hoping to find?'

'We need to know where the starseed was taken when Corlainn surrendered it after the battle. The purges that followed his arrest threw the Suvaeon into chaos. Our records from that time are patchy at best, but we know a number of gifted Knights fled south to the Daughterhouse in El Maqqam. I'm hoping there's something in the books and papers they took with them, or that they left records while they were there.'

Gair stared at him. 'You mean you don't know whether there's anything useful to find?'

'Not for certain, no, but there were always rumours. It's a more likely place to start than anywhere else.'

'You dragged me down here on the strength of *rumours*, and now you want to throw me into a Suvaeon Daughterhouse? Blood and stones, Alderan!' Renewed anger tightened Gair's chest. *All this time wasted on a hunch!*

'Do you fancy your chances of getting into the Suvaeon archives in Dremen instead?' Alderan snapped. 'That's the next place we'll have to look if we come up dry here. The fate of the Veil could rest on that stone, Gair. We have to find it before anyone else does.'

'You mean before Savin does.' Even saying the name was painful. It clawed at Gair's throat like a fever-cough.

'Yes. The damage he could do with it is incalculable. He could rip a hole in the Veil wide enough to expose the whole Hidden Kingdom, and he could keep it open, destroying the balance between worlds for ever. We can't let that happen.'

I can't let him live.

Shahe's muzzle nudged at Gair's hand. He looked down and saw his knuckles gleaming white on the bucket's leather strap. It took an effort to relax his grip and lift the bucket up for her. She drank noisily.

'Then let's get on with it,' he said, offering the remaining water to Alderan's grey.

He felt the old man's eyes on him as he folded and stowed the bucket and swung himself onto Shahe's back, but no words were spoken. Just as well. He did not think he would have been able to answer Alderan civilly with such a foul taste in his mouth.

24

INTO THE SNOWS

❖

The chill gouged Teia to the bone. She had dressed as warmly as she could, but the winter mocked her layers of fur and sealskin, pinched her heavy breasts until she wept and then froze the tears to her lashes. Her hands and feet ached as if her marrow had turned to ice, every muscle so stiff with the cold she could not even lift her head to look beyond Finn's drooping ears at the endless white.

She would find no rest here. No shelter, no safety from the winter. For three days she had pushed on into the teeth of its spite, knowing she had gone too far ever to go back before she had even left the caves. Her family's fate, the fate of her entire people, was in Ytha's hands now. Or Maegern's. She had rolled the bones and lost. There was nothing left to do now but go on, into the maw of the wind, and follow the frigid stars east to the pass that would take her into the Empire.

If she had kept quiet, swallowed her fears and been the dutiful daughter, she would be warm and snug beneath her furs this night, not plodding through snow that was belly-deep on her horse with a glassy crust that cut skin like a blade. She would have a fire on which she could make soup, perhaps even a wedding to look forward to that would secure her status and her family's for as long as the chief lived. Instead she had this world of snow and sky and wind and only the vast darkness for company.

Finn stopped. Teia saw nothing ahead but more snow and the shoulders of the mountains rearing up, even blacker than the night behind them. She squeezed her calves into his ribs to urge him on. He whickered but stood his ground. Teia tried again.

'On, Finn,' she urged. She could hardly say the words, her cheeks were so stiff. 'Come on.'

Finn tossed his head, chewing his bit. His ears flickered back then forwards and his feet shifted restlessly in the snow. Why was he being so stubborn? A few miles more and they would be far enough away that Drwyn's scouts would not bother to pursue her and now her stupid horse was balking. Did he want her to be caught? They would drag her back to the caves for sure, to Drwyn's fists and Ytha's spite, and that she could not allow.

Forcing her sluggish muscles to work, she kicked her heels hard into Finn's sides. The horse shied and her numbed fingers nearly missed their grip on the saddle horn. She kicked again. 'Get on, you stubborn lump!'

Finn leapt forwards and plunged up to his chest in black water. Chunks of ice fountained around him as he forged on, staggering and stumbling when the cold current beneath the ice threatened to drag him under.

Teia yelped, feeling the water soaking her boots even as terror gripped her heart in a fist. The river! It would be the death of him in this cold, and of her, too. Clamping her hand around the saddle horn, she yanked his head back the way they had come. Somehow he found the strength to lunge up onto the bank, hitting his knees in the snow and surging back to his feet, shivering and rolling his eyes.

Now Teia could see the sinuous track of the river winding beneath the snow, a barely perceptible dip in the otherwise featureless plain. Macha's ears – she had to do something for him, and quickly. Quickest of all would be to use her gift to create warmth, but she wasn't sure how – and didn't dare waste time experimenting, or risk charring her horse's hide to a crisp if she succeeded too well.

Heart pounding, she dismounted and fumbled at the blanket-roll tied behind the saddle. Her hands were clumsy on the knots; she dragged her mittens off with her teeth and attacked the fastenings with bare hands, trying to loosen them before the cold stiffened her fingers to uselessness. At last the thongs came undone and the blanket billowed open. She gathered it up in big handfuls and started rubbing Finn's legs down as briskly as she dared.

'I'm so sorry,' she told him over and over as she worked. 'I'm so sorry, Finn. You knew – you knew the river was there and I ignored you!' Hind legs, forelegs and back again; her hands soon numbed to claws but she kept working: if her horse dropped with cold-water shock it really didn't matter whether or not she could feel the reins. Her teeth chattered. The icy wind pushed its fingers into the smallest gaps in her clothing and its touch made her shudder. Cursing her stupidity, she dragged herself on her knees around to Finn's forelegs again, rubbing and rubbing and praying to Lord Aedon to take pity on him and blast her for a fool.

Eventually the thick blanket tumbled from her grasp. Panting with exertion, she tried to pick it up again but her hands wouldn't grip, despite the warmth at her core that had sweat prickling under her breasts and down her spine. She sat on her heels to catch her breath. Finn stood beside her with his back to the wind, head down but eyes alert. He didn't appear to be shivering too badly, but they had to find shelter soon.

Macha, her hands were so cold! She tucked one into the opposite armpit and pawed through the snow with the other for her dropped mittens. They'd blown a little way off; she'd have to walk or crawl to fetch them. She tried to lever herself onto her knees but her legs were as stiff as dried elk-meat.

Twisting around, she grabbed for Finn's stirrup. Maybe she could pull herself up that way. She scrabbled at the leather but her cold-stiffened fingers slid uselessly off it, unable to get a purchase. She tried again and managed to shove her numbed fist through the stirrup far enough that she could pull down with her wrist. It was sufficient leverage, just about, but Macha's ears, it hurt. Sobbing, she hauled one knee up, got one foot under her. Movement forced blood back to her muscles, making them burn and throb. Cold wind stung her wet cheeks like a slap and she realised she was weeping. Leaning on the stirrup again, she lumbered to her feet. More tears; she was helpless to stop them spilling over with pain or relief or a little of both. She was up, she was moving and by the Eldest she would go on.

Picking the blanket up took two attempts. Getting it slung over Finn's back took two more, then she staggered off in pursuit of her mittens, towing the big dun after her with a fist knotted in the blanket around his neck.

'Good lad,' she panted, lugging her unresponsive feet through the snow. 'Good lad.'

She caught her mittens as they flopped and flapped in

the wind by stamping on them. Shook out the snow, forced them over her clawed fingers. Turned Finn towards the hills and kept walking, one unsteady step after another. Keep moving, that was the key. Keep moving, and eventually they'd find somewhere out of the wind to rest.

Cold. So cold. The pale snows looked endless, too deep for either of them to run. It was difficult enough just to walk. Ahead the white-cloaked shapes of the hills marched ever away from her, shoulders hunched and backs turned. Teia swayed, leaning on Finn's shoulder to stay upright. They never appeared to draw any closer. She would die out there. Die for her pride and Ytha's folly and change not a whit of the clan's doom.

Oh gods, let me sleep.

Finn stumbled and fell heavily to his knees, knocking Teia from her feet. Numb hands scrabbled for the reins, for a handful of mane, anything to stop her fall, but it was too late. Something struck her head and the stars spiralled into darkness.

❧

Pain. Pounding in her head, her blood throbbing in her ears. If she could feel that much pain, she couldn't be dead, could she? Macha's ears, it *hurt*.

Someone lifted her eyelid. Bright firelight stabbed her eye and Teia twitched her head away from it. Movement intensified the pain and she groaned.

'She's awake.'

'Macha be praised! I was right feared for her.'

'What about the little one? Will the child be all right?'

Too many voices. Too loud. Teia tried to raise her hands to cover her ears but she couldn't lift them from her sides. Something warm and heavy kept them pinned and she was too weak to shrug it off.

'You rest there,' said the first voice that had spoken. 'I'll fetch you something to drink.'

Footsteps. Movement. The crackle of a fire and a low, animal sound. Horses? *Finn!* She forced her eyes open but could see little more than dark shapes in the flickering orange light. A woman's face appeared above her, brown and wrinkled as a dried berry, framed by stringy, greying hair.

'Finn?' Teia managed. 'Is he hurt?'

'No, lass. Your baby's fine, far as I can tell.' The woman, first-voice, smiled, revealing a missing tooth.

Stupid woman. 'Not the baby. My horse!'

'Weren't no horse when Baer found you. All on your own, you were.' No Finn? The woman turned back the blankets that had been tucked around Teia and eased her into a sitting position.

'Here now, you drink this and you'll feel a mite better.'

Steadying Teia's head with one hand, she brought a cup to her lips. The first taste told Teia what herbs the drink contained and she spat it straight out.

'No.'

'Come on, lass, it won't hurt you. It's for the pain.' The woman brought the cup up again. The more Teia struggled to turn her head away, the tighter the grip on the back of her neck became.

'No!'

Flailing her arm, she managed to dash the cup away, spilling some of its contents. 'That's crowsfoot – it'll make me sleep.'

Fresh pain bloomed through her skull. She put up her hand and felt a rough bandage around her head.

'Yes, yes, sleep,' the woman prattled in a sing-song voice, as if she was speaking to a child. 'Sleep's what you need, a nice long rest . . .'

She proffered the cup again and Teia fended her off clumsily, her other hand held to her throbbing head. If she drank crowsfoot with a head injury, she'd probably never wake up again. The woman might as well have offered her bitter aconite to drink. *Macha's mercy, it hurts!*

'. . . and then you'll feel better—'

'No!'

She shoved the woman away again and tried to swing her legs around, get them under her. Her vision swam then settled, wobbling with every pulse of pain behind her eyes. With a bit more effort she succeeded in kicking off the blankets, though her limbs felt only marginally under her control. More pounding in her head followed the exertion, nausea churning her stomach. Macha's ears, maybe she should lie down again, as the woman was urging. No. She couldn't sleep. She had to find Finn.

Teia squinted into the leaping shadows. A cave. Low-roofed, but deep enough to accommodate perhaps twenty people, huddled in small groups around bundles and baskets. Silent, unreadable silhouettes against the fire burning in the cave-mouth, they kept their heads down, looked neither right nor left, as if they were too exhausted to spare even the energy it took to be curious. The only faces she could see were those of the woman kneeling next to her and two others crouched close by.

'Where's my horse?' she asked them.

'Must have wandered off. Weren't no horse when Baer found you—'

'Leave off, Gerna!' said one of the other women, pushing forward. 'She's tired of walking, wants your horse for herself. We've only two, see? We have to take turns.'

She glared at Gerna, who tossed her stringy hair and retreated into the shadows, taking her cup of crowsfoot tea with her.

'Lazy old baggage,' the woman muttered. Her companion stifled a giggle with her hand and Teia realised she was much younger, though the gloom made it difficult to guess her age.

'Anyway,' said the other. A raw-boned, rather angular creature, she had weathered skin and coarse black hair cut in a practical crop. Without any apparent effort, she hauled Teia's heavy saddlebags closer. 'Your bits of things are here. Baer said to take the provisions for the group. I'm sorry.'

Both women looked apologetic. Now that Teia's vision was clearing she could see how pinched and tired their faces were. Perhaps that explained the others' indifference: they were too beaten down to manage a thought for anyone but themselves.

'That's all right, I understand. When there's little enough to go around, everyone should share. But where is Finn, my horse? Please.'

'Over there.' The woman pointed. Teia glimpsed a broad dun back in the shadows beyond a couple of scrubby ponies.

Teia felt suddenly weak with relief. She would never have forgiven herself if any harm had come to him, especially after he'd tried to save her. 'Can you tell me what happened? And what are your names?'

The younger of the two women smiled shyly. 'I'm Lenna. That's Neve.' She turned her head towards the older woman and the firelight gleamed on a poorly healed scar on her cheek, still angry and new. 'Baer was leading the hunters back to camp when he found tracks in the snow. A bit further on, he saw a horse standing over someone on the ground, and it were you. You'd hit your head on a rock. Half-hour more and you'd both have died out there, he reckons.'

The other woman, Gerna, had mentioned this man Baer. 'Is he your leader? Your chief?'

'We don't have no chief,' said Neve. 'We don't have

no clan.' Her lips thinned, then her face softened a bit, the tight lines easing. 'But yes, my man's the closest to a leader we've got.'

'Lost Ones.' Teia felt dizzy again.

'Aye, right enough.' Neve said it with a brisk pride that dared Teia to make mock of her. 'What are you doing out here in the cold, getting so near your time?'

Teia touched the bandage again. 'I questioned the Speaker to her face. I stood against her, before the entire clan.'

'And she sent you away.' Neve nodded, as if that was all they needed to know about how Teia had ended up there. 'I'll find you something hot to eat.'

She pushed herself to her feet and wove through the others to the fire, sparing a scornful glance for someone on the way, probably the luckless Gerna.

Lenna moved closer and Teia saw she also was pregnant, the size of her belly unmistakable even through layers of bulky clothing. Her age was more apparent, too: about the same as Teia's.

'Don't you have no man to care for you?' Lenna asked softly. 'No family?'

'No. I dishonoured my family when I left. I'm no longer welcome amongst the Crainnh.'

Lenna lowered her eyes. 'We don't speak our clan names here. Baer says it's better to leave it all behind, make new lives, not mourn what we've lost.'

'Baer sounds wise,' said Teia. 'Is he here?'

'Outside, making sure no one followed you. We've little enough without folk trying to take it from us.'

She rubbed absently at the edge of the scar on her cheek and Teia guessed she'd earned it when someone had tried to rob her of whatever possessions she had. Other Lost Ones, most likely. 'Does that hurt?' she asked.

Abashed, Lenna snatched her hand to her lap and ducked her head, so that her dark hair hid the mark. 'Sometimes. A bit.'

'Let me see.'

Without thinking Teia spun a light and reached to turn Lenna's face towards it, but the girl blinked and scrambled backwards on her rump, eyes popping like a field mouse's.

'You didn't say you was no Speaker!'

'I'm only an apprentice.' Teia held out her hand. 'I won't hurt you, Lenna. It's just a light.'

The girl was not convinced and shrank back further, hugging her unborn child protectively.

'I only want to help – look, I have a salve . . .' She opened her saddlebag and began rooting for her simples, but Lenna shook her head, darting fearful glances at the little globe. Teia let it go and closed her bags again. Whatever trust she'd begun to forge with the girl had been shattered – the wide-eyed stare said she expected Teia to transform into a monster at any moment.

A tense, silent minute later Neve returned with some soup – thin and not particularly good, but it was hot – and Teia felt better for eating it. Strengthened, she made her way unsteadily across the cave to check on Finn.

He looked happy enough; he'd been rubbed down properly after his soaking in the river and his saddle blanket was still spread out over a rock near the fire to dry. Teia stroked his nose, and apologised again for not trusting him. Looking back to where she'd left her bags she saw Lenna whispering with Neve, and guessed they were talking about her and the light she'd made. She tried to ignore the occasional stares from the younger woman that slid her way like knives.

Over by the horses the firelight was in her favour and she could see the Lost Ones more clearly: men and women old before their time, faces hardened and closed. They were frightened, she realised, all of them: frightened of starving, frightened of being alone, or being robbed by others like themselves who perhaps had even less than they did. She and Lenna appeared to be the youngest. There were no children – exile was a hard place to raise a child. She touched her swollen belly briefly. Soon there would be two.

Someone whistled sharply and an answering trill came from outside. Three figures trooped in from the cold, kicking snow from their buskins and shrugging off bows and quivers. One was a gangling boy of maybe fourteen summers, hiding his youth under a fuzzy, uneven beard. After him came a lad no more than five or six years older, with the broad face and sturdy, close-coupled build of a prize ram, crowned with shaggy brown curls well in need of shearing. He went straight across the cave to Lenna, who scurried into his arms.

The third man was past his prime but still hard of face and limb, with a sinewy toughness like sun-dried meat. Sharp eyes flicked around the cave and found Teia standing by the horses. He strode over, shaking snow from a long iron-grey braid.

'You must be Baer,' she said.

'That I am.' He rested his bow on his shoulder and assessed her from bandaged head to burgeoning belly, gaze lingering on her cheek and the absence of a wedding tattoo. 'I suggest you go home, girl. This is no life, no matter what you're running from.'

'I'm not running.' He snorted and Teia bristled. 'I'm travelling. South through the mountains.'

'In winter? And had you thought about how you'd keep yourself when your stores ran out?'

'I have my own bow. I can hunt as well as any man,' she said hotly.

'With that belly?' Baer barked a laugh. 'Aye, after you've pupped, mebbe! Swallow your pride and go back to your mother, girl. For your babe's sake, if not for your own.'

Angry now, Teia straightened up and stood as tall as

she could. 'I can take care of myself. I'll be gone at first light, then I'll trouble you no longer.'

She pushed past him, heading back towards her bags. Out of the corner of her eye she saw Lenna with her man, heads together, the girl's hands talking as eloquently as any words. They both fell silent and stared as she passed.

How dare he presume to judge her? How *dare* he! He knew nothing about her, nothing about what she'd seen.

Kneeling, she emptied her saddlebags to see what else she might have lost when her provisions were taken, but everything appeared to be there, if hopelessly disordered. Anger sour in her stomach and her head still pounding, she began folding the spare clothes and her blankets and jamming them back into the bags. After a few minutes she heard footsteps approaching, but didn't look up.

'You've got a spark about you, girl,' said Baer from behind her. She ignored him, starting on the other bag. 'Not many who find us are so proud.'

'My pride is about all I've got left,' she snapped. 'Give me my provisions back. I've a long way to go.'

'You're not going anywhere. It's the middle of winter.'

She flung her sealskin jerkin to the ground and stood up to round on him. 'Do you think I don't know that?' She was shouting, but she couldn't seem to bring her voice down, even as the rest of the group's stares sharpened with hostility. 'I have to do this, Baer. I'm cold and I'm tired and I've no idea how far I have to go but I *have* to do this, and Macha as my witness, you'll not stop me. Now, will you return my provisions or do I have to steal them as I leave?'

He stared at her, face carved from granite, then lashed out with the flat of his hand. In a blink Teia had reached for the restless magic inside her and Baer's palm rebounded off something invisible but very solid. For all he tried hard to hide it, she saw him wince.

'So it's true,' he said, rubbing his hands together.

'So what's true?' She let her weave unravel and knelt down again to continue packing her bags.

'That you have powers. Lenna told Isaak you made a light out of plain air, right in front of her.'

'I wanted to see her face more clearly. I thought I could do something to heal her wound.'

'You know healing?'

'A little. Herbs that harm, herbs that cure.'

He grunted. 'None of the other bands has a Speaker.'

'I'm only an apprentice. Besides, I'm not staying.'

'Your gifts would be very valuable to us.'

'And what would you do with them, eh? Make war on the others? No.' She shook her head and immediately regretted it when the pain made her queasy. She pressed her hand to her stomach: Neve's soup was not sitting well.

Baer hunkered down nearby. 'You could help keep us safe.'

Teia fastened the last buckle and sat back on her heels. One side of Baer's face was in shadow, the other carved into hard lines by the firelight.

'There is something I have to do,' she said tiredly. 'The fate of my clan rests on it – maybe of all the clans. I have the foretelling, Baer. I have seen it.'

'Seen what?'

'Slaughter. Bloodshed. The Wild Hunt riding loose across the plains.' She pushed her saddlebags away, suddenly too exhausted to mistrust him. Even the Lost Ones deserved a warning.

'Let the clans deal with it. If they have brought this doom down upon themselves, it's no concern of ours. They made that clear when they sent each of us into exile.'

'No, Baer, listen to me. It will be a disaster. No clan is

safe, no people are safe – not even exiles. If you have any care for these folk, lead them south through the mountains. Get as far away as possible.'

His lips twisted. 'Into the Empire.'

'Their iron men withstood the Hunt once before. They can do it again.'

'You are sure of what you saw? The Hunt . . .' Baer shook his head, disbelieving. 'The Hunt is a campfire story to frighten children. If you stay amongst the Lost Ones you'll learn there is worse to fear than bogles and hobgoblins. Like your fellow man.' He turned and spat. 'Ten years,' he said bitterly. 'Ten long winters skulking in these hills like a jackal, unable to ride the plains of my ancestors. Now you suggest I run to the Empire because the Hunt is coming? You ask too much, girl.' He levered himself to his feet.

Ytha had belittled her, called her *child* too many times to stand for it from a man who knew nothing about her. Her head aching and her patience about at an end, Teia stood and advanced on Baer, so close that he took a half-step back out of sheer surprise.

'My name,' she said, 'is Teia. And yes, I am sure of what I saw. I witnessed the summoning. I saw Maegern appear in the fire and I heard Her speak. Ytha, Speaker of the Crainnh, means to summon the Hunt and use it to reclaim the lands lost by Gwlach, but she'll never bend the Raven to her will. Once She's free, Maegern will bow to no one. This I have seen.'

With both hands she dragged open the layers of clothes at her neck. The claw-marks had barely faded, blue as tattoos across the upper slopes of her breasts. Baer's stone-black eyes widened.

'Her Hound marked me, Baer. I speak truth. Make of it what you will.'

Then she strode past him, out towards the cave-mouth. Her head was pounding so fiercely she could scarcely see straight. The firelight was too bright and the shadows too velvety-dark to make out the faces that turned towards her as she passed through a sea of whispers that ebbed and flowed around her.

Sourness climbed her throat. She swallowed it down but that wasn't enough. Falling to her knees in the blown snow at the entrance to the cave, she vomited up the soup she'd eaten in a stinging, stinking gush. The child squirmed.

Oh, Macha, make me a stone, she prayed. *Make me a stone that cannot feel, that cannot weep.*

She shut her eyes, but images from her foretelling stalked across her vision, stark and bloody as ever. The night wind touched her face with frigid fingers and sighed away into the dark. Bitter saliva flooded her mouth. Stomach cramping violently, she bent over to vomit again and as she retched she felt a hand on her back, another scooping her hair out of the way.

'There, lass.' Neve's voice, gruffly soothing. 'There now.'

A cup of water was offered and Teia groped for it to rinse out her mouth. Neve wrapped a blanket around her shoulders; she let the older woman lead her back into the camp and lie her down, wipe her face with a damp washcloth as she clutched the blanket under her chin and shivered as if she had the killing ague. She was cold, so cold. She pulled her knees up as close to her chest as she could and closed her eyes against the sick throbbing in her head.

Why had she tried to convince Baer? She could have stolen back her provisions and left with the dawn. There was no time to waste. Ytha wouldn't be sitting idle, she could be sure of that, not with two Hounds at her heels and the scent of victory in her nostrils.

Teia let her head fall forwards, burying her face in the blanket. Macha's ears, why had she ever thought this would work?

✢

'Girl. Teia.'

The unfamiliar voice woke her and she blinked drowsily at the shape squatting between her and the distant fire. Baer's hard features swam into focus. Somehow the cave felt warmer now and she struggled out of her blankets.

'Baer.' Teia rubbed her eyes and stifled a yawn. Her mouth tasted foul.

'What you said before – that was a true telling?'

'It was true.'

She sat up. Sleeping bodies were laid out across the floor of the cavern like rows of fruits for drying save for one man on watch, barely visible against the black night outside. 'It's late, Baer.'

He didn't appear to have heard her, or didn't think her demurral worth respecting. His hands fiddled with something in front of his chest that she couldn't see. 'The Wild Hunt will ride?'

'If Ytha finds the key to Maegern's prison, the same that locked Her away, then yes. And her feet are on that path.' She smothered another yawn with her hand. Her baby dealt her a petulant kick and she winced. 'The Raven sent two Hounds as a token of Her intent. When they arrived, I knew the Speaker would never listen to me, no matter what I said.' *I had to go. I'm so sorry, Mama. I had to go, for the sake of the people. Macha watch over you when the darkness comes.*

Baer did not look up from his restless fingers. 'The stories tell that the iron men took the starseed from the battlefield. They don't say where.'

Maegern's voice scraped around inside Teia's head again. 'It's in the city of seven towers,' she said, the unfamiliar words making awkward shapes in her mouth. 'I don't know where that is.'

'I heard tell of a city once,' said Baer, 'in the lands we lost. Dwellings of wood and stone, and all people living close in one place. All the time, in one place. They called it Fleet.'

A destination. Somewhere she might find men of the Empire. It gave her a little hope. 'Then I shall go to Fleet. Perhaps someone there will know this city Ytha seeks.'

Baer shook his head. 'They are no longer kin to us, girl. They won't aid you.'

'I have no other choice.'

He dropped what he'd been fidgeting with and she realised it was the end of his braid. Hard fingers closed around her arm.

'Twelve clans surrendered. Their chiefs broke spears and gave their honour to the Empire. What chance do you think you will stand amongst them?'

'I have to try.' She eased her arm from his grasp. 'I know the Empire has no reason to care for us, but even they will not be safe if the Hunt rides free.'

Baer sat back on his heels. Silhouetted by the firelight, his face was unreadable. 'Brave talk for a bit of a girl, on her own and with a babe on the way.'

'Moonstruck foolish, more like!' put in Neve, from somewhere behind Teia. ' 'Twas the Empire as sent us here and no good can come from treating with them now.'

'Neve.' Baer's tone held a warning. She made an indelicate sound and rolled herself in her blankets again, her point made.

Shaking his head, Baer looked out across the sleeping forms of his people. 'There's not a one of us wouldn't give their all to return to our homelands,' he said. 'Every true-blood warrior would die for the chance to win them back. After all this time, if your Speaker promises we can go home, why should we stop her?'

'She has no idea what she's turning loose. She thinks she can call the Hunt to heel like herd-dogs, but she can't.'

He looked back at her. 'You know this for fact?'

Teia thought of Ytha, how she had stood eye to eye with the Speaker of her clan, and tried not to shudder at the memory. 'When I defied her she ordered Maegern's Hounds to kill me. They refused. They obey none but the Raven. In my dreams, I saw the land torn apart in blood and flame and Ytha was powerless to prevent it.' She kneaded her aching head. 'I speak truly, Baer. You do not have to believe me, or follow me. I ask nothing of you but the provisions I need to see me southwards.'

Another lengthy pause. 'When?'

'The spring full moon. Drwyn will gather the war bands at the Scattering and ride at their head with Ytha and the Hunt by his side.'

That rocked Baer back. 'Old Drw's crossed over?'

'In the autumn, before the Gathering. Drwyn's been Ytha's creature for years and she means to see him do what Gwlach could not. He'll be raised Chief of Chiefs at the Scattering, if not before.'

He rubbed his chin. 'Less than a moon away.' Baer pushed himself to his feet, hands now in fists at his sides. 'Go to sleep, Teia. We'll talk again tomorrow.'

25

DOUBTS

❧

From the promontory she could see almost the entirety of the Mere, from the foaming column of Belaleithne Falls, veiled in spray, to the island at the far end on which Carantuil stood, its pale walls and indigo clay tiles gleaming in the morning sun. With the waters perfectly reflecting the blue of the sky and the green of the enfolding hills, Tanith felt as if she had somehow stepped into the crystal sphere surrounding one of the intricate coloured glass sculptures for which the craftsmen on the Western Isles were so rightly famous.

According to the stories Tanith's father had told when she was younger, and curious about the parent she only hazily remembered, this had been her mother's favourite view. She'd sat on the moss beneath the birches for hours at a time, he'd said, capturing the changing moods of the waters with her sketchbook and paints. Whenever the pressures of being High Seat had grown too much for her, an hour here had restored her more thoroughly than meditation, more thoroughly even than sleep. In a way, she was there still. Certainly Tanith always sensed something of her mother's spirit lingering in that place, no matter how many years had passed since she died – something that was absent at the snowy marble mausoleum in the palace grounds that was her formal resting place.

Hello, Mama, she said to the air, and sat down on a rock. Her bandaged foot throbbed; she'd ridden most of the half-mile or so from her house, but she'd left her

horse at the end of the steep path and walked the last
hundred yards through the dense birch-woods, and now
she was suffering for it. With such a deep cut she should
have sent for a Healer, but perversely she'd cleansed and
dressed it herself and left it to mend in its own time. The
pain was a reminder to be careful where she trod, in
more ways than one.

*I'm sorry I've been away for so long. I tried to speak
to you almost every day whilst I was on the Isles – I
hope you could still hear me.*

Around her the birches shivered in the breeze. She
looked down at the spray of white flowers she held and
touched their waxy petals. In the dappled shade of the
trees they were so pale they almost glowed.

*I brought you some morningstars – I know how much
you love them.* The flowers nodded, and she plunged
on. *I have so much to tell you I hardly know where to
begin. I want to tell you all about my training, how
proud I was when they gave me my Master's mantle
and asked me to join the faculty after just four years.
Can you believe it? I've been teaching classes!*

But that wasn't what she'd come to say, and she
couldn't keep up the bright chatter when so much else
weighed so heavily on her mind. She bit her lip, tried to
marshal her thoughts, but they leapt and skittered
about like saelkies in search of sweets and refused to be
herded into any sort of order.

*Now I've come home again. I had to. It was time –
past time. I . . . Mama, I don't know what to do here.
The politics, the juggling of influence and interests –
I've tried to understand it, truly I have, but it doesn't
come naturally to me and I've been away from Court
for so long I think I've forgotten everything Papa tried
to teach me. Not that I listened much,* she admitted,
with a twinge of embarrassment that had her ducking
her head even though there was no one else around to
see her. She turned her mother's favourite ring around

and around on her middle finger, where she'd worn it
since her hand had grown enough for it to fit properly.
*I missed you terribly when I was growing up, but I'm
glad you weren't there to see it. I don't think I did much
to make you and Papa proud.*

All she'd done was make her father despair. Fallen
headlong in love at barely sixteen and sneaked out of
the house late at night to be with him when she should
have been sleeping. Devoured medical texts and treatises on surgery when she should have been studying
statecraft. And then she'd run away from a life she
thought of as stifling, just to find herself face to face
with it again five years later, still unprepared.

She twirled the morningstars back and forth through
her fingers. *What a mess.*

Gently reproving, the trees shook their heads. Sunlight touched her face through the shifting leaves, and
just for a second she imagined the warmth was a hand
cupped to her cheek as her mother told her not to
worry, everything would be all right.

If only she could believe that.

*Mama, I don't think the Ten quite know what to
make of me. I've been living in the human world since
before I was seventeen, and now here I am stepping up
to the High Seat of our House. They don't know me the
way they knew you and I'm not sure they'll trust me.
They're frightened by all the turmoil in the world and
they're on the brink of withdrawing behind the Veil,
and I have no idea how I'll ever persuade them that
running away from trouble isn't the answer.*

The irony of her words was bitter gall in her mouth.
Overhead, the golden leaves on the birches rustled a
sympathetic sigh.

*There's something else, too. Ailric. Do you remember
me telling you about him, before I went to the Isles?
He's asked Papa's blessing to seek my hand, but I can't
marry him, Mama. He's become too much like his fa-*

ther, too arrogant, too inward-looking. He regards humans as little better than animals – I think he'd be happiest if the world outside Astolar ceased to exist.

She fell silent, listening to the distant murmur of the falls and the eerie cry of a diver-bird somewhere out on the water.

I think you'd have liked the Western Isles, Mama. It's a beautiful place, and the people are . . . people. Humans are more like us than we realise. Yes, they can be fractious and stubborn, but so can we, and I saw as much nobility and wisdom in them as I see in the best of us. They suffer from most of the same ailments we do, they birth their children the same way – I should know, I've delivered more than a dozen! When things are funny they laugh, and they cry when they are sad – sometimes they laugh when they should be crying. They put others before themselves, take hurts so others don't have to and somehow find the courage to keep going even when their hearts are breaking.

Tanith realised she was no longer speaking of humanity in general but of one person in particular, and bit her lip. She'd seen Gair's heart break and had been unable to do anything about it. For all her physician's training, she'd been helpless to save the piece of him that died with the woman in his arms. Her eyes flew closed, the scar on her forearm burning. Oh, spirits!

I'm sorry I can't stay long, Mama. I'm to present myself at Court today as High Seat and I have to prepare. I'll come back later and tell you everything, I promise.

Limping carefully to the edge of the promontory, she lifted the morningstars to her face and breathed their delicate scent one final time. It reminded her of her mother's perfume so powerfully her hand began to shake.

'I miss you, Mama,' she whispered, and threw the spray of blossoms out into the Mere.

⚜

Lord Elindorien sighed.

'How I wish your mother was here. She should be the one to have this conversation, not me,' he muttered, pinching his brows. 'You are the only daughter of a noble House, Tanith. You are heir to the oldest realm in these lands. Sometimes we do not have the luxury of choice.'

She stared at him. 'You're telling me to marry him?'

Her father shot her a rueful smile. 'I would never attempt to *tell* you to do anything, daughter mine. But time is passing, and you are past the age at which marriage is customary. Ailric's offer is a good one. House Vairene is a fine family and he holds you in high esteem.'

She began pacing again and could not make herself stop. Even the pulses of pain from her bandaged foot did not break her stride. 'I won't do it.'

'But why not?' Exasperation tinged her father's voice. 'You and Ailric were close once – surely you could kindle that closeness again.'

'We are not a good match.' *Not any more.*

He folded his arms. 'The Leahn. Yes?'

'No.'

'He is not for you, Tanith.'

'He never was.' Back and forth across the pale carpet, skirts whipping around her legs. 'Gair has nothing to do with my decision.'

'So why will you not consider Ailric for your husband? His enduring regard for you tells me he will be a loyal and steadfast consort, and he is close to you in age.'

'And no other young men are likely to come forward for my hand, is that it?'

'I did not say that,' replied her father in a tone of voice that told her it was exactly what he had been thinking. 'Our race is dwindling, Daughter, and with every year that passes we grow less fruitful. The time for a harvest is now.'

'Harvest?' She almost laughed. 'Don't be so coy about it, Papa. We are animals, no different from the horses and cattle in our fields. You want me to breed.'

At her choice of words Lord Elindorien's nose wrinkled. 'Must you be so crude?'

'It is what you meant.'

He sighed. 'We cannot allow our line to fail, Tanith. There must always be ten Houses.' Her father, who so rarely allowed his emotions to rule him, sounded sharp, and tired, and even a little afraid. 'If you enter the chamber with Ailric at your side, it will sway the Ten. It may even guarantee you High Seat Morwenna's support in the vote – he was always her favourite grandson. But if you antagonise House Vairene it could make things very difficult for you when it comes your time to rule. You will need allies amongst the Ten, not enemies – especially now, with the Court so divided.'

'I know. You gave me Barthalus's *Essays on Government* when I turned ten years old.' Even then she'd been expected to know what it meant to be a Daughter of the White Court.

He came around the table and took hold of her shoulders, turning her to face him. 'You are the last Elindorien, my daughter. If your mother had lived and I could have given her more children, this burden would not have to fall to you, but ifs and could-haves are of no use to us now. We have only what lies before us. You must see your duty clearly.'

'My duty,' she said. 'To my House and my people.' Anger, unbidden and unstoppable, clawed at her stomach with fiery talons. 'What about my duty to *myself*?'

'Daughter—'

'Ailric embodies the very worst qualities of nobility,' she spat. Her father blinked, startled by her vehemence, but she couldn't stop herself. 'He's an arrogant, entitled

snob. Or would you see me tied to a man I despise simply to see me wed?'

'Of course not, but—'

'And what about you and *your* duty? Why did you
never marry again, Papa?'

'I could not!' he snapped back, his face despairing.
'Your mother was my only love. Once she was gone, I
could not bring myself to join with another.'

'Just as I cannot bring myself to join with Ailric.'
With a great effort Tanith gentled her tone and took his
hands in hers. To her surprise, they were trembling. 'I'm
sorry, Papa, but I must choose my own husband and it
will not be him.'

Lord Elindorien looked at her, his tawny eyes veiled
with more layers of emotion than she could fathom.
'You loved him once,' he said quietly.

'I loved a boy who played the lute so beautifully the
birds themselves fell silent to listen to him. That boy
doesn't exist any more.'

'He is the same boy, grown now into a man.'

The anger inside her dwindled to nothing as fast as it
had risen. Tanith shook her head and smiled for what
was gone. 'Ailric the lutenist died a long time ago, Papa.
I'm a good Healer, but I cannot bring a relationship
back to life when it was not meant to live.'

Lord Elindorien looked down at their hands. 'No, I
suppose not.' He sighed, rubbing his thumb across her
knuckles. 'Do you still have it? The Barthalus?'

'I do.'

A smile tweaked at the corner of his mouth. 'You
cried when I gave it to you because you really wanted
some book about the adventures of a human prince.'

'*Prince Corum and the Forty Knights.*' Fat salty tears
of disappointment rolling down her cheeks, and in
those years after her mother died her father hadn't
known how to console her. But a few days later he'd
brought her a copy, and she'd hung from his neck and

cried even harder as he patted her back in baffled wonderment. 'I remember.'

Across the Mere the Queen's herald blew the summons on his silver-chased horn. The solemn double note shivered the air like thunder. In the silence afterwards, even the Mere itself was stilled.

'It is time,' said her father at last, releasing her hands.

Tanith nodded. 'It is time.'

She smoothed her dress over her hips. After the simple gowns she had worn on the Isles the heavy white satin weighed her down, its pendant sleeves and trailing skirts dragging at her like sea-anchors. The inner sleeves with their pearl buttons from wrist to elbow clung to her as inescapably as her duty.

She blew out a long breath. 'I'm ready.'

He offered her his arm. With one hand to lift her skirts and the other on her father's bronze brocade cuff, she allowed him to lead her outside and across the mossy lawn to the many-tiered towers of the palace.

26

TO SERVE
THE GODDESS

Ansel could hear the Elders arguing without even opening the side door of the Rede-hall. They hadn't stopped since the tourney ended the day before, not for a minute, huddled in groups in corridors, strolling in the cloisters. Only in the silence of the refectory was there any relief from their endless bickering. There and during the Knighting ceremony that morning in the Sacristy, for twenty-two of the thirty-two novices who had competed in the lists, which had been conducted in an outraged silence that said more than words.

He eyed the liveried sentry beside the door.

What do you think? Does it matter, in the eyes of the Goddess, what lies beneath the mail and surcoat so long as there is an honest heart?

The sentry's face remained impassive, his gaze fixed on some detail of the tapestry on the far wall at a height that avoided the Preceptor's eye. For a moment Ansel contemplated asking him the question, then thought better of it. Any answer he received would be nothing more than what the man thought his superior wanted to hear.

More's the pity.

Hurrying footsteps sounded behind him and he turned, leaning on his staff. Danilar strode towards him in black formal robes, draping his crimson stole around his neck. His expression boiled with unasked questions.

'Chaplain,' Ansel said evenly, starting down the stone-flagged passage towards him. 'Will you walk with me for a moment?'

Danilar fell into step with him and slowed his pace accordingly. When they had retraced his steps along the corridor to the corner and were out of the sentry's earshot, Ansel turned to face him.

'Very well,' he said. 'Spit it out.'

'Did you know Selsen was a girl?'

'I knew.'

'Why didn't you tell me?'

'There was too much at stake. I couldn't tell anyone.' *There are some things I still cannot tell you. I pray you'll be able to forgive me, in time.*

The Chaplain looked away to hide his hurt. 'We've been friends for more than forty years, Ansel. You couldn't trust me with this?'

'I couldn't trust anyone. Not even my oldest friend.' He touched Danilar's arm. 'I'm sorry. It was better that no one knew, apart from me and the Superior at Caer Amon. That way if it all blew up in our faces, no one else would be hurt. I didn't want to expose you to the risk of a scandal.'

A grunt was all he received by way of reply. Danilar refused to meet his gaze and fidgeted with his stole, straightening it repeatedly even though it didn't need it. 'So this was your plan all along? To bring women into the Order?'

'My plan, if you recall, is to open admission to the Order to everyone who wants to join. Our numbers have never recovered from the desert wars. We need all the Knights we can train – now more than ever, with the news out of Gimrael.'

'But *women*!'

'*Everyone*, Danilar,' Ansel reminded him. 'And why not? Selsen's desire to be a Knight gave me the idea, and she has more than proved that a woman can stand toe to toe with the best of our men.'

Even before he'd finished speaking, the Chaplain was shaking his head. 'On the field, perhaps, but women and men living side by side in a House of the Goddess represents great temptation. A Knight cannot serve Eador with his whole heart when he is preoccupied by . . .' Danilar hesitated, clearly flustered. 'Worldly desires.'

Leaning on his staff, Ansel laughed. 'My dear Chaplain, I do believe you are blushing.'

'Ansel, please! This is serious.' Now his old friend faced him and his eyes were pleading. He pointed towards the door beyond the waiting sentry. 'They won't support you. What you are asking them to do goes against everything they have been taught, everything they have believed since the novitiate.'

'If all goes to plan, they won't have a choice. I have

the law and the Articles on my side – they'll have to support me.'

'When you go through that door you'll have a fight on your hands that will make Samarak look like a border skirmish. You do realise that, don't you?'

'I think I've got one more scrap left in me.'

'It might be your last!'

Ansel shrugged. 'If it is, so be it. I'd rather die fighting for something I believe in than end my days as a mindless ruin in the infirmary, unable to wipe my own arse.'

Danilar stared at him. 'Blunt, but apposite.' Sighing gustily, he scrubbed his thick fingers through his hair. 'Very well. Have it your way. Just don't expect me to say a blessing over your bloodied corpse when the Rede is done with you.'

With a deep breath, Ansel straightened up and automatically checked that he had a bottle of poppy syrup tucked into his pocket. Chances were good he would need every drop of it before this day was done.

'You knew it wouldn't be easy, Danilar. I told you that.'

'You did and I've been with you from the start. I cannot deny that I have reservations about the practicalities of what you're advocating, but we can fight about them later. I am your friend, Ansel. You can count on me.'

Ansel eyed the Chaplain fondly, seeing not the grizzled bear of a man in front of him but a scab-kneed boy in a too-short novice robe, scrumping apples with him in a long-ago orchard. He'd hoped to delay this particular storm of words until after Selsen's ordination, but hoping didn't make it so. The battle had come, and the best he could do was fight with what weapons he had.

'One last charge, old friend?' he said softly. 'For the Oak and the Goddess, to our last breath?'

Lips set into a determined line, Danilar squared his blacksmith's shoulders and tucked his thumbs into his girdle. *If he had his sword on his hip*, Ansel thought, *he'd be loosening it in its scabbard right about now.*

'One last charge.' A decisive nod. 'And may devils take the hindmost!'

⚜

'Impossible!' thundered Elder Festan.

'It's already done,' Ansel said.

'Overturn it! It's within your power as Preceptor. A female cannot be a Knight and that's the end of it.'

Expressions of support rumbled up from the benches.

'Why not?'

'It is not permitted!'

Another Elder surged to his feet without waiting for Festan to yield the floor. 'Women have no place on a battlefield, Preceptor. You of all people should know that, after the desert wars.'

'And why is that, Jago?'

'They are physically . . . unsuited to the rigours of combat.'

'What's that you say?' For comic effect, Ansel cupped a hand around his ear. 'Speak up, man. Physically inferior?' Someone snorted. 'So when I watched Selsen take three strikes in the lists from an experienced Knight, I imagined it?'

Discomfited, Elder Jago launched a new argument. 'The other novices were completely taken in. She'd been living amongst them in the dortoir for almost two months, pretending to be what she was not, deceiving her way into their confidences and their lives. If they were so taken in, how do we even know Hengfors was correct?'

Standing, the lanky physician cleared his throat and glared down his considerable nose at the objector. 'Although I am a member of a cloistered Order, Elder, I am first and foremost a surgeon, and well versed in anatomy. The patient on my table yesterday afternoon was most certainly female.'

'So how did she pass for a boy, being so abundantly female? In the bathhouse, at the garderobe?'

'It is not so difficult to arrange a little privacy for these things,' said Hengfors. 'Her physique is well trained and muscular, and her feminine attributes –' Jago blushed '– are modest. With care for how she walked and some strapping around her chest, we all saw what we expected to see.'

Arranging his robe around his heron-like frame as if settling his feathers, Hengfors perched back on the end of the witnesses' bench below the lowest row of Elders, next to the martial Masters. Jago plumped into his seat with his face flaming to the roots of his ash-coloured hair.

Festan opened his mouth again, but before he could utter a word another Elder was standing up to address the Rede.

'But Elder Jago's original point was well made,' Ceinan said. 'The very qualities we most prize in womankind, and which we are sworn to defend, are the same qualities that make them unsuitable to be soldiers of the Goddess. They are nurturers, not warriors. They bring forth new life from their bodies. Surely we should not ask them to take life away?'

Nods and murmurs of agreement met his words. Standing uncomfortably at the witness stand with her left arm strapped across her chest, Selsen stirred, her face tight with anger. She tried to sign something then had to give up; thieftalk was impossible with only one useful hand. She turned a look of appeal towards Ansel. His fingers flickered discreetly.

I understand.

'Forgive my speaking on Selsen's behalf,' he said, 'but we are not asking her to do anything at all. She is asking us.' Selsen nodded vigorously.

'With all respect to her,' Ceinan said, bowing to Selsen just enough to appear polite, 'this Elder at least must refuse. Call the vote, Preceptor. Let each man here follow his conscience on this matter.' With that, he subsided gracefully into his seat.

Festan remembered he had the floor and shook himself like a large dog coming out of the sea. 'There's no point calling for a vote,' he rumbled. 'Even if we wanted her to be Knighted, she couldn't be. Honestly, Preceptor, I don't understand why you persist with this folly when it's patently impossible.'

'Selsen completed the trial-at-arms with high honour, one of the finest novices our Order has ever produced. What more must she do to prove her worth?' Ansel leaned forward a little, the better to make his point. 'You were there, Festan, sitting right in front of me in the pavilion. You watched the events, you heard the judges' decisions, just as I did.'

'Yes, but—'

'But what?' Ansel attempted to rein in his temper but his patience had worn too thin to make a good leash. 'All that's happened since is you've discovered the novice you watched is of the fairer sex. It doesn't change her achievements, so why do you object to her receiving due credit for them?'

Festan threw up his hands as if appealing to heaven to intervene. 'It is forbidden under the Articles! A woman cannot become a Knight!'

'Under which Article would that be, Elder?' put in Danilar mildly.

Thanks be to the Goddess! Whatever his own reservations about the matter at hand, Danilar remained a man of his word.

The interruption threw Festan from his stride. 'Chaplain?'

'Under which of the Articles of Knighthood are women excluded from service? Forgive me – I'm getting older and my memory's not what it was.' The snort from before returned, this time developing into an outright chuckle. Ansel suspected he knew who it was but he didn't dare scan the rows of Elders to find out for sure. Besides, Festan's apoplectic features were an entertainment in themselves.

'Well, I don't recall exactly, but—'

'Elder Morten is right there, with a copy of the Articles,' Danilar said, indicating the Elder and his equally aged brother Tercel seated at one the clerks' desks, a leather-bound book open before them. 'Perhaps he could check?'

Morten's reedy voice failed to carry over the hubbub of assertion and counter-assertion. Ansel rapped his staff on the dais for silence and the white-haired Elder tried again.

'I don't need to check, gentlemen – and milady.' He turned and gave Selsen a half-bow. 'Nowhere in the Articles is there a reference to gender except in the form of the personal pronoun "he" which, as any student of the law will know, can refer to either sex and requires no disambiguation.'

Ceinan leaned forwards in his seat. 'Are you saying, Morten, that this woman's ordination should be permitted on the strength of a bit of legal shorthand?'

Elder Morten spread his frail hands. 'I am saying there is nothing in the Articles to specifically proscribe it.'

'But there's nothing that specifically permits it, either?'

'Correct.'

'But—'

Tercel held up a knobby finger and Ceinan, surprisingly, fell silent. 'In law, the position has always been: that which is not prohibited *is permitted*. It is one of the pillars of jurisprudence.'

Ansel bit his cheek to contain his glee. *Thank heavens for Morten and Tercel and their unsurpassed reverence for the niceties of consistorial law! They were experts on it before I was out of the novitiate. Does anyone want to argue with them?*

The Elders muttered like a pot on the boil, but no one raised an objection strenuous enough to force it to be acknowledged. Too soon, far too soon to be hopeful, but Ansel's fingers twitched to pin the gilded oak leaves on Selsen's shoulder. 'Let us be absolutely clear about this, gentlemen,' he declared. 'Elder Morten, please list for us the requirements for Knighthood.'

'Under Article One, the candidate must be hale of body, sound of limb and at least twenty years of age. Under Article Four, a minimum of six years must have been served in the novitiate and under Article Eight, the candidate must demonstrate sufficient skill at arms in the presence of authoritative witnesses.'

Not once did Morten have to refer to the worn pages of the book in front of him. He turned to Selsen, a kindly smile creasing his wizened features even further. 'Novice Selsen, are you qualified under these Articles?'

Selsen nodded.

'Can you not speak, milady, so that your answer might be recorded by Brother Chronicler?'

On the opposite desk the clerk finished writing and waited, pen poised. Selsen shook her head.

'The girl is mute from birth,' Ansel put in. 'I have a letter that attests to it, which can be entered into the record.' *Please don't call for it, Morten. I've risked enough to get her this far. It has to be enough!*

'I don't think that will be necessary, Preceptor. Your word is sufficient for the purpose of these proceedings.' Morten folded his hands in front of him. 'And I believe Selsen has demonstrated the necessary skill at arms, eh, Masters?'

Across the hall on the witnesses' bench, the Master of Swords, Master of Horse and Master of Arms all nodded, though only Selenas looked comfortable about it. A hint of a smile played about his lean jaw.

It was you who chuckled before, wasn't it? If you didn't, you look like you want to now.

'Could you discern that the novice was female?' Ansel asked. They all shook their heads. 'You saw only an aspiring Knight and made your judgement on that basis, devoid of prejudice?' Once again, they nodded. 'So all that remains is for her to serve her vigil. She is qualified under the Articles. I fail to see what further objections can be brought.'

He raised his staff in preparation to strike it and end the debate, but Festan was not finished.

'I find it morally objectionable,' he declared. 'There are perils faced by women, and only women, which must exclude them from situations where they have to engage the enemy directly.'

'Specifically?' Ansel said. *I was expecting this, but I never expected Festan to be the one to suggest it.*

'Specifically pertaining to their treatment if captured.'

The word hung in the air, soundless but as loud as thunder. Every man in the room heard it. They could not do otherwise: it was part of a Knight's duty to protect women from such assault with strength of arms, with his body or, when all else failed, with his life. Regardless of how high or low their station, a woman was the embodiment of the Goddess's power of creation in physical form, and to profane that form with violence or ill intent was to commit a profound sin. But the central tenet of Knighthood, upon which all others depended, was to act in defence of what was right, no matter the cost.

Someone has to say it. It might as well be me. 'Rape.'

Festan looked uncomfortable, fidgeting with his sleeves and unable to meet Selsen's eye. The rest of the Curia fared little better, save those accustomed to hiding their emotions behind a mask of dispassion. More than a few sported blushes to rival their robes for hue.

'In a word, yes,' replied Festan. 'This is not a peril the rest of us must face.'

You'd be surprised, Festan. The Saint Benet's Day massacre at the Daughterhouse in El Maqqam showed us that rape was not the furthest depth to which the Cult would stoop.

An urgent clicking sound dragged his attention to Selsen – she was snapping her fingers. When she had his eye she mimed writing with her good hand.

'You wish to add something?' Her eyes imploring, she nodded. 'If the Rede has no objection?'

No one demurred. Selsen stepped down from the witness stand and hurried to Brother Chronicler's desk. She grabbed one of his spare quills and a sheet of paper and scribbled several lines, then handed the page back to the clerk who looked uncertainly from the girl dressed in novice robes to his Preceptor and back again.

'Please read the witness's statement, Brother,' said Ansel.

'"I ask only for the right to defend my faith to the best of my ability. If I feared the consequences, I would not ask for that right. It is my life's wish to be a Knight; if it be the Goddess's will that I take hurt or die in Her service, then let Her will be done."'

The clerk lowered the sheet and laid it on the desk, staring at it as if it was an adder that might yet bite him.

'Surely if a woman wishes to serve the Goddess, she can do so by taking holy orders,' interjected Elder Eadwyn. Several other voices chorused their agreement. 'There is no need for her to don armour and trade blows with a sword.'

'Why not, if that is what she wants?' All eyes turned to a new speaker. Selenas, the sinewy Syfrian Master of Swords, was on his feet. 'If she wishes to shoulder the responsibility of Knighthood, surely that is her choice? Or are we reduced to making women's decisions for them and telling them what they may and may not do for their own good? I rather think our Goddess would take a dim view of such paternalistic presumption on our part.'

One or two scandalised gasps flitted through the assembled Curia at Selenas's own presumption to speak on Her behalf.

'It is a man's duty to protect a woman, and even more so a Knight's,' said Eadwyn to general approbation, and sat down.

Selenas cocked his head to one side. 'And what if she doesn't want our protection? What if she feels she is capable of protecting herself and anyone else who needs it? I have faced Selsen over crossed swords, gentlemen, and I can assure you, the person requiring protection that day was not the lady.'

He swept her an elegant bow, bending his whipcord frame at the waist with his right hand over his heart. After a moment's startlement, Selsen returned the compliment.

Eadwyn rose to his feet again. 'Surely you can see that women lack the necessary aggression to overcome an enemy hand-to-hand. She may have all the martial skill, but does she have the steel inside to press home her attack, when doing so might put her own life at risk? Will she fail when blood and worse are sprayed across her face?'

'You've obviously never stepped into a stable where a mare has a foal at foot,' said the Master of Horse gruffly.

'Indeed,' said Ansel. 'Women have the hearts of lions, Elder Eadwyn, of that I have no doubt. All Selsen asks is for a chance to prove it.'

In the uncomfortable pause that followed, Ceinan rose again.

'Are we not still overlooking something, my brothers?' he began. 'There is another moral question to be addressed. Women serving alongside men, at close quarters, lays both open to the temptations of the flesh. How are women to preserve their modesty and their virtue under such circumstances? How are the men?'

How indeed? If a Knight can fail and break his vows when all his comrades are men, what hope is there for him when he fights shoulder to shoulder with women?

'That, I think, is a question we cannot answer in debate,' Ansel said. 'We can only answer it in the field and trust to our faith that we are strong enough to prevail.'

Again the urgent snapping of fingers. Selsen held up the sheet of paper so all the Elders could see. In block letters on the reverse, so forcefully that the quill had split and sputtered, she had written: I WILL NOT FAIL. When Ceinan raised his eyebrows she scowled and brandished the paper before her like a shield.

'It appears I am outmatched, my lady, and must cede the field,' the Dremenirian said. He spread his hands and bowed his head, but not before Ansel had caught the twitch of his lips that hid a smile. 'My objections remain. I have no need to restate them.'

He sat down and Ansel nodded.

'Your objections are noted, Elder. Is there any further comment before we put this to the vote? Eadwyn? Festan?' Meaty arms folded across his chest, Festan shook his head grimly. Returned to the witness stand once more, Selsen made the sign of blessing over her breast and closed her eyes. 'Then so be it.'

Staff ringing on the stone dais, he called for the vote.

27

SIGNS

꧁❦꧂

Darkness. Soft, silent, suffocating. It enveloped Teia like the blackness of the womb and in it a nightmare waited to be born. She heard its heartbeat, sensed the shape of its dreams. Felt it stretch and grow, and knew its mother's name. She screamed.

Hands caught her shoulders as she struggled with her blankets.

'Gently, gently now, Teia,' said Neve. 'It's all right. Everything's all right.'

'She's coming,' Teia whispered. She drew in a shuddering breath. 'I felt it. She's coming!'

Neve frowned. The slaty light seeping into the cave was not kind to her face, hardening it, deepening the lines etched into it by her years of exile. Like water runnels carved into stone.

'Who's coming? You've had a bad dream, that's all. It's over now. Everything will be all right, you'll see.'

Prescience's icy hands remained clamped around Teia's heart and she shivered. Cold. She was so cold, the warmth at her core leaching out of her in the face of what was to come. 'No, it won't. Nothing will be all right ever again.'

'Teia?'

'She's almost here, Neve.'

'Who?'

'The Raven.'

Oh, Macha keep me safe from the storm.

❈

'I've never seen a woman so afraid, Baer.'

Neve stood beside him at the lookout, hugging herself against the cold, as the bone-white hills revealed themselves under a paling sky. Her man said nothing, but his eyes never stopped moving, scanning the snow for tracks, for signs of pursuit.

'She said it over and over, that *She*'s coming, that nothing will be right again.'

One of the Eldest. What the girl claimed she had seen. Was it true that the Raven had been summoned by the Speaker of the Crainnh? The girl had no reason to lie. What Teia was attempting was so reckless, surely only the truth could spur her to try – or what she believed to be the truth, anyway. He had yet to settle his own mind on whether it was or it wasn't and, once it was settled, he still had to decide what to do. There were two-dozen souls in his care now, with winter upon them; the same stubborn spirit that had got him sent into exile in the first place said he should hunker down in the lands he knew and wait it out, but there was a restless disquiet in the corners of his heart that he couldn't ignore.

'Maegern,' he said quietly. Out of the corner of his eye, he saw Neve make the sign of protection. 'Superstitious, Neve? You?'

'She had a look about her. Faraway, but looking into me at the same time. Fair chilled me, it did.'

'A foretelling?'

'I don't know. Maybe. She wouldn't talk about it no more, just set to gathering up her things.'

'It wasn't simply a nightmare?'

'Powerful dark, if it was.' Neve shook her head. 'You should have seen her face, Baer. Then you'd understand.'

He grunted. 'If only I had some proof.'

'She's got the Talent, you've seen that, and after the way she looked at me I don't doubt she's got the sight, too.'

Now there was a thing, if it were true. Eyes narrowed, he asked, 'Banfaíth? You're sure?'

'I reckon.' Settling her shawl around her shoulders, Neve gave him that look he had come to know well: the one that said this was women's business and he had best not argue. 'Women know sometimes,' she said. 'T'ain't something as can be taught. T'ain't something as can be put in a box and showed to you. We just know, in our bones.' Arms folded, she shrugged. 'It's why Speakers are always women.'

He searched the horizon again, for the hundredth, the thousandth time since his watch began. Lost Ones could never be too careful.

Banfaíth. Speakers were trouble enough, to men and women both. Useful, no doubt, and powerful, but always trouble. But the Banfaíth were . . . other. They listened to the wind and it told them its secrets. They had the knowing of things hidden from others. How to read dreams. How to read a man's heart.

His fingers clenched and unclenched restlessly on the bow lying across his shoulders. *She's just a bit of a girl. Like my own I left behind.* 'I'll go to her, soon as my watch is over. I promised I'd talk with her again.'

His woman kissed him quickly, fondly, on the cheek. 'Best be quick. I think she's on her way.'

⊰⊱

Finn stood quietly, saddle blanket spread across his broad back. Getting the bridle on him had been easy enough, but the saddle was proving more problematic. Hampered by her bulging belly, Teia simply couldn't stand close enough or hoist it high enough to get it onto Finn's back.

After the third attempt she dropped it and kneaded her lower back with both hands. Stupid thing. If she had a rock to stand on, even a bale of dung, she could manage, but she didn't and oh her back ached now from trying. She was getting closer to her time. Carefully she rested one hand on the firm globe of her abdomen. Fifteen weeks to go or thereabouts, if she'd reckoned up correctly, although lately her size had made her begin to wonder whether she'd made a mistake. Then, with some pain, she would be rid of it for good and all.

Guilt spasmed inside her. It wasn't the child's fault. An infant had no say in her conception, in her allotted parents. How could Teia blame her? If anyone was to blame it was the unborn's father.

Thinking of Drwyn fired her with enough anger to heave the saddle to shoulder height and fling it towards Finn. He grunted but stood still. Almost there. One more heave and she could—Macha's ears, the blanket was slipping. On her tiptoes, Teia strained to steady the saddle against her upper chest whilst tugging the blanket straight again, but the combined weight was too much for her.

Down the saddle crashed. She stepped back smartly and it missed her feet, thumping to the ground with a jingle of buckles. Finn sidestepped away, the blanket slithering from his back to top the saddle in a heap.

'Du bagh na freann!'

Tears of frustration pricked at her eyes. She'd come this far, survived a confrontation with Ytha and Drwyn both, and now she couldn't even saddle her own horse. She wanted to scream.

'Now, now,' said a voice behind her. 'A pretty wee girl shouldn't know words like that.'

Teia swung around, face burning. Anger and shame, she couldn't have said which was the hotter. But Baer winked when he caught her eye and that so flustered her that she bent down for the saddle blanket and took her time spreading it just so in order to hide her confusion.

When she reached for the saddle itself, Baer scooped it up and set it on Finn's back with practised ease. The dun lunged for him with his teeth and Teia smacked his nose.

'None of your nonsense,' she told him firmly. He flicked his ears.

'Got a temper, that one?' Baer asked, reaching for the girths.

'A bit, if he decides he doesn't like you.'

'And he doesn't like many people, eh?' He shot her a sidelong look and Teia couldn't help but smile.

'Not many, no. Thank you, Baer.'

He straightened up and rested one arm on the saddle, watching her curiously. 'You sure you won't stay with us?'

'I'm sure. My way lies on a different road.'

She nodded south, towards the mountains rearing above the foothills that surrounded the cave, and tried not to think about how far she had to go. Out of the lands of her people, into the unknown.

The silver moon was setting as the sun rose, the dawn moon high in the southern sky. As she watched, the first sunlight hit the highest peaks and the forked summit of Tir Malroth stabbed up at the dawn moon's belly. Premonition crawled along her spine.

That way, Macha keep me. The Haunted Mountain. She bit her lip. *The one place the clans won't go.*

Baer was speaking. 'I'd best bring you those provisions, then,' he said. Something in his voice told Teia he'd had to say it twice to snag her attention.

'I'm sorry, I was away with the wind.'

'You've a long journey ahead. I wish you luck.'

She smiled at him and nodded her thanks. He strode away, leaving Teia to watch the moons on their patient journey across the sky. They were approaching trinity.

It would occur about the same time as her daughter was born, perhaps a little later. Thoughtful, she rested a hand on her belly. What if she gave birth under the trinity? What would that portend for her daughter, out there, amongst strange kin?

❦

Kael reined up near the edge of the scrubby alder trees that fringed the river. 'Hold,' he said tensely.

Duncan and the four scouts riding behind him halted. He scanned the surrounding trees for anything amiss but saw no tracks disturbing the snow underfoot, and the trees grew too densely to allow him to do more than glimpse the thickly snowed plain beyond, and the twisting dark ribbon of the river that cut across it.

'What is it?'

Kael didn't answer straight away, casting about him like a questing hound. The scar that gouged his face from temple to jaw shone red against his sallow skin, his newly grown beard not even close to hiding it. 'Dead men.'

'Here?'

Without looking, the scarred clansman lifted his arm and pointed out to the plain. 'There.'

'You're sure?' Duncan asked, and Kael gave him a disgusted look. Of course Kael was sure; he was *always* sure.

Even after all this time, Duncan had no real understanding of how his lieutenant did what he did, how he knew what he knew. On careful consideration, he wasn't even sure he *wanted* to know. Sometimes the extent of the seeker's awareness of the dark places in men's hearts was downright disturbing.

He motioned to the four scouts. 'Off you go. See what you can see, and be back here in an hour.' Needing no further instructions, they divided into two pairs and set off, one upstream, one down.

He slid a sideways glance at Kael. The man had always been ill at ease with the world around him, but since they'd tracked Maegern's Hound across the mountains his discomfort had grown markedly worse. The beast's stench appeared to linger in his nostrils, leaving his lips permanently twisted with distaste and his disposition more sour than ever. He wouldn't even look towards the plains and whatever he could sense there.

Leaving his horse with its reins over a branch, Duncan picked his way through the last of the alders in the direction Kael had pointed. As the cover ran out he hunkered down to survey the undulating snows. Even from a distance he could see where they'd been churned up by many feet some time before the last snowfall. Tracks led in and tracks led out, blurred by the fresh snow but still visible. In the middle of the churned area, between the alders and the river's lazy swoop, were two irregular shapes, roughly man-sized and almost completely covered with snow.

'I see them,' he said. He didn't need to raise his voice; his words would carry well enough on the cold, still air. He looked left and right again to be sure no one was watching – straight ahead the plain was as empty and undisturbed as a fresh-made bed, all the way to the horizon – and then walked out to the bodies.

No attempt had been made to build a cairn or honour them in death; they had simply been left where they fell, limbs all tumbled about. He hunkered down and brushed the snow away from their faces with his sleeve. One corpse lay on his back, and scavengers had already torn into his features – only empty sockets and a lipless grin remained. Duncan tried and failed not to shudder. He'd seen his share of dead men, but never the likes of this.

The other man had fallen across his left arm. The right side of his face had been stripped almost to the bone, but the left, when Duncan managed to heave him up, still held enough ashen-grey skin to show a clan tattoo, high on his cheek. Three lines, one long and swooping suggesting the head, neck and back of a running horse, the others short strokes to make the forelegs. His lips tightened, and he lowered the corpse back onto the ground. Clan Morennadh. His clan.

Quickly he swept aside more snow from the bodies, exposing the bloody and frost-stiffened buckskins each man wore. Their furs and winter gear were gone; boots and weapons, too. Most of their fingers were missing – to animals, he thought at first, then noticed the cleanly-severed edges of the bones on one hand, still visible despite the gnawing of rodents. Hacked off, then, presumably for a ring that couldn't be removed any other way.

In this cold, there was no telling how long ago they'd died – long enough ago to be frozen solid; not long enough yet for them to to be dragged apart by the wild creatures. He searched them as best he could for anything that might help identify them, but nothing of any value or use remained. All he found was a small bead-and-bone charm stitched to missing-finger's belt.

Carefully, Duncan slit the stitches with his knife. He turned the charm over in his hand and recognised the sigil for safe travelling carved into the bone. It hadn't done the poor fellow much good.

Straightening up, he tucked away his knife and turned back towards the trees, slipping the charm into his pocket. Maybe someone from Sor's ride would recognise it and give him a name, so the dead could be properly sung – and maybe, in time, vengeance properly taken.

When he reached Kael, the scar-faced seeker still had his back set resolutely towards the plain and its grim burden. Duncan couldn't say he blamed him. From the looks of it, the two Morennadh had died hard.

'Two Morennadh,' he said. 'Stripped of anything of value, right down to their boots. How did you know they were there?'

Kael spat, scowling. 'Smelled what was done to 'em.' He scrubbed his palm across his nose, as if the foetid stench that troubled him was something physical that could be wiped away. 'Smells bad.'

The cold had kept the bodies from stinking; only the faintest odour of corruption on the air had betrayed that they were on their way back to the earth, but that wasn't what Kael was referring to.

'Do you know who did it?' Duncan hardly needed to ask; this side of the Archen Mountains, the north side, the culprits could only be Nimrothi.

Kael shook his head. 'No, but I can tell you where they went – towards the pass at Saardost.' He scrubbed his nose again. 'This place stinks.'

Saardost made sense: it was the lowest of the three passes through the an-Archen and the easiest to travel – passable with care even at this time of year, before the thaw was under way. But the tracks he'd seen indicated only a small party, nowhere near large enough to be the war band. Scouts, then, and they'd run across two of the Morennadh's own.

A short time later, the rest of the patrol returned and made their report. As far as they'd been able to follow the tracks in the time allotted, they'd seen spoor for only a half-dozen horses at most, which confirmed Duncan's theory of a scouting party, hugging the foothills as they headed towards the pass. Of the Nimrothi war band there was no sign. They could be further out on the plain, or nowhere within a hundred miles; it was impossible to say.

'But now they know we're looking for them,' he muttered, hands on hips.

'Also means they're between us and the pass.' Kael scratched at his beard, carefully avoiding the tail of the scar. 'The scouts are, anyway. We could take the long road, and go back through King's Gate. Only two days from here.'

Duncan was shaking his head almost before his lieutenant finished speaking. 'It's still too early in the year to be sure the Gate is passable – we might end up in snow to our noses. No, we follow them east, back the way we came, rejoin the rest of the ride then go through Saardost in numbers. The Nimrothi know we have scouts of our own here, but they won't know that *we* have discovered *theirs*. As long as they think they're undetected they won't risk a confrontation with a larger party.' It was what he would do in their position: stay out of sight, observe, report back. He wouldn't risk a battle if there was a chance his men might come off worst.

Though the odds were in his favour, it was still a gamble. It was also the only option open to him. Sor was at Saardost Keep, and he needed to know what had happened to his men.

'All right.' He took his horse's reins from Kael and swung up into the saddle. 'Let's go, whilst there's still some light.'

A couple of the other riders exchanged looks. 'We're not going to honour them?' one asked, nodding towards the fallen clansmen.

'If we do, and more Nimrothi scouts come this way, they'll know they've been discovered.' Duncan hated himself for saying it, but it had to be so.

'What's the point?' Kael snapped, jerking his horse into a tight turn. 'Waste your *uisca* on them if you want, but what made them men is already gone. What's left will go back to the earth either way.'

He dug in his heels and his horse leapt forward, recklessly fast for the conditions. The other scouts shared another dubious look then filed after him at a more sensible pace. Duncan brought up the rear, chafing at having to leave kin unburied and chewing over how he would break the news to Sor. His brother took his responsibilities as a war captain no less seriously for being the chief. If anything, he was happier being just a war captain, though his wife fretted constantly that their children would grow up fatherless – and if that came to pass, Duncan would find the Morennadh clan torc around his own neck. He shuddered at the thought. He was barely ready for a wife yet, much less that responsibility.

As his horse plodded through the snow, the travelling charm in his pocket pressed against his thigh. He glanced back in the direction of his dead kinsmen, now out of sight behind a thick screen of alders and scrubby winter-bare bushes. Some ill luck had been at work there, to bring them into conflict with the Nimrothi. Neither side would have wanted to betray their presence to the other, but the results had been deadly.

Sor would not be best pleased, but they had a direction of travel for the Nimrothi scouts, and by implication for the war band following along behind: east, to Saardost Keep. He hoped the restored defences of the ancient fortress would be ready in time.

⊰⊱

Teia left the Maenardh at the last good ford along the river. It ran wide and fast over a bed of gravel, bone-achingly cold but shallow enough that Finn could cross it without chilling too badly.

The farewells were stiff. Neve hovered at Baer's shoulder and fretted her bottom lip with her teeth; Baer himself simply cautioned her to have a care for rock-wolves in the hills, then turned east along the river, the rest of his little band straggling behind him. Lenna and her man were the only others who could or would meet her eye, and they did so with a fear and hostility that did not abate even when she raised her mittened hand and waved them out of sight.

Alone again. As I always seem to be.

She swung Finn southwards. Up into the hills first, then she would pick her way from there. According to the stories there was a good pass below the Haunted Mountain, but it was high, perhaps too high to have thawed by the time she reached it. She looked up, shading her eyes against the brightness of the peaks rising into the mussel-shell sky. In the centre, Tir Malroth brandished its tusks. Unreachable, implacable, forbidding.

All her life she had lived in the shadow of the Archen Mountains. Sometimes close, when wintering in their foothills, sometimes distant, when the clan followed the plodding elk across the plains. They spanned the horizon from sunrise to sunset, the southern limit of her world. The rest, the Empire and its lands, were only tales to her, dangerous voices on the wind.

The enormity of the task she had set herself sank like a stone in her chest. *Macha watch over me. Lord Aedon protect me. I don't know what else to do.*

Even the longest journey had to begin with a step, and every step she took would make her journey shorter. She couldn't go back, nor could she stay where she was. Clicking her tongue, she urged Finn further into the hills.

28

DAUGHTER OF
THE WHITE COURT

❧

The Ten hadn't listened, as she'd known they wouldn't.

Oh, they'd heard her well enough, but when Berec and Denellin spoke the Court listened to them instead of the newly presented High Seat of House Elindorien who had spent so long with the humans that she had come to think like them, share their fears. They hadn't said it in so many words, but the implication had been clear. The Ten thought she cared more about humans than her own people.

Tanith gripped the arms of her chair tightly, the pale wood cool against her sweat-slick palms. Didn't they see that the danger was real? Didn't they realise that if the Veil fell, Astolar would no longer be safe – nowhere would be safe?

Across the high-domed chamber with its intricately tessellated floor, Denellin was still arguing for reclusion and the number of heads nodding agreement with the points he made dismayed her. Four voting for the realm to isolate itself, her father had said. Now it looked as if there might be six.

'In conclusion, it seems only prudent that we should close our borders and insulate ourselves from the civil unrest so prevalent across the human Empire. Rioting in Yelda last year, clashes of faith again in the desert this. These are troubled times, Majesty, and we would do well to distance ourselves from them.'

Murmurs of assent followed him back to his seat from the speaker's circle in the centre of the floor. Berec being one of those to agree was only to be expected. Time had gouged deep lines into his face and the hair spilling around the shoulders of his garnet robes had the translucence of spider-silk. But Taren Odessil too? And House Vairene?

This was her one chance to urge them towards unity instead of division; stalwart defence instead of self-interest. Heart pounding, Tanith stood up.

The Chancellor, in the twelfth seat, directly opposite the Queen, nodded to her. 'The Court recognises the Seat of House Elindorien.'

She walked to the circle, keeping her hands busy holding up her skirts so that they would not be seen to be trembling. As a Daughter of the White Court it was her duty to speak out for the best interests of the realm, as she had done that morning, and they hadn't listened. If she didn't say something now, it would be too late: they would vote for reclusion and hide in their marble halls as the world fell apart around them. Then when their own walls crumbled, they would look around and find no one left to help them.

'Majesty, if I may be so bold, Lord Denellin overlooks a crucial fact. The human Empire to which he refers is also our Empire. We are a part of it, by solemn treaty and the custom of ages. We trade in its markets, teach in its universities; its troubles are our troubles. We cannot isolate ourselves as he suggests without severing our ties with the Empire altogether.'

Tanith looked around the chamber, at the men and women of the Ten in their House colours beneath their velvet banners. Gold and silver thread winked in the sunshine filtering down through the filigreed dome.

'As my father likes to remind me, we are not a war-like people. We are a people of alliance, of negotiated peace, the kind of peace to which we swore ourselves in this very chamber centuries ago. Would you have Astolar secede from the Empire and break those oaths?'

Grey heads shook gravely and leaned towards their neighbours', the susurrus of whispered words too soft for her to hear. She was the youngest in the chamber by thirty or more years; many of the Ten had been ageing when her mother had ascended to the High Seat – Berec had made toys for her when she was a child! How many members of the Court still saw her as that child, playing at being Queen in the empty chamber, marching her wooden horse across the speaker's circle? Perhaps her father had been right and Ailric's presence at her side would have lent her some gravitas. Too late to worry about that now.

'But more importantly, we must face the fact that the Veil which protects our world is failing. Worse, there is a reiver loose who has the power to tear a hole in it, and if he is not stopped, he could rend the whole Veil. Without it there will be nothing to secure us from the dark realms. The Hidden Kingdom will be exposed and its denizens given free rein to invade the daylight world. We must stand against this reiver, or deal with worse than rioting apprentices.'

Hisses of distaste. The Queen turned her head aside, lips pressed into a thin line.

'You are certain of this? You have seen this reiver?' asked Taren, the next youngest after Tanith. He was slender and dark enough to belie his years, if one did not look closely enough to see the crow's feet, the silver-brushed temples.

'I have seen his handiwork and that was enough.' Despite her best efforts, Tanith's trembling had reached her voice, and the more she tried to suppress it, the sharper her tone became. 'A young man was attacked, his body so torn he almost bled to death as I fought to Heal him. His mind, his memories, utterly violated.' A single hot tear spilled over her lashes and coursed down her cheek at the pain of the memory. 'I had to shield him from the Song itself to give him peace.'

'Does he live, this young man?' asked Denellin.

'He lives. More by luck than any skill of mine, but he lives.' Tanith fumbled open the tiny pearl buttons on her left sleeve, one by one.

'Who is he? Can he be brought before us, that we might question him?'

'He's no one important, no scion of a noble house. Just a human.' She wrenched her sleeve back. Two or three pearls burst their stitching and rattled across the tiled floor. 'The reiver's creatures did this to me.' She brandished her scarred forearm before their shocked faces. 'Does this make it real for you? Is this evidence enough that the threat to the Veil, and to us, is real?'

Uncomfortable, Denellin shifted in his seat. 'Please, Lady Elindorien, compose yourself.'

'No!' Another scalding tear fell. 'I will *not* compose myself! I will *not* be calm and restrained and dignified when there is a reiver loose, who can do this –' she shook her raised arm '– and this –' she flung an illusion into the air of a procession bearing twenty-four linen-wrapped corpses towards unlit pyres, and peppered it with more images: Chapterhouse's failing shields, Donata's horrified face frozen in death, the yammering horde of demons attacking unarmed men '– and you will do nothing to stand against him. Don't you see? This affects all of us, every one. If the Veil is brought down there will be nowhere left for us. We will be rendered as defenceless as they were, and if we isolate ourselves now, who will we turn to for aid when the demons come for us?'

'Daughter.'

The Queen's voice was incisive, steely as a blade. Dashing the back of her hand across her cheeks, Tanith faced the highest Seat of them all.

'Majesty?'

Queen Emelia was the eldest member of the Court, a
reed-like woman in a gauzy pearl-grey gown that draped
her seated form like dusty cobwebs. Her white hair was
piled atop her head, held in place with long pins from
which crystal ornaments danced and sparkled with her
slightest movement. Yet there was nothing fragile or
ephemeral about her face. It was handsome – aquiline,
even – rather than beautiful, save for her eyes. Large and
luminous as tiger-jade, they fixed Tanith in place as if she
was a moth skewered on one of those very hairpins.

'You speak with great conviction, Daughter. Your
passion does you credit, even if it is at some small cost
to the dignity of these proceedings.' A blush heated
Tanith's cheeks but she kept her head up, the anger and
frustration boiling inside her hotter by far. 'You are
quite correct when you say we are part of the Empire
and that we have profited from it over many years. But
the troubles it faces now are not our troubles. They are
of human making, therefore humans must find their
own solution. We cannot provide a solution for them,
nor will I risk harm to any more of our people by further embroiling them in the troubles of men.'

Shock drove words into Tanith's mouth. 'But the
Veil—'

'The Veil, Daughter, is as strong as it has ever been. I
have examined it myself.'

Any hope Tanith had held that the Queen would
hear her faded. Mastering her disappointment before it
showed on her face, she asked, 'And the reiver?'

'He is human, you said? Humans have not possessed
the power to rend the Veil in a thousand years, not
since the northern clans were broken and their talisman
lost. What damage he can do is inconsequential compared to the future facing our people. *Your* people,'
Emelia added, with a fraction more steel. 'Let the humans mend what humans have wrought.'

She sat back, refractions from the crystals in her hair jewelling the floor.

Tanith looked around the chamber again. Berec and Denellin, who had no daughters of their own and whose granddaughters were mere infants, stared back impassively. Taren, whose sons had yet to produce any progeny, looked past her. Likewise the High Seat of House Nevessin, a widower whose family tree was so tangled it might take the Chancellor a generation to find a female heir. The representative of House Ione did not attempt to meet her eye, nor did any of the others save Morwenna, the High Seat of Ailric's House, in the last seat. The only other woman amongst the Ten, nearly as old as Emelia, she gave Tanith a sad ghost of a smile and shook her head.

Tanith took a deep breath, surprised to find her trembling had ceased. It was over. But at least she'd fought for them.

'Majesty.' She curtsied deeply. 'High Seats of the Court. I thank you for your indulgence in hearing me. I only regret that your self-interest and insularity blinds you to the dangers before you. Perhaps you will heed my words before it is truly too late for us all.'

Turning her back on their outraged exclamations, Tanith walked from the speaker's circle with her head up, her back straight, heading not to her seat but to the tall double doors behind the Chancellor. There was no point in staying: she would not receive a fair hearing now, no matter what she said. Out of the doors she strode, along the marble corridors flooded with the endless sunlight that felt so very cold today, past startled court officials and dozing heralds. Down the palace steps, her footsteps quickening until she lifted her skirts and ran across the mossy lawns. Ran back to the serenity of her house, slammed the door behind her, fell to her knees and wept.

※

The sun was setting when her father came to her. Tanith heard him close the door, heard his steps pause in the hallway as he no doubt noted the packed saddlebags, the good warm cloak folded atop her riding leathers. The bow and quiver leaning against the wall.

She wrapped her arms tighter across her chest and stared out over the Mere, bronzed by the sunset. She would not cry again. Her weeping was done and there was no point in any more.

'Tanith?'

When she said nothing he moved closer, the sound of his footsteps changing as he stepped onto the terrace but came no further.

'Daughter?'

Out on the lake a saelkie popped its head from the water then dived again with scarcely a ripple to mar the molten surface. A pang of loss pierced her heart. If the Veil fell, the saelkies would not be safe either.

'They wouldn't listen, Papa. They heard me out, but they wouldn't listen.'

'So I hear,' he said wryly. 'You caused quite a stir. When I said you would shake the Court to its foundations, I did not expect you to begin with your presentation address.'

'What better time? Begin as you mean to continue, it's the surest way to succeed.' Bitterness twisted her mouth and she clamped it shut, blinking treacherous wetness from her eyes. She would *not* cry!

'You knew it would be difficult. Berec and Denellin, Morwenna, they have all sat at Court for many years. They would not have been easily shifted from their position.'

'They've sat there so long they've ossified,' she spat.

'Perhaps if you gave it some time, tried to speak to them individually when things have calmed down—' '

Tanith shook her head. 'It'd take too long. Besides, I refuse to grovel in front of the Court and apologise for *their* inability to see what's in front of them.'

'Tanith—'

The chiding tone was enough to whirl her around, her braided hair bouncing off her shoulder.

'No, Papa! Don't tell me I was rude, or how many rules of the Court I broke. I had to speak as I did, from my heart, because I know no other way. I had to try to make them see the threat Savin poses – not just to Astolar, or to the Empire, but to everyone who walks the earth and breathes its air.' Tears broke through her resolve, trembling on her lashes, ready to fall. 'He endangers everyone, Papa.'

Lord Elindorien was silent, face schooled to stillness. He looked out over the Mere, tawny eyes faraway. Across the water, shadows lengthened, the trees whispering in the evening breeze.

'May I see it?' he asked at last. 'The hurt you took?'

Tanith pushed up the sleeve of her robe and offered her forearm. With the sunset's colours masking its redness the scar did not look quite so ugly, but only she knew how deep the wound went.

Lord Elindorien traced its course from elbow to wrist with cool fingers. 'It was not Healed.'

'Too many other injured needed help for the Healers to waste their time on me.' *Lying to my father. Oh, spirits, is this what I have become?*

'How?'

In a heartbeat she was back on the parapet with a longsword in her hands as Gair spread his arms and took up the shield that two dozen Masters couldn't hold. Did he even know what he had achieved that day? Did he know how many lives he had saved, at such cost to himself?

'Demons attacked Chapterhouse,' she said. 'They broke through our shield. We had to fight them, hand to hand, until it was restored.' She shivered, cold despite the warmth of the evening. 'I was defending people who couldn't defend themselves.'

'You never told me.'

'I didn't want to talk about it.' She pulled her sleeve back down, hiding the scar from sight, though she would never be able to hide what it represented. Not from herself, anyway. 'I still don't.'

'That was a brave thing to do.'

'I was far from the bravest that day. I saw children defending each other with hoes and rakes from the kitchen garden. I saw a woman torn apart—' She broke off, turned away, eyes searching for something, anything else to look at but the image rising from her memory that made her eyes burn. *Oh, Gair, I'm so sorry.*

A long pause followed. The sun had dipped behind the hills above Belaleithne Falls, turning the Mere steely as the mist stole out of the distance and covered the water like a veil.

'Must I lose you again?' her father asked quietly. 'So soon after your return?'

'There is nothing more I can do here,' she said. 'I've shown the Court the danger facing us and they refuse to see it. The Guardians are doing what they can, they'll continue to patch small tears in the Veil, but the only sure way to save it is if we find Savin, or find the starseed before he does.'

'So where will you go?'

'Mesarild, to warn the Emperor.'

'That's over three hundred leagues.' More than six hundred miles, as humans reckoned it – some fifteen days on horseback, with a single mount and some care. Her father clicked his tongue against his teeth. 'Tanith, are you sure?'

'I'll go through Bregorin. If I can find a guide I'll be there in less than a week.'

'Travel the wildwood? And what then? Will Theodegrance be any quicker to understand what a threat to the Veil means? The humans do not trust the Song as we do, Daughter. They see it as something evil.'

'Not all of them, Papa. I'll just have to find a way to make them understand.' Brave words when she'd failed so utterly with her own people, but she had to try.

He frowned, narrow brows drawing down. 'Will the Emperor even see you?'

'I think I have enough titles in my pedigree to guarantee an audience. If not . . .' She shrugged. 'I'll seek out the Warlord. An Arennorian clansman will pay heed to the Veil even if Theodegrance will not.'

A smile alleviated some of the gravity in her father's face, gave a little light back to his eyes. 'Oh, my daughter, I would that your mother were here, to see what a firebrand the fruit of our love has become.'

'Papa?'

'When she passed on you were still a little girl in ribbons,' he said. 'If she could see you in riding leathers, with a dagger in your belt and a bow on your shoulder . . .' He turned and took her hand in one of his, pulling something from his pocket with the other. 'I believe she would be proud of you.'

Into her palm he poured a number of pearl buttons, some still trailing fragments of white thread. Closing her fingers over them, he added, 'She hated court gowns, too.'

Tanith flung her arms around his shoulders and hugged him tight. 'I'll miss you,' she whispered into his neck.

Taken aback, Lord Elindorien was slow to return her embrace. He did so a little awkwardly, as if uncomfortable to be displaying such open emotion, but when they stepped apart to arm's length once more, Tanith detected an uncharacteristic thickness in his voice as he spoke.

'Will you not take an escort?'

'What do I have to fear from the woods of Bregorin? Besides, I can move faster alone, without tents and trumpeters.'

His eyebrows twitched. 'Not even a handmaid? You are a lady of the Court, after all.'

She laughed. 'Papa, I survived five whole years at Chapterhouse without a maid. I think I can manage a ride in the forest.'

He held up his hands, conceding. 'Very well. I would be happier if you were not alone, but you are no longer a child. When do you intend to leave?'

'Tomorrow. First light.'

'Then may benevolent spirits attend you until you return.' Gravely, Lord Elindorien kissed her on each cheek. 'I will take your seat at Court again as your regent.'

'Thank you. They'll probably be relieved to see you after what I said this afternoon.' She bit her lip, suddenly unsure how to explain why she wasn't the daughter he'd hoped for. 'I know this wasn't what you wanted for me, Papa. I know you expected me to marry well and take my place at Court as Mother did, but this is important. I have to do this.'

He smiled. 'I think I understand better than you know, daughter mine. After all, I married your mother – against her father's wishes, I might add.'

Surprised, she said, 'I never knew that.'

'Yes, he had an Amerlaine boy in mind, I believe, not some upstart younger son of a very minor House.' He took her hands back into his and this time she saw his heart in his eyes. 'But he could no more deny his daughter her heart's desire than I can deny mine.'

'Oh, Papa.' She kissed him again, feeling fresh tears brimming. Loving ones this time, not the bitter juice of frustration.

'Only promise to come back to us, Tanith. If we are

to survive this age, Astolar needs you and daughters like you.'

'I promise.'

Squeezing her hands, he said, 'Then go, and with my blessing.'

29

STORM

❧

The sandstorm had begun not long after dawn. First a muddying of the horizon, then within an hour the sand-clouds had become a seething wall advancing across the desert at the speed of a galloping horse, hissing, roaring, swallowing the sun and smothering everything in its path.

Gair crouched over Shahe's neck, her mane lashing his face, and urged her level with Alderan's pounding grey. The storm was almost upon them, hot as the breath of a furnace.

'We have to find shelter!' he yelled. The sand-veil muffled his voice, but he didn't dare lower it: the grit in the air stung exposed skin worse than a swarm of bitemes.

Alderan pointed ahead at the looming wall of the city. 'We're almost there, see!'

The Lion Gate of El Maqqam reared out of the whirling dust. Gaping jaws framed the gates, the watchtower windows beneath the beast's scowling stone brows blinded by wooden shutters. One of the heavy studded gates was already closed, two hazy figures wrestling with the other.

'How far to the Daughterhouse?' Gair shouted back.

'Not far once we're inside. Come on, before they close the gates!'

The approaching storm growled and whined around the walls. In the gateway, one of the blurry figures gestured, beckoning them to hurry. Gair gave Shahe her head. She overtook Alderan's grey in the space of five yards then raced for the arch, pounding beneath it into a square lined with blocky half-visible buildings. He reined her up and looked back over his shoulder in time to see the old man galloping in with the sand already billowing around him. The thickly veiled guards hauled the second gate shut so close behind him they almost clipped the grey's tail. They lowered a massive beam slung from chains into brackets across the gates, then vanished into their guardhouse without a word and slammed the door shut behind them.

Within the walls there was much less wind but gusts still swirled restlessly around the square, carving the dusty earth into rippling patterns like a beach at low tide. Gair chanced lowering his veil.

'Friendly folk,' he panted, breathless after the race against the sandstorm.

'They just want to get out of the storm, same as us,' Alderan said. 'If we'd been caught outside it would have flayed the hide off us – it still can, so we'd better hurry up and get to the Daughter-house. They have a guest hall where we can rest.'

He led the way across the square and down a broad street. Few citizens were visible and all were hurrying home, heads down and sand-veils or *barouks* held across their faces. Dust-devils danced between the rosy stone buildings with their barred shutters and closed doors, springing up and dying as if stirred by capricious fingers. Palm trees planted along the median of the street thrashed their heads in the rising wind.

More and more dust thickened the air, darkening the tea-coloured sky. Blown sand stung exposed skin and hands, left grit between the teeth. Within minutes of entering the city they were forced to dismount and lead their horses with rags tied across their eyes as the storm shrieked over the rooftops with the sound of steel on a grindstone.

'How much further?' Gair shouted.

His head turned against the wind, Alderan pointed into the haze. Veils of sand shrouded the street ahead, in which buildings were visible only as vague shapes. Even with a hand shielding his face, Gair had to keep his eyes slitted and stumbled into Alderan's horse when the old man stopped abruptly.

'This is it.' He pointed at a pair of massively studded doors set into the weathered pink stone of a high wall. His knock was lost in the roar of the wind; he had to pound on the door with the hilt of his belt-knife to make himself heard.

After a minute or two a small square port slid open behind a grille in the door.

'Yes?'

To Gair's surprise, the voice belonged to a woman. He squinted at the grille but saw little more than the edge of a brown cowl. What was a Tamasian sister doing at a Suvaeon Daughterhouse?

'Bless you, Sister!' Alderan replied. 'We are travellers seeking shelter. This is a bad day to be abroad!'

'You must find shelter elsewhere, *sayyar*. I cannot let you in.'

The port began to close.

Alderan leaned into the meagre shelter of the wall and lowered his veil. 'The storm is on us, Sister. There's nowhere else for us to go.'

Anxious eyes flicked from Alderan to Gair and back again, then looked away. 'I'm sorry, the guest hall is closed. You could try the merchants' inn, by the river.'

'The river is half a city away!' the old man exclaimed. 'We'd never make it there in time!'

Stepping up to the door, Gair shoved his fingers through the grille and stopped the port cover from sliding shut. 'The house of the Goddess is never closed to the faithful.'

The nun peered at him through the narrow gap in the port. 'Saint Tamas and the lepers,' she said. 'Book of Lessons, chapter fifteen. You are Eadorians.'

'We are.' With his free hand, Gair pushed back his *kaif* to show more of his face. 'Please, Sister, we'll be welcome nowhere else!'

Her eyes closed as if in a brief prayer, then he heard bolts shoot back. 'Come in, quickly, before the Superior finds out.'

'Thank you, Sister.'

'Do not thank me until you know what gift you have been given!'

The nun held the door open against the wind until they and the horses were inside, then Alderan helped her heave it closed and bolt it behind them. Hunched against the wind, one hand holding her cowl forward to shield her face, she led them past a shuttered-up porter's lodge and, hugging the walls for shelter, around the dirt-floored yard towards a cluster of rosy stone preceptory buildings looming out of the whirling dust. A square-towered chapel dominated one end, barely visible through the rising storm; at the other a two-storey annexe ran at right angles to the central cloister, ending in a row of stables and stores. Alderan took the horses that way whilst Gair followed the brown-robed sister to the annexe. As soon as she opened the door it was snatched out of her hands by the wind; he gestured the nun in ahead of him and had to put his shoulder to the thick timbers to heave it closed again.

Inside was a long room with a hearth at the far end and a wooden staircase in the corner. The walls were whitewashed plaster, set with shuttered windows along one side and iron brackets for lamps along the other, but the brackets were empty and the tiled floor, now liberally strewn with blown sand, had not been swept in some time. Apart from a farmhouse-style dresser against one wall, the only furniture was a heavy table with a bench on either side in front of the fireplace, though the room could have accommodated at least three more of like size.

'You must forgive the welcome,' said the nun, pushing back her cowl and swatting dust from her skirts. She was small and solid, like a fox-terrier, with close-cropped wiry black hair. Her face, though deeply tanned and lined by sun and wind, did not look desert-born. 'The guest hall here has been closed since Firstmoon.'

Closing the doors to travellers was unheard of, but it explained the lack of fuel in the scuttle beside the hearth at the far end, the film of dust on the table and dresser.

'Has there been trouble in the city?' he asked, and she nodded.

'Our Superior is fearful for our safety. Please, rest here. I shall fetch some tea.'

After the nun left, Gair stripped off his gloves and dusted his hands clean of the fine sand that had found its way inside them, then shook a considerable quantity more of the stuff out of the folds of his *barouk*. Tucking his gloves into his sash, he explored the guest hall. The door to the right of the fireplace led to a small kitchen, its iron range cold and the pantry shelves empty but for a few sacks of dry goods and some jars of seasonings. Upstairs were the guest quarters, but when he peeked inside the first room he found the bed stripped of linens and the pallet rolled up. The next one he tried was the same. Even the air smelled closed-up and stale. He left the two rooms with their doors ajar to freshen them, then returned to the common room. As he arrived, the nun, who was presumably the Daughterhouse's hospitaller, returned with a stack of sheets and blankets in her arms.

'Here, let me help you with those.' Gair moved towards her, hands outstretched.

Her eyes widened and he realised, too late, that he should have kept his gloves on to conceal the witch-mark branded into his left palm.

'Hidderling,' she breathed, barely audible above the storm's shriek. She stared at him, the stack of bedding sagging in her hands.

'I'm sorry, I didn't mean to startle you.' Gently, Gair took the linens from her and set them on the table.

Button eyes unblinking, like a mouse before a cat, the nun backed up a pace.

'I should never have opened the gate,' she whispered, her face pale beneath its tan. One hand groped for the simple wooden Oak suspended from a thong around her neck and held it out in front of her in a warding gesture. 'Holy Mother forgive me, I have admitted an agent of the Nameless onto holy ground!'

Saints, how to explain it? The Suvaeon certainly believed that to be true. 'I'm not what you think, Sister . . . ?'

'Names give the Hidden power!' The nun continued to back away. 'The Superior was right – unclean things walk the streets of El Maqqam!'

She began to pray under her breath, still retreating, ready to bolt at any second. Though he couldn't quite hear the words, he recognised the shapes her lips made: she was reciting the confession. *These are my sins that I lay before Thee, O Mother; with open heart I come to Thee, a penitent soul . . .* The sturdy little nun was in mortal fear and preparing herself to meet the Goddess.

Sweet saints.

'Please, Sister, you are in no danger from me.' To make his height less intimidating, Gair sat down on the nearest bench and dragged his *kaif* from his head to sit around his neck. 'My name is Gair. I mean you no harm, I swear.'

Behind her the outer door banged open to admit Alderan in another gust of sand and wind, carrying their saddlebags. As he heeled the door shut behind him the nun whirled around, brandishing her Oak.

'And you? Do you also bear the mark of a witch?'

Alderan shot a look at Gair who spread his hands helplessly in reply.

'No,' the old man said, lowering the bulky bags to the floor. 'You have nothing to fear from either of us, Sister. Gair was raised in the faith by the Suvaeon Knights.'

She darted a wary look back over her shoulder. 'Truly told?'

'I went to the Holy City at the age of eleven,' Gair said. 'Sister, we only want shelter from this storm, and to consult the books the Knights left here. Then we'll go.'

The hand holding the Oak lowered a little. 'And the mark on your palm?'

Before Gair could think of a way to answer without telling an untruth, Alderan saved him the trouble.

'He was falsely accused,' he said, dragging the saddlebags across the tiles to the table. 'By the time the truth came to light, his sentence had been carried out.' If he was at all perturbed about lying to a nun, he showed no outward sign of it.

She chewed her lip, looking anxiously from one to the other. 'How can I know this for truth? I have only your word, and the Father of Lies—' The sister broke off and narrowed her eyes at Gair. 'Show me your Saint Agostin medallion.'

'I can't. I don't have it any more.' The silver pendant was long gone, yanked from his neck even before he'd been sentenced.

'All who trained to be Knights should have one.' Suspicion honed an edge on the nun's voice.

'The marshals took it from me when I was arrested. I never got it back.'

The conversation was going nowhere. He was an offence against everything the sister believed, and he had no further stomach for keeping an innocent woman in fear for her life.

He stood up, heaving his saddlebags onto his shoulder. 'Coming here was a mistake, Alderan. I think we've wasted enough of the good sister's time.'

With a formal bow to the nun, Gair headed for the door. He'd bed down in the stables with Shahe until the storm ended, then figure out whether to stay to help Alderan or obey his itching feet and go back north.

To his surprise, the nun called after him. 'Wait.'

He half-turned, enough to see she'd let the Oak drop back onto the breast of her habit.

'I cannot let you stay here on consecrated ground, but in good conscience, as hospitaller, neither can I turn you out into a storm. You spoke truly, at the gate – the house of the Goddess is never closed.' Then she sighed and smoothed her dusty habit. 'So let us say no more of this and pray Goddess it does not reach the Superior's ear, or I will end my days doing penance.'

'Is your Superior . . .' Alderan hunted for an appropriate word.

'She worries,' the nun said brightly, folding her hands. 'She fears for our safety in this city, fears the presence of strangers in our midst. Were it not for the lack of a suitable escort, she would pack us all up and return to the cloister in Syfria.'

'Once upon a time, no woman of the cloth would have needed an escort wherever she chose to go, within the Empire or without,' Gair said.

She turned to him with a sad smile. 'Once, sir Knight, our habits were indeed enough protection. Now we need steel.'

'What about the imperial garrison?'

'The soldiers were sent west two weeks ago – some trouble at the Sardauki border. There are none to spare for us.' At the door, she paused with her hand on the latch. 'And my name is Sister Sofi.'

30

BANFAÍTH

Teia woke with a start. She held her breath, ears straining for the sound that had roused her. Nothing. Only Finn's snoring, the thin hiss of the wind past her shelter of blankets and pine branches, and the hammering of her own heart. Slowly, she exhaled, silvery breath coiling in front of her face.

So what had woken her? Gathering a blanket about her shoulders she shuffled to the shelter's entrance and peered down into the snowy valley. She saw no tracks but her own and Finn's between the black ranks of the trees, the edges glittering with frost. Further back into the forest she couldn't see anything but vague shapes, and her imagination instantly peopled the shadows with watching wolves.

She swallowed, scanning the trees again. She'd been careful when she decided to camp here and checked for spoor. There hadn't been tracks for anything bigger than a hare, but that didn't mean a wolf pack hadn't come ghosting by to see who had strayed into their territory. Maybe she'd end up like Joren, dead almost before he knew he was hurt. Heartbeat quickening, she groped over her blanket for her bow.

Then she heard it again: the twang of bowstrings from further down the trail, this time followed by a muffled cry. Sound carried far on a clear night, but who was attacking whom? And would they follow the tracks in the snow and come after her next? Bow and quiver in hand, she slipped outside.

Once out of the cosy fug of her shelter the cold bit deep. Finn stirred and she quietened him with a hand on his neck, then tightened his girths and mounted up as stealthily as she could. After the disastrous attempt to ready him herself four days ago, she'd had to leave him saddled and silently promised to make it up to him later as she steered him down the trail.

Soon the sound of her horse's hooves crunching through the snow was lost in the growing noise. Shouts and women's cries, the snap of arrows fired. Around a bend in the trail she found a band of men and women struggling up the slope towards the trees, whilst five or six others with bows held off another, larger party, well armed with short spears. Several javelins porcupined the snowdrifts, with here and there scarlet smears amongst the churned footprints. The bowmen were retreating in good order, a pace at a time; one of them looked back and Teia saw a long grey braid swing over his shoulder.

Her magic rose up to her will. Thrusting out her arm she spun a globe of light the size of her head and flung it high over the trail. Startled gasps greeted it.

'Hold hard!' she shouted, mountain air and magic lending her voice a resonance that stopped the advancing attackers in their tracks.

'The Talent!' cried one. 'She's a Speaker!'

A luridly tattooed man at the forefront of the attacking group snorted. 'She's no Speaker – she's naught but a girl.' He brandished a feather-decked war-axe. 'Back to it, boys!'

His warriors roared. Desperate, or simply eager for the kill, they lumbered up to a run in the thick snow. Off to the right, one of them hefted a javelin. Before he'd cocked his arm Teia had smacked the weapon from his hand with a fist of air. Unbalanced, the man staggered back. Two of his companions, wild-eyed and wilder-haired, readied their own weapons, and with another fist she disarmed them both.

The charge faltered, the men looking about uneasily, but they kept coming. Out of the corner of her eye Teia saw Baer take advantage of their confusion to rally his people up the trail towards her.

She drew herself up in the saddle. 'These people are under my protection. I suggest you don't challenge it.'

'There are more of us than of you,' snarled the tattooed man, hefting his axe. 'We do not fear your magics!'

Teia gathered Finn's reins, ready to run if she had to. Behind her, a woman screamed a warning and she looked up to see a javelin arcing from the back of the attacking group, shining against the night sky like a shooting star.

Time slowed. Wrapped in the lambent gyre of her magic, Teia had nothing to fear. Not in that place, where she was the master and power moved as she willed it. She raised her hand and magic tingled through her muscles like the return of blood to a cramped arm. The javelin reached the apex of its flight; humming, it began to fall towards her.

Easy. Just like stopping Ytha's fist. Reaching out as it fell, she closed her hand around the wooden shaft. The sudden arrest of the spear's movement wrenched her shoulder, but she kept her grip. Someone gasped. Ahead, the advancing warriors halted. Their leader waved his axe again, urging them forward with yells and curses.

Teia hefted the spear, cocking back her arm. 'Yield!' she shouted. 'I have warned you!'

Yelling obscenities, the tattooed man broke into a trot. She remembered her father's words, when he'd taught her to defend herself with a knife: *When you've a weapon in your hand either use it or don't, but don't hesitate. Hesitation will get you killed.* Gritting her teeth, she hurled the spear as hard as she could.

It thudded into the man's thigh and he dropped with a cry, blood spraying across the snow. The men behind him milled uncertainly. One or two edged forward, but several more made signs of protection and would not move.

'Take your man and go.' Teia felt queasy but somehow her voice did not tremble. Finn fidgeted as Baer's retreating people crowded around him. 'Leave these people alone or worse will follow.'

The warriors lowered their weapons but made no move. The tattooed fellow thrashed and screamed until the two men closest darted out, seized his coat and dragged him back to the group.

'Get out of here!' Baer added his voice, his bow at full draw. 'Go on, go!'

Muttering, casting fearful looks over their shoulders, the other band retreated down the trail. Frightened, tired people clustered around Teia's horse, clutching their bundles, clutching each other. Two blowing ponies, one or two men with bloody rents in their clothing being fussed over by anxious women, and Neve, laughter bubbling through her fear as she squeezed Teia's hand.

Baer pushed through them and stopped at Finn's shoulder, leaning on his bow. His hard face gave nothing away. 'Teia,' he said.

'Baer,' she greeted him gravely.

'Is there good shelter ahead? We have wounded to attend to.'

'There's a thicket of pine trees up around the bend. You can make shelters, find fuel for fires.'

He inclined his head, just once. 'Thank you.'

Slinging his bow over his shoulder, he walked away up the trail, issuing instructions. Soon everyone had their tasks and fear was replaced by the will to work together.

Teia sat her horse and watched them go. Neve had been right. Baer was as close to a chief as those people had. *And am I their Speaker now?*

She watched the other band trudging back down the slope. More than one threw an uneasy glance at the light she had conjured, still hanging over them like a full moon. That appeared to have made even more of an impression on them than a spear through their leader's leg. Battle injuries they would no doubt be accustomed to, but an aggressive demonstration of the Talent was something else entirely. They had spent too long away from their clan Speakers. A grim little smile tugging at her lips, she waited until all the attackers were well out of sight before she let the light go.

When she returned up the trail the thicket was all activity, the air heady with the scent of pine resin. Baer's people were busy cutting fuel, rigging tent-skins between trees, scraping out a communal fire-pit. The small ring of stones outside her shelter had been swept free of ash and a new fire laid; all she had to do was light it. Teia looked for Baer but he was off in the darkness of the trees somewhere, issuing orders. Neve, however, caught her eye and waved.

Wearily, Teia swung down from Finn's saddle and kneaded her aching back. Four days of riding, almost constantly uphill since she'd left the river, had taken a toll on her. After a couple of hours her womb would tense and harden, taut as a drum-skin under her clothes, and she would have to shift around in the saddle or get down and walk until it relaxed again. Now her belly felt loaded with rocks instead of a baby.

Someone appeared from the night and, with a nod to her, took Finn's reins. She was too tired to protest. As he led the horse away towards the sheltered spot where the ponies were tethered she realised he was Lenna's man, Isaak. Strange. She looked around for other faces she recognised, but the little clearing was all a-bustle and amongst the trees the light was too poor to make out more than shapes.

It was too much to take in. She crawled into her shelter, back into the faint warmth of her blankets, and closed her eyes. Morning would be soon enough to worry about it.

⟡

Peering at her reflection in a basin of water at the entrance to her shelter, Teia unwound the bandage covering her forehead and held her breath as the dressing came away.

A thick black scab ran from above her right eyebrow up into her hairline, as long as her hand was wide. Around the edges her skin was an angry red, crusted with dried blood. The cold air stung on her newly knitted flesh, but after almost six days it was time for the wound to breathe; keeping it covered for too long would only slow the healing.

She touched the scab tentatively. It felt tough as shield-leather, like the scale of some monstrous serpent. Underneath there would be a scar, a bad one, but she'd been lucky to escape with just that. A few inches to the right and that rock would most likely have spilled her brains.

Using the wadded-up bandage, she brushed away the dried blood as best she could. Most of it was still on her scalp, clumping her hair into spiky tufts, but the wound had been deepest there and was still too tender to scrub at it. Besides, her scalp – her whole body, come to that – itched for the want of a good bath, and touching only made it worse.

Losing patience, she threw the bandage down and bent over the basin to sluice water on her face. As she fumbled dripping for a cloth to dry herself, her reflection caught her eye, wavering in the water. Grey sky surrounded her face, reflected from outside. She'd seen that image before. Even the tired shadows bruising her eyes looked familiar. All that was missing was a tangle of wet hair to make it the vision that had haunted her scrying for over two years.

She dried her face, watching the image steady. No, it wasn't quite the same, but close enough to make her think. There'd been no opportunity to look into the waters since Ytha had taken her for the blood scrying at the start of winter. Her future might have changed since then. Only one way could she be sure.

Resting her hands on the basin's edge, she glanced around the camp outside. Everyone she could see was bustling to make up for sleeping late: breaking down the shelters, stowing the gear. Puffy white breath rose amongst the snow-capped pines, every sound too loud in the brittle mountain air. No one was looking her way. It shouldn't matter any more, now that she was so far away from Ytha, but habits were as hard to crush as fleas.

Legs crossed, she drew the basin close between her knees – her back was still aching from the ride – and waited for the water to settle again. Then she reached for her magic. The power sprang up eagerly, like a hound-pup hearing its name called. A few glimmers of blue crawled over her fingers.

Show me.

Her reflection changed, the scab melting away and a lock of white hair snaking back from her brow above that same bleak, dead-eyed expression she'd seen so

many times before. It had been true telling, then. She
felt a cold coil of trepidation in the pit of her stomach.
Had the rest been true telling, too?

Show me Drwyn.

White filled the basin, white that swirled and shifted
as if carried on a fitful wind. At first she could see nothing, then her viewing swooped in like a bird through
the veils of snow to a camp on the undulating plain.
Dispirited horses huddled in a corral with their backs
to the wind; clusters of tents stood crusted white down
one side and gathering low drifts at the base. Here and
there tiny pinpricks of fire glittered in the murk.

The clan was on the move already, camped somewhere north of the winter caverns, she guessed, unable
to discern enough detail through the blizzard to be sure
of the location. It was early to be moving for the Scattering. Drwyn – or more likely Ytha – was growing impatient.

Down her viewing swept, dizzying her with the
plunge. Towards the camp, towards a large tent set
slightly apart from the others, with lamplight glimmer-
ing round the door curtain. Then through and into a
cosy golden cave where Drwyn paced back and forth,
wrapped in his plaid. Idly, she noted an absence of war-
gear and that the furnishings were arranged with a
woman's care, and wasn't surprised she'd already been
replaced. He was frowning, drinking frequently, absently, from the cup in his fist, quite clearly waiting for
something.

A gust of snowy air as someone came in turned him
around.

'What word from the Speaker?' he snapped, inside
the vault of her mind.

The other person came closer, and Teia recognised
the moustache and dirty blond braids.

'The storm will blow on into the west by noon,' said

Harl, shaking back his furs and shedding snow over the chief's carpets.

Drwyn cursed. 'We'll lose a day's travelling!'

'The going will be easier once the snow stops. We'll make up time tomorrow.'

'The Speaker said that as well, did she?' He tossed the last of his drink into his throat and swallowed it down. His hand flexed around the cup; if it hadn't been horn he'd have crushed it.

'Er . . . yes, my chief.' Harl hesitated. 'So. The girl.'

Teia's breath caught. Did he mean *her*? Even in the small circle described by the basin, she saw Drwyn's lips thin.

'What of her?'

'We're not riding after her? I thought you said—'

'It's none of your concern,' he said shortly. 'She's lost to us now, if the winter hasn't already claimed her.'

One hand fidgeted with the edge of his plaid cloak, plucking at it in a way that put Teia in mind of the twitching of a crag-cat's tail when its prey was out of reach. He wasn't coming after her, not right then, but he hadn't forgotten about her either. She shivered, and the image in the water shivered with her.

'A pity, that,' said Harl. 'She had a fine pair of—' The last word was choked off by the chief's hand clamped around his neck.

'Forget the girl!' Drwyn snarled. 'The Scattering is what concerns me now. When the wandering moon comes full again I will be Chief of Chiefs, and I will lead our people south to reclaim our ancient lands from the usurpers. Do you understand?'

Wheezing, Harl clutched at the fingers constricting his windpipe. He was unable to resist as the chief brought his face very close, almost nose to nose with him.

'But should we happen to find her,' added Drwyn, voice pitched dangerously low, 'she – is – *mine*.'

Harl sputtered incoherently, his pocked skin turning an unwholesome colour.

'I will not hear words like that again?'

'N-no!'

'Good.' Drwyn released him like a hound dropping a rabbit and Harl staggered. 'Was there anything else?'

'Only that the Speaker asks you to attend her to discuss the Scattering.' Rubbing his throat, Harl added, 'Directly, my chief.'

'I'd best not keep her waiting, then.'

Drwyn tossed his empty cup onto the carpet and strode for the door.

Teia sat back and let the power go, scattering the image held in the water with a swirl of her hand. Much as she would have liked to spy on Ytha, she dared not venture too close with her power when she didn't know whether it would be detected. Best to let the Speaker continue to think she was dead, and be content with observing Drwyn.

Oddly, knowing he was not pursuing her did not come as a relief. It meant the Speaker was pressing ahead with her plans to see him anointed Chief of Chiefs, and that only gave Teia more incentive to keep moving.

Neve poked her head into the shelter. 'I've brought you some tea,' she said, setting down a teapot and bowls. Teia put the basin to one side and hitched herself closer.

'I can make my own, you know,' she said, but accepted the bowl she was handed. 'Thank you.'

'It's no bother.' The older woman turned away and began fussing with the kettle on its tripod over the fire.

Teia watched her, fragrant steam curling around her face as she sipped. When she'd woken, her fire had already been lit and the kettle set to boil. Now she was half-inclined to think Neve had a hand in that, too.

'Up you get, Gerna – the day's a-wasting, woman!'

The familiar voice barking instructions made Teia look up. Baer was striding across the camp, long braid swinging as he chivvied his little band of outcasts along. Command came so naturally to him, he must have been a war captain once, or had learned from one. He reminded her a little of her father.

'Baer,' she called to him. He altered his course towards her. 'Will you join me for some tea?'

'That would be welcome, thank you.' He squatted down next to the fire and rubbed his hands together for warmth whilst she poured another bowl for him.

'How are your wounded from last night? I have a few medicines that may help.'

'They've only knocks and scrapes. They'll mend.' He thanked her for the tea and cradled the bowl to his lips.

'Who were they, those men who attacked you? More Lost Ones?'

'I reckon so.' He sipped. 'They'd harried us back west for a day and a night, probably looking to steal what we had. We turned south into the hills for a bit of shelter and found ourselves following your trail. Lucky for us, eh?' he added, with a show of teeth.

Teia topped up her own bowl from the teapot, considering. She had a good horse, supplies, she was as well prepared as she could be for what she was likely to face in the mountains, but she'd expected the predators to walk on four legs rather than two.

'Are they likely to come back, do you think?'

'Not if they've any sense,' he said, chuckling. 'Especially not after you put the fear into them like that! I told you a Speaker was a useful thing to have.' Eyes narrowed shrewdly, he studied her over the rim of his bowl. 'Are you afeared of them?'

'A little bit,' she admitted. 'Against one, I think I could give a good account of myself, but not against that many.'

He sipped. 'And you're still set on crossing the mountains?'

She had no other choice. 'I have to.'

'Then we ride with you for a day or two, until the trail is clear,' he said firmly. 'Those skulkers will think twice about coming after the lot of us, now that we've shown them our mettle.'

Startled by both his generosity and his all-settled tone of finality, Teia stared at him. 'I don't mean to take your people out of their way. I'll manage.'

'And then who'll protect the rest of us?' He laughed, then sobered quickly. 'No, it's safest all round to travel together. I confess, though, I don't know this trail. Can you scry our way ahead?'

Teia bit her lip, glancing at Neve, but the older woman's back was turned as she stirred something in a pot over the fire.

'I don't know,' she whispered. 'I was only learning—' She broke off. She'd puzzled out viewing for herself; scrying the way into the mountains couldn't be all that different. Perhaps now was the time to explore what she could do.

Suddenly determined, she nodded. 'All right. I'll try.'

The basin she'd used to spy on Drwyn was nearby. She drew it closer and scanned the upper part of the valley to fix it in her mind. Then she reached into the waters.

Focus was not easy to maintain. If someone in the camp called out a name or she recognised the voice, her attention flashed to that person, so at first the image in the water slewed wildly around the little encampment. As Teia sank deeper into the thrumming music inside her and closed her ears to the others' chatter, the sounds of Neve cooking, the viewing steadied. She saw the smoking fire-pit, the tents beyond it, the trees that clothed the valley's slopes, and imagined herself walking towards them.

In the water, the image changed, tracking the path of her thoughts. Through the trees where the snow was not so deep, along the flank of the mountain, slowly climbing. She dared to push a little faster. Now she was a bird, gliding above the treetops, seeing the forest thin as the land surged up and the clouds pressed down from above.

Her temples began to pound and she realised she was holding her breath. Exhaling made the image wobble, then turn abruptly grey. Teia forced herself to breathe deep and slow; with it her mental flight steadied and she ducked down out of the clouds again. That was better.

Now the valley was narrowing, growing shallower as the two flanks came together, and she emerged onto a wind-scoured ridge running up towards the hidden peaks. Snow fell thickly there, sleeting across her vision as if driven by a gale. It made visibility difficult and dizzying, and she had to let the viewing go.

'I'm sorry,' she gasped, the basin wobbling under her hands. 'I think that's all I can do.'

Baer said nothing, and she looked up. Half a dozen of the Lost Ones were standing around her fire, staring at the fading images in the water. Isaak, with Lenna clinging to his arm. Neve, a porridgey spoon in her hand dripping into the snow at her feet. A couple of other men she hardly knew.

One by one they lifted their gazes to her face. Uneasy with all the attention, she swallowed. A cold, clammy feeling spread across her spine and her palms began to sweat.

'Banfaíth,' someone whispered. She didn't see who; with their slack-lipped expressions, all looking as if they'd been gut-shot, it could have been any of them. Teia felt slightly sick, wiping her hands nervously on her trews.

'It was just a viewing, to show the way ahead,' she said, but she could see from their faces, their wide eyes, that they weren't hearing her. Nothing she said would make any difference.

'She sees . . .' One of the men – a stringy fellow with a bloody rip in the sleeve of his coat – dragged his eyes away from Teia to look at Isaak and Lenna, who burrowed under her man's arm and peered anxiously around him, a field mouse peeping from its nest. 'So it's true,' he breathed. 'Banfaíth.'

No one else spoke. No one else moved. On the far side of the camp the rest of the Lost Ones continued to work, oblivious to what was happening, but even the thumps and rustles they made sounded muted, swallowed up by the breathless silence expanding outwards from Teia, kneeling at its centre.

She cringed inside. Macha's ears, what had she done?

Banfaíth was an old title, maybe even older than the title of Speaker. It meant the one who sees, the one with the gift of foretelling. The sight, as the elder folk called it, in the old way.

'Didn't I tell you, Baer?' said Neve, shattering the moment so completely Teia half-expected to hear it break, like glass. Everyone started, staring at her. 'Women know.' She popped the spoon in her mouth and licked off the remaining porridge, then with a satisfied nod went back to her cook-pot.

Baer set down his tea-bowl and heaved himself to his feet. 'Aye. So you said.' Then he clapped his hands together so sharply it made Lenna squeak. 'That's enough gawping here,' he announced, a little more loudly than necessary. 'We've a bit of a climb ahead of us and there's snow up there, so best get on.' The others were slow to move, dragging their feet as if frozen to the earth, and he gestured irritably. 'Go on, now. There's tents to strike and packs to load, and I'm not doing it for you.'

They drifted away, casting looks back over their shoulders. Teia couldn't bear to watch, her eyes fixed firmly on the basin of water in front of her. Over and over, she scrubbed her hands on the stuff of her trews, though the sweat was long dried. She couldn't seem to stop.

'Never shown anyone before, have you?' said Baer.

She shook her head. 'Only the Speaker.' Looking down at her hands, reddened by cold and rubbing, she added, 'I never expected that.'

'Well, it was probably my fault,' he admitted, and she looked up. He scratched at the root of his braid, face twisted up, maybe to hide his expression. 'Varn over there came to ask me summat and saw what you were conjuring in the water. Before I could stop him he ran to get the others. By then it were too late.' He spread his hands. 'Probably best they all know, if'n we're riding along together. They'd only have started to mutter otherwise.'

That made sense. 'I see.'

Leaning down, he cupped a hand under her elbow to help her to her feet. 'Up you get, girl. Catch your death down there in the snow.' With his other hand he beat the crust of snow off her lower legs, but the wool beneath was already wet. Renewed circulation burned and tingled its way down to her feet.

'I never doubted you,' he said quietly as he worked. 'Not after what you did last night. With what Neve said I think I already knew, but now I've seen it.' He straightened up, met her gaze levelly and dipped his head. 'Banfaíth.'

She hesitated, then returned the nod. 'Baer.'

And that was that.

Before she could turn around, Neve was there with a bowl of porridge for her, and clucking over the state of her trews like a hen over her chick. By the time she'd finished eating, her shelter had been struck, tent-skins and blankets rolled, and Isaak was leading Finn over, saddled and ready.

'Banfaíth,' he murmured, and made a stirrup with his hands to help her mount.

From the vantage point of the gelding's back she could see knots of people form and scatter as the Lost Ones scurried to finish their tasks, and knew the word was spreading. Instead of being hostile and mistrustful, the glances shot her way now were curious, even awed.

The foretelling was not a common gift. Ytha had claimed to have it, though Teia had never seen her manifest it in any way that she could compare to her own experiences. There again, if Ytha was tormented by dreams as dark and savage as her own, she wasn't likely to let them show on her face and reveal to the rest of the clan that there was actually a woman of flesh and blood beneath the snow-fox robe.

Of course, that was before the Speaker had been launched into a frothing fury in front of half the clan . . . Teia shut her eyes at the memory. Macha's mercy, she'd *struck* the *Speaker*. Strangely, the notion didn't horrify her nearly as much as it once would have. The Crainnh had needed to be shown that their Speaker was human, like them. They needed to know that she could be wrong. That she *was* wrong.

Teia opened her eyes again and looked up the valley towards the saddle of the next ridge. She could only hope that she wasn't too late.

31

SCARS

❧

In Gair's dreams, it was always the same. How she had looked that day. Sea-coloured eyes still glowing with what they had just shared, a flash of white teeth over her shoulder, then she opened the door and was gone. The click of the latch as it swung closed behind her always woke him and in the instant between sleep and wakefulness, between memory and truth, he could still taste her on his lips.

Aysha.

Crackling parchment snatched him back to the present. A scroll had fallen from the heap in the middle of the table and rocked to a halt in front of him. On the far side of the heap, Alderan was engrossed in a book. Carefully, Gair set the scroll back on the pile.

Alderan turned a page. 'Find anything?'

Gair looked down at the book on the table between his hands, still open at the same page, at the familiar name. Ishamar al-Dinn. One of the few fragments of Gimraeli that he could read – that she had taught him to read. *How long have I been sitting here?*

'No. Not yet.' He closed the book and set it to one side, away from the others, letting his hand linger on the cracked leather binding. 'Just some poetry.'

Ishamar al-Dinn, who'd risked a prince's wrath for love. Finding that book of verse amidst the maps and breviaries had arrested him as surely as a hand on his sleeve. He'd read no further than the name on the title page – he didn't need to, not with her voice already filling his mind.

Ai qur'ash-ashann; el majar e binh ey fahl majani, al-ashann iyya el habbir a baranjor. His throat tightened. *The thornbird sings; my tears fall upon the dust as his song falls sweet upon my heart.*

He remembered her reading it to him as they lay in her bed, lovemaking still warm and heavy on their limbs. Her voice rippling over him like a caress. *Aysha.*

Alderan was looking at him. Afraid that he had said her name aloud, Gair thrust himself out of his chair. The sudden movement started fresh sweat across his chest and back but even over by the windows there wasn't a breath of a breeze to stir the torpid air. Not even the illusion of coolness to be obtained by looking outside; the embrasures were too high and deep to show anything but silver-blue sky beyond the wrought-iron screens. He plucked his limp shirt away from his skin. Now that the storm had passed, El Maqqam was once more pinned down by the sun's glaring eye.

'Surely we should have found something by now,' he muttered. Restless feet took him the length of the room, hand skimming over the piled manuscripts and books still waiting to be sorted on the crowded shelves. 'Are these all books the Knights brought with them?' he asked as his prowling carried him behind Alderan and along the opposite side of the room.

'So Sister Sofi told me.' The old man closed his book and moved to the next, quickly discarding it. 'Children's stories.' He reached for another. 'The Sisters found this room when they moved here from Syfria.'

'I thought this was a Suvaeon Daughterhouse.'

'It was, until the Order abandoned it. The building had been locked up and empty for almost thirteen years when the Sisters of Saint Tamas took it on.'

Gair looked around him. Battered leather folios were crammed together with rolled maps and volumes of all shapes and sizes, some spineless and scarred, others stained by salt water or worse, piled up in no kind of order. Evidence of a hasty departure for an uncertain destination.

'Why did they leave?' he asked, and then he remembered. Of course. The Saint Benet's Day massacre, which led to the Lector of Dremen declaring a crisis of the faith, which led to the desert wars and to some soldier on his way south to Samarak slaking his lust with a Leahn girl. *Which led to me.* 'Never mind. It doesn't matter.'

'I didn't think you would be one to forget.'

Yet he had forgotten. Embarrassed, angry at himself, Gair clenched his teeth. 'It – doesn't – *matter.*'

One thousand, eight hundred and nineteen deaths on the first night of the massacre. Eadorian merchants, their entire families, even their employees, all slaughtered. Churches put to the torch with their congregations inside, the doors nailed shut. And the first the rest of the Empire had known about it was when some Zhimandari fishermen began hauling up more than yellowtails in their nets.

The news had taken too long to reach Dremen. By the time the Knights set sail it was already too late; not a single northerner was left alive in El Maqqam. Those that had escaped the Cultists' curved swords had perished in the pitiless heat of the desert. The Knights who had tried to defend them had died nailed to thorn trees in a gruesome parody of the Goddess they worshipped. And now war was stirring again.

I shouldn't be here.

His hands were knotted into fists. An effort of will was required to unclench them, more effort still to hold them at his sides and not sweep the nearest shelves clear of all that useless paper and—Gair shut his eyes and took a slow breath, letting it out even more slowly. Then another. The thunder of his pulse in his ears began to quieten.

At the far end of the room, by the door, the shelves were empty, ready to be refilled. He ran his fingertips along one of them. Despite a dusting, it still bore the ghostly outlines of the texts that had stood there undisturbed for so long.

I should never have come. 'There's nothing here, Alderan. There can't be. After two days, surely we'd have found it?'

The old man looked up from the books he was sorting into stacks. 'Perhaps,' he said. 'Perhaps not. We can't know unless we look.' He picked up the largest pile. 'These are all religious texts. Why don't you start refilling the top shelf?'

'We're wasting our time here!'

Alderan's expression remained unmoved, the books held out before him like a gift. With poor grace, Gair snatched them from him and the topmost book slithered off onto the floor. After shelving the others, he stooped to pick it up.

It was a psalter, fallen with the cover open. A name and date were inscribed on the fly-leaf in faded ink. The day its owner received his spurs, perhaps; the book a gift from a doting parent. Gair looked again at the date. Three years before Corlainn sacrificed himself for his beloved Order. He closed the book and slipped it onto the shelf with the others. A dark stain down the pale leather spine did not augur well for the unknown Knight's fate.

He was maybe only a year or two older than me. Did his mother wonder what happened to her boy? He felt a brief pang. *Does mine?*

A knock sounded at the door, then a Tamasian sister let herself into the room. Her cowl was drawn well forward over her face and she kept her head down as she carried a teapot and cups on a tray to the table.

'That was a kind thought, Sister, thank you,' said Alderan from the far end of the room.

She set the tray down and turned to leave. As she did so, her face caught the sunlight angling through the high windows. Angry scar tissue gleamed on her cinnamon cheeks.

'Sister?' Gair moved towards her. 'Are you hurt? What happened?'

The nun retreated, shaking her head mutely. He lifted his hand towards the edge of her cowl and she shrank away, backing into the doorframe in her haste to leave. Then she was gone, sandalled feet pattering down the corridor at a run.

'Her face!' Gair turned back to Alderan, who stood motionless with another stack of books in his hands. 'Did you see her face?'

'I saw.' He held out the books. 'Medical reference.'

'Don't you care what happened to her, who did that to her?'

'I care, but what's done is done – I can't change it for her. This –' he gestured with the books '– I can do something about and maybe change countless lives.'

'But she's been mutilated! A woman of the cloth!'

'There'll be worse than that done if the Veil comes down, believe me.' Alderan thumped the books back onto the table in a cloud of dust and cocked his arms akimbo, blue eyes hard. 'Where should I spend myself, Gair? On the one, or the many? The sand is running through the glass. Why don't you tell me how I should use the time that remains?'

Gair had no answer for him. Alderan was right. Like a Healer on a battlefield, he had to work where he could do the most good for those most likely to live. Anything else was wasted effort. Numb, he took the stack and carried it to the shelves, shock and despair sitting uneasily in his belly. His hands worked methodically to arrange the books on the shelf, but all he could see was the nun's face, the scars all the more terrible for being shadowed by her cowl.

Knife-cuts. The edges had been too clean to be anything else. Recent, too, judging by the inflammation, the livid spots where stitches had been. Was whatever had happened to that nun the reason Sister Sofi said they needed an armed escort out of the city?

A hand snatched at his arm and dragged him around, the last few books tumbling from his grasp.

'What did you say to her?' Sofi's face was white with fury. 'What did you do?'

'Nothing, Sister, I swear!'

He knelt to pick up the fallen texts but she dashed them out of his hands. With her rage behind her she loomed over him, her shoulders hunched, fists tightly balled on her broad hips.

'Resa's distraught because of something you said or did, so you tell me what it was, or by Saint Tamas himself I'll—' She bit off the rest of the threat, lips clamping together.

Pushing himself to his feet, Gair spread his hands. 'I saw her face and asked if she was hurt, that's all. I thought maybe I could help.'

'Help?' Sofi's lips twisted. 'You can't help her. No one can. It would have been a mercy if the Mother had seen fit to gather her up that day.'

Gently, Gair asked, 'Sister, what happened to her?'

Eyes closed, Sofi calmed herself with a deep breath in and a slow exhalation. Then she looked away, jaw working on the words before she spoke. 'There are so many poor in the city, so many who have no means to bring up their children. We help where we can. Resa was singing to entertain the little ones whilst Sister Avis distributed food from the cart. Nonsense verses, clapping games. She loved to make them laugh.'

Her shoulders slumped, face crumpling in on itself, and she did not resist when Gair turned his empty chair around and steered her to it. She looked down at her hands folded in her lap. 'She's desert-born – the first

Gimraeli novice our sisterhood has seen in two generations. A gentle child with a ready smile. We were so proud of her. Then the Cultists came.'

Her lips drew back, mouth open, waiting for words that would not come. Gair poured tea, added plenty of honey and pushed the cup into Sofi's unresisting hands.

'They said she was preaching to them. Corrupting them. Sister Avis tried to intervene and they knocked her over. She hit her head on the wagon, on the wheel-rim. And then they took Resa's voice.' Tears spilled onto Sofi's face, shining in the afternoon light. 'They took her voice!'

Now he knew what the knife-scars signified. 'They cut out her tongue.'

'She fought them. Fought like a sand-tiger.'

It was horribly easy to picture. The girl struggling, the knife slipping. The wonder was that she hadn't choked on her own blood.

'Where is she now?' Gair asked.

'The chapel.' Sofi lifted her head, eyes unseeing through her grief. 'She prays for the men who did this to her. For forgiveness, though how even our blessed Mother could forgive them I do not know.'

He looked along the table at Alderan, who nodded and said, 'Go on. I'll stay here.'

⚔

Gair saw no one as he loped through the corridors and cloisters of the Daughterhouse towards the chapel. Sofi said the rest of the sisters would be tending the gardens, repairing the worst ravages of the storm, so he was unlikely to encounter anyone who would report his presence to the Superior. Nonetheless he kept his pace up, just to be safe.

The Tamasians had taken an abandoned Suvaeon house and made it their own, turning the tilt-yard into an orchard and vegetable garden, and the armoury and forge into a workshop for more mundane metalworking. Yet signs remained of the buildings' original purpose: the worn stone thresholds of doors, scarred by spurred feet, the refectory and dormitories that could have accommodated ten times the number of nuns. This had once been a house of warriors.

Bas-relief Knights flanked the entrance to the church, the branches of the carved trees behind them reaching up to form an arch. The door stood ajar and opened silently at Gair's touch. Inside, banners of coloured light swept across the Daughter-house's chapel, as if the stained-glass saints between the roof-trusses shone with the Goddess's own grace instead of the sun outside. The rows of pews stood empty, the thick Book on the lectern closed, waiting for the Evensong service. On the high altar, a few candles flickered, their flames reflected in the bronze leaves of the Oak above, giving the illusion that they were stirring in a gentle breeze.

On the altar steps knelt a slender figure in Tamasian brown. Resa's cowl was down, her head bowed in prayer like one of the saints in the windows. Short, raven-dark hair gleamed in the candlelight.

Gair hesitated in the doorway. The patient, dusty silence of a church was achingly familiar. He smelled hot wax and old wood, paper and stone. As an excommunicate he shouldn't be there, on sacred ground – in truth, as Sister Sofi had originally said, he shouldn't even be within the Daughterhouse precincts. On cue, the witch-mark on his palm began to burn. He rubbed it firmly with his other hand and tried to convince himself the pain was in his imagination. What was done was done.

Then for the first time in almost a year and a half, he dropped to one knee and genuflected before the Oak. Right hand over his heart, left palm held up and out.

Forgive me, Mother.

The burning did not lessen.

Gair pushed himself back to his feet and walked towards the altar. He was halfway there when Resa stirred. Scar tissue shone briefly on her cheek, then she tugged her cowl forward and shuffled sideways, out of the light spilling around her from the high windows.

He stopped, not wanting to intrude. 'I came to apologise, Sister.'

Her posture remained tense, uneasy, like a wild thing poised to flee.

'It was wrong of me to stare. Forgive me.'

A slim hand gestured him forward and indicated the steps next to her, then she folded her hands together and bowed her head again. Gair guessed she was asking him to pray with her. Carefully looking nowhere but straight ahead, he walked the rest of the way to the altar steps.

In front of the great bronze Oak on the wall stood a smaller, leafless tree, set in the centre of the pristine white altar cloth. It had been fashioned from nails as long as his hand and as thick through as his index finger, dull and black as oak galls. Threaded through the iron tree's branches was a silver chain, from which hung a medallion no bigger than his thumbnail.

A lump formed in his throat, big as a fist, and he knew, with numbing certainty, that the tree held two nails for every man and boy who had once called this Daughterhouse his home.

Goddess be with you, Brothers.

After ten years at the Motherhouse, he couldn't help but be moved by what the nameless blacksmith had done, taking the cold iron of a horrific death and transforming it into a symbol of life. He bowed his head and said a prayer for them, but the words echoed hollowly inside him, as if spoken into an empty room. After the final amen he waited, but all he heard above the rippling sound of the Song was his own heartbeat.

Making the sign of blessing over his breast, Gair looked up towards the Oak. Should he really expect anything different? The Goddess had been silent for many years. Perhaps it was now too many.

He reached for the rail to push himself up to his feet. Quick as an adder, Resa's brown hand caught hold of his left wrist. He looked at her.

'Sister?'

She kept her head down, hiding the worst of her scars, and turned his hand palm uppermost.

Seeing the brand no longer shocked him. He'd become accustomed to its ugliness, the lingering stiffness in the small muscles underneath it that made him think, after a year and a half, he would probably never regain full flexibility in that hand. To a believer like Resa, it was a symbol of everything she had been raised to shun. *Suffer ye not the life of a witch.*

But unlike Sofi, she did not recoil from it. Instead she tilted his hand towards the light and slowly traced the witchmark with her fingertip as if committing it to memory.

Lifting her head, she looked him full in the face.

The Cultist's knife had taken a path from the left corner of her mouth almost to the angle of her jaw. On the right, it had slashed up towards her cheekbone and the cut had tightened as it healed, distorting her upper lip into a sneer.

Dark-brown eyes watched him for his reaction. Not challenging, not defiant, as Aysha had been, but composed. Only a little redness around her eyes betrayed that she had been weeping.

He had no name for what he felt. He wasn't sure if it even had a name. It was dark and hot and surged up from his gut in a wave, making his palms itch for the hilt of a sword.

'Sister, I'm so sorry.'

She wagged a finger in the gentlest of admonitions. He had nothing to be sorry for, it said. Then she pointed up at the Oak, bronze leaves shimmering in the candlelight. What had happened was the Goddess' will – or maybe she meant Holy Eador would judge the culprits when they came before Her. Either way, there was nothing he could do.

Or was there?

Even as the thought entered his mind the Song rose up, a glorious cascade of possibility. Its potential thrummed in his every nerve, waiting for his will to give it shape.

A voice at the back of his mind cautioned that there might be a witchfinder in El Maqqam, but the voice was as small and buzzy as a trapped insect, easily ignored. What had been done to this girl was barbaric. Inhumane. So many different kinds of *wrong* that it offended every principle he had. He had to do something, somehow, to put it right.

With the power singing inside him, he reached out his free hand to Resa's cheek. She shied away from it, frowning, fearful.

'I won't hurt you,' he said, 'but this will feel strange.'

What do you think you're doing? We're— He pushed Alderan's voice away, blotting it out. The weaving required all his attention.

The Song tingling through his fingertips, he cupped his hand over Resa's cheek. Her eyes flew wide. Her spine stiffened, then her mouth fell open as shock melted into a spreading wonder. She looked exactly as Gair imagined it must feel to be touched by the Goddess's grace.

Her own Song was a fragile thing, pale and weak as a plant kept too long in the dark. It shivered at his touch, its few clear notes almost drowned by the jangle of pain at its core. With only his instinct and a memory of Tanith's Healing to work from, he wrapped his Song around it and turned it towards the light.

The buzzing intensified. It had grown from the barely audible whine of a biteme to the harsh, sawing drone of a horsefly. Frowning, Gair renewed his focus on the

Song and the joyful rush of it along his nerves. He never tired of this. It was exhilarating, so alive—

Pain seared across his mind, blank and white as if he'd struck his head. His nerves screamed, the music of the Song transformed into a shrieking cacophony. He recoiled from it and his weaving broke apart into whirling white-hot shards that drove into his brain like the talons of a predator.

Holy saints, it hurt. Every beat of his heart sent hot pulses of pain through his head; he only barely managed to catch Sister Resa as she fainted. Holding her against his chest, he screwed his eyes shut and waited for the pain to pass.

When it had diminished enough that he dared to move, he checked the nun's pulse and respiration to be sure she was just in a faint, and laid her carefully on the floor with her cowl folded into a pillow. Then he sat on the altar steps with his head between his hands.

He must have made a mistake, got something seriously wrong. Hardly surprising, attempting something as complex as Healing without any instruction – if Tanith ever found out, she'd tear strips off him up one side and down the other. Besides, Resa's wounds were old, already closed. He doubted anyone could have helped her, not even Tanith or Saaron. Why had he ever thought that he could?

Propping his chin on his hand, he looked over at the unconscious nun. Thick red furrows still distorted her cheeks, so at least his clumsy meddling hadn't made anything worse. His skull felt as if it had been rung like a chapel bell; he could only hope he hadn't hurt her.

He raked his fingers back through his hair and let his hands fall. Time to face the consequences.

Ask Sister Sofi to come down here, he sent to Alderan. *Resa needs somewhere quiet to rest.*

She's already on her way. A pause. *You and I need to talk. Now.*

I'll be there in a minute.

Make it sooner.

When Sofi arrived, Gair told her Resa had fainted when she stood up from her prayers. It was only a small untruth, but the elder nun accepted it though her eyes remained hard with suspicion. Not long after that Resa woke, and Sofi became too concerned with the girl's well-being to spare a thought for him. He lingered long enough to be sure the young nun had come to no harm, then took advantage of Sofi's distraction to slip quietly away.

He climbed back up the stairs and walked along to the storeroom that held the Knights' books. On the way he tried to sort through what he might have done to cause that sudden discord in the Song. The most likely explanation was that he'd simply been careless: too caught up in his emotions and his concentration had slipped. It wasn't the first time his temper had got the better of him.

Alderan was busy shelving books when he let himself back in, though the piles of texts on the table and against the walls looked no smaller. The old man glanced at him then turned his attention back to the stack in his hands.

'I hope you're proud of yourself,' he said, thumping the books into place.

Gair's head was still throbbing with the after-effects of the failed Healing. 'Not particularly.'

'We're supposed to be hiding our presence here. You do remember that?' More thumps punctuated Alderan's words. 'If there's a witchfinder within a hundred miles of El Maqqam – or, Goddess help us, if Savin is – you just lit a signal fire for them. You're strong, boy, but by the saints you're about as subtle as a rockslide. You can't just pour everything you've got into the weaving and hope for the best.'

'Well, excuse me,' Gair bit back. 'I haven't had the benefit of all your years of experience.'

The old man snorted. 'Clearly.'

Frustrated, already angry with himself, Gair slammed the door behind him. 'Damn it, Alderan, what was I supposed to do – just leave her disfigured like that? Leave her in pain? I had to try to help her!'

'And did you?'

'No.' The anger drained away and left him feeling raw, scoured out. He leaned on the back of a chair and let his head fall forwards. 'I failed.'

'You can't Heal a wound once it's scarred, Gair,' said Alderan.

'I know.'

But he'd tried anyway, too moved by Resa's scars not to. He'd taken a reckless chance, perhaps betrayed their location, and seen no gain from it. Alderan said nothing but the reproof was there anyway, loud as a shout. The old man fetched the next stack of books from the table and sorted them onto the shelf.

'Is she all right?' he asked eventually, not looking around.

'She seems to be. Sister Sofi's looking after her.' Gair straightened up and scrubbed his hands over his face. 'I know there is a point beyond which Healing doesn't work. I don't know what I thought I could achieve. I simply had to try.'

Turning towards the light, Alderan studied the last book. It was a fat, heavy thing, the size of an heirloom Book of Eador, and its binding had flaked so badly that whatever title had once been blocked on its spine was now almost impossible to read. He rubbed his fingertips lightly over the remaining letters then stood it carefully on the shelf next to the others.

'Maybe you thought that if you could Heal Resa's scars, there would be some chance for yours.'

Gair opened his left hand. Sweat glistened in the creases of his palm, almost as if the eye-shaped witchmark was weeping.

'That hadn't occurred to me,' he said. He wiped his hand dry on his trousers. 'She saw it. Sister Resa. Then she showed me her face.'

Alderan hefted another stack and began filling the next shelf. 'She's a brave girl. Many wouldn't have wanted to live on after an attack like that.'

Inside, Gair felt a lick of that dark fire again. 'I think she finds a lot of comfort in prayer.'

'The faithful usually do.' Book after book slid onto the shelf. 'Do you miss it? Prayer, I mean. The round of the hours.'

As a child, the morning service had simply been a part of Gair's day. He'd been too young to question it; the household went to prayers so he went to prayers, and sat in a pew behind the family with the other foster boys to listen to Father Drumheller fulminate at the lectern. Later, at the Motherhouse, where the full liturgy was observed and attendance was mandatory, he'd had no choice – even though he no longer heard the Goddess speak.

'I missed the routine at first – I still can't shake the habit of waking up early. But prayer?' Gair lifted another pile of books from the table to help Alderan. 'No, I don't miss it. The Church holds nothing for me any more.'

Before today he had been in chapel only once since he left the Motherhouse. After Low bell, when all of Chapterhouse was sleeping, he had knelt in the faint glow of the sanctuary lamp with grief scalding his cheeks and tried to open his heart to the Goddess, but his hands had stayed in fists at his sides. He had known then that his faith, such as it had ever been, was gone.

One by one he shelved the books, then returned to his seat and the next unsorted pile. The book of verse, twin to the one under his pillow in the guest hall, remained where he had left it. He touched the scarred cover, the ragged edges of the pages that had come loose

from their binding, then added it to the appropriate
stack for shelving and opened the next book.

Perhaps he would read some more tonight, when he
couldn't sleep. Try to puzzle out a few more words by
the clear silver light of Lumiel, or just hold the book in
his hands and remember Aysha's voice. It didn't salve
his pain, but it gave him more comfort than prayer had
ever done.

32

TIME TO DANCE

❧

The labourer's tunic was coarse and scratchy, and more
than a little tight across Gair's shoulders. He also suspected that he was not the only creature inhabiting it.
But a disguise was necessary to be out in the city, and a
deep desertman's *barouk* would not help him pass for a
humble carter. With a homespun *kaif* to hide his fair
hair and veil his face, he slouched on the wagon-seat to
minimise his height and steered the two plodding mules
through the streets under the direction of the spare-
framed, angular Sister Avis sitting next to him.

Resa had come to him in the archive that morning,
apparently none the worse for his clumsy attempt at
Healing. With pointing and mime she indicated that she
intended to go out to feed the poor, undeterred by the
attack she had suffered the last time she had done so.
She'd asked for his help, although he'd already decided
to offer his sword. Alderan was out somewhere on
business of his own so there'd been no one to stop him.

Besides, after three days inside he needed a chance to get out of that room, to breathe fresh air instead of the dust of dead men's books.

El Maqqam's streets were busy, for all that the hour was early, with traders setting out their stalls and shop-keepers opening shutters and sweeping steps. Small boys dodged through the crowd, chasing after each other and the scruffy dogs that haunted the bazaars for scraps.

On doorposts and lintel-stones, Gair saw the image of a many-rayed sun. Some were faded by the weather, but many more were as vivid as if freshly painted.

'Sister Avis?' he whispered. 'The sun signs over the doors – do they mean what I think they mean?'

'They mean the householder is faithful to Silnor. A Cultist. There are more of them now than ever.' The bony nun looked disapproving. 'The city is not what it was.'

Gair watched the hurrying stream of folk part and re-form around the wagon. This close to the southern gate the square thronged with citizens and merchants, produce-laden carts and drovers with livestock brought in from the farms that patterned the river valley. It could have been market day in any city, anywhere in the Empire; only the darker skins and flowing clothes marked it as a desert city – that and the almost complete absence of northern faces.

No one caught his eye or gave him any sign of a threat, but neither did anyone look up from their business. Fear had already taken root. Even the native Maqqami felt its touch. Keep quiet, stay small, don't attract attention. With the toe of his boot, Gair nudged the *qatan* hidden under the wagon-seat a little closer to hand. Given enough of a spark, fear could ignite like dry grass at summer's end.

Resa, I hope you know what you're doing.

Following Sister Avis's pointing arm he guided the

wagon across the square to a spot where the beggars huddled under the wall, out of the sun's gaze. As it came to a halt the huddle became individuals, mostly women and ragged children. Hesitant waves became whoops of delight when Resa hopped down from the wagon-bed and the children clustered around her skirts. They, at least, appeared unafraid. Small hands touched her scars, but she smiled and kissed their puzzled faces then went to help Avis uncover the sacks of provisions.

As an untidy queue formed beside the wagon, Gair let his gaze rove over the square, careful not to linger too long in any one place. Most of the scurrying citizens kept their eyes firmly in front of them and paid no heed to the two nuns, but a few made a point of crossing to the other side of the dusty plaza, with hard expressions and harder stares directed back over their shoulders.

If Resa saw them, she gave no sign. Though she wore her cowl up, it was not pulled forward enough to completely cover her face and she smiled as she handed out loaves and fruit. With her free hand she made the sign of blessing and if it was not returned, she neither frowned nor faltered. Food was given freely and equally, regardless.

Maybe it was because she was smiling, but the scars did not appear quite so livid today, though it was hard to be sure from any distance. As if she'd sensed his gaze on her, she looked up. Her smile this time was just for him, and then she inclined her head. He nodded back.

She'd made no mention of what had happened in the chapel. He didn't know whether she'd realised what he'd done or whether she simply didn't remember, because when he'd tried to apologise she'd waved it away as if it was of no consequence.

All at once the crowd of women scattered, stumbling and dropping their meagre provisions. Booted feet kicked them out of the way, rough hands shoving their children, too, and the littlest ones began to wail.

Gair turned on the wagon-seat. Five men were pushing their way towards the two nuns, sand-veils hanging loose on their chests. Their clothing was dusty and unremarkable save for their bright-yellow sashes, through which well-worn *qatans* were thrust, but they carried themselves as if clad in the raiment of princes.

Yellow sashes. Sun-yellow. Cultists. Not wearing their allegiance under their shirts, like the ones in Zhimandar, but proudly, their thumbs tucked into those same sashes to draw the eye. Even the way they stared around them ensured they were the centre of everyone's attention.

Gair edged the sword closer still.

The biggest, broadest of the five swaggered to the front of the group, smoothing his luxuriant moustaches with finger and thumb. Resa had knelt to soothe a crying child and Avis positioned herself in front of them, trying to shield them both, but the younger nun was having none of it. She stood at Avis's side and faced the Cultist, her head up and her hands folded at her waist. The sniffling child peeked around her skirts, his face still wet with tears.

'Back again?' the swaggering fellow sneered in common, presumably intended to intimidate the northern-born Avis. He spat on the ground at Resa's feet. 'I thought you would have learned your lesson.'

A slow burn of anger began in Gair's chest. That vainglorious bastard had something to do with the attack on the sisters.

'We are doing good work here,' Avis said, but there was a quaver in her voice. 'There is no harm in our feeding the poor.'

'We can tend to our own,' snapped one of the others. 'We have no need of your corruption.'

The leader picked up a fallen loaf and broke it in two, making an elaborate show of sniffing it. 'Poisoned?' he asked, then threw it aside. 'Or do you just poison our children with your lies?'

He grabbed the child by the shoulder and dragged him away from Resa, ignoring his sobs and outstretched hands. The little boy wriggled out of the man's grasp and ran back to the nun to cling to her legs. She wrapped her arm protectively around him.

The other Cultists scowled and rested their hands on their sword-hilts. Hoping their attention would remain fixed on the sisters, Gair stooped to grasp his own blade.

Sister Avis shook her head. 'The word of the Goddess is no lie. Only truth.'

'False truth!' the man spat. 'There is no Goddess!'

Spittle sprayed with the words, right into the nun's face, and she flinched. The Cultist snatched her wooden Oak from the breast of her habit and snapped the leather thong around her neck with a jerk of his hand.

'Where is Her power now, eh?' He dropped the Oak into the dust and stamped on it, smashing it into pieces. Avis blanched but stood firm. 'She has no power here.'

'Her power is in the hearts of all good men,' said the nun. 'She is in us all, if you only let yourself hear Her.'

'Lies!'

The Cultist backhanded Avis across the face. She staggered into Resa, blood on her lip.

Gair grabbed the sword and leapt down from the cart. 'Enough!'

In a half-dozen strides he put himself between the five men and the sisters. 'These women have no quarrel with you.'

'The faith of the *ammanai* is not welcome here,' said the Cultists' leader. 'The desert-born are sun-born and answer to no other!'

Resa pushed in front of Gair and the Cultist's lip

curled. He made to speak but she raised her hand to silence him. Pointing up to the sky, then down to the earth, she spread her hands to encompass the whole square around her, then pressed those hands to her heart. Gair understood. All things, all people, were one under the Goddess. It was the simplest, most eloquent statement of faith he had ever heard, though not a word was spoken.

'Idolatrous witch,' the Cultist growled. His sword hissed into his hand. 'You have fallen from the true path, and for that you will die!'

The blade slashed towards the nun. Gair drew his *qatan* and lunged, and the two blades screeched together at waist-height. 'I said, that's enough.'

He stepped past Resa and levered the other sword up and away, forcing the Cultist back a pace.

The moustachioed fellow grinned nastily and tossed his *qatan* from hand to hand. 'So they have found a Knight-protector. Take care that the fate of the last Knights to walk these sands does not also befall you.'

'I am no Knight,' Gair said, 'but I will stand between you and these women until one of us falls.'

A familiar music had begun to stir in his blood. He brought the *qatan* to the salute as if it was his longsword. The searing sun winked along the blade, yet he felt cold as carved stone.

'The veil may hide your face but your voice betrays you, *ammanai*.' The Cultist twitched his fingers and the rest of his men drew their swords. 'Out of the way.'

'Back on the wagon, Sisters. We're leaving.' Gair passed his empty scabbard to Resa.

'So you can spread your corruption in another part of the city?' The Cultist scowled. 'El Maqqam stands in the light of Silnor. You are not welcome here!'

He raised his sword again, his four companions doing likewise.

Gair set his feet in readiness. 'Quickly, Sisters!'

It was time to dance.

Shouting in Gimraeli, the Cultists closed in. Steel rang on steel as Gair parried the first blows away, whirling on his heel to meet a man closing in from behind. No time for finesse; he simply hacked across the man's shoulder and down through his collarbone.

Blood sprayed across the skirts of Avis's habit. 'Merciful Mother!' she exclaimed, blessing herself as the man fell sobbing, clutching his ruined shoulder.

Gair paid him no mind as the dance went on. He was already wheeling again, the *qatan* fluid in his hands as it turned away blade after blade and kept the Cultists at bay. With each arc of the sword, scarlet drops pattered onto the dusty cobbles.

In the periphery of his vision he saw the two nuns scrambling onto the wagon-seat, Resa's frightened face staring at him. Two Cultist closed, forcing him into an inelegant parry. As he turned one blade away, the other sliced him along his left ribs.

Swearing, Gair fell back a step. His side burned. Somewhere in the crowded square a woman gasped and men turned to follow the clash of weapons. He thought he glimpsed a flash of yellow amongst them, then the two Cultists charged. Gair had barely enough time to recognise the blood on one of the blades as his own before pain and fury veiled his mind and all restraint fled.

He didn't know the meaning of the words he shouted as he swung. He didn't feel the judder in his wrist when his blade bit bone, nor hear the silky sound of steel parting flesh. Again and again he spun and struck, until no one was left to strike back.

A touch on his arm swung him around, blade ready.

Avis, leaning down from the wagon-seat, pulled her hand away. 'Come,' she said, white-faced and glancing anxiously at the onlookers. 'There's no more time.'

Gair looked into the staring crowd, at the hostile eyes. Three men lay still at his feet, a fourth in a spreading pool of scarlet a few yards away. The fifth, the one with the moustache, was bleeding from a slash to the fat of his thigh but still on his feet, his hands flexing around the hilt of the bloody sword held steadily at an advance guard. Behind him, the crowd began to seethe.

Avis was right: it was time to go.

He threw the *qatan* into the wagon-bed beside Resa and tried to vault up after it, but pain flared white-hot in his side and he fell awkwardly across the tailboards. Muttering, the crowd advanced. Gritting his teeth, he scrabbled for purchase with his good right hand, then Resa thrust her arms beneath his armpits and hauled him up enough that he could pull himself the rest of the way.

'Go!' he shouted. Some of the men pushing through to the front of the crowd were clearly armed. '*Go!*'

'Hyah!' Avis yelled and snapped the reins across the mules' rumps. The wagon jolted forwards and rattled across the cobbles away from the square.

Lying amongst the sacks and baskets in the wagon-bed, every jounce brought Gair fresh pain. Resa bent over him and ripped apart the rent in his smock.

'I'm all right,' he gasped. 'I don't think it's deep.' He was lying; it burned like a brand.

She shushed him with a gesture and used a piece of the smock to wipe away the blood. Rummaging amongst the provisions she found a flask of water and upended it over the wound. He bit down on a cry as her fingers probed around it, then she nodded, satisfied. She tapped one of his ribs and with her other hand mimed a blade slashing.

'Scored the rib?'

Resa nodded again. Not too serious, then. Her hands threaded an imaginary needle – it needed stitching.

The wagon bounced over a rutted cross-street and he swore again.

'Sorry,' he panted, when the pain had subsided. 'It stings a bit.'

Slumped amongst the sacks and baskets, Gair closed his eyes and tried to shut off his awareness of the wound. More stitches. The first set was still in his shoulder. No doubt Alderan would have some choice words to say when he returned to the Daughterhouse.

33

PORTENT

※

Snow was falling again when Teia emerged from her shelter. Fat white flakes, settling thickly on the tents, piling up against trees already stooped under the weight of snow on their branches like old men weary of winter's burden.

It was barely dawn but the fire outside was already well alight, a kettle steaming on the stones. Lenna was hunkered beside it, a snow-dappled blanket over her shoulders for a cloak, swirling the teapot to hurry the brew along.

For the Banfaith. For me.

Four days, now. Teia had insisted that she could manage, take care of herself, yet as soon as she turned her back one of the women was there to serve her food or pour her tea – even Gerna took her turn, so stickily ingratiating when she did so that Teia was glad when it was over. Each afternoon one of the men would build her a shelter or tend to Finn as diligently as if the dun was his own horse. And no one would say who had given them their instructions.

'Good morning, Banfaíth,' Lenna said, pouring tea into a bowl. 'Your tea.'

'Thank you, Lenna.'

Hands wrapped around the cup to make the most of the warmth, Teia sipped her tea and yawned as she watched the camp stirring. In the dull, shadowless light, people moved through the falling snow like figures from a dream, distant and not quite solid. Even the tracks they made quickly began to fill, almost as if the snow was patiently erasing them from the mountain's face.

As if we had never been. As if people of flesh and blood do not belong here.

She shivered and glanced up at Tir Malroth, but the cloud was too low to see the mountain's forked peak. No wonder her dreams had been so dark of late, when every stride took her closer to the Haunted Mountain.

Last night had been no exception. She'd been back in the caves, and Drwyn's wolf-skin had torn itself from the curing frame and stalked her through endless tunnels, snarling that she had no place with the Crainnh. When she'd finally found the way up to the air, she'd emerged onto a stark mountainside above a plain of ash and smoke and death as far as her eyes could see.

She'd woken gulping for air, her throat raw and lungs aching as if she'd been running for miles. The underground chase had surely been nothing more than a bad dream brought on by recent events, but the blasted plain . . . that had the shine of a foretelling to it, and had so spoiled her sleep for the rest of the night that the least sound from outside the shelter had been enough to wake her with her heart racing.

The touch of a hand on her elbow almost made her leap out of her boots.

'Oh!'

Lenna snatched her hand back. 'Is everything all

right, Banfaíth?' She looked half-terrified, field-mouse eyes staring, the scar on her cheek livid in the cold.

'Sorry. Yes, everything's fine.' Teia managed a smile. 'You startled me, that's all.'

'I wanted to know if you're done?' Lenna gestured towards the shelter. 'So I can put up your blankets?'

For a moment Teia thought about telling her no and doing it herself, but having been so badly frightened by that first conjured light, and then the revelation of her gift for foretelling, it had taken almost two full days just to get Lenna to speak to her without cringing. It might be kinder simply to let her be, however unaccustomed Teia was to being waited on.

'I'm done,' she said, and the girl disappeared inside.

A figure approached the fire. Shoulders hunched inside his coat and his footsteps creaking in the deepening snow, Baer greeted her with a nod. 'Banfaíth.'

'Baer. Will you have some tea?'

'Aye, I will.'

Teia poured him a bowl from the pot keeping warm on the stones at the edge of the fire. Tea with Baer had become a daily ritual. He would tell her of the band's progress the day before and his plans for the day to come, just like a chief to his Speaker.

Was that how she was regarded? Sipping her tea, she watched him from the corner of her eye. If he was expecting her guidance, she wouldn't have much to offer. Whatever her gifts, there weren't many ways in which a mere girl could counsel a veteran such as him. Even the time she'd spent with Drwyn had taught her little of a Speaker's role; Ytha had always been careful to keep her guidance for the chief's ears alone.

'The lookout saw some game this morning,' he said eventually. 'Like elk but smaller, he tells me, and spotted like the fawns of the hill deer. I've sent two men to bring one down, to see if it makes good eating.'

It was the first game bigger than a bird that they'd

seen on their journey into the mountains. Not a one of the band looked to be carrying an ounce of fat so Teia knew they were accustomed to hard bread and short rations, but away from the familiar plains and the places where they knew game could be found, even in winter, there were lean times ahead for them.

'A good thought,' she said. 'We need fresh meat – the men especially, if they are to maintain their strength.'

She stopped, feeling suddenly foolish. Baer had been exiled for ten years; surely he already knew how to feed men so that they survived the winter. What could she possibly tell him that was new? Ducking her head to hide her blushes, she concentrated on her tea. The best she could do was play the role in which the Lost Ones had cast her, and hope she didn't make even more of a fool of herself.

As she finished her tea, Baer bolted the last of his as if it had been a signal that their conversation was over. But then he looked down into the bowl and rolled his tongue around his mouth, hunting for the right words to say.

'Speak, Baer,' she said softly. 'I'd rather know your mind than be forever guessing at it.'

'Perhaps the others haven't noticed yet,' he began, still studying the dregs of his tea, 'but it seems to me our path is set for Tir Malroth.'

'And that worries you.'

His eyes flicked up to hers, then slid away. 'It does.'

'It's the only safe route through the mountains. Drwyn sent scouts to the other pass, I know that for sure. They'd never let us through.' *And what if he sent scouts to the pass below Tir Malroth, too? What if they capture us, hand me back to Drwyn – or to Ytha?* She squashed that thought, hurried on. 'No one ever goes this way.'

'Aye, for good reason!' he retorted. 'It's Tir Malroth, girl – the Haunted Mountain!' He stopped, biting back whatever he'd been about to say. His jaw worked. 'Forgive me, Banfaíth. I misspoke.'

'Baer, I'm young enough to be your daughter – you don't have to apologise to me.' Tentatively, she laid a hand on his arm. She would miss the company if she left them here, but this was her task, not theirs. 'I appreciate all the help you've given me to get this far. You didn't have to come with me and I'm grateful you did. I will understand if you come no further.'

'And let you go on alone?' He snorted. 'Neve would kill me. Besides, there's better shelter here in the mountains than there was down on the plains. And maybe game now, too.' He squinted against the falling snow to study the clouds and put down his bowl. 'We'd best be moving soon. The trail ahead is steep and those clouds have plenty more snow in their bellies. I can smell it.'

❈

Four hours later, a sharp whistle from up ahead stopped the trudging column in a wide forested valley. Teia looked around from talking to Neve and saw Isaak and Varn weaving through the trees ahead, the former with a deer's carcass over his broad shoulders, the other man carrying both their bows.

Baer strode up from the back of the group and nodded to Teia. 'Will you join me, Banfaíth, and see what Isaak has found?'

She steered Finn out of line and followed him to where the two men were slogging through the knee-deep snow towards them. The pair of them were caked in white but grinning fit to break their faces. Teia dismounted carefully and kneaded her aching back whilst she waited for the hunters to reach her.

Isaak slung the spotted deer off his shoulder and laid it at Teia's feet. He'd made a clean kill, one arrow to the heart; only a little blood stained the doe's chestnut breast and her wide dark eyes still held the last light of life.

'Is it good?' he asked.

Kneeling in the snow, Teia stripped off her mitten and laid her hand on the doe's flank. The rest of the band crowded around, whispering and peering over each other's shoulders to watch. Their eager attention made her nervous so she closed her eyes, and the whispers fell silent.

Ytha had scarcely taught her the trick of using her magic like this, out beyond her body. She concentrated on the texture of the hide under her palm, the faint, lingering warmth seeping from the organs beneath, and called up her power. Just a thread at first, which she allowed to flow along her arm, down through her hand and into the deer.

No new music greeted her because the beast was dead, but there was something . . . Almost an echo, or a space where something used to be that now was gone. She strained to feel the shape of it and was deluged in sensation. Not sight, not touch, but it filled her awareness with a sense of richness that all but made her mouth water.

Opening her eyes, she smiled up at Isaak. 'Yes, it's good. Very good. And this hide,' she stroked it, 'will make fine leather, soft enough for clothes.'

The shaggy young man grinned and drew his knife.

Teia levered herself to her feet and left him to it, unable to stomach the sounds and smells of butcher-work, however necessary it might be. Her back was aching again and walking seemed to soothe it a little, though her gait was becoming more and more like a duck's as her belly, impossibly, continued to grow. Drwyn's old trews had been let out at the seams as far as they could go before she left the caves but had begun to dig into her uncomfortably. Her breasts were tender, too, her once-dainty nipples now swollen and dark.

Perhaps they should stay a while in that valley. It was sheltered from the worst of the wind, with densely forested flanks and a stream that flowed too fast to freeze completely. They could hunt more, build a smoke-tent to cure the venison and the coarse sausage made from the offal. Rest the animals and themselves. After four days in these conditions . . . She kneaded her back and sighed. Rest would be good.

But time was against them, an enemy greater than the Wild Hunt and Drwyn's war band combined. If she presented her warning to the Empire with time enough for them to prepare, there was some hope. If she was too late, she might as well not have come at all.

Ahead of her the trees petered out amongst the tumbled rocks surrounding the river that leapt and chattered the length of the valley. The snow was falling faster now, making up for its smaller, drier flakes with twice as many thrown down twice as hard. She could barely make out the opposite bank. At the edge of the trees she stopped; close to the water the stones were thickly sheathed in ice and crowned with caps of snow. The footing there would be chancy.

She brushed snow from a fallen tree at the edge of the rocks, where its neighbours provided a bit of shelter, and eased herself down to sit on it. No sooner did her back cease aching than her feet began; some part of her always hurt, as if the pain never went away, just took up residence in some other part of her body. Praise Macha, it would all be over in three months or so.

Mountains ringed the valley, their peaks lost in the low cloud and swirling snow. Without sight of the skyline she could not orient herself in relation to the great forked crown of Tir Malroth; she did not even know for sure that they were following the right trail. Picking their way was like chasing a mouse through the folds of a rumpled blanket: after a while the mazy valleys all looked the same. Snow and trees and rock; everything grey and white with scarcely a scrap of colour to be seen.

How far still to the pass? Another five days? Six? Baer would not be drawn on it, not even to hazard a guess. This trail was foreign to them all, knowledge of it having been lost with the lives that gave the fishtailed peak its name. She would have to look into the waters again to plot their course.

Except her dream was preying on her mind. It had left such a sense of dread behind, as brooding and formless as her sense of the Haunted Mountain looming nearby, but so thick it was almost something she could taste. She pulled from her belt-pouch the small bronze basin she had taken to carrying since her journey began. She scooped snow into it from a nearby drift and used a little of her power to melt it to water. Basin balanced between her hands on the roundness of her belly, Teia opened herself to whatever the waters would show.

Fires on the plains. Running. Dying. Maegern's steed rearing. Scarlet and black, ashes and blood. Nothing new. The image reformed into the staring eye on the Raven's shield, hideously alive, knowing her, down to her deepest fears and most secret desires. Then it blinked, opening again as a human eye so blue as to be almost violet in a pale, dirt-smudged face.

It took a moment for her to realise it was her own face, hollowed and hardened into the face of a stranger. A lock of white hair hung over the savage wound on her brow. Instinctively she touched it and in the water the woman – her – lifted a hand to touch her scar, too.

True telling. She'd found the first white strand when she combed her hair that morning using the little looking-glass Drwyn had given her. Only short, newly grown, but a portent for what was to come.

Show me.

Darkness.

Show me.

Darkness so absolute the basin in her hands became a hole in the world. Daylight did not pierce it, nor the breeze ruffle its surface. She closed her eyes and concentrated, throwing herself as wide open to the vision as she knew how. There had to be more to her future than this.

Show me!

But the darkness remained, flat and fathomless. Frustrated, Teia flung the water out of the bowl and it fell sparkling over the rocks at her feet. If only she could have learned more about her gift for scrying from Ytha. The last two attempts had been the same – only the familiar images and then blackness. Did it mean death? Loss of her Talent? Or did it simply mean Maegern and the Hunt would triumph?

The empty bowl tumbled from her hands onto the rock, ringing as it bounced, and Teia pressed trembling fingers to her mouth. Oh, Macha, was she leading them all to their doom on the Haunted Mountain?

'Banfaíth?' Baer's voice sounded amongst the trees behind her, the snow creaking as he trudged through it.

Quickly she straightened up, fumbled for her scrying bowl and made a show of shaking out the last drops of water as if she was done. The chief could not see the Banfaíth at a loss – or worse, weeping. Not when he had placed his trust, and that of the entire band, in her.

'Are you well?' he asked when he reached her. Were her eyes red?

'I am well, Baer.' She sounded calmer than she felt. 'Is Isaak done with his catch?'

'Aye. We'll eat well tonight, I think.' He peered up at the sky. 'There's no more'n an hour or two of daylight left. We should make camp early, here, and take some rest whilst we can.'

'I agree. I'm sure the ponies will appreciate it, too. The last few miles have been hard on everyone.' More time lost, but rest and hot food now would make them all stronger to face the demands of the days to come.

Forcing herself to appear confident, Teia tucked the bowl back in her pouch. 'In the morning we press on.'

Dark eyes studied her face. 'Our course holds true?'

She nodded firmly. 'Our course holds true.'

It was all they could do.

⊰⊱

A hot supper was good for everyone's mood. Fresh meat, tender and rich, improved it further, and the atmosphere around the fire became relaxed, almost jovial. One or two folk glanced up uneasily at the fishtailed mountain, but with little to see on such a cloudy night they soon found the contents of their bowls more interesting. Even Gerna ceased complaining, stuffing venison into her mouth until her chin shone with grease.

After the meal, Baer doubled the lookouts. Watching him with half an eye whilst Lenna brewed tea, Teia noted that each man was well armed. The band had collected the javelins the other Maenardh left behind when their leader fell, and those men with bows had used their rest time that afternoon to replenish their quivers with new arrows. After Lenna had gone to her own supper, Teia waited until Baer passed close by.

'Won't you join me for some tea, Baer?' she called. He hesitated, then walked towards her. As he hunkered down to take the bowl she asked quietly, 'Is something wrong?'

'No, Banfaíth. Naught's amiss,' he said, but she knew him well enough by now to recognise the forced tone.

'You've doubled the watch and sent them well back down the trail, away from the fire. My father is a warrior, Baer – I know about night sight and how a lamp or torch spoils it.' He looked uncomfortable, like a child caught shirking his chores. 'What are they watching for?'

'Maybe something, maybe nothing,' he admitted at last, scratching at the root of his braid. 'Down in the last valley, the lookout thought he saw a fire. Far off, a day or more behind us. He told Varn when he relieved him and Varn told me.'

'So you've seen it, too?'

'Aye.' He blew on his tea whilst Teia considered.

'How many people, do you think?'

He shrugged. 'Can't be sure. Can't even be sure how far away they might be. Distance is hard to judge here, when your eyes are accustomed to the plains.'

Pursuit, then? But who would follow them? They'd long left clan lands behind, and even if Drwyn still believed she carried his heir, his thoughts were turned towards the Scattering now and being raised Chief of Chiefs. He'd have his pick of girls then. Prettier, more obedient girls. Every clan would want to provide a wife to the Chief of Chiefs; even his prodigious appetite would be sated.

She gnawed at her lip, bowl forgotten in her hands. If not Drwyn's warriors, who would be following them through the mountains? Then she knew.

'Lost Ones.'

Baer blinked. 'Are you sure?'

'I'm sure.' And she was, sure to her bones, though she couldn't have told him why. 'They're people like us, Baer, I know it.'

'And women know,' he muttered, and shook his head. 'Aedon save me. Can you scry them out?'

'No. For a viewing I need a hook to catch on to at the start – someone I know, or a familiar place to guide me.' Self-conscious, she ducked her head and sipped at her tea. 'I don't know as much about working the Talent as you seem to think.'

'Then I'll have to send a man back down there to see what they're about.' Baer finished his tea in two quick, deep swallows. 'Perhaps they want to join us,' he said sourly.

'Maybe they do.' Teia could see how little he liked that idea. 'It may not mean trouble, Baer.'

'More'n likely does, though,' he grunted. 'That last band outnumbered us two to one. If you hadn't put the fear into 'em, we'd not have survived.' He shook his head again, braid swinging. 'If it's them and they close on us, we'll lose everything.'

'If they joined us, we'd have more spears to defend ourselves,' Teia countered. The further she thought about it, the more right it seemed.

'Extra mouths to feed,' he replied. 'We've scarce enough for ourselves as it is.'

'Additional hunters to catch game. We'll be out above the trees in a day or two – game might be hard to find until we've crossed the next ridge.'

His jaw stuck out pugnaciously. 'We'll manage.'

'We might manage better with greater numbers.'

He fixed her with a flat stare, eyes like polished stones in the firelight. 'I don't like it.'

'I won't leave people behind, Baer, not even Maenardh. Not as prey for the Wild Hunt.' She swallowed, remembering her last look into the waters. 'Every day, I feel Her drawing closer.'

The chief-who-was-not-a-chief continued to stare, then finally dipped his head, lips twisting in a way that said he was still unhappy, but knew better than to continue to argue.

'As you wish, Banfaíth.' He sighed, breath steaming on the night air. 'I'll send a scout on one of the ponies. He can catch up with the rest of us on the far side of the ridge.'

Then he set down his bowl and strode off into the night.

In the morning, when Isaak appeared at her fireside

instead of the man who was chief in all but name, it appeared the scout Baer had sent back along their trail was himself, and she would have to lead his people on alone.

34

WILDWOOD

Tanith sat with her back against the bole of a lightning-struck oak tree, keeping one eye on the simmering pot over the fire, and waited for a guide to appear. She had built the fire carefully, on bare earth, well ringed with stones, and had used only fallen wood. In the forests of Bregorin, it was unwise to be careless with a naked flame if she expected the forestals to grant her their aid.

Ancient woods surrounded her. Beeches broad as bridge-piers, chestnuts whose massive boughs stooped so far under their own weight that they almost touched the ground, all draped in thick moss like swathes of tattered velvet. Even the air beneath the leafy canopy overhead felt dense and heavy with time.

With its cloven crown and froth of bright new leaves, the oak tree marked the furthest point to which Tanith had been able to penetrate the forest. Not that the going was difficult; quite the opposite, in fact: the trees were widely spaced and easily tall enough to ride beneath, but whichever direction she travelled, no matter how carefully she kept to a straight line, she found herself back at the oak tree within a few minutes. The forest simply did not wish her to go any further. She must wait here for her guide.

So all day she had waited. Baked bread, read her book. Sat with her back against the oak and watched deer ghosting through the trees, listening to the forest breathe around her, and waiting for her guide to show himself. She suspected he already knew she was there.

She stirred her pot of rabbit stew then covered it again, setting the spoon on her plate. Even the chink of metal on metal was muted, deadened by the thick air. In the distance a woodpecker drummed, a fusillade of sharp raps, then fell silent.

As soon as she'd arrived at the edge of the forest, after a five-day ride from her house on the edge of the Mere, she'd sensed a presence in the woods. At first she hadn't been sure whether it wasn't simply the patient stillness that always gathered underneath such venerable trees, but then yesterday she'd felt someone watching her. Awareness had brushed her colours like a strand of gossamer over her face, so subtle she barely registered it at all and when she reached for it she'd found nothing. Not with her eyes, not with the Song. All she'd sensed around her was life. Slow and slumberous in the trees, acid-sharp in the ferns unfurling amongst the mossy rocks, bright and scuttling in the unseen birds. The forest teemed with it: beetles and centipedes, voles, lichen-patterned moths. A thousand eyes, but none of them belonged to her watcher.

Tanith made herself more comfortable against the furrowed trunk of the oak and closed her own eyes. She must be patient; he would reveal himself at a time of his choosing. If she tried to seek him out or hasten their meeting, it was very likely he would never appear at all and she would have to ride the long leagues to Mesarild. The Bregorinnen were slow to share their secrets with outsiders, even with Astolans whose race was as old as their own.

Overhead, a wren trilled, his song purling down through the branches above her, then he whirred away to the other side of the clearing and began again. Between the end of one phrase and the start of the next, something in the wood changed. She opened her eyes.

The forestal stood on the far side of the clearing, half-hidden by a tree. Soft, shapeless clothing in browns and greens blurred his outline, rendering him all but indistinguishable from leaf and bark and rock. Then he pushed back his hood, revealing mahogany hair and quick dark eyes in a face as brown as bogwood.

'Well met,' she said, standing to greet him with a half-bow, as was proper. Just as well – she would have felt foolish attempting a curtsey in riding leathers.

'Lady.' He dipped his head. His voice was deep and somewhat sonorous. A braided leather band across his brow kept his unruly mane off his face. 'What brings a daughter of Astolar into the forest?'

'I have a long journey to make in haste. I hoped to shorten it, with your help.'

'You wish to travel the wildwood.' His tone was flat.

'If you will be my guide.'

He leaned on what she had at first thought was a staff, but now saw for what it was: a longbow, sturdy and almost as tall as the man who wielded it. Arrows peeped from a quiver on his shoulder. 'Few ask, these days. Fewer still are granted the gift.'

'Please.' She spread her hands. 'I would not ask if the need was not great. I have to reach Mesarild as soon as possible. The Veil between worlds may depend on it.'

Dark eyes searched her face, assessing. 'There is danger at hand?'

'Great danger. The Veil is weakening and there is one with both the will and, I fear, the means to bring it down – a reiver. I must warn the Empire to prepare for war.'

'War means men need timber. Ill tidings for the woods.'

'Ill tidings for everyone, if the reiver has his way.'
Briefly, she described the weakening of the Veil Masen
had observed, and the demons Savin had sent against
Chapterhouse in pursuit of the tools to rend it completely.

'If what you say is true . . .' The forestal looked uneasy. 'The King must be warned.'

'Take me to him and I will explain, as I have to you.'

He shook his head. 'Impossible. The King sees no one
from outside the Grove.'

'But it's important!'

'Forgive me, but this is the King's will. I cannot make
it different.'

'Is there someone else I can speak to?'

The forestal's eyes hardened, black as oak-galls. 'You
will not be permitted inside the Grove, my lady, so do
not ask. I will guide you through the wildwood to the
forests north of Mesarild, but no further or deeper than
that.'

Reining back her frustration, she bowed again. 'Then
I thank you. Please join me for supper. There's plenty –
fresh bread, too.'

With a nod she indicated the bannock she had baked
in the coals that morning, now wrapped in a cloth.

'A gift from the hearth,' he said, coming forward into
the clearing.

'And a gift from the hill,' Tanith finished the words,
'so hearts and minds remember still.'

His stony expression relented a little and he studied
her with a touch of curiosity. 'Not many still know the
old ways, even amongst your people.'

'I read a lot,' she said, shrugging. 'I didn't want to offend.'

'You have not.' Stooping, he plucked a sprig of leaves
from a blue-flowered plant growing amongst the rocks
near his feet and held it out to her.

'What's this?'

'Wood vervain. It goes well with rabbit.'

Tanith bruised the leaves in her fingers and cupped them to her nose. 'It's good. Piquant.' She smiled. 'Thank you. I'm familiar with most herbs, but I didn't recognise that one.'

'It only grows here, in the forest.' He squatted on his heels, bow held loosely between his hands.

Shredding the leaves into the pot, she asked, 'Does it have medicinal properties? I'm always looking for new remedies.'

'A tea brewed from the flowers is sovereign against headaches. Beyond that—' He broke off. 'I thought you were here alone.'

Tanith lowered the cook-pot lid, disquiet prickling down her spine. 'I am.'

'Then you were followed.'

In a heartbeat he was on his feet, an arrow nocked and the string drawn back to his ear, aiming at something behind her. 'Show yourself, stranger,' he commanded.

Tanith dropped her hand to the hilt of the dagger at her belt. She should have nothing to fear here, in the fringes of the wildwood, but the forestal's wariness had set her instincts on edge. Peering into the trees, she made out the shape of a man leading a horse. As he drew closer she recognised his pale-blond hair and sharply handsome features.

'It's all right,' she said, sighing. Ailric had followed her? 'I know him.'

The forestal lowered his bow but kept a finger over the arrow. 'You are certain?'

'Yes. He means no harm.'

Ailric stopped at the edge of the clearing, hands spread to show he held no weapons. He was dressed for riding, with well-stuffed packs tied behind the saddle of his black horse.

Tanith's heart sank like a stone. He'd come prepared

for a long journey. 'What are you doing here, Ailric?' she asked.

'Protecting you, I thought.' He tethered his mount to a tree next to her own brown mare. 'When I called at your house and found it empty, I was worried about you.'

'So you went to my father?'

'Tanith—'

'Did he send you after me?'

'He told me where you were bound.' Coming towards her, he reached for her hands. 'Please, Tanith, do not blame him for my decision. The human lands are no place for a Daughter of the White Court, not unescorted.'

She folded her arms, tucking her hands in her armpits out of his reach. 'I am not made of porcelain, you know. I'll be perfectly safe.'

He let his own hands fall to his sides. 'We hear reports from the Empire almost daily. Bandits, thieves – even the highways are not safe, and now your news of this reiver . . . I cannot allow you to ride into that alone.'

The nerve of him! 'You cannot *allow* me?' she echoed. 'You are not my father, Ailric, nor my husband, to *allow* me to do anything at all. Besides, I won't be alone. The forestal will see me to the edge of the Great Forest north of Mesarild. From there it's less than a half-day's ride into the city. I'll be fine.'

'Forgive me, I misspoke.' Somehow he was closer now, gaze tender, anxious. 'My only concern is for your well-being. I could not bear it if something were to happen to you, love,' he said softly.

'Go home, Ailric.'

Hurt clouded his expression. 'Why so angry with me?'

Thrusting her hands in her pockets, she looked away. The forestal, waiting on the far side of the fire, was near enough to have overheard most of the exchange. Spirits forfend.

She lowered her voice. 'Don't do this. There's nothing between us.'

Long fingers cradled her cheek, turned her back towards him. 'Is there not?'

His gold-flecked gaze caressed her face. Such beautiful eyes, the colour of flame, that warmed her and melted her like butter in a skillet and robbed her of the strength to resist as he bent his head and kissed her.

My love, he whispered into her thoughts. *My only love my Tanith my bride I am yours I have always been yours be mine again.*

His kiss, his scent of cedarwood and bay, was achingly familiar. The touch of his colours conjured a flood of memory. Strong hands at her waist, lifting her onto the mossy lakeshore. Wet bodies sliding over and against each other, and fingers stroking, plucking, strumming her as deftly as a lute, until she sang with desire.

It had been wrong then, and it would be wrong now. Breaking away from his lips, Tanith stepped backwards.

'No. Not any more.'

Her voice trembled – with anger, with desire, with too many tangled emotions to unpick. She despised what he had become and despised the part of her that still, despite it all, responded to his touch.

'Don't do that again.'

He spread his hands, taking a half-step back. 'Only let me accompany you. For your father's sake, if not for mine.'

The Bregorinnen stirred. 'I agreed to guide one, my lady, and one only.'

Ailric turned his easy smile on him. 'Are two so much more hardship than one?'

'You would not ask if you knew what you were asking.' Obviously put out, the forestal sighed. 'Very well. I will guide you both. But heed this: the wildwood is not a pleasure park. You must obey any command I give on the instant and without question, otherwise I cannot answer for your safety.'

'Understood,' Ailric murmured and inclined his head almost far enough to pass for a bow. To Tanith, he added, 'Please? If you are set on this course, at least let me see you safely to your destination. That is all I ask.'

He sounded sincere. She didn't know what he had said to her father, but Lord Elindorien would worry less if he thought Ailric was with her. He would have enough challenges, of her making, to face when he returned to the Court in her stead. If it spared him a little worry, she could put up with Ailric for a while longer. Besides, she could not afford to alienate him completely, not when she might one day need House Vairene's vote in the Council chamber: however she had offended the Ten, she remained House Elindorien's heir, and Second Ascendant to the throne after Morwenna. Eventually she woud have to rebuild the bridges she had burned that day. Ruefully she wondered – yet again – if allowing Ailric to escort her would have made a difference to the way her address was received, and then thrust the thought from her mind. Second-guessing herself would not help matters now.

'Very well,' she said, 'but only as escort. Nothing more.'

'Of course.' He laid his palm over his heart. 'My lady.'

He crossed the clearing to attend to his horse, and Tanith watched him go. Riding leathers flattered his lean, narrow-hipped physique in ways that left her biting her lip against a sudden heat surging through her. Whatever else Ailric had become, he remained an extraordinarily attractive man.

Blowing out her cheeks, she ran her hands back through her hair, acutely conscious of the warmth in her face. Oh, spirits keep her, that kiss! She had all but fallen for him again. All but forgotten what had driven them apart during the time she spent on the Isles, amongst the humans he regarded with such contempt; the selfish demands that she come home to Astolar, to him, and give up her dream of being a Healer. Her body could not be allowed to overrule her mind a second time.

To busy herself she attended to supper, setting out plates and cups, slicing bread. When the forestal appeared silently at her side with a leather bucket of water she started.

'Oh!'

'My apologies. I did not mean to startle you.'

'It's my fault. I'm a little distracted.' He did not miss the glance that strayed towards the horses and she cursed herself. 'I never asked you for your name. I'm Tanith, and that's Ailric.'

'True names have power,' he said sternly. 'They should not be used lightly, lest they be used against you.'

The power of the name. It was the oldest of magics, older than horseshoes and hazel twigs and toasting a newborn with wine. Old as the Song itself.

'I trust you,' Tanith said and smiled. When the forestal remained silent, she added, 'So what should I call you by?'

For a long moment he looked away into the woods, his expression closed.

'Owyn,' he said, then turned to leave. 'We begin our journey into the wildwood after supper. Be ready.'

⊰⊱

As the sun settled on the Astolan hills in the west and stretched its long golden fingers into the forest, Tanith and Ailric broke camp, carefully erasing any trace of their presence. The firestones were scattered, the ashes buried, even the flattened leaf-mould where she had sat and slept was stirred up again. Ailric's expression told

her he didn't understand, but he followed her directions and when they were done, the forestal gave her a
satisfied nod.

'You have read well,' he said.

As she mounted up, Ailric leaned forward in his saddle. 'What did he mean, you have read well?'

'I read a little about Bregorinnen customs before I set
out. They see it as their duty to tend the forest. It is
courteous to tread lightly in these woods.'

Owyn handed each of them an acorn, green-gold and
plump, still snug in its cup. 'Keep these close to you,' he
said. The nut felt heavier in Tanith's hand than she had
expected and her palm tingled. 'It will protect you from
harm and help prevent you from becoming lost. I will
lead your horse, my lady, and you will lead your companion's. Do not stray from the path, whatever you may
see or hear.'

From inside his boot he pulled a wooden flute and began to play. An elfin, airy little melody, it danced like
leaves in a breeze, twisting and shining and never the same
twice. In it Tanith heard fragments of bird-calls, running
water, even laughter. Threads of music trailed into the air
around them, winking in and out of sight like gossamer.

*Like seeing the Song in a complex weaving, except
there is no warp and weft. It's following our path – or
we're following it.*

She tucked the acorn into a pocket and reached her
hand up into the music. Bright threads tangled around
her fingers then slipped free, drifting into the darkening
wood. She rubbed her fingers together. She'd felt something, briefly; spider-silk, maybe, as insubstantial as a
breath, yet it had raised the hairs on her arm.

'It's beautiful,' she whispered.

Owyn looked back over his shoulder at her, dipped
his head in acknowledgement and played on.

Deep into the woods they rode as the day dwindled and

shadows clustered beneath the spreading trees, through pillared halls of mighty beeches hung with banners of sunset light. Across misty glades, past silent pools, until they reached a clearing where two weathered stone columns thrust up from the dark leaf-mould like broken bones. There Owyn stopped and lowered his flute.

'Wait,' he said, pacing slowly around, head cocked as if listening for a sound only he could hear. After fully a minute, Ailric urged his horse up past Tanith's, his mouth framing a question. Owyn's hand came up, though he did not turn. 'Please, wait.'

Tanith reached out to touch Ailric's arm. 'He knows his way. Let him be.'

The Astolan made no attempt to hide his irritation, but kept his thoughts to himself.

After a moment or two more, Owyn padded back to them, tucking his flute back into its case in his boot. 'We can go no further this day,' he said. 'You should rest.'

Though he spoke quietly, his voice sounded loud in the absence of music – in the absence of any sound at all, Tanith noticed. She dismounted, looking around at the trees that ringed the glade. Not a feather stirred amongst their branches. The clearing was silent as a midnight chapel.

'How far have we travelled?' Ailric asked as the forestal led their horses away.

'I've no idea – time flows differently in the wildwood. You'll have to ask Owyn.'

He made a non-committal sound and lowered his voice. 'I do not think he cares for me. Are you certain he is trustworthy?'

'Be nice,' she chided him. 'He's agreed to guide us, and he's given us no reason to think he is anything but honourable. Don't think so ill of strangers, Ailric.'

A mark on the surface of the nearest stone caught her

eye and she stooped to examine it. Centuries of weather and a crust of grey and golden lichen had all but obscured it, but the closer she looked, the more she saw. The entire surface of the pillar had been carved with symbols, spirals and intricate knot-like patterns so softened by time as to be barely distinguishable from the grain of the rock.

'Do you see these markings?' she asked.

Ailric peered over her shoulder. 'Is it language of some kind?'

She traced one of the flowing shapes with her fingertips. 'I'm not sure. I don't recognise it at all, but something tells me it's not purely decorative either.'

There was meaning in those symbols, she was sure of it. Whoever had carved them had intended them to endure, so their message must be significant. A warning, perhaps? A marker, like the milestones alongside the imperial highways, showing the distance to the next town?

Across the clearing, Owyn finished hobbling the horses and straightened up. 'Please, you must rest,' he said. 'Light no fires in this place and do not leave the clearing. I will return shortly with water for the beasts.'

Before Tanith could ask him about the stones, he'd loped off into the trees, the silence closing after him like a heavy curtain.

Woodland was rarely so still. There was always something rustling or chirping, but in that strange clearing she and Ailric were the only creatures stirring. Not even a biteme. To distract herself from the unsettling quiet, she laid out her bedroll then fed the horses and fetched some provisions from the saddlebags. When she returned, Ailric had laid his own bed close by, but not so near that she felt compelled to move hers. After a cold meal washed down with water from their canteens, they settled themselves to sleep.

The air remained close and still, for all the centre of the clearing was open to the sky. Ailric kicked off his blanket irritably. 'Too warm for spring,' he grumbled, settling himself again only to sit up a minute later and shrug off his jacket as well. 'Too warm for leathers!'

Hiding a smile, her own blanket folded under her head as a pillow, Tanith lay on her back and watched the first stars appear in the deepening blue. By her reckoning Lumiel would be rising soon, though she suspected the trees around them were too dense to see the second moon until it was well up in the sky. They hid the Evenlight, too, it appeared. Miriel should be over there in the west, beneath the Dragon. Except the Dragon constellation wasn't there.

She sat up, alarmed. 'Ailric, look at the stars.'

He sighed and turned over, his shirt pale as silver in the dark. 'Yes. Very pretty.'

Tanith thumped his shoulder. 'They're wrong!' She pointed. 'No Dragon. No Huntsman. That could be Amarada, but it looks stretched somehow, out of proportion. Where *are* we?'

Ailric stood up and walked to the centre of the clearing, near the stones. Hands on hips he stared up at the sky, turning in a slow circle. 'A better question might be *when* are we,' he said, then looked back at her. 'Time flows differently here, correct? Perhaps we are only now beginning to appreciate how differently.'

That made sense. Storybooks were full of tales of the Bregorinnen guides and how they found short cuts through the wild-wood. Why had she come looking for one herself, if not to hasten the journey to Mesarild? She should have expected this, or something like it.

'Of course,' she said, lying down again. 'I didn't think.'

Ailric returned to his bed and sat, supporting himself on one arm. His pale hair gleamed, silvery like his shirt. 'You need not fear, love. You have your guide and I will keep you safe.' He lifted one hand as if to touch her then thought better of it. 'Sleep well.'

'And you.' Tanith took one last look at the unfamiliar stars, then turned on her side and closed her eyes.

35

REPROOFS

❧

'Idiot!'

Gair winced. He lay naked but for a towel on the Daughter house infirmary table as Alderan fumed and clattered through the bottles on the shelves. Dust-motes glowed in the afternoon light slanting through the shuttered windows.

'What were you thinking? I told you to stay out of sight and what did you do? Chopped four Cult warriors into pieces in the middle of the square. You're an *idiot*!'

'I heard you the first time,' Gair muttered, turning his head aside.

Alderan thumped a bottle down on the table and bent over to glare at him, only inches from his face. 'Idiot,' he repeated, slowly and precisely.

'The sisters were determined. I couldn't let them go alone.'

'Then they're idiots, too!'

Unstopping the bottle, Alderan poured the contents directly onto Gair's wound. The liquid scoured his raw flesh and he convulsed.

'Sweet saints, what is that stuff?'

'Spirits of iodine.'

'Ow!'

'You'll get no sympathy from me, not after your actions today. We had little enough time here as it was and there's still half the books to sort. Now you've brought the Cult down on us and the sisters, too. You're an—'

'Idiot, yes. You said.'

Alderan scowled and thumped the stopper back into the bottle.

Using a curved needle he closed the gash with crisp, angry stitches. Gair made himself lie still for the duration but had to bite the inside of his cheek at each stab of the needle. The spirits of iodine had left his side excruciatingly sensitive – even a breath of air across the wound felt like a nettle-sting – and Alderan was not being particularly gentle.

When he was done, the old man snipped out the stitches in Gair's shoulder, then hooked a thumb to indicate he should sit up. He did so, carefully, and held his arms folded over his head whilst the latest wound was salved and dressed.

'I don't know what you were thinking,' Alderan muttered as he tied off the bandage. 'Not thinking at all, most like. I swear, the Goddess created Leahns to teach the rest of us the meaning of stubborn.'

Gair eased himself down from the table. 'You heard what Sister Sofi said – I couldn't leave the nuns unprotected in the city, not after what happened to Resa.'

He fetched his clothes from a stool by the wall and began to dress. The old man washed his hands, drying them on the discarded towel.

'You might not have sworn the vows,' he said, without looking up from his hands, 'but you are a Knight in your heart, true as any who stood vigil for his spurs.'

'A Knight needs to have faith in the Goddess.' Gair pulled a clean shirt over his head and tucked it into his trousers. 'I only did what any man would have done in the same circumstances.'

For the first time Alderan's expression softened a little, though it was a long way from a smile. 'What any idiot would have done.'

Gair made a face but said nothing. He fastened his trousers, tied his sash about his waist and sat down on the stool to put on his boots. The bending and tugging did his wound no favours, but he gritted his teeth against the pain.

'First three, now five,' the old man said quietly. 'How many will it take, Gair?'

'I didn't know how many there would be. My only concern was protecting the sisters.'

Alderan didn't answer. When Gair stood up, he was alone.

⁂

The stringy-haired guard outside the chief's tent swallowed nervously, gaze flicking from Ytha's face to the carved whitewood half-spear cradled in her arms. 'Um.'

She raised an eyebrow. 'Is there a problem, Harl?'

'The chief is not alone,' he blurted. 'He told us he was not to be disturbed.'

She stared. Harl wilted, his pocked face twisting. 'Um.'

'Macha's ears!' Rolling her eyes, Ytha pushed past the discomfited warrior and into the tent.

Upended cups and *uisca* flasks littered the carpets. Discarded clothes added their own earthy odour to the air, already thick with drink and sweat and rut. Shadowy figures moved behind the hanging that screened Drwyn's sleeping quarters. Growled words and a girl yelped.

'No, please!'

The silhouette of an arm rose, fell. An open palm cracked onto skin. 'Get back here, bitch.'

Sobs. A groan of pleasure, then the rhythmic slap of

flesh on flesh. The girl wailed, the sound abruptly stifled, either by a cushion or a large palm.

Ytha's nostrils flared. This was her Chief of Chiefs? Slaking himself with a girl when the chiefs of sixteen other clans were waiting on him? He was grunting now, nearing his completion, which came with a roar like a bull elk.

'You're done,' he panted, pushing the girl away. 'Get out.'

Schooling her face to stillness, Ytha waited. A shadow crept past the lamp and ducked when something was flung at it.

'I said get out!'

A skinny girl stumbled through the hangings with her clothes in her arms. Bruises were already blooming on her shoulders, red teethmarks on her barely budded breasts. Ytha glimpsed a tear-streaked face and bloody lip before the girl fled out into the night with a moan.

She frowned. The fourth in as many days. All young, all with their buttocks spanked crimson, their maidenhood no more than a smear on Drwyn's cushions. The Scattering's wedding fair would do a brisk trade.

'Get dressed, Drwyn,' she said. 'The chiefs are waiting.'

Moments later he jerked the hanging aside. He was dressed in just a pair of trews, and those only buttoned enough to stay up around his hips. Sweat gleamed on his thick arms and darkly furred chest. Resting on his collarbones, the wolf-heads on his torc glittered in the lamplight with every breath.

'Ytha.'

With a glimmer of amusement in his dark eyes he watched her, as if waiting for her reaction. She ground her teeth. By the Eldest, he tried her patience at times!

'No one but your guards has seen you for almost a week. Now the other chiefs are here – they will expect you to greet them.'

He picked up the one *uisca* flask still standing and emptied it in great gulping swallows, then dragged the back of his arm across his mouth. 'I've been busy.'

'Amusing yourself with those girls?' Catching his scent, she wrinkled her nose. 'Faugh! You need a bath.'

'It's sweaty work, getting an heir.' He scratched the line of hair that plunged down his belly from his navel and grinned. 'Don't you care for the smell of a man, Ytha?'

His insolence knew no bounds. 'I care about not turning the stomachs of the other Speakers!' she snapped. 'The Scattering is already a day old – this is not a good way to garner support from the other clans.'

Drwyn nodded at the spear she held. 'Is that it? The battle-chief's spear?'

Imbecile! 'No. Gwlach's spear was lost with him, centuries ago. I had this made for you over the winter from the same wood used to make a Speaker's staff.'

She held it out and he took it, examining it from the rune-carved shaft to the gleaming bronze head with its intricate engraving. He fingered the point and jerked back his hand when it cut him. 'It's sharp.'

Ytha suppressed a smile. *Serves the whelp right.*

'Of course. What use is a blunt spear?' She folded her hands at her waist. 'Whitewood holds a charm the best of any wood. There is protection for the bearer spelled out in those runes. As long as you carry that spear, no harm should come to you.'

He traced the deeply incised symbols with his fingertip. 'Magic?'

'Of a sort. It will turn a killing stroke to one that only wounds and diminish a wounding one to almost nothing. Enough to preserve your life in battle, though it cannot deflect a blow entirely.'

What a working that had been. She had carved the runes herself, using her sky-iron knife in the clear light of the silver moon's waxing. She had tied the white cords that bound it with sacred knots and woven her power into every one. All she hoped now was that her efforts had not been in vain.

'You cannot become Chief of Chiefs until you are acclaimed so by the other clans,' she said softly, slowly.

Drwyn turned the spear over and over in his hands and its point's reflection winked in his eyes. He didn't appear to be listening, his head no doubt stuffed with *uisca*-fumes and dreams of glory.

She grasped the shaft between his hands and held it still. 'Hear me, Drwyn.'

He glanced up. 'I hear you, Ytha. One hour.'

'Eirdubh and the others grow impatient.'

'One hour,' he repeated and made to jerk the spear from her grasp. In a blink she had called her magic and strengthened her grip with air, and however hard he tugged he could not take it from her. He scowled, like a child denied a favourite toy.

'This is not yours yet.' She met his gaze and held it until he unclenched his hands and let go. 'When the others have pledged their allegiance, then it will be yours by right, but not yet.'

His lips twisted sulkily, but he nodded. Good. Pride was always a bitter drink to swallow, but when his victory came, it would be more than sweet enough to take the taste away. Sweet enough for both of them.

'I will meet the chiefs in an hour,' he said.

Ytha smiled. 'Then I shall leave you to your bath.'

Inclining her head, she made her way to the tent door, the spear cradled across her body on her arm like an infant.

At the threshold his voice arrested her. 'The girl. Teia.'

She half-turned. 'What of her?'

'You promised me she would give me an heir.'

Ytha studied his face. The black hair and beard were so like his father's, but the truculent jut of the jaw, that was all his own. Was it just the desire for a son that troubled him? No, he'd filled more than enough ripe young wombs with his seed since. Then was it the girl herself? The way he'd ignored his daughter, she'd never thought him capable of forming a lasting bond.

'You must let go of her, Drwyn.'

Dark eyes burned. 'And let go of what she carries, too?'

'She was never part of our plans, and neither was her child. She's of no concern to us now. Let the winter have her.'

His jaw worked, still chewing on resentment. 'What if she bears a son? My son?'

'If she bears a son. If she survives the snow. A lot of ifs.'

He looked away. 'Nevertheless.'

'Once you are raised Chief of Chiefs, what can she do that we should be concerned over?' Ytha firmed her tone, reaching for the outer curtain. 'She does not matter, Drwyn. Even if she is still alive, she does not matter. Remember that.'

❦

Closing the door behind him, Gair looked around the stuffy storeroom. Shelves lined the walls, neatly ordered by the door and below the windows, but the rest overstuffed and thick with the dust of years. Yet more books were piled on the square table in the centre of the room or stacked on the floor around it, leaving barely enough room to walk on either side.

So many texts remained unsorted, but after all the hours he'd spent turning those crackling pages, leafing through unbound sheets, the less likely it seemed that they'd contain some clue to the starseed's location. It was the oddest collection of books he'd ever seen: tales for children mixed with medical texts and philosophical treatises, maps centuries out of date, stores and requisitions lists for quartermasters long since gone to dust. He and Alderan had found no relevant histories or personal journals, and not a single document bearing the Suvaeon's seal.

What a dust-choked, frustrating and strangely poignant waste of time.

Still, he owed it to Alderan to at least try, even if the weight of his given word hung around his neck like a horse-collar. He eyed the crowded shelves again. If there truly was anything to be found in all that . . . wreckage of lives.

With a sigh, he returned to the pile of books he had been sorting when Resa came to find him that morning. Better to travel hopefully than to arrive, as the saying went. Then he realised exactly where that saying came from and almost laughed. Proverbs, chapter eighteen, verse twenty-one. There was so much scripture in his head, but no faith in his heart to make it any more meaningful than an old saw.

By the time the sky in the high windows had purpled into dusk and the bell rang for Vespers, Gair's side was throbbing. He shifted in his seat, fingering the bandage through his shirt. Alderan had not returned from whatever mysterious errand he'd been about since leaving the infirmary, so he'd been working alone – and fruitlessly – all afternoon. Two more shelves were now sorted, though he could only tell because he knew where he'd started.

His stomach growled, reminding him that he'd eaten nothing since a fruit pastry at breakfast. He was thirsty, too; his tongue felt glued to the roof of his mouth. He looked down at his dust-darkened hands and grimaced. Before he did anything else, he needed a wash.

After he'd cleaned up in his room, he went back downstairs into the guest hall common room. It had been swept and dusted since he and Alderan had arrived, the hearth laid with wood and kindling, the scuttle filled. On the table, plates had been set for a meal, with covered dishes that proved to contain baked chicken in a sticky glaze and some kind of cold cooked grain mixed with chopped vegetables. Another bowl held plump fresh dates.

Gair filled a plate and sat down to eat. No more than five minutes after the chimes that signified the end of evening service, the door swung open with enough force to rebound off the wall. He looked up, expecting Alderan, but the formidable figure that strode in was definitely not him.

The Superior was not tall, especially compared to Gair, but in terms of sheer presence she towered. She had the kind of comfortably rounded country-born handsomeness that belonged in a farmhouse kitchen with its sleeves rolled up. Dressed in a stout black habit with her starched white wimple shining like snow atop a mountain of anger, she bore down on him across the common room in much the same manner as an avenging angel.

'The guest hall was closed for a reason,' she barked. Pale-blue eyes snapped sparks. 'The city is too dangerous for us to allow strangers within these walls.'

Standing up, Gair bowed formally.

'Good evening, Superior. Sisters,' he added, with another bow for the nuns scuttling in after her. Sofi was there, looking chastened, along with Resa and Avis, dressed in a clean habit but with a swollen purpling lip.

'What is your business here?' the Superior demanded. 'Sister Sofi has told me what she knows, but I sometimes wonder whether her head is stuffed with forcemeat instead of brains, so I would hear you for myself. Well? Speak up, boy – my time is short.'

Before he could even begin to explain, she marched up to him and seized his left hand, peering at the brand on his palm. Her lips compressed into a hard line.

'A witchmark. So that at least is true.' Several of the sisters blessed themselves anxiously as the Superior looked him up and down. 'Are you also a Knight of the Suvaeon Order?'

'A novice only,' Gair said, 'and an excommunicate, as you see.'

Her eyes narrowed. 'And you dared ask for sanctuary within these walls? When you know Church precincts are forbidden to you?'

'I asked only for shelter from a storm.'

'The storm has been over for three days, yet you are still here.' Drawing herself up to her full height, she folded her hands inside her scapular, the golden Oak on her breast gleaming. 'You must leave immediately.'

'But Superior,' Sofi put in, 'guest-right has been given. We cannot withdraw it without good cause.'

'One of our order coming home beaten and bloody is cause enough for me,' the Superior said tartly. 'Very well. One more night, since Sister Avis tells me you were injured in her defence, but after that, I do not expect to see you again. We have spent many years taking care to avoid bringing the Cult's attention down on us, and up until the start of this year we were successful. After what happened to Sister Resa the last thing we needed was to provoke them, and you, young man, have done precisely that. It is dangerous enough for us here in El Maqqam, outside the enclave as we are, without this as well. Good day to you.'

With a curt nod, she swung on her heel and marched out of the room, the other sisters clustering after her. Resa lingered and snagged Sofi's sleeve to halt her as she passed. When the others had gone, they came over to the table.

'I feel as if I was just trampled by a runaway horse,' Gair said as he sat down. Resa hid a smile behind her hand.

Sofi gave him an apologetic gesture that was halfway between a nod and a shrug. 'Our Superior is . . . forceful. But she is a good woman, and cares deeply for our safety. That is why she is so concerned about allowing strangers inside the Daughterhouse.' She hesitated. 'I'm sorry. You took a hurt to save Resa and Avis today and we should show more gratitude for that.'

'Don't worry about it, Sister.'

He pushed some food around his plate but the honey-glazed chicken reminded him too much of a picnic on the beach that he'd never taken, and now never could. Any enthusiasm to eat died with the memory and he dropped the fork.

'What did she mean, about the enclave?'

'There has been trouble in the city of late. Blood spilled, property destroyed.' Sofi looked uncomfortable, fingers fretting at a frayed cuff. 'The northern merchants claimed Cult hotheads were to blame and pressed the governor to take action, but all he did was order a wall built around their enclave and set a curfew on them. For their protection, the decree said.'

For their protection? The governor had as good as penned the northern folk like cattle for slaughter.

'When was this?' Gair asked.

'Early last year. It stopped the house-burnings and the outright violence, but many shopkeepers have lost trade – businesses owned by northerners, merchants with whom they traded. Even the ones who traded with us.' She shrugged. 'You know how it goes, I'm sure. People are afraid.'

'Can't you go into the enclave?' It was a prison in all but name, but at least it would be safer. For a time, anyway.

The nun shook her head. 'We cannot purchase property here, even if we had the means. No one would sell to us for fear of reprisal. Besides, the city governor has forbidden us from consecrating any land.'

'Then you should leave, before things get any worse.' Before the noose closed around them completely. 'How many of you are there?'

'Thirty-four.'

He couldn't defend that many, not without using the Song and that would draw even more of the wrong kind of attention to the Tamasians – and probably terrify them half to death into the bargain. They were already scared of an excommunicate; what would they make of a witch?

Gair glanced at Resa but her face revealed nothing. She had to have realised what he'd tried to do for her in the chapel, but she didn't appear to have told anyone. She was skilled at communicating her meaning with hand gestures and pantomime; he was sure she would have told Sofi, at least, who appeared to have a bond with her.

'Would the governor not spare some men from the city guard?'

Sofi spread her hands. 'We asked. He is too fearful of unrest taking hold in the city to lend us a single man.'

Perfect. The governor did just enough to be seen to be doing something, but not enough that either faction could point a finger of blame when the whole city exploded into violence – as it surely would, and soon.

'You know I will offer my sword, if it helps.'

'I know.' Sofi said it a little stiffly, and didn't meet his eye. She still didn't trust him, not entirely. 'If we had soldiers to aid us we could leave here tomorrow and sail back to Syfria, but we haven't, and that's that. We must put our faith in the Goddess to steer us through these troubled times.'

Faith was a powerful thing, but faith alone wouldn't stop an angry mob. It hadn't shielded Avis today, and it certainly hadn't protected Resa. Her soul, maybe, but not her body.

Sweet saints, they needed help. Perhaps he and Alderan . . . ? Gair dismissed that thought unfinished. The old man wouldn't abandon his search for the starseed; he'd made that quite clear.

So it's down to me.

Sofi touched his arm, as if guessing at his thoughts. 'This is not your responsibility, Gair. All will be well, you'll see.'

'I'm not sure even your faith will be enough to guarantee that, Sister.'

He pushed his plate away and fingered his side when it twinged. Today there had been five. Tomorrow there might be fifty, or five hundred, turning El Maqqam into a charnel house again. He thought of the little Oak on the chapel altar, made from thick black nails, and shivered at the sudden chill in his soul.

36

TRAPPED

⚜

Gair sat in the guest hall, cleaning his borrowed *qatan* by glim-light. He'd scoured the guard and fuller thoroughly – blood salts would start rust if left staining the blade for too long – and dressed the edge with a stone, although it hardly needed it. Even after hard use, Gimraeli steel remained sharp.

He turned the blade over across his hand. Such an elegant weapon compared to the swords he was accustomed to. Light, graceful, balanced for fast handling – quick as thought in the hands of someone who knew what they were doing. If he'd had the time, he'd have enjoyed learning to master it.

The inscription winked in the light of the hovering glims. He tilted the blade to study the flowing script but

his Gimraeli was limited to the courtesies and few simple
phrases, nowhere near enough to attempt a translation.
Pity he hadn't thought to ask N'ril what it said; maybe
the blade had a name, like the swords in stories: *Spite*
or *Kingkiller*, or Prince Corum's blade *Thorn*.

That got him thinking about his own sword, which
he'd left in Zhiman-dar with N'ril. A plain soldier's
weapon in a worn scabbard that his foster-father had
flung at him in a moment of bitter recrimination. It was
the only possession he'd brought out of Leah; everything else, bar the clothes he'd stood up in, he'd had to
leave behind. In time he'd grown into the sword's length
and weight, wearing it across his back even though he'd
been tall enough to carry it on his hip since he was thirteen, and he'd made it his own.

It hardly needed a name, but if he were to give it one,
he knew what it would be.

Vengeance.

His knuckles whitened on the *qatan*'s long hilt. In the
pit of his stomach he felt the sick lurch that told him he
was far from where he ought to be. Most days it was no
more than a vague discomfort, like something he'd
eaten that wouldn't digest. At other times it rose up into
his throat so thick and fiery he thought he'd choke on it.

I can't stay here.

Except he'd given his word and, damn it, he was no
oath-breaker.

Nothing had gone right since they'd stepped off the
docks at Zhiman-dar. An ambush in the souq, a sandstorm, more Cultists than even Alderan had expected,
and they had naught to show for it. Under his shirt,
the cut along his rib throbbed steadily. Nothing but
scars.

I should never have come.

He growled in frustration. Sometimes, trying to do the
right thing just turned around and bit you on the arse.

Carefully, he sighted along the blade one last time to

be sure there were no nicks or burrs he'd missed with the stone, then ran it through an oiled rag a couple of times before slipping it back into its scabbard. No harm in being cautious, even in a dry climate. He couldn't imagine much worse than needing to draw a sword in a hurry and finding it stuck.

Somewhere outside, a cat yowled, then another, and a brief, shrill fight ensued. He frowned, realising how late it was: long past curfew – more than an hour past Low bell, in fact – and Alderan still had not returned.

He got up and cracked the shutters on the nearest window to peer outside. Across the moon-washed foreyard the preceptory stood shuttered and dark, the sisters long abed. No sign of anyone moving, and apart from a shutter banging closed some distance away, he couldn't hear any activity on the nearby streets.

'Damn it, Alderan,' he muttered. 'Where the hell are you?'

Too tired and sore to stand for long, he prowled back to the table only to find himself too restless to sit. Even the idea of working in the archive palled: he hadn't been able to concentrate for more than an hour after supper before he'd found himself pacing like a beast in a menagerie, measuring the limits of its confinement.

He touched the teapot next to his cup. Cold. Making another pot would at least give him something to do. He refilled the kettle from the cistern in the kitchen, hung it over the fire and stoked up the coals under it. Then he wandered back to the window to worry and watch for Alderan whilst he waited for it to boil.

Outside, the sky was clear and velvet-dark. Miriel, the first moon, was near setting; a gibbous Lumiel stood high over the distant towers of the governor's palace, bright as a diamond on a black crown. The third moon, Simiel, wouldn't rise until nearer dawn, after the first had set, but the interval was shortening by a few minutes every day as the trinity approached. In less than three months, Lumiel would catch up with her larger, slower sisters again. All three moons would hang in the morning sky together, and ships everywhere would ride it out on deep water. Not even the sea-elves would risk a landfall under a trinity moon, not when the tides raced and fought like spring hares.

In the stories he had devoured as a child, the trinity was always a portent to some dire event: the rise of a tyrant, or a catastrophic flood like the one that had drowned Al-Amar. He was not much given to superstition, but with the Veil weakened and a trinity rising . . . well. The coincidence was striking.

The kettle began to murmur and he scanned the foreyard again. 'Come on, old man. We need to get out of here.'

Still nothing to see. He was about to turn away when a flicker of movement caught his eye. A dark shape changed the silhouette of the wall by the gate – another cat, perhaps, running along the top of the wall on its nocturnal patrols. Then the shape leapt down into the yard and he realised it wasn't a cat, not unless the cat was the size of a small man.

A thought extinguished the glims. Someone slipping over the wall like that could only mean trouble.

Scooping up the *qatan* from the table, he loped for the guest-hall door, butter-soft Gimraeli boots almost silent on the tiled floor. At the door he pressed his back to the wall, straining to hear any sounds from outside. There. A faint squeak, as of a bolt being drawn, then the rising burble of the kettle drowned anything more. Damn it. His pulse quickened and he eased the sword from its sheath.

Heavy breathing sounded right outside the door, and a strange snuffling. At least two people, then, or a man and a beast of some kind. Carefully, Gair lowered the scabbard to the floor to free his left hand and waited.

The latch lifted and slowly the door swung in, away

from him. A moon-shadow spilled across the floor in the shape of a *barouk*-clad man. The one hand he could see held no weapon. Where was the second man?

The intruder took a couple of steps into the guest hall, head turning as he scanned the common room. Dressed in black from *kaif* to boots, he was averagely tall for a desertman, which gave Gair a full head height advantage.

He let the fellow take one more step inside then launched himself forward. His left arm went around the man's neck to seize his opposite shoulder and he used the leverage of his greater height to wrench the intruder around to face the way he had come, and anyone who might be following him in. The fellow struggled and Gair levered the man's head back with his forearm as he brought up the naked *qatan* to just below his veiled chin.

'Stand still or I'll cut your throat,' he said.

The struggling ceased. A hand slid up the inside of his thigh and took a firm, confident hold of his stones. 'Not if I geld you first, Empire.'

The woman spoke common with a sensuous purr that in other circumstances would have been acutely distracting – particularly with her hand between his legs. Two more figures appeared in the doorway, one supporting the other who was head-down and clearly close to collapse.

'This man is hurt,' said the able-bodied one, through gritted teeth. 'And I assure you our intentions are honest.'

'Honest intentions usually knock. Bring him inside.' Gair put up his sword and released the desertwoman. Her grip on his stones eased, but she did not let go. He stared at her. 'Do you mind?'

Sloe-black eyes regarded him over her sand-veil, tilted up with an unseen smile. Pushing herself off his chest, she treated his masculine parts to a deliberate caress and murmured, 'I did not mind at all.'

Only as she walked away did Gair see the dagger in her other hand. She twirled it nonchalantly over her fingers then tucked it away somewhere inside her *barouk*. He swallowed, his mouth suddenly dry.

Ouch.

The fellow in the doorway sighed. '*Sayyar*, may I remind you that this man is bleeding? And also heavy.'

He shifted his grip on the injured fellow and the man's head lolled back. It was Alderan, eyes swollen shut, his face sheeted with blood that looked like black paint in the moonlight.

Holy saints.

Gair scabbarded his sword and shoved it through his sash, then hurried to help the grumbling desertman. Between the two of them they managed to get the old man laid out on the table. He was barely conscious and, judging by the noises he was making, having some difficulty breathing.

Light, first, so he could see what he was doing. Gair summoned half a dozen fist-sized glims above the table and heard the woman gasp behind him. Her companion took a half-step backwards, eyeing the blue-white globes warily.

'Sorcery?' he asked.

'You can call it that.' Gair started stripping off Alderan's *barouk*. 'It'd take too long to explain.'

The Gimraeli, all in black like his companion, shook his head. 'And you thought we might be a threat to *you*?'

'People dressed in black sneaking around in the dead of night? I didn't know what to think.'

The wadded robe went under the old man's head to support it. His face was a mess. Bruised and swollen, his lip was split and his nose thoroughly broken. Most of the blood appeared to have come from a deep gash on his brow that ran up into his hairline.

'I need some warm water. The kettle's boiling, and there's a kitchen through that door there.' Using his belt-knife, Gair began cutting off Alderan's ruined shirt. Bruises were developing on his chest and shoulders, too, purple-black on his weather-browned skin. He'd been beaten hard, a while ago, with feet as well as fists. A less hale man of his years might not have survived.

When neither of the Gimraelis stirred, Gair glared at them. 'Well? Are you going to help me or not?'

The man simply folded his arms and looked away. His friend, perched cross-legged on the furthest bench, picked a date from the bowl by Alderan's feet and dropped her veil to pop it into her mouth.

'Blood and stones!' He drove the knife point-first into the table and stalked into the kitchen.

A trawl of the cupboards found some dishcloths and a large basin which he half-filled with water, laced with a handful of salt. Back in the common room, he topped it up from the kettle and set about bathing Alderan's wounds as carefully as he could. His patient stirred, then drifted back into unconsciousness, blood bubbling in his mashed-up nose with every breath.

'What happened?' he asked as he worked, striving to keep his tone neutral. His injured side burned, enough that he thought he might have torn a stitch lifting the old man onto the table, and it wasn't helping his temper.

'We found him like that,' said the black-robed man. He'd crossed over to the window and closed the shutters to the merest slit that was still possible to see through. 'In the street.'

About as helpful as a paper andiron. 'How did you know to bring him here?'

No answer. Gair looked up again and caught the woman watching him. She spat the date-stone into the hearth and smiled impudently, then selected another, larger date and pushed it slowly into her mouth, her full lips pouting around it as if it was, well, something else entirely.

That took him to the limit of his patience. Angry at

her goading, stricken by the memories that filled him, he straightened up and hurled the bloody dishcloth into the basin. Water slopped over the side and dripped on the floor.

'All right. Talk. Who the hell are you two?'

The man turned from the window.

'Does it matter, so long as your friend is safe? We are done here,' he said and walked towards the door.

As the desertman thumbed the latch, the Song leapt to Gair's will. Solid air slammed the door back into its frame and held it there.

'I've had enough of this,' he growled. 'Tell me what I want to know or by the Goddess neither of you leaves this room.'

The woman surged to her feet, reaching into her *ba-rouk* for her knife. Gair drew his sword and knocked the dagger from her hand. As it skittered away across the floor he grabbed her shoulder, kicked her feet from under her and sat her down hard on the bench again with the tip of the *qatan* hovering at her chin.

'I meant what I said about cutting your throat.'

Her mouth tightened and she gave him a surly glare, but spread her hands. A sound behind him whipped Gair's head around, sword flicking out to stop the approaching desertman in his tracks. 'Give me one good reason not to, after the day I've had today.'

The man glanced at the *qatan*, then his dark eyes crinkled with a smile. 'Days like that are not unfamiliar to me.' He lifted a hand towards his sand-veil. 'May I?'

Gair gave him a cautious nod. The face beneath the veil was younger than he'd expected, middle- to late-twenties at the most, finely carved, with a neat, short beard framing his mouth. His bold nose and the set of his brows were similar enough to the girl's to suggest a family resemblance – siblings.

'You know N'ril?' he asked.

'N'ril al-Feqqin?' The man nodded. Gair kept the

sword levelled, uncomfortably aware that he had taken his eye off a woman who might be carrying more than one dagger in her sash. 'I know him.'

'We are . . . friends of his.'

He caught the hesitation. 'Open your shirt.'

Eyebrow crooked – with curiosity or amusement Gair couldn't tell – the desertman did as he was asked. There was no sun tattoo on his chest, but he had a puckered scar below his right nipple, from an arrow by the look of it. Whoever this man was, he believed in something enough to wager his life on it.

'Thank you,' Gair said, releasing the air-Song. 'Perhaps we can start again.'

He sheathed the *qatan* and stepped away from the woman. She pouted, pushing out her bosom enough that he couldn't fail to notice how perfectly rounded it was.

'Don't you want to look inside my shirt, too?'

Mother have mercy, she was relentless. She wielded her sensuality like a weapon.

Just then Alderan groaned and Gair hurried to his side. 'Easy there,' he said. 'You're a bit battered.'

Bruised eyelids struggled to part. One blue iris was ringed with scarlet; the other eye was too swollen to open at all.

'Gair?' he managed.

'I'm here. Can you tell me what happened?'

'Somebody hit me. With a house, I think. Sweet saints, *ow*.' Alderan reached up to touch his face, but Gair steered his hand away.

'Better not. Your nose is broken. Maybe other bones, too.'

'That explains why I can't breathe.' The old man's square brown hand gripped Gair's, some of his strength returning. 'Help me up.'

Supporting his shoulders with one arm, Gair assisted him into a sitting position on the table. Gobbets of congealing blood dribbled from his nose, which he wiped away with the wet cloth.

Alderan's one good eye focused on the two figures in desert robes. 'And these two are?'

'They brought you here. I've yet to establish who they are.'

The two exchanged a look. The woman had retrieved her dagger and was using it to trim her fingernails, seated cross-legged on the bench once more. Her companion concentrated on refastening his clothes.

'Well, they didn't gut me in the street, so I suppose that makes them friends of a sort.' Alderan did not sound particularly trusting, which given the state of his face was hardly unexpected.

'He claims to know N'ril,' Gair said, nodding at the man, who bowed.

'Your servant, *sayyar*.'

Holding one hand to his ribs, Alderan grunted. 'We'll see.' He hawked and spat bloody phlegm into the fire, where it hissed. 'Gair, fetch my scrip, will you? My head's ringing. You two, make some damn tea before I get more cranky than I already am.'

With unexpected alacrity, they disappeared into the guest hall's kitchen. Gair stayed at Alderan's side.

'It'll be days before you can see properly,' he said. 'I can Heal you.'

'The way you tried with Resa?' Alderan shook his head. 'Goddess, no. You need a lot more practice.'

'I can do it!'

'No, Gair. A couple of days' rest and some flagwort ointment to bring down the swelling and I'll be fine.'

'Maybe. But the Superior wants us out of here tomorrow!'

A bloody blue eye fixed on him. 'She knows we're here?'

'Sister Avis told her, I think.'

Alderan swore. The other two emerged from the

kitchen with a fresh teapot and a tray of cups. As the tea brewed and was poured he skewered his two rescuers with a glare that was all the more intimidating for being delivered by just the one eye.

'Some introductions are in order, don't you think?' he growled.

'I regret we cannot give you our true names,' the man said, hands spread apologetically. 'We would rather not be linked to tonight's events in any way, for our own safety, and for yours. But I spoke truly when I said I know N'ril, though he does not know me.'

'Clear as mud,' grunted Alderan. 'So what should we call you?'

'You may call me Canon and my sister Tierce.'

Gair gaped at their choices. 'You're joking.'

'They seem appropriate ciphers, given our current location.' Canon folded his arms, outwardly calm, but he radiated wariness like a cat curled up with its eyes half-open. His sister shot him a disgusted look, then went back to paring her nails.

'You're *jihadi*.' Careful of his split lip, Alderan sipped his tea.

Canon raised his eyebrows. 'What makes you say so?'

'Ciphers? Secrecy? Credit me with a little intelligence, please.' Making a face, the old man put down his cup. 'Gah. Tastes like blood.'

'I fear you are mistaken, *sayyar*,' said Canon neutrally.

'Really.' Sarcasm dripped from the word.

'I assure you—'

'I went into the city today to visit a teahouse recommended to me. I ordered a pot of Isfahan Black, no honey, and asked my server if he knew what time the flower-market would open tomorrow as I wanted some orchids for my wife.'

Tierce's hands stilled. Her grip on the knife altered a

fraction, almost as if she was testing the weight, preparing to throw. Gair rested his hand on his sword hilt. That woman was altogether too fond of her knives.

But Canon merely shrugged. 'I'm afraid your wife will be disappointed. Orchids are out of season now – you should try later in the year.'

'That's what the fellow told me,' said Alderan. 'So I asked directions to the jewellers' quarter instead and he recommended a shop called the Jade Elephant, which he said was owned by a friend of his.'

'I cannot say I know it.' The Gimraeli's expression was smooth, carefully bland, and Alderan showed his teeth.

'I am surprised. It's been a *jihadi* safe house since the desert wars, although I'd guess it's rather less safe these days.'

Gair blinked, then mentally kicked himself. By now he ought to be accustomed to Alderan knowing far more than he let on. Nothing about him should be a surprise any more.

'When I left the teahouse, the server should have run after me saying he'd miscalculated my change and palmed me a note with directions so I could meet my contact. Instead a couple of Cultist thugs ambushed me a few streets away. Your security's been broken, Canon,' Alderan said, and now his tone was serious. 'The Dragon *jihad* has been compromised.'

For a full minute Canon said nothing, then the coiled tension drained out of him and he dropped onto the opposite bench.

'We know.' He pushed his *kaif* back off his head and rubbed his hands over his face, looking suddenly very tired – and very young. 'Rather, I should say we had begun to suspect after what happened to Uril last year. We were on our way to the teahouse to investigate. By pure chance we cut along the alley behind the winemerchant's that those Cultists had chosen for their work and we found you.'

'Then for that, I thank you.' Alderan inclined his head.

'Thank Tierce, it was her idea. Sometimes I think she likes skulking in alleys just for skulking's sake.'

Tierce stuck out her tongue at her brother. She took off her *kaif*, too, and shook out a mass of black hair, spilling in waves around her shoulders. With a final flourish, the silvery blade flashing between her nimble fingers, she tucked her dagger back into its sheath in her sash. One of a pair, Gair noted, to his chagrin. She saw that he'd seen and smirked.

Trying not to show how much she discomfited him, he asked, 'So what happens now? We have work of our own here, Alderan.'

The old man looked thoughtfully at Canon, who leaned his elbows on the table with his head between his hands. 'I went looking for the *jihad* to find out how bad things had become here. That question appears to have answered itself, so perhaps we can help each other.'

'We have no love for the Empire, old man.' Tierce dropped her feet to the floor either side of her bench, ready to spring. 'Nor any need for your help.'

'We have a saying in the north,' said Alderan. 'When a nail needs driving, any hammer will do.'

'We have plenty of hammers of our own,' Tierce said and muttered something else in Gimraeli. She turned to Canon. 'There are too many Cultists on the streets tonight. We should go.'

Her brother propped his chin on his palm. 'Tell me how you knew the passwords.'

'Tell me how you knew to bring Alderan here,' Gair interjected, patience evaporating.

Canon held up a hand. 'Please, *sayyar*. My question is of the greater import, I think. Lives may depend on it.'

Alderan dabbed a little more blood from his nose with the dishcloth. 'I knew Uril. He told me what to ask at the teahouse, if ever I needed to find the *jihadi*.'

'Then you also know Uril is dead?'

'I know.' The old man nodded. 'N'ril told me.'

N'ril is involved with the jihadi? Gair frowned. 'I'm sorry, who's Uril?'

It was Tierce who answered, and did so in a snarl. 'You should know, Empire. You carry his sword.'

N'ril's brother. Of course. The similarity of their names should have given him a clue.

In icy tones, Tierce added, 'It would please me to learn how you came by it.'

'I know N'ril. He suggested I carry this sword for the duration of my time here.'

Her lip curled. 'Then be sure you do not dishonour it.'

'Tierce,' said Canon, with the tired patience of a parent having to repeat instructions to a wilful child, then continued his tale. 'We have lost six cells since he was taken. Nineteen people, including Uril, butchered like animals.'

'Less than animals,' snarled Tierce. 'At least animals have their throats slit before their bellies are opened.' Hunger for vengeance glittered in her eyes, dark and hard.

'Forgive me the question,' Alderan said, 'but is it possible that Uril betrayed you, under duress?'

Canon shook his head. 'No. I am sure of it – I knew him well and he was one of the strongest of us. I must believe that we have another enemy, an enemy within, yes? A Cultist agent, or someone who values gold more highly than the trust we placed in them.'

'Or was coerced,' the old man suggested.

Canon tilted his head, conceding. 'That is also possible.'

Beside him, Tierce glowered. 'Traitors.' She spat on the floor, earning a frown from her brother.

'This is a house of the Goddess, Sister.'

'Not my Goddess.'

'Nevertheless.' His tone sharpened. 'Be respectful, or we are no better than those we are sworn to oppose.'

She tossed her head. 'What do I care?'

'Perhaps you should learn to,' he snapped back. 'When we were still children the Goddess's soldiers gave their lives to save this city from the Cultists. You should honour that sacrifice!'

'My enemy's enemy is my friend?' she sneered. 'Those who bed down amongst dogs rise up with their fleas, Brother!'

In a whirl of black robes she was gone, slamming the door behind her.

Canon sighed and took a moment to compose himself.

'Please, forgive my sister,' he said. 'Sometimes her grief speaks instead of herself. She saw Uril, after they were done with him. He . . . took a long time to die.'

'They were close?' Alderan asked gently, but Gair already knew the answer.

He stared into the fire, arms folded tightly across his chest, over the sudden sick hammering of his heart. He knew that grief. Knew its name, had felt its breath on him. Pain boiled in his veins as he saw her again, opened up like a fish, leaking her life away into a rain-puddled yard. *Aysha*.

The bench scraped across the floor as Canon stood up. 'I think perhaps I should leave. It is not safe to linger outside after dark, even for us.'

Controlling himself with an effort, Gair faced him. 'You never told us how you knew to bring Alderan here.'

'We didn't. Once we saw his face and knew he was not desert-born, there was nowhere else we could take him. The Empire quarter is under curfew and the gates are manned by city guards, not all of whom are . . . sympathetic. Even if they had granted us admission, we would have made ourselves targets. The sisters here are known for their charity.' He bowed, formally, in the desert style. 'May you find better fortune in the days to come.'

As he turned to go, the door to the guest hall flew open in his face to reveal Tierce, veiled again, her eyes alive with a dangerous light.

'They're coming,' she said. 'Cultists. Lots of them.'

37

WHAT'S RIGHT AND WHAT'S NECESSARY

A cold knot formed in Gair's belly.

Goddess help him. He'd provoked the Cult by defending the nuns in the square; now they were coming in numbers to make the sisters pay.

'Could they have followed you here?' he asked Canon, to be sure.

The Gimraeli looked doubtful. 'I do not think it likely. We saw no one after we left the alley.'

'But that doesn't mean no one saw you.' Alderan pushed himself to his feet. 'Gair, fetch my scrip.'

'There's no time!' Gair snapped. If he'd brought the Cult down on the Sisters, it was up to him to see to their safety, and do it fast. Already he could hear a growing rumble from the street outside. 'Canon, watch them.' Refastening his *kaif* and veil, the desertman trotted for the door. 'Tierce, did you bolt the street door after you?'

'Do I look stupid to you?'

He bit back a sharp retort. 'Then go and rouse the

sisters, quickly. Tell them to take only what they can't bear to leave behind.'

She curled her lip. 'I will accompany my brother. Let their own soldiers defend them.'

Exasperated, he swore. 'They don't have any soldiers, Tierce! These are holy women, consecrated virgins. What do you imagine the Cultists will do to them if we don't see them safely out of here?'

'Then who slew four Cultists by the south gate this morning? *Holy women?*' Tierce sneered. 'Three Knights, I heard, disguised as carters.'

'There was only one,' said Alderan, neck craned awkwardly so he could use his good eye to peer through the narrow gap between the shutters. Orange light from torches in the street beyond the wall rendered his face a ghastly mask. 'He's an idiot who causes enough trouble for three.'

For the first time, Tierce's arrogance was shaken. She stared at Gair. 'You?'

'Apparently,' he said. 'Go and rouse the sisters. They number thirty-four, including the Superior. Make sure no one is left behind.'

She darted away and he turned to Alderan. 'This is my fault. If I hadn't gone out with them this morning—'

'We'd very likely have ended up in exactly the same situation, only with two dead nuns on your conscience,' the old man finished for him, still squinting between the shutters. 'I don't think you started anything that wouldn't have happened anyway, as soon as Resa showed she wasn't afraid of them – although I'd have liked a little more time to work through those books after coming all this way.'

He straightened up, dabbing at his still-leaking nose with the back of his hand. 'Damned thing. I thought you were going to fetch my scrip.'

'And I told you there's no time.'

Before Alderan could protest, Gair seized his head

between both hands and opened himself to the Song. Brilliant colour flooded his mind, sweeping through him and into the other man in a rush of glorious music. It was too late to worry about subtlety now.

When he let go, Alderan reeled against the wall, breathing hard. Sweat shone on his brow.

'Holy Mother Goddess!' he gasped. 'You definitely need practice. That was brutal.'

'You can see out of both eyes now, can't you?' Gair snapped, heading for the stairs.

In his room he snatched up his few things and stuffed them into his saddlebags, a chilly foreboding gnawing at him. Nothing, not a single thing, had gone right so far. He looked around to be sure he hadn't left anything, then did the same for the old man's belongings and carried all of their baggage back down to the common room.

Alderan was still watching out of the window. The torchlight outside looked brighter now, and someone had begun pounding on the street door to the rhythm of an angry chant.

'Sooner or later one of them will figure out which is the business end of an axe,' he muttered. He palpated his still-swollen nose tentatively. 'You could at least have straightened it.'

Gair ignored that. 'Where's Canon?'

'I sent him to fetch the horses.'

'What about Tierce?'

'She hasn't come back yet.'

Blood and stones. The wretched girl had probably followed her brother and to blazes with anyone's skin but her own. Gair loped for the door.

'I'll find her, then meet you in the yard.'

Outside, the increased number of torches in the street beyond the wall had polluted the clear silver-blue of the moonlight to a muddy-river brown that gave the yard an unfamiliar aspect. Shadows lurked and leapt as the torches moved, creating a hundred places amongst the outbuildings and stores where Cultists could have hidden, if any of them had given thought to climbing over the wall instead of targeting the gate. Each heavy thump shook the thick door in its frame.

Across the yard the stable door opened, sending out a widening beam of lamplight that pushed the shadows back. A black-robed shape followed, soon recognisable as Canon, leading Alderan's grey gelding. There was no sign of Tierce with him. She must have gone into the main preceptory building after all.

At the head of the steps the iron-strapped door was closed and no lights burned within the Daughterhouse that Gair could see. Instead each upper window blazed with reflected torchlight from the street as if the entire place was on fire. In Zhiman-dar the Cultists had burned books. If the ugly tone of the chants and the resounding blows against the street door were anything to go by, the ones in El Maqqam were aiming a little higher.

The door was unlocked and opened easily when he lifted the latch. Only a little moonlight entered through the high windows, draping the stone-flagged entry hall with shadows. Summoning a glim at his shoulder he hurried towards the stairs. He had only the vaguest idea where the dormitory might be, but it was reasonable to assume it would be on one of the upper floors.

On the first landing he heard muffled voices and followed the sound to a side passage where a group of nuns fluttered in the darkness like startled doves. Tierce stalked back and forth, hissing and growling at them to hurry up, and her impatience only added to their nervousness.

'For pity's sake,' Gair muttered and threw half a dozen more glims into the air overhead. People always felt safer when they could see.

Several sisters squeaked in alarm at the sudden illumination, but they stopped fluttering. Frozen in place, they stared at him with fear-bright eyes.

A sturdy grey-haired nun was the first to recover herself. 'Merciful saints!' she exclaimed, drawing herself up. 'Who are you, bringing this deviltry into the Goddess's house?'

Gair spread his hands placatingly, palms down to keep the witchmark out of sight. There was enough panic in the air already.

'I'm here to help, Sisters, that's all. It's no longer safe for you here. You need to leave.'

The nun stuck out her jaw. 'Absolutely not. We are doing the Goddess's work here – we will not be driven away by ignorance and mindless hate.'

Avis and Resa had tried much that line of reasoning in the square that morning, without success. 'There's no time to argue about this, Sister,' Gair said. 'There are Cultists at the gate, a lot of them, and they're very likely armed. We have to go.'

He took a quick headcount of the women clustered around the sturdy nun and came up several short without spotting any familiar faces.

'Isn't the Superior here?' he asked Tierce, who shrugged.

'How should I know? They all look the same to me.'

Addressing the nuns, Gair raised his voice a little. 'Where's the Superior? What about Resa? Sofi?'

The sturdy one frowned. 'Sister Sofi has gone to fetch the pyx-chest,' she said. 'I think Sister Avis went to the Superior's lodging.'

Better hurry, Alderan sent, pressing urgency into Gair's mind. *They'll be through the gate before long!*

At the prospect of having to comb the corridors of the Daughterhouse to round up the missing sisters Gair almost swore, but remembered himself just in time. 'Is there another door to the street? A lepers' gate, some other way out of here?'

'There's a lepers' gate behind the chapel,' the nun said. 'What's happening outside? Who are you?'

'A sinner, Sister Martha,' said the Superior crisply,

appearing from the far end of the corridor. Sofi, clutching a small chest, scurried in her wake.

The senior nun had donned her black habit but hadn't bothered with a wimple, and lacking its stern frame her face looked younger, softer, surrounded by short brown curls that showed barely any grey.

'A sinner with a sword, no less. *Barouks* to cover your habits, Daughters, then meet Sister Avis and the others at the lepers' gate.' She clapped her hands. 'Quickly now, we have no time to waste.'

A familiar voice issuing instructions was all it took to galvanise the nuns and they hurried away. The Superior eyed the glims drifting along the vaulted corridor, then fixed her shrewd, pale gaze on Gair.

'And other gifts, too, it appears,' she murmured. 'Who are you, my son? Truly?'

'Please go with them,' he urged her. 'They're frightened. We'll join you as quickly as we can.'

'You haven't answered my question.'

There was no *time*! 'I am what you see, Superior – a sinner with a sword. Now please, hurry!'

'You have surprised me,' she said, 'and I have not been surprised in a very long while.' Inclining her head, she gathered her black skirts and glided after the departing nuns.

Tierce stalked back down to the yard behind Gair. Both horses were saddled and ready, tethered to a ring in the wall by the guest-hall door. Alderan limped out in his bloodstained *barouk*, a bundle of robes in his hands. Both his eyes were open now, if magnificently bruised, and the cuts and scrapes on his face had scabbed over. Dried blood had left stark lines in the creases of his skin, wild tufts and spikes in his hair; instead of a genial old lion, he resembled some tattooed shaman from the Belisthan forests.

He tossed the robes to Gair. 'These are yours. Are the nuns leaving?'

'The Superior's assembling them behind the chapel.'

'Good.' A splintering thud shook the outer gate and the crowd in the street roared their approval. 'We've not much time. Get upstairs and help Canon with the books.'

Barouk half-on, Gair stared at him. 'But what about the Sisters?'

Alderan gave him a terse shake of the head. 'They'll have to make their own way out. We haven't time to ride shepherd if we're going to get any of these books away from here.'

Gair couldn't quite believe what he'd heard. 'You're serious? You'll just abandon them?'

'If I had the choice, no, but there is more at stake here.' The old man made an exasperated, impatient sound. 'Look, the sisters have lived here for years. They know this city – they'll be fine. Those books won't be, unless we can take them somewhere safe.'

'So you'll just leave the women to the Cult? Let those bastards cut their tongues out and worse? Good Goddess, Alderan!' Gair tugged the *barouk* across his shoulders, slung his *kaif* around his neck. 'No. Not while I'm still breathing.'

A slow fire burned inside him. He knew what Alderan was saying, that depending on what the books contained potentially thousands of lives could be saved, but that was in the abstract, an impersonal rationalisation that would never have the same gut-punch immediacy of the very real, very present danger facing the sisters. He could not countenance abandoning them, not when he'd brought that danger down on them in the first place. It smacked too much of cowardice.

Frowning, Alderan cocked his fists on his hips. 'Gair, I thought you understood. Those books might hold the knowledge we need to preserve the Veil. If they're destroyed—'

'And that makes them more important than the sisters' lives?' Saints and angels, the man was bloodless. 'I came here with you like you asked and I've helped as much as I can, but I can't do any more. I won't. I caused this mess, and it's up to me to get the sisters out of it.'

Gair jerked Shahe's reins from the ring on the wall and flipped them over her head. He'd wasted more than enough time on those books; he wasn't prepared to waste even a second more.

Canon emerged from the Daughterhouse with a stack of books in his arms that reached his chin. His sister went straight to him and they spoke urgently in Gimraeli. Her eyes gleaming over her veil, she snatched the grey's reins and was off at a run.

'I'm disappointed in you, Gair.' The old man's eyes were glass-hard, almost silvery in the strange light. 'This is our best hope of stopping Savin in his tracks with the least blood spilled. You know that. I thought it's what you wanted, to make him pay for what he did to you.'

His hand on the saddle horn in preparation to mount, Gair paused. 'Oh, I want to make him pay all right.' His voice trembled with the effort of keeping his emotions in check. 'I want it so much I can taste it, but I won't throw those nuns to the wolves to get it.'

He swung up into the saddle and Shahe immediately began to dance, unsettled by the smoke and chanting, the furious passions in the air.

The old man threw up his hands. 'You don't understand! This is the only thing to do if we're going to have any chance of stopping him—'

'No, it's not! You're wrong!' Good Goddess, couldn't the man hear himself?

'It's *necessary*!' Alderan snarled. 'Get down off your Knightly high horse for a minute and you'll see it, too.'

'What's right and what's necessary are not the same thing.' Gair reined Shahe about in a tight circle, his heart thumping hard against his breastbone. 'The nuns are my responsibility now – I'll see them safely back to Syfria on my way north. You and your damned books can go to hell.'

A blazing torch whirled over the wall and bounced across the earth in gouts of sparks, close enough to make Shahe crab away, head tossing anxiously. Whooping voices followed it, the words unclear but the intent plain. He had to get the nuns out.

Behind him the thudding and chanting continued, regular blows shaking the stout door in its frame. A new-moon sliver of steel burst through the sun-whitened wood; the crowd outside cheered and more torches were hurled over the wall.

'Then go with the Goddess,' said Alderan as Gair brought his mount back under control. His voice was coloured only by a quiet resignation. 'If you can, find Masen – he's somewhere in the far north. You might be able to help each other.'

Then there was no time left and nothing more to say. Gair gathered Shahe up and urged her towards the chapel.

⚜

Tanith woke from an unsettling dream with her heart thundering in her ears and her hand across her throat, expecting any second to feel the kiss of a blade. A pale and pearly dawn seeped through the trees, the air heavy with the scent of damp leaf-mould – and something else, something dank and faintly rotten.

Sitting up, she looked around the clearing. The horses were tethered where they'd been left, their tails spangled with dew, but apart from a bucket of water for them to drink from there was no sign of the forestal.

Beside her, Ailric's blankets were empty. The tall Astolan stood near the stone pillars, one hand on each as he leaned between them.

'What is it?' she asked, getting to her feet. Her leathers felt uncomfortably damp and clung to her in a way that said her skin was patterned head to foot with crease-marks. She rubbed at a particularly sore spot on her hip and found a hard lump in her pocket that dug into her. The acorn. She turned it over in her hand, then tucked it away again.

'I heard something. Shouting. The clash of swords.'

'Was it not just a dream? I woke up convinced someone was about to slit my throat.' She stretched. 'Where's Owyn?'

Ailric shrugged. 'He has not returned.' He leaned a little further between the stones. 'I hear it again. There is a battle somewhere near here.'

'In Bregorin? They have no enemies. Half the world believes they don't exist.'

'I tell you, I hear fighting.'

Tanith walked to stand next to him and listened. The clearing remained preternaturally still, without so much as the *whirr* of a bird's wings to shatter the silence. Even her own pulse sounded loud in her ears. Faintly, she heard men shouting. Screaming horses. Swords on shields.

'Do you hear it, too?' he asked.

She nodded, straining to hear more. Something *splinked* off the stone next to her face and left a stinging line across her cheek. Her hand flew to touch it and came away smeared with blood. 'I'm cut,' she exclaimed.

At once Ailric laid his hand over her cheek. A simple Healing rushed through her, shivering her body into gooseflesh. In the space of a few seconds the cut tightened with a scab and even the soreness at her hip was washed away.

'Thank you,' she said, then flinched as he reached into the neck of her shirt. 'What are you doing?'

'Hold still a moment.'

He fished around inside her collar, his touch conjuring up more memories. She wanted to pull away, but another treacherous part of her revelled in the sudden intimacy.

'There.' He held out his hand. A stone chip lay in his palm, no bigger than her thumbnail and sharp as a blade.

'I heard it, but I saw nothing.' Tanith fingered the new scab. 'Where did it come from?'

Ailric began casting about for what might have struck the chip. More shouting voices, closer now and louder than the other battle sounds, made him turn.

A man crashed through the undergrowth on the far side of the glade and ran towards the stone pillars. One hand gripped a naked sword, the other pressed against his ribs, where blood seeped through his fingers to stain his plaid shirt. His rasping breaths and desperate eyes said he was close to his limits. Bowstrings sang and he staggered. The sword fell to the ground, then the man pitched onto the dirt with a white-fletched arrow sprouting from his back.

'It must have been an arrow, look.' Pointing at something on the ground, Ailric stepped between the stones and vanished from sight.

'*Ailric!*' Tanith lunged for the stones.

A hand on her arm dragged her back. 'Don't go through,' said Owyn.

'But he's gone!'

'I know, I saw. But you cannot go through the stones or you will be lost, too.'

Tanith wrestled her arm out of his grasp, fighting sudden tears with anger. 'You said the acorns would keep us from being lost!'

The forestal sighed. 'They should. Does Ailric have his?'

'I don't know. I think so.' She scrubbed her hands across her face and remembered. Last night, Ailric taking off his jacket. Standing at the stones that morning with his fine shirt crumpled and flecked with dirt from the forest floor. 'No.'

Owyn's face grew grim. 'Can you find it?'

She ran to the discarded jacket and hunted through the pockets until her hand closed on the cool, distinctive shape and pulled out the acorn.

'You still have yours?' She touched her pocket, nodded. 'Good. Bring his – and a weapon, if you have one.'

Quickly Tanith snatched up her belt with its long knife and buckled it around her waist. Then, with the Song already rising to her will, she hurried back to the stones where Owyn was tying running loops into either end of a length of rope he'd taken from his satchel. He slipped one loop around the wrist of his non-dominant hand and the other around hers. There was perhaps three yards of slack, enough for freedom of movement and to defend herself, if need be.

'Whatever you do, keep hold of this rope. I can find you if we become separated, but it won't be easy. Are you ready?'

'Where has he gone, Owyn?'

'Explanations must wait. We go now or not at all.'

With that, he stepped through the stones.

38

FIRE

✥

The sisters were waiting when Gair arrived at the lepers' gate, an arched opening in the thick outer wall behind the chapel only a little taller than Shahe's shoulders. One nun held the wooden door barely ajar and kept a careful watch on the alley outside. The others clustered around the Superior, occasionally casting anxious glances in the direction of the porter's lodge, out of sight beyond the chapel's buttresses but not out of earshot.

'Are you ready?' he asked, dismounting. The Superior nodded. 'Then let's go.'

Shahe baulked at being led through the low gate, as uncomfortable with the nuns crowding behind her as with the archway ahead. In the end Gair had to throw a fold of his *barouk* over her head to blind her and coax her through the arch into the alleyway beyond. The nuns followed, their few valuables bundled into burlap sacks. In plain desert robes with sand-veils across their faces, they were scarcely recognisable as women to a casual eye.

'We need to keep off the main thoroughfares,' Gair said, shrugging his own robe back into place. 'If that mob catches sight of us there might not be much I can do.'

The Superior nodded her understanding. 'We can keep to side streets and alleys for most of the way.'

'Then lead on – you know the city better than I do. Take the horse.' He held out Shahe's reins.

'Thank you, my son, but no. I fear you may have a more pressing need of her than I.' She pointed along the alley. 'This way to the second corner, then we must turn right.'

Right would take them away from the route Gair and Alderan had taken from the Lion Gate when they arrived in the city, but he assumed the Superior was choosing the way that had the greatest chance of them staying unnoticed. Mounted once more, he led the way through the alley. The dry earth underfoot muffled Shahe's hoofbeats; nonetheless he strained his ears to catch any sound that might draw attention to them.

Once out of the lee of the preceptory buildings, the rumbling chant from the Daughterhouse gate became louder, punctuated by the sound of steel on wood. Flames leapt high above the wall, one of the outbuildings now well ablaze.

At Shahe's shoulder, the Superior made the sign of blessing over her breast. 'Vandals,' she muttered.

'What are they chanting?' Gair asked.

'I wouldn't soil my mouth with the words,' she replied tensely. 'All kinds of vileness.'

He dared a glance along a narrow side street. Some of the mob appeared to be women. As he watched, one threw back her head and gave an eerie ululating cry, instantly taken up by several others. Men howled their approval and fire roared into the sky.

If he'd never come south, this might never have happened.

He forced himself to look ahead again. Self-flagellation wouldn't change anything – all he could do was use his guilt as a spur and keep moving. Nudging Shahe on, he left the Daughter-house behind.

The alleys of El Maqqam were often only wide enough for the nuns to pass two abreast – and sometimes barely wide enough at all for Shahe, or so hampered with laundry-lines Gair had to dismount and lead her through the piles of junk and refuse, haunted by dead-eyed, scrawny cats that skittered around and away from the mare's hooves. The smell told him he didn't want to know what he was stepping over or, occasionally, when he had no other choice, in.

Turn after turn took them further away from the route he vaguely remembered. Without a clear sight of a moon at this hour he soon lost his bearings, but the Superior never faltered, directing him with gestures or a quiet word, as familiar with the city in the dark as if the sun had been high. She was tireless in her care for her anxious flock, too, reassuring them with a smile or a touch on the arm and never once betraying her own concern, even when a rat broke from a pile of nameless waste almost under her feet.

At the corner of an open square she stopped, her hand on Shahe's shoulder. The buildings opposite stood silhouetted against a paling sky and birds chattered amongst the dead skirts of the palm trees ringing the public well in the centre. Already people were visible around the square: three women with water-jars gossiping at the well, shopkeepers opening shutters and folding out awnings as they readied their stores for the day's trade. On the far side, one fellow yawned in a doorway, watching the women with their water-jars. Someone shouted something to him and he laughed, scratching his ample belly, then shouted back.

'We have to cross the square,' the Superior whispered.

Gair eyed the fellow watching the women, then scanned the square for a way across that wouldn't pass through the man's eyeline. He didn't find one. 'We'll be seen,' he said. 'How far to the Gate from here?'

'Not far, but it won't open until dawn.'

Crossing the square would have been easy if they'd had a wagon or two: the sisters could have hidden in the bed, undercover. Gair chewed at his lip, then stopped himself. No point fretting over what they lacked. They must make do with what they had.

'Is there another alley that leads onto this square? One you can reach from here without being seen?'

'Almost certainly.' The Superior looked round at the nuns. 'Sisters?' Several of them nodded.

'Split up,' he said. It was the best they could do. 'Small groups, no more than three or four of you at once, and don't cross too close together. If you can find water-jars or something to carry to help you blend in, so much the better.'

The Superior pointed at a shadowy passage between two shops. 'That alley there, beside the oil-merchant's, stays gloomy until almost noon. We will meet there, then press on for the Lion Gate.'

'But for the love of the saints don't hurry,' Gair added. 'It'll only attract attention.'

Reluctantly, with hugs and blessings, the nuns separated into smaller groups, most of whom retreated down the narrow street they were on before peeling off into various alleys and cuts between backyards. Gair watched them go and groaned inside at their tensed shoulders and scuttling birdlike movements.

Following his gaze, the Superior guessed his thoughts. 'They'll be fine,' she said, patting his arm. Then she turned to the three sisters who remained, one of whom, Sister Martha, had her arms wrapped tightly around a sack. 'Off you go, Daughters.'

The nuns stepped out into the square. Almost at once the corpulent merchant's head swung around to watch them. Gair searched for a sun-sign over his door but the shop's awning hung too low for him to see. He swore, under his breath but still too loud not to have been heard by the Superior standing beside him.

'Forgive me,' he apologised. 'I forgot I have company.'

To his surprise, her eyes crinkled up with a smile.

'My father was a quartermaster for the Tenth Legion. Believe me, I've heard far worse – although I have to say, for a young man raised in the Church you have a remarkably colourful vocabulary.' She nodded towards the nuns. 'Look.'

Sister Martha had opened the top of the sack and all three women had their heads together over it as they walked, as if it contained something extraordinary. The merchant looked away, his attention attracted now by the women coming from the well, swaying gracefully with their water-jars balanced atop their heads. His eyes followed them all the way back across the square and he grinned. Just a lecher, then, enjoying the morning view.

Relieved, Gair blew out a long breath.

'Our turn,' he said. He offered his arm and kicked his foot out of the stirrup so the Superior could use it to mount.

'I haven't ridden astride since I was a little girl, behind my da,' she said. She began kilting up her habit with her girdle, then paused. 'I'd take it as a kindness if you didn't look.'

Dutifully, Gair kept his eyes fixed on Shahe's ears until with a breathless prayer for forgiveness, the Superior had heaved herself up behind him. She arranged the voluminous *barouk* to ensure her legs were decently covered.

'Ready,' she said.

'You might want to hold on to me, in case we have to move smartly.' He nudged the horse into a walk and out of the alley.

Sister Martha's group had made it across the square and were disappearing into the shadowed side street, still apparently intent on the contents of the sack. Another group set off from further around the plaza, having cut through the alleys to the next street over. Five of them. Too many, and moving a little too fast.

'They should have waited,' Gair muttered. Instinctively he eased the *qatan* in its sheath. 'They should have waited!'

'Goddess in heaven.' The Superior's hands knotted in the folds of his robe. 'Behind us.'

Gair dragged his gaze away from the frightened nuns and looked around. Oily black smoke billowed into the bleaching sky from another part of the city, with flames leaping at its heart. He checked the eastern sky for Simiel, spotting the edge of the moon's yellowed disc edging above the rooftops. The smoke was rising to the south of it, which could only mean one place. His heart sank.

'The Daughterhouse,' he said, and hoped Alderan had seen sense at last. The breeze tasted of burned paper and regret.

In moments the rest of the city realised something was ablaze. Merchants and their families spilled out of their houses around the plaza to point and stare. Children whooped excitedly, the flames lighting up their eyes and laughing mouths. Even though they were only children and knew no better, Gair felt sickened.

More in hope than expectation of an answer, he flung out a hail attuned to Alderan's colours. After a heart-stopping pause, the reply came back: *Get out of the city.*

Sensing Gair's anxiety, Shahe started to prance and the Superior tightened her grip on his waist. *Alderan—*

No time – just go, damn you!

Abruptly the familiar colours of brandy and jasper turned muddy and dim. Every instinct screamed at Gair to go back, even though the flames and the thickening column of smoke said the Daughterhouse was already beyond saving.

Are you all right? he sent. Only silence answered.

Holy saints, no. *Alderan!*

All he heard was distant cheering, distorted by the intervening buildings; an ugly, vicious sound, like the drone of some poisonous insect. He sent out one last hail, then reluctantly let Alderan's muted colours go.

Guilt assailed him. 'I should go back. There might be something I can do—'

He made to turn the horse the way they'd come but the Superior squeezed his arm.

'You saw the size of the crowd at the gate,' she said. 'You'd never get through.'

'I can't just leave them!'

Those blasted books. Shahe danced, and he stared at the smoke staining the sky. If anyone had been caught inside the Daughter-house, they were surely lost now.

Her fingers dug into his biceps. 'My da used to say you have to do the job that's in front of you. Besides, the lepers' gate we used is on the far side of the precep-tory. They may have escaped.'

She was right. She had to be, but somehow he couldn't make himself believe it, and his shoulders slumped. 'Maybe.'

Even to his own ears his voice sounded strained, and no amount of swallowing would clear the tightness in his throat. *I should never have come to Gimrael.*

'We'd best keep moving,' he said, when he could speak again. 'The sooner we get out of the city, the bet-ter.'

Clicking his tongue at Shahe, he started her across the square. Nuns appeared from side streets in twos and threes, clinging to each other and darting fearful looks back over their shoulders, his urgings forgotten. Not that it mattered now; with destruction to watch no one was paying them any heed as they converged on the alley beside the oil-merchant's shop.

The cheering abruptly grew louder, as if the crowd had turned a corner onto the main street into the square. Chanting rather than cheering – Gair made out words and phrases repeated over and over, though the only one he understood was *ammanai*. The chant growled and snarled, the crowd a beast with a thousand voices.

He dared a glance over his shoulder. A mob surged into the square from the southeastern corner carrying a bare-chested, thickset man on their shoulders who was brandishing an axe above his head. A yellow sash circled his waist. Ululating women danced around him, skirts swirling, their veils gone. Long black hair flew like banners.

A victory mob. He urged Shahe to a brisk walk and soon caught up with the others in the relative safety of the alley's gloom. There he handed the Superior down from the mare's back and twisted in the saddle to watch the Cultists manhandling something to the front of the crowd. Bronze leaves gleamed in the early light: the Oak from the Daughterhouse chapel at a guess. It clattered onto the cobbles and was lost in a chanting, stamping mêlée. He turned away, glad the nuns couldn't see over the heads of the crowd.

Three more figures clustered uncertainly in the mouth of an alley directly across from the oil-merchant's. At a nod from Gair, the Superior waved them over. With the citizens so intent on the Cultist mob, they hiked up their robes and ran into the arms of their sisters. He counted. Fifteen now on this side of the square, still less than half the number who had set out. Standing in his stirrups, he searched the other streets he could see that opened onto the plaza and found the shapes of four more nuns, maybe five; the pre-dawn shadows between the buildings prevented an accurate count.

He turned to the Superior. 'Take this group to the gate. I'll bring the rest.'

She shook her head. 'Sister Martha can take them. I'll stay here until I know they're all safe.'

'I don't want to have to choose between protecting you and protecting your flock if this crowd turns ugly.'

As soon as the words left his mouth, Gair realised arguing with her would be fruitless. She simply folded her hands in her scapular, serene and immovable as a marble saint. 'As you wish.'

He swung Shahe around and walked her back out into the plaza. At the sound of hooves on the cobbles a few spectators glanced towards him; when all they saw was a lone deep desertman ambling his horse across the square their attention quickly returned to the spectacle in front of them. By the time he reached the other side, the waiting nuns had increased in number to seven and crowded about his mount.

'We saw smoke. What's happening?' demanded one. Her sagging veil revealed a pinched, pale-lipped face.

'There's a fire on the other side of the city,' he said, unsure if he should tell them the absolute truth. He needn't have worried.

'The Daughterhouse,' the nun moaned, clutching at Shahe's reins. 'They've burned the Daughterhouse!'

The black mare tossed her head until Gair disengaged the nun's hand. 'Easy, Sister. I'll see you safely out of the city, don't worry.'

She seized his arm, her fingers cold with fear. 'Merciful Mother, what are we to do? Where do we go? They've burned the Daughterhouse!'

Sobbing, she slumped to her knees. At once Resa was beside her, an arm around her shoulders. The older nun clung to her and buried her face in the girl's robe.

Gair searched the group for other familiar faces but found none. 'Where are the rest of you?'

A nun carrying a sack with bulky, awkwardly shaped contents answered him. 'Sofi took them further up towards the Lion Gate. She said she used to visit the poor by the north wall and knew another way through.'

Damn it. They were three separate parties now instead of one. At least when the sisters were all in the same place there was a chance he could shield them if it came to it, but not any more. The Song surged restlessly in response to his unease.

'Very well,' he said. 'We'll cross the plaza together whilst everyone's busy watching those Cultists. I'll stay between you and the crowd, so keep together until we get to the other side. The Superior's waiting for us. Ready?'

Six nods, of varying degrees of confidence. The weeping nun was still sobbing into Resa's shoulder.

'Let's go.'

As one, they moved out into the plaza. Gair kept half an eye on the Cultists as he rode across. The man with the axe was holding court, the bronze Oak trampled to pieces at his feet. Shouting in Gimraeli, he scooped up a handful of the twisted metal leaves and brandished them at the crowd before flinging them back to the ground. He spoke too fast and too passionately for Gair to pick out even the bones of what he said, but the gestures with fists and axe, the growls and cheers of the crowd that greeted his words, made his meaning plain.

Just like in Zhiman-dar. Nothing but contempt for anyone who does not share their faith. Gair's stomach soured. The Superior was right about that as well: they were vandals – and if they were prepared to attack Church property, it was surely only a matter of time before they turned on the Empire's merchants, if they hadn't already.

The thickset man thrust out an arm, pointing at him. No, past him. Gair looked up the main street, his hand already closing around the hilt of the *qatan*. Several men in yellow sashes were swaggering into the square, grinning widely, their arms spread in welcome. The Cult followers began to cheer, but all Gair noticed was the way one of the yellow-sashed men was limping.

The moustache. The cocky, look-at-me strut. His fingers tightened on his sword hilt, the cut along his ribs burning with the memory.

'Stay with me, sisters,' he hissed. 'Keep walking. Don't look up!'

The sister with the awkwardly shaped sack did just that. She squeaked and stopped in her tracks. Another walked into the back of her, the impact jolting her hard enough to tip the bulky sack forward in her arms. From it fell a thick, heavy book, landing with its cover open at a gorgeously coloured frontispiece of the Goddess on the oak tree.

Another sister snatched the book up, but the limping man had seen enough. *'Ammanai!'* he snarled, pointing.

The nuns froze in place.

'You godless ones are not welcome here.' He drew his sword. A heartbeat later the rest of the yellow-sashed warriors followed suit.

Gair swore and wheeled Shahe around to put the nuns behind him, his heart sinking. No more than a hundred yards separated them from the oil-merchant's shop and the robed figures clustered in the shadows at the alley's mouth, but it might as well have been a mile.

He drew his sword and let it hang down by his leg, ready but not threatening. There was little to be gained by offering the Cultists any provocation: seven or eight swords afoot were more than a match for one man on horseback. His mount would be hamstrung in a matter of seconds, and he would barely slow them down enough to buy the women time to escape – never mind what would happen when the rest of the crowd beyond the well realised what was happening. His spine prickled, anticipating the bite of that axe.

Holy saints.

Quelling a sudden flutter of fear, he addressed the moustachioed one, who was clearly the leader of the group.

'There doesn't need to be any trouble, *sayyar*,' he said. 'Let the women pass.'

'Their presence is an insult to Lord Silnor, and they

must answer for it,' the fellow spat. His eyes narrowed in recognition. 'You! I thought I'd finished you yesterday.'

Bluster – the fellow was saving face in front of his men. It was tempting to offer a pointed rejoinder, but Gair held his tongue. Baiting the man would only provoke him, and there was still a chance that the situation wouldn't come to blows – but it did no harm to be ready just in case. He took a deep breath in, all the way to the bottom of his lungs, then let it out slowly, settling himself just as if he was about to work the forms in the practice yard.

'Let the sisters leave,' he said.

The Gimraeli sneered. 'I take no orders from northern barbarians. I answer to my God alone!'

Gair opened himself up to the Song. Power sang along his nerves and set them tingling. Just holding it sharpened his senses to almost painful clarity, set them alive to the weave of his clothes against his skin, the smell of baking bread on the morning air and the warm horse beneath him. Behind him, one of the nuns prayed to the Goddess for protection in a fervent whisper, and he heard every word as if he was kneeling at her side.

'Let the sisters leave,' he said again, 'and we can all walk away from here.'

'And if I don't?'

A smile tugged at his lips, feral and unexpected. 'Then we don't.'

Moustache growled something in his own tongue and the warriors behind him began to fan out. 'Stand aside, Churchling, or you will die here!'

As the yellow-sashes spread out, Gair could no longer keep them all in view at the same time. If one or more of them got behind him he'd be finished, but he no longer cared. Alongside the power of the Song, a little madness bubbled in his veins.

Raising the *qatan* to his lips he kissed the blade, the

way the Knights in his childhood storybooks had blessed themselves before battle. His blood was singing.

'Then so be it.'

Gesturing with his sword, Moustache barked another command that sent the two outermost pairs of his men surging into a run. Gair flung a shield over the nuns and gave Shahe his heels to charge the nearest pair, unable to engage them all simultaneously. It was time to dance.

The *sulqa* barged the first man off his stride with her shoulder. Gair swung hard at the other and the sword took the Gimraeli in the side of the neck with a disconcertingly wooden sound. The man dropped without a cry.

Whipping his blade free, Gair heeled the mare to face the first Cultist again as he recovered himself. He met steel with steel, parrying once, twice, as quick on his feet as a dancer. His blade snaked out beneath Gair's guard and only Shahe's battle training spared her its bite. The *sulqa* jinked and lunged with her teeth, and as the Gimraeli stepped sideways to dodge her, Gair reversed his too-high blocking stroke into an upward sweep of steel that opened the other man's chest to the bone.

The Gimraeli's screams attracted the attention of a few outliers of the crowd on the far side of the well. Several figures exchanged glances then began drifting across the square, but Gair had no time to spare for them. Two other yellow sashes of the four sent against him remained unaccounted for. He wheeled Shahe again, his blade held ready.

They had separated in an attempt to flank him: too far apart to get in each other's way, but too close together for him to target one without leaving himself or his horse exposed to the other. He swore under his breath, reining Shahe a couple of steps left then right as he tried to keep both swordsmen in sight. Behind him the nuns were praying fervently, and he hoped their prayers would be heard. A little divine intercession would not go amiss. Time was running out.

More folk were watching now, a ring of them forming around the battle. Faces turned towards him; arms pointed from the crowd. Swirls of movement in his peripheral vision pulled at his eye. He didn't dare take his attention off the approaching yellow-sashes to look, so instead his imagination provided images of *barouks* swept back from the hilts of knives and hands swooping down to the ground for stones.

Khajal.

If he was going to do anything, he had to do it quickly. As the citizens drew closer, they cut him off from the far corner of the square and the oil-merchant's shop. Moustache's four remaining warriors were advancing, too, their blades shining, but the nearer two were the greatest threat for now. He could not afford to let himself be distracted by what might come next.

With a snap of his wrist he flicked the blood from his blade before it trickled down to his hand and affected his grip. Scarlet drops spattered the ground like paint and behind him one of the nuns moaned, 'Blessed Mother!' in a gulping voice that sounded as if she was about to be sick.

'Be ready to run, Sisters,' Gair said, still not taking his eyes off the two men approaching.

Flexing his fingers on the *qatan*'s long hilt, he tried to remember everything N'ril had taught him. Though he'd spent the last decade with a sword in his hand, he was accustomed to a heavier weapon and a school of combat that bore more resemblance to hewing wood than to the supple-wristed, slash-and-gone desert style. It would take more than a couple of crowded hours in N'ril's rooftop garden to make him as fluent as the men he faced.

Something struck him hard on the point of his left

shoulder. He shied from the blow, and it took him a beat to recognise the object as a stone. In that moment's distraction, the two yellow-sashed warriors darted in.

Gair gave Shahe his heels. She leapt forward and he swept his left arm up and across his body in a shield of the Song as if wrapping himself in a cloak, then pushed it out ahead of him. One of the Gimraelis ran into a wall of solid air and tumbled onto his backside right underneath the hooves of the charging *sulqa*. The other reeled sideways from the impact but recovered quickly, blade coming up to meet Gair's. Steel shrieked on steel, then Shahe was through.

A twitch of the reins brought her around again, almost in her own length, her shoes slipping on the dusty cobbles. The man on the ground was no threat, curled in a foetal arc clutching at his belly, but the other fellow was circling to follow Shahe, his blade at the guard. Gair flexed his tingling hand and kept the mare moving. If he stood still, he and the nuns would die.

More stones flew and thudded off his shield. Shahe grunted and jinked sideways when one got through and hit her on her unprotected flank; another struck Gair's back to one side of his spine and twisted him about, swearing in pain. Like the tide up the beach, the gathering crowd surged towards him.

Blow after blow jolted his shield. Stones, cudgels, he hadn't time to see what they were. His attention was on the yellow-sashed swordsman doing his best to gut him. Burning pain and a tell-tale wetness on his side said his wound had burst at least one more stitch but he kept slashing and thrusting at anyone who came close enough.

Shahe began to plunge and kick, whinnying as more blows found her, too. Her steel-shod hooves exacted their own retribution but her unpredictable movements were as much hindrance as help to Gair as he fought.

His Gimraeli opponent grinned, flicking out lunge after lunge. He knew where the advantage lay.

Desperation began to lick at the edges of Gair's concentration. He'd lost sight of the nuns in the heaving crowd, and no matter how quickly he thrust, how light Shahe was on her feet, there were too many threats to track them all. Already his body ached with repeated impacts from stones and sticks, and cuts burned where his defence had been a shade too clumsy or too slow.

A raised hand appeared near him, grasping a long knife. He chopped down hard. As the man fell away clutching the gouting stump of his wrist, Gair urged Shahe into the space he'd created. Men ducked out of her path and she made a yard or two back towards the nuns. Another, heavier missile hammered into Gair's shield at neck-height: a cobblestone, big as a loaf of bread. His weaving trembled and the Song buzzed angrily in his head.

This was beyond dangerous. If a stone that size hit Shahe it could break her leg and then they'd both be swallowed by the mob. He couldn't shield her from all sides at once and still fight. Abandoning his shield, he wove the air into something else and flung his hands out from his sides.

Music reared up inside, wild as a torrent of white water. Wind slammed into the Gimraelis around him with the force of a sandstorm and tumbled them from their feet amidst billowing clouds of dust. A few strides ahead he saw the nuns, cowering with their arms above their heads as if for protection. Sticks and loosened cobblestones littered the ground around them, along with half a dozen dusty, dazed young men.

'Sorcery!' someone cried. 'Devils' work!'

Other voices took up the cry. Beyond the well, more faces appeared in the crowd as they turned to see what was happening, then started to advance towards the coughing Gimraelis on the ground. Saints. He'd bought the sisters even less time than he'd hoped he might.

Inside him, the Song responded to his anxiety and surged up against his will. Discordant yowls distorted the melodies but he shoved them down, wheeling Shahe in a tight circle and dropping the nuns' shield. He had no time to worry about what that dissonance in the Song meant. There were only a few seconds in which to get out before the crowd closed in even thicker than before.

'Run!' he yelled. 'Quickly, get across the square!'

Even as one weaving dissolved he gathered the Song into others. Whips of flame cracked across the faces of the crowd and halted their advance. With a fresh wall of air he swept aside the remaining Cultists in his immediate path, clearing the way for the sisters. They got to their feet slowly, stumbling and supporting each other, peering about through the dust.

'This way!' he roared at them. 'Hurry!'

Galvanised by his voice, the nuns hiked up their skirts and ran. Heads down, looking neither right nor left, they pelted past him and through the gap in the crowd towards the outstretched arms of their sisters. Several folk made to follow but Gair cracked his fiery whip again, striking sparks from the stones at their feet.

'Stay back!'

Each snap of the lash made the Song inside him howl. Little jolts and quivers skittered up his arm, setting his muscles twitching like serpents beneath his skin.

The Gimraelis he'd up-ended were picking themselves off the ground, sullen black stares on him as they dusted themselves off. Others who'd been less stunned or who were quicker to recover prowled back and forth just out of range, like wild dogs held at bay by a burning branch. Occasionally one would dart out as if to test how fast he could flick the lash, and how close.

He had to move, and now.

With a squeeze of his calves he urged Shahe into a

fast walk. The young men fell back only as far as they felt they had to, flat-eyed, their lips curling. The nuns were about twenty yards ahead of him and through the thick of the crowd. In a few seconds they'd be safe. In a few more, with a little luck, so would he.

Someone growled behind him. Pain burst in his back like a punch to the kidneys: another stone, thrown from close range. Cursing, he swung Shahe to face the threat. The young men had closed in behind him and they had weapons in their hands.

He flung out his sword-arm, the bloody blade smoking with the power coursing through him.

'Back!' he snarled.

The nearest of the youths sneered, bouncing a rock in his hand, then cocked back his arm to throw. Gair seized more of the Song to shield against it and the buzzing dissonance sawed through his thoughts, shredding the weaving before it was formed. The fire-weaving he held ready twisted under his will, horribly alive and suddenly searingly hot.

He gasped and flung it away. Flames belched up from the cobbles ahead of him, scattering the crowd there and racing towards the palms around the well. Sparrows burst from the dry fronds, chattering in alarm. In seconds the trees were engulfed in flame.

But the burning sensation did not relent. It skittered wildly up the nerves of his arm and spread throughout his body, hotter than a fever. Muscles spasmed, bending his back like a bow. A white light of pain exploded inside his skull.

He didn't hear the crowd close around him. He hardly felt the hands that grabbed the *sulqa*'s harness and tugged at his *barouk*, trying to drag him from the saddle. His mind was gripped by fiery talons, and all he felt was pain. Pain worse than he'd experienced in the chapel when he'd tried to Heal Resa, worse than anything he'd ever known before except the reiving.

Gair screamed.

Goddess have mercy, it hurts!

Shahe's shrill whinny of distress drove into his ears like an auger. Rearing in panic, she pitched him to the ground. The impact knocked the breath from him, turned the scream into a groan. Other screams scraped at his ears, mixed with the crackle of fire. Inside him, the Song roared with a fierce and terrible heat.

Fresh flames scorched along his spine, down his legs. His hands contorted into claws and the *qatan* fell into the dust. Plunging hooves crashed around him, detonating explosions of pain in his skull as he burned and burned and burned.

Wait for me, Aysha. I'm coming.

EPILOGUE

❦

Eirdubh was the first, as he had promised. The sinewy chief of the Amhain knelt in the melting snow and wrapped his right hand around the shaft of the white-corded spear. With his left he offered up his own clan spear in pledge of fealty. Drwyn smiled and inclined his head. Reaching out, he grasped the Stone Crow's spear to close the circle. It was begun.

Standing at Drwyn's side, Ytha watched the other chiefs come one by one to make their pledges. With every bowed head and gruff-voiced vow, the surging bubble of excitement in her breast grew. Stone Crow. Silverthorn. White Lake. Clan by clan, six, seven of them. Yes. This would be a mighty war band, perhaps mightier than the one Gwlach had raised and squandered, but this time they would not fail. This time they would hold a blade to the iron men's throats. They would cast the Emperor from his usurped throne and drive his men from their lands!

Patience, she reminded herself, *patience*. It was too soon to be thinking of glory. That was how Gwlach had failed: he'd had his eyes fixed too far ahead and failed to see it when his plans crumbled right in front of his feet. Not her. She had laid better plans, stronger plans, and she had made a stronger chief. A Chief of Chiefs.

Broad-backed and upright, as a warrior should be, Drwyn wore a new shirt and trews, his plaid fastened about his shoulders with a jewelled pin. His hair and beard carefully combed, his bearing was as magisterial as Drw's had ever been. Kingly, even, and the other chiefs could see it. It reflected in their eyes.

They see what in their heart of hearts they have always wanted to see. Ruler, father, protector. Someone to lead them home.

And I have given him to them.

Knowing that, she struggled to keep the grin from her lips and remain as impassive as a Speaker should be. Her cheeks ached with the effort.

Eight clans now. Nine. The tenth to come forward, the hawk-faced, white-blond Conor Two Bears, did not kneel. He met Drwyn's gaze full on, with not an ounce of softness in his eyes.

'If I give you my war band, Drwyn, will you use them wisely?' he said. 'I will not see my clan go the way of the Black Water.'

To Ytha's surprise, Drwyn did not falter. 'We lost too many men to Gwlach's foolishness.' He offered his spear, white cords swinging in the restless wind. 'I am not Gwlach.'

'I pray not.' Dropping to one knee in the snow, Conor grasped the whitewood spear and held up his own. 'Do not disappoint me, or I will swear blood feud on the Crainnh until the last Eagle falls.'

Oh you will, will you? Ytha frowned. Though he had seen the Hounds, Conor was if anything less convinced now than he had been at the Gathering. The Eagle Clan held lands adjoining those of the Feathain near the coast. Over the years they'd mingled their blood with the whalers and seal-drivers of the White Sea and inherited some of their outlandish notions along with their pale hair. Living in longhouses with soft beds and warm fires, halfway to forgetting they were horse-lords.

Her knuckles whitened on her staff. They might have to be reminded.

But before she could speak, Drwyn closed his fist around the feather-decked spear of the Eagle Clan and repeated, 'I am not Gwlach.'

Teeth bared, Conor nodded. 'I am relieved to hear it, my chief.'

Ten clans, then, but she would have to watch Two Bears to be sure his allegiance held. Binding his Speaker to her with the others would help, but still. It would only take one clan to fall away for others to follow.

But ten clans became twelve, thirteen, then Conor's brother-in-looks Aarik of the Feathain stepped up to make his pledge and she held her breath. When he'd made his vow she released it and cursed herself for doubting. This was her plan. It would not fail.

And then it was done. Sixteen pledges given to the Chief of Chiefs. A war band more than forty-five-thousand strong, if the other Speakers had given her accurate numbers of men under arms. Drwyn had his warriors and she would have her war.

He stood up, the enspelled spear cradled on his arm, and looked at his chiefs.

'My brothers,' he declared. Like his father's, his voice was strong and resonant, and needed no subtle bending of the air to carry it. 'This is a momentous occasion. For the first time in the history of this Broken Land, we are united in a common purpose. We speak with one voice and by all the Elder Gods I mean to make our voice heard. Tonight we feast!'

That met with a roar of approval from the watching warriors.

'In the morning, my Speaker will ask Maegern's Hounds to show us the way to victory. We will fall upon our enemies as the wolf falls upon the lamb.' He thrust the spear up towards the bright spring sky. 'And we will take back what was ours!'

ACKNOWLEDGEMENTS

It's been a hard, lonely road this one. The first book was a fluke, a mix of white-hot creative fury and time. The second was born in much the same way, but on its journey to completion it had to fend off illness, unrealistic expectations, attacks of self-doubt and all the other demons that assail the new novelist when faced with doing it all over again, only better – oh, and this time, to deadline.

As with any journey, friends have helped share the burden, especially Greta, Jenny, Mags and Jo, whose continuing faith in me never fails to both humble and inspire. Much love also to Mum and Dad, my brother Ian and niece Mia. Special thanks go to my redoubtable agent Ian Drury, my editor Gillian Redfearn and all the team at Gollancz, without whom etc.

But most of all I want to thank my husband Rob, who not only manages to live with the snarling monster that is me in a creative funk, he also picks the monster up when she stumbles, makes her laugh when she feels like crying, and brings her endless cups of tea. Every writer should have one.